Forbidden Child
A Tale of the '70s

Sylvie Chartrand

FORBIDDEN CHILD

A tale of the '70s

Sylvie Chartrand

First edition

Library and Archives Canada Cataloguing in Publication
Chartrand, Sylvie
Forbidden child : a tale of the '70s / Sylvie Chartrand

ISBN 978-2-9701077-1-2
eISBN 978-2-9701077-0-5

Cover artwork: Lydia Hoekstra
Text design and typesetting: Emma Smart Publishing Services

To Lucie and France

Disclaimer

All characters appearing in this work are fictitious. Any resemblance to real persons, living or dead, is purely coincidental.

I wish I could have put all the lyrics I meant to include in this book but I was warned that by doing so I could end up having legal troubles. Copyrights can be rather expensive, so I took all the lyrics out. Since this book wouldn't have been written if it weren't for the music of the '70s inspiring me, I decided to "describe" the songs I was listening to while I was writing, instead of putting the actual lyrics. I hope the reader will recognize, if not all, at least some of them.

The songs appearing at the beginning of each chapter are not meant to be in chronological order. These are the songs I was listening to while writing this book.

Author's note about Québec

Some people are not aware that Québec is the only French-speaking province in Canada. Eight million French "froggies" are drowned in a population of thirty-five million Canadians. The rest of Canada speaks its own brand of English, which sounds neither American nor British.

The French language spoken in most parts of Québec has a little more spice than its European counterpart. For instance, in France, *gosses* means "children." In Québec, the word is slang for testicles. When the French say *branler* they mean "to masturbate"; however, in Québec, this term is used whenever one indulges in a little procrastination. These two examples demonstrate how alienated we sometimes feel from our European cousins.

Another distinction: the accent. The distinctive French accent that is so widely known has little to do with what you'll hear in Québec. For one thing, France speaks an octave higher than Québec. This is especially true of French women who sound, more often than not, like Minnie Mouse on helium gas to Québécois. French people like to express their apparently above-average, intricate selves armed with a vocabulary most of us in Québec consider suspicious on account of its military precision.

The French are also known to add English words to their *Larousse* dictionary. People in France look for a *parking* space. They go out *shopping*. They even face *challenges*. The accent is conveniently stripped of its Anglo-Saxon consonance, and, *voila*, these words get their French passport for life. This linguistic abandon is common in the Old Country. France doesn't suffer from the phobia of losing its identity. On the other hand, in Québec, the French language is like a runaway teenager. You manage to get her back home, but you never know when she'll be out running wild again. In France, inserting English words into a conversation is perceived as chic; in Québec, it betrays a lack of education. Damn, we even have a French word for e-mail: *courriel!* In canine terms, when it comes to protecting the French language, France is a poodle and Québec a Rottweiler.

A good proportion of Québec's population lives in constant apprehension of being robbed of the right to express themselves in French. Squeezed between English-speaking sisters on both sides *and* a somewhat troubled big brother, the United States of America, to the south, the shy French Canadian is on guard 24/7.

Not that we speak perfect French. Far from it, actually. Our accent is neither pretty nor racy, and I've been told more than once how annoying it sounds. Ironically, the average Québécois understands the French spoken in France pretty well, but the French can't grasp half of what we say unless they have spent a considerable amount of time in La Belle Province.

They'll tell you it's the accent.

For reasons I can't even explain to myself, I wrote this story in English. I had the audacity to do so because I've been living and working half of my life in English. I can express the deepest workings of my mind with no difficulty, if not always perfectly, in both languages. I have no doubt of my ability to make myself clear, *en français* or in English, though I sometimes need to juggle my words, or I translate literally from one language to the other. Although most of the conversations contained in this story took place in Québécois, I chose to write them in English simply because that's the language my brain uses whenever I reminisce about this period of my life.

In the early 1970s, Québec was in the middle of its own peace-and-love era. A new generation of kids led the way. They didn't play hockey and they didn't like country music. Hair grew past shoulders, pot was everywhere, French-speaking bands with political messages emerged. A sudden post-Beatles British invasion took no one by surprise. Québécois kids found new heroes in a country they fervently hated and sang in a language that otherwise made them spit whenever they forced themselves to use it. But the music was good, too good to be loathed. Québec's political orientation was shifting, and there were serious reasons to believe that in the near future the province would, hopefully or not, become a sovereign state. It was a time of economic ease. Kids were able to do things their parents could have only dreamed of at that age, such as living on their own or travelling the world with an army surplus backpack as their only luggage. Québécois teenagers left the province by the hundreds. Some hitchhiked to California, some went picking grapes in Europe. Others drifted to Asia and South America. The ones who spoke English were a bit more adventurous than their French-only counterparts. But this was not a rule.

Prologue

*Listening to Tom Waits singing there is no devil out there,
it's just God getting drunk.*

MOTHER EARTH MIGHT AS *well have ceased her itinerary
throughout the galaxy. The Andes might as well have collapsed
into the ocean. It was an event no one expected. Something
forgotten and buried deep in our minds, along with a thousand
other impossibilities we assumed should not, could not, and
would not happen. Something left undone because there were no
decent ways of doing it right. In fact, it hadn't been discussed in
months. Possible it was, but only in the distant future, and only
if a miracle took place. And of course, only if it wasn't too late.
But certainly not at this time of our lives and definitely not on
the near horizon.*

Even Holiji was against it.

Chapter 1

Listening to the Beatles singing about an unhappy boy named Jude

J UDE WAS NO ORDINARY dope dealer. He got high on his own stuff but never too stoned to lose track of things. He always remained on top and ready to bounce. He was permanently on the lookout and—let's face it—he was smarter than any Royal Canadian Mounted Police agent because he never was caught. When Jude was a mere sixteen years old, he could already tell where the narcs would hit next and who would be dumb enough to end up in prison for selling or simply for possessing some grass or hashish.

Even though they did everything to conceal it, guys were intimidated by Jude, especially when girls were around. He was not the kind of man any girl in her right mind would want as a long-term partner, but Jude had money, and he was wild and handsome. He radiated an enticing aura of pure excitement with a little danger thrown in. Not that he looked different from the others—the fashion code of Levi's jeans topped with a T-shirt was rigorously followed by all—no, it was because of his larger-than-life style. Most girls were smitten, if not for a lifetime then at least for a couple of weeks. I know, because I too stood in the cattle line, eagerly waiting to get some of Jude's attention.

I already had a boyfriend when I met him. Well, kind of. Since we had lost our respective virginity together, I suppose Jean-Luc was a serious boyfriend. We had known each other since the age of twelve. He was very good-looking: tall, blond—all the attributes that make a young girl want to graduate from drooling over idols in teen magazines to dating real men. Jean-Luc was my whole life (or so I thought), and our future was bright and clear. We would marry and have 2.3 children as the statistics dictated, though Jean-Luc was hoping for half a dozen. He'd work at the garage owned by his dad while I'd stay home with the kids. My parents adored Jean-Luc. He was every mama's dream for her daughter. Unfortunately, good boys rarely last long in good girls' minds. Sooner or later, they are discarded as a distraction from the ultimate but misguided pleasure and satisfaction of attempting to turn a bad seed into a healthy plant.

It was 1973. The younger generation was feeding its heart and soul on the new sounds of what was loosely called "progressive rock." The legends of the '60s were dead (most of them choking on their own vomit), and the '70s kids were impatiently waiting for some magnificent bird to soar from the ashes. The Beatles were beatified, the Stones would eternally remain the bad boys of rock and roll, and you could finally declare your admiration for both groups without being labelled a traitor. The Doors, though still extremely popular with the young crowd, were just about to be called "the most overrated group of all time" by a popular music magazine, and the Who were on their way to perform their last concert in Montreal (they vowed to never come back after having been arrested and thrown in jail for destroying their rooms at the posh Bonaventure Hotel).

Genesis, Yes, Emerson, Lake & Palmer, the Moody Blues, Gentle Giant, Pink Floyd, King Crimson, Focus, and countless others were the flavour of the day. We read every lyric (without understanding half of them) with such intensity you'd have thought our next meal depended on it. Locally, the music scene was also evolving with bands like Harmonium, Offenbach, Octobre, Beau Dommage, and the Ville Emard Blues Band.

About to turn seventeen, I attended CEGEP (Collège d'enseignement général et professionnel), the Québec pre-university school designed as an educational parking lot for moderately zealous kids secretly aspiring to embrace an establishment they outwardly despised. At CEGEP Maisonneuve, we were spoiled. Two cafeterias, three cafés, a reading room, and a semi-Olympic swimming pool. We even had André Ménard—the future co-creator of the Montreal Jazz Festival—in charge of selecting the weekly movie presented at the auditorium for the ludicrous sum of fifty cents. But we knew all that fun would have to stop one day, either by going to jail for possession or else by being kicked out of school for ingesting LSD before class. But more likely—though nobody was willing to admit it—it would stop the day we joined a university and pursued the career path intended by our parents.

Jude would have none of this nonsense. No Canadian was about to tell this boy what life was all about. Jude had big dreams. American dreams, that is, not that second-class Canadian stuff suited for accountants and dentists. Jude's aim was so high that none of us could really grasp what the hell he was looking for. We admired him, but that was something we never told him. Jude was not the type of guy you wanted to compliment. He was so full of himself that he didn't need any praise. Whenever he showed up at the apartment with a sample of his latest arrival of hashish coming from places we could not even pronounce, let alone locate on the small plastic globe in the living room, he was everybody's favourite boy. After a couple of joints, everyone would congratulate him for his incredibly good dope, the best hashish and grass available in the world. By way of holy smoke, Jude made us visit faraway lands such as Afghanistan, Morocco, Kashmir, Thailand, Mexico, and so many other places we doubted we would ever see with our own eyes.

Chapter 2

*Listening to Grand Funk Railroad singing about getting
nearer to home*

NOVEMBER 1973. I MET Jude the night Alain, a boy I knew from school, invited me to a gathering of a bunch of hippies at their communal dwelling. This was not an opportunity an aspiring free spirit like me could afford to miss. Jean-Luc was light years away from my mind and conveniently miles away at another school, which was a good thing because he wouldn't have approved. Alain and I left CEGEP around 5:00 p.m. We took the subway up to the Honoré Beaugrand metro station, then walked a couple of blocks east and took a turn on Sherbrooke Street.

The building was old and grey. A welfare haven, no doubt about it. Alain headed straight for the basement. Down the short flight of stairs, we landed in a cramped space with a single door facing us. It looked like a closet to me, but I could clearly hear music and laughter coming from the other side. A wrought-iron number *1* hung on the door on a loose nail. If you looked closely enough you could see the dirt contour of a *0* next to it, making it apartment *10*, a conclusion I reached while waiting for someone to let us in.

You'd think this missing digit would have been a major drag for any tenant leading a normal life, but Alain said nobody ever bothered to ask the janitor to affix the *o* back in place.

Alain banged on the door repeatedly. At last it opened. The only thing that got to my senses was the distinctive smell of hashish. The *man* at the door—he appeared at least twenty—had a lit joint in his mouth, fire in, and nothing more than the homemade filter coming out from his lips. He offered Alain and me a blow, which meant inhaling the smoke he was exhaling through the filter. It was almost like kissing, but the joint guaranteed no tongue would be involved. I took a long drag, my lips tingling at the contact of the man's moustache.

After this welcome puff we were led to the kitchen, where about fifteen kids sat wherever they could, cramped like Japanese commuters in a subway. All the windows were shut. A thick fog of cigarette and hash smoke floated over their heads like in a Turkish bath. Even the Siamese cat up on the fridge looked as if it was having a good time. On the wall was a popular poster, Robert Crumb's *Stoned Again*, picturing a cartoon face gradually melting down to liquid.

Everybody was laughing and talking, exchanging what seemed to be an endless joint. Alain introduced me, but I was hardly noticed. I sat on the floor, trying to memorize names, overwhelmed by it all. This was my first meeting with bona fide free spirits. These kids were my age, maybe a little older, but they lived free of parental supervision.

Looking back, I can say it was a momentous evening that would change the course of my life. Of course, I couldn't know that then. At the time, I was far too shy to talk, and I didn't. Alain quickly joined the conversation, and I was left to myself in the last free corner of the kitchen floor. Only two other girls were present. They both glanced at me furtively, measuring the level of threat I might represent in their male harem. Simultaneously, the boys discreetly weighed the size of my tits and ass. According to the general reaction, I understood I was no babe. I looked innocent and naïve and couldn't possibly be of any interest to them, worldly smokers. Mind you, I suspected that probably no earlier than the week before, one of them had sat right where I was, but had since been promoted, either for his or her wit, tits, or capacity to smoke.

Still, I felt like a zit. A leper in the presence of kings. A hippie version of the hunchback of Notre Dame. They were out of my league, and my ineptitude was blatant. (For instance, between the really cool poster of the Beatles from the White Album and a psychedelic picture of Jimi Hendrix stolen from my brother, you could still see the smiling faces of David Cassidy and Bobby Sherman hanging on my bedroom walls. These two were nothing more than remnants of my younger, sillier years, a time that apparently had come to an abrupt end the moment I set foot in that kitchen.)

A newcomer burst through the doorway, and in a split second I was totally forgotten. I took this opportunity to take a good look at everyone. Some were too stoned to be interesting. I concentrated on the others. Those were the ones I liked. Those were the ones I wanted to be like, to be with. They were about to become my best friends in the world, and I would soon know everything about them.

There was Hugo. It was hard not to notice him because he was suspended halfway up the kitchen doorway, his back against one edge of the frame and his feet pressed firmly against the other. How he stayed there so effortlessly, I had no idea. But he seemed comfortable there, smoking joint after joint while maintaining perfect balance. When he wasn't at school, I later learned, Hugo worked for the phone company. His job consisted of climbing telephone poles and fixing whatever had to be fixed up there. Like many of us, he counted North American Indians in his family tree. I recalled my dad saying that pure blood Indians did not fear heights, something about their genes. Hugo spent his days rotting in CEGEP just like the rest of us. He was good-looking, with long, straight, raven-black hair, and you had to be blind not to let your eyes wander down to his perfect ass whenever he left his perch.

There was also Frankie, the "man" who had let us in. Frankie was an acidhead, a breed sheltered by most hippie crowds in the '70s. Everyone knew one, took care of one, made sure one got home safely. It turned out Frankie was twenty-three, the senior in that crowd. His ancestors had travelled to Canada all the way from Scotland in 1907, a feat Frankie was terribly proud of, as if they had been the only Europeans intrepid enough to consider the journey. His entire life revolved around Jimi Hendrix and LSD. He sported a thick moustache. The hair situation on this guy was totally out of control. The skin on his face had to fight to be exposed to daylight. Maybe it had something to do with all that LSD he was taking. Frankie seemed like a good guy, if not terribly smart. He didn't work or attend school. He didn't have enough neurons left for either activity. He still lived with his parents, who were desperate to see him get married and raise a couple of lads and lasses. Fat chance. Frankie's mind was way out there, diving in and out of reality like a playful hairy dolphin enjoying a sunny day. I soon understood that he was a priceless addition to the group because he owned a car, an old beat-up gold Impala with a white vinyl top. Frankie loved to drive his buddies around town, but the space in his car was limited. To make more room, he got rid of every seat except for the driver's and opened the back space all the way to the trunk. Up to ten kids could squeeze in, sprawled on pillows, listening to loud music, and smoking dope. For a long time, Frankie's Impala was our sole means of private transportation. That we weren't killed in that car is proof that there is a god for innocent, doped-out-of-their-minds children with no bad intentions.

That same god seemingly made the rusted Impala invisible to police cars patrolling the streets of Montreal.

Sitting next to Frankie was Alex, obviously the leader of the clan. As events will show, I would grow to know Alex far better than all the others. He was tall, with a fair complexion and eyes as blue as those of the Siamese cat on the fridge. Relying on standard stereotypes, one would have never guessed that Alex was Greek. Even Hugo with his Comanche nose and straight black hair looked more Greek than Alex. His ancestors came from Crete. I'd heard somewhere that the best-looking guys on earth are bred on this island amid olive groves, tomatoes, and goats. Alex's eyes were piercing and inquisitive. When he was stoned, his mouth played tricks on him. It became hopelessly dry, and each word seemed to chap his lips. One feature, however, was instrumental in making him the chosen one to lead, or at least that was my conclusion at the time. Whereas the iris of his right eye reacted normally to light, the other remained the size of a pinhead, like a dysfunctional marble staring at you. It gave Alex a halo of specialness. The only other person with a fucked-up eye like his was David Bowie, and we all knew he was definitely from another planet. Not unlike an African albino officially elected witch doctor of his village because of his light skin, Alex ruled because of his fucked-up eye. He hated school. He had no time to waste on mathematics and geography. His aunt owned a small construction company. He worked for her here and there, and that was it. The rest of his time was spent on dope and music, the latter being his passion in life.

Camille sat right beneath Hugo in the door frame. She was leaning on what seemed to be her boyfriend, judging by the way she was sticking her tongue in his mouth. She was the girl every guy wanted to be with. Not a classic beauty, but pretty, in command of herself, clearly one of the boys. Her long and curly strawberry blond hair fell down to her waist. Her laugh was contagious. It cracked you up even when you had no idea what had gotten her started. A sexy gap between her two front teeth added to her charm. Her beau, Claude, was the serious one in this kitchen.

Camille became as close as a sister to me over the ensuing years. She went to CEGEP Rosemont and worked in a pastry shop on weekends. Although Claude too was a dedicated smoker, he spent an awful lot of time studying to become a civil engineer. Everyone seemed to be rather proud of Claude's goal in life. His dedication lent an air of refinement to the group. Claude was taking the easy way out by complying with what society and his parents expected of him, but we admired him nonetheless. He and Camille were inseparable, and their lovemaking moans, I was soon to discover, could be heard through the apartment's walls at any time, day or night.

Another girl, Grace, was sitting on Alex, but I could tell she wasn't his girlfriend. She came from a Québécois family not that different from mine. She was named after Grace Kelly, her mother's favourite actress. Unfortunately, in French the name Grace phonetically transforms itself into *grass*, but it's worse in Québécois—something like *grrawss*. Also, in French, *grasse* means fat, something laughable since Grace was as thin as a fishing pole. She was the skinniest thing I had ever seen, no more than eighty pounds. Everything about her was bones and teeth. She had a pretty smile, though, the kind of smile you'd want to wake up to, and from what I quickly gathered, many guys seemed more than willing to see that girl's face at the crack of dawn. She was never without a date. Despite her Lilliputian size, Grace could seriously party. She could outdrink just about anybody of any size, something remarkable in those days of smoke and acid. A girl who could hold her drinks was exceptional. Grace could smoke, drink, put a man to bed next to her, *and* award him with a smile in the morning light. Quite a date. Good-sport-there-for-fun girl. Foul words cascaded out of her mouth like a fountain of filth, totally unlike Grace Kelly. It was surreal to think she was the personal secretary of an Anglo big shot in the industrial part of town. Grace disliked me the minute I was introduced to her, I could tell. But I didn't give a damn. Being stoned can make you either paranoid or aloof. Ordinarily, I am of the second group, though I was definitely more self-conscious that evening.

Two guys sat on the kitchen counter by the sink. One was older, also in his early twenties. He talked loudly as if he meant for part of Saskatchewan to hear what he had to say. The other, a little younger, hung on his every word. Milou and Tintin.

In case you're not familiar with the classic Belgian comic heroes, Tintin is an audacious journalist always on the lookout for international intrigues. He never leaves home without his brave companion, a little white terrier he calls Milou. *Les aventures de Tintin et Milou.* In this kitchen, though, it was clear that Milou was the one calling the shots. Tintin told me later he was convinced that as long as he remained in Milou's shadow, filling the role of his ever-present sidekick, nothing bad could ever happen to him. Nobody knew much about Tintin's past or ever bothered to find out his real name. The teachers in school called him Tintin, his neighbours called him Tintin, even his own mother called him Tintin. Like a witness in a protection program, he had adopted this new name with the conviction that his future depended on it.

Milou, on the other hand, did not appreciate one bit being called by the famous dog's name. Then again, he had only himself to blame for it. At a younger age, he had felt the urge to change his first name. The one appearing on his Notre Dame Hospital birth certificate, the one his family had always used to get his attention, was the unbelievable appellation of Hilarius. His grandmother swore that her side of the family counted an ancestor with that name. According to her, he was canonized in the late fifteenth century. *St. Hilarius.*

It made you feel sorry for the saint. I mean, who can take you seriously when your name is Hilarius? But she had insisted that one of her grandchildren bear the name, and Milou was the chosen one.

When he turned thirteen, an age when humans tend to become incredibly sensitive about things that didn't matter one bit the day before, Hilarius couldn't take it anymore. He decided to change his name to Milou, and he ordered everyone around to call him by the white terrier's name. He figured this would bring him tons of friends since everybody loved Milou-the-dog. At first, it was hard for his friends to comply, and a few heated arguments arose along the way, but with time, good will, and patience, it was as if he had never been called otherwise. Hilarius became Milou to everybody. That is, everybody but his family. This made him Hilarius at home and Milou everywhere else.

A few years later, Milou-who-was-once-Hilarius read in a *Playboy* magazine a very serious and non-illustrated article about the impact of a name on its owner's destiny. Hilarius— he could only climb to the top of the world with a grand name like that! How stupid to have changed it! Milou backtracked and tried to return to being Hilarius, but no matter how hard he tried to reverse the situation, people kept calling him Milou. It was as if the dog's name was painted all over his body. His new friends knew him only as Milou, and his old friends told him there was no way in hell they would go through that ordeal one more time—they had lobotomized Hilarius out of their heads. A snake needs rough stones to shed its dry skin, and Milou was a desperate diamondback rubbing his scales ferociously on a bed of satin sheets. "Milou" stuck on him like the nose on his face. That was pretty much the end of Hilarius.

Milou was a part-time stripper. That's how he made a living. He performed on stage, shaking his hips to "Maggie May" while being distracted by the noisy comments of drunken women sitting in the front row asking the "doggy" where his "master" was. Tintin didn't strip. As Milou put it, his sidekick was "unstrippable." In other words, he was too fat to look cute in a leather-laced G-string. Milou deplored this inconvenience. He figured that if there were a bill downtown announcing that Tintin *and* Milou were taking their clothes off, they could end up in Vegas in no time—a perpetual dream of his. He kept pestering his friend to stick to a diet, and Tintin did try repeatedly, but he never managed to shed a single pound.

Upstaging Milou was virtually impossible. He too was ruling in that kitchen on my first visit there, but as a court buffoon. Tintin's best friend was done with school. He liked to say that his feet had gotten lost somewhere between CEGEP and university. He was convinced that somewhere, somehow, somebody would realize what a gold mine he was, just by being himself. Milou didn't have the body of an Adonis, but according to the owner of Le Chaton Rose Strip Club, he looked good enough to take his clothes off four evenings a week in front of a crowd. At the time, nobody in his circle of friends (or in his family, who had long given up on him) had ever bothered to visit the strip joint where he worked. They said it was embarrassing enough just to know he was parading his naked butt somewhere downtown.

Milou sported a Zorro outfit day in and day out throughout the hottest summer ever in Montreal. He always wore outrageous clothes. His reputation was so legendary that he had to work hard to live up to it. Whether stripping was really the best move of his life, nobody cared to ask. This was the kind of thing people expected him to do. In some ways, Milou's striptease career had a lot to do with my own destiny. But we'll get to that later.

Don't get me wrong—these kids weren't losers. They were like me. They had parents who cared for them. They went home for Christmas. They knew they could always count on their folks. And they loathed school just as much as I did.

Then there was Jude. Neither quieter nor less formidable, he was sitting at the kitchen table, rolling the biggest joints I had ever seen and drooling from his Mick Jagger mouth whenever he laughed. Jude looked a lot like the singer of the Stones. Same wide mouth, same puppy eyes, same Chinese astrological sign. There was a miniature Rider tarot deck on the table next to an enormous piece of hashish that had to be his, considering the way he was carelessly handling it. The cards sat there, waiting to become a piece of conversation. Jude was like that—he liked to flash stuff bought or stolen from stores downtown. Indian incense holders, jazz records featuring musicians unknown to us but world famous, tarot cards, crystals. Even Anglo girls from his Anglo college.

Jude could easily get front-row tickets to any show in town. He had connections. He knew people. He spoke English as easily as French, and for a boy named Jude Caron (you don't get more French Canadian than this), to be perfectly bilingual without a hint of an accent was a curiosity. Something definitely unpatriotic, but darn awesome.

Jude knew about Maharishi Mahesh Yogi and Baba Ram Dass, and he told incredible tales about a group of entranced priests he had once seen in a New York mosque, the Whirling Dervishes. Jude was also a liar. That first night he bragged about a girl he claimed to have coaxed into having sex with him on a horse. The best sex he ever had, he said. He explained how the motion of a horse was ideal for intercourse. I thought, *that's bullshit*. Of course, I was much too shy to tell him I thought he was making this up. I know about horses, and there's no way in hell you could talk a horse into that kind of nonsense. *You ride, you ride. You fuck, you fuck. None of that gooey stuff on my back*. To my surprise, everyone bought it. The guys looked at him with envy. The girls analyzed silently whether they would be willing to go that far to reach orgasm.

Thus, from the start I knew Jude could lie, and I suspected this wasn't his first try at it. Liar or not, he was charismatic, and he had the most beautiful hands I had ever seen. His long fingers rolled the hash in little pellets while he talked, often louder than Milou. He glanced in my direction a couple of times, and I felt he was trying to impress me. Impressed I was, especially when he started singing Led Zeppelin's "Living Loving Maid" with the real words. Not just the pathetic phonetic sounds we hummed to the music. He was singing the actual lyrics.

What a guy! I thought.

Chapter 3

*Listening to the B-side of a Genesis album in which
Peter Gabriel reminds his blue-eyed lover that
dinner's served*

*H*OW COULD *I* HAVE *ever lived without them?* They all
looked so gentle and decent, yet there was something
definitely rebellious about them. I wanted a life of rock and
roll, drugs, and sex—in that order—and it looked as if they
did too. They just had to get to know me a little. I wanted to
be part of them as soon as humanly possible.

In that apartment, there were no parents and no domestic
chores. Their own place. Their own jobs, their own studies,
and according to Alain, managing it all as they wished. So
free. They looked beautiful to me. They played nice music
too. Yes, Genesis, Jethro Tull, the Stones. Joints were huge
and burned perfectly. Everybody was funny, witty. I knew I
was finally at the right place.

My overwhelming experience in this New World kitchen
had made me forget how badly I had to pee. I gathered the
courage to get up and ask Frankie for directions to the bathroom. He seemed friendly enough to be approached with
such a mundane request. There was a lot of noise, and Frankie

misunderstood what I said and thought I was asking for a beer. To my surprise, he grabbed a screwdriver and opened the fridge door. The handle had disappeared God knows where. There was nothing but beer in there. An unidentified yellowish liquid floated in the vegetable drawer. For a second, I thought this was where people relieved themselves, and I mumbled that I didn't have to go after all. Frankie shrugged as if he didn't care one way or the other. I crawled back into my corner.

Time passed. There had to be a toilet somewhere. I really had to go. Sitting down on the cold floor just made it worse. I got up again and headed straight for the corridor, walking under Hugo and over Camille and Claude in the process. I made it look as though I knew exactly where I was heading. Nobody paid attention, but I could have sworn I saw Jude wink at me.

The corridor showed four doors leading to bedrooms, but there was no bathroom in sight. I followed the music and ended up in what seemed to be the living room. Someone had switched the lights off and changed Led Zeppelin for the B-side of Genesis's album Foxtrot. I heard Peter Gabriel whispering about blue eyes and true love.

I stood in the dark for a second. I could feel a presence in the room. An invisible hand reached for a lamp, and then right in front of me was a bare-breasted girl swinging her hips from side to side.

She smiled at me. "Isn't this divine?"

I didn't know if she was talking about the room, the song, her tits, or the joint smoking in the ashtray next to her. I smiled back, not wanting to compromise myself at this stage of our relationship. A black-and-white hand-painted scarf wrapped around her waist concealed her G-stringed behind. She was singing and dancing by herself, oblivious to the party going on at the other end of the corridor. Her long hair flowed around her. I was hypnotized by the grace of her movements, but I couldn't stand there just staring at her—*what would people think?*—and I still badly needed to pee. I exited the living room. She didn't seem to notice. The lights went off again. That was Marie, I soon discovered, and she was Hugo's beloved girlfriend.

I finally found the john right next to the kitchen. I must have been pretty nervous to have missed it. Everybody saw me going in, and I prayed to God I wouldn't make an audible fart or do anything embarrassing. So far spotless in my behaviour, I rejoined the kitchen crowd and went back to my corner. Someone passed a joint and another asked me something I can't remember today, but my reply was clever and funny, and everyone laughed and made room for me to get closer to the table. I saw Jude wink at me. This time, I was sure he had.

The clock hit 1:00 a.m., and people left in a hurry. It was a particularly cold night, and nobody wanted to miss the last bus. Alex, Hugo, Marie, Grace, Camille, and Claude, who lived on the premises, went to bed. Frankie packed his car with human flesh and took off. No one bothered to tidy up the apartment. The place was a mess—ashtrays full of cigarette and joint butts, empty beer bottles, as well as a few souls too stoned to make it home and already fast asleep on the living room carpet.

I was still sitting in the kitchen, on a chair by then, alone with the Siamese cat and Jude. He got up to put his coat on and offered to take me home. I accepted with a little too much enthusiasm. I'm sure he detected that. *My loss, his gain.* I said I had to check what Alain was doing. Luckily for me, he was with the others sleeping on the living room floor.

Jude and I were halfway through the door when Camille stepped out of her room wrapped in a faded pink bathrobe. I asked her to let Alain know I had to leave. "Tell him I'll be fine."

Jude was waiting for me up the stairs. Camille stretched

her neck to take a look at him. In a half-sweet, half-bitchy tone, she said, "You can't imagine just how fine a ride home you'll get, girl."

I pretended not to hear and ran up to join Jude.

Chapter 4

*Listening to Loggins and Messina warning a man about
the pitfalls of glory*

OUT THERE, THE WIND was inhumanly cold. One of those
nights that makes us Canadians wonder why the hell
we go on living in this country, and why so many people
inhabiting perfect-weather paradises dream of migrating
here. Mind you, I'd bet Canada is not their first choice.

Our backs against the wind, Jude and I headed for the
corner of Sherbrooke and Lacordaire. We jumped up and
down, flapping our arms like convulsive penguins in a vain
attempt to keep ourselves warm. By then, it was certainly too
late to catch a bus, and I assumed we would have no other
alternative but to hitchhike. I held my thumb high, gusts of
cold air licking the inside of my sleeve like an open flame on
a dry piece of wood. There was not a single car in sight.

We made it to the middle of the street, half running,
half laughing. Deprived of the protection of the buildings,
I shuddered as the wind cut sadistically through my clothes
like the razor of a maniac. The boulevard was deserted.

"Man, I hate the cold!" I gasped.

Jude noticed the back of my jean jacket, where my sister

Simone had embroidered an orange, pink, and red sun. Carried away by inspiration, she had also thrown in a yellow bird, but had placed it too far left. The result looked like a mustard stain. The bird was meant to fly around the sun, but he never made it there. The poor thing was freezing her butt off just like the rest of us.

"That's pretty, Geneviève. Did you make it yourself?"

"Yes," I lied, with an expression meaning he had yet to see what I was most certainly capable of.

"You'll have to design something on mine one of these days."

"Sure," I said. "Whatever you want."

I swallowed. Following this claim, I would have to bribe my sister big time to convince her to stitch something on Jude's jacket *and* keep her mouth shut about it. But I didn't feel guilty about embellishing the truth a bit. After all, I had caught Jude lying twice in a matter of hours. First, that silly story of him screwing on a horse, and second, he couldn't seriously mean what he had just said about that nonsense on my jacket. But I didn't mind—that second time he had lied to be nice to me. Now I had lied to him too. I felt we were even.

The early winter silence fell on us. No snow to muffle our steps, no engine sounds in the distance, no beating hearts but our own. It looked as if the city was about to roll up the sidewalks and fly south until April.

"Hey Geneviève, could you stitch, let's say, a map of the world on my jacket?" he asked. His eyes were hooded with doubt.

I shrugged as if he were asking Picasso to draw a cube. "Just about anything you like."

I sure knew how to make an ass of myself. Not only would I have to spend the next ten years of my life paying my kid sister for her work (the whole thing based on a solid installment plan she'd surely impose on me), but I would also have to get her some serious drawing lessons. My sister did have some artistic talents worth pursuing, but let's get real here—the bird on my back looked like a cross between a seagull and a kangaroo. A crescent moon maybe, but a map of the world? *Me and my big mouth.* I considered moving to Siberia and freezing to death just to avoid the embarrassment.

"That would teach me ..."

"What?"

"Nothing." Mouth betraying thoughts. It still happens to me all the time.

Being angry with myself did not make me feel any warmer. Jude took my arm. It made the skin on my neck shiver. He promised we'd be warm soon. And he was right. Far in the distance, headlights were heading our way. I braced myself, ready to pull my thumb out of my pocket and let it fall off from frostbite if I had to. Then I recognized the yellow light of a cab.

"Shit!" I muttered.

Without a word, Jude hailed the taxi emphatically, as if he were trying to get the attention of a pilot flying a plane. I couldn't believe it. Who in their right mind would spend money on a taxicab in Montreal?

The car stopped, and Jude ran to the driver, making a sign for him to roll down the window. The driver hesitated for a moment. He was obviously concerned for his safety. He locked the doors one at a time and rolled down the passenger window by an inch, right in front of *me*, ignoring Jude right by his side. I stood there speechless, my mouth frozen.

Jude cursed and ran to join me. He leaned toward the warm air coming from the narrow opening and, wiping his drippy nose on his sleeve, shouted, "How about five bucks to take us to Outremont, with one stop along the way?"

A chic residential area in Montreal? So that's where he lives? A rich kid?

I could tell the driver was considering leaving us out there in the cold. Or hell. Or whatever fucked-up place we undoubtedly belonged to. Reading his mind, Jude pushed his fingers in the opened window a second before the man had time to react. The cab driver didn't move, just looked at the windy road in front of him. He had yet to utter a word. I'm pretty sure he was considering stepping on the gas and fleeing from this possible trap. But something made him stay and listen, his facial expression ping-ponging from empathy to disgust as if begged by a blind man to practice mouth-to-mouth resuscitation on his obviously dead-for-days dog.

Jude pleaded relentlessly. With his big lips blue and frozen, you really had to pay close attention to understand what the hell he was saying. This temporary speech impediment also had the misfortune of making him look drunk. The driver cocked his head and took a disgusted look at me. I tried to appear as distinguished as possible, pushing away the locks of hair stuck on my wet cheeks. He didn't even smile. Jude persisted.

"Come on, man, be cool. The streets are empty, you have no customers, and it's *fucking cold!*"

I thought the "fucking" and the screaming were risky additions to his plea. The driver asked to see the moncy, and Jude flashed the blue bill. The man took the cold tender from Jude's shivering hand, and the back door magically flipped open. We jumped in, the warmth engulfing us like motherly arms.

The driver seemed just as impressed as I was. Here and there his eyes shifted from the road to Jude in the rear-view mirror. You need to have balls to bargain with a Montreal taxi driver. The driver and I both knew there was something special about that boy.

And now we were on our way home in a cozy taxi. I too was looking at Jude here and there, but mostly sideways. Between the driver and me, Jude was bombarded with glances. I couldn't help myself. I was amazed. Jude had guts, plus he was cute and clean—his body and clothes. He was perfectly bilingual. *And* he seemed to have an opinion on everything. *The ideal man.*

The taxi driver was from the Caribbean—Haiti, judging by the small flag spread on the dashboard. To make sure he wouldn't have to suffer what he probably assumed would be a moronic conversation between teenagers, he pushed a tape in his 8-track cassette deck and cranked up the volume. Calypso music. *Yuck.* Then again, for five bucks we couldn't complain too much. My jaw had stopped shivering, my blood flow was returning to normal, and I wanted to keep it that way.

Jude leaned over the front seat and tapped the driver on the shoulder. "You have something else we can listen to?"

The nerve! The man shook his head.

"Then can you try CHOM-FM 97.7? Thanks, I appreciate it."

The taxi driver pulled the mammoth cassette out and turned the radio dial left and right looking for CHOM, peeking more than ever in the rear-view mirror. At that point, he seemed not to care if Jude noticed. He didn't seem angry or afraid. He wasn't doing what Jude asked because he had to but because he was impressed. I covered my mouth to laugh. That was something.

Jude was whispering. He said he wanted me to learn something from what he had just done. He said I should know it was always easier to bargain with black drivers because a lot of potential customers are racist enough to refuse to take a ride with them, especially at night. I wondered how Jude, when he had hailed the cab, could have known from a distance whether the driver was black, white, or lime green. I wasn't sure and didn't dare to ask just yet. I added this question to the little pile of questions I was already gathering for him in my head. The driver located CHOM. Loggins and Messina sang about how careful we should be on the way to glory.

I felt strangely awake despite the late hour. Jude and I

talked about music and tarot cards (a topic I smartly brought into the conversation) and, of course, about the people back on Sherbrooke Street. He said he was closer to Alex, Hugo, and Milou. They had grown up on the same street and had attended the same elementary school, inseparable up to Grade 8. Then Jude was sent to an English high school in the west part of town. This was a bold move for a Québécois family originating from Rimouski, a region in Québec where being English or speaking the Queen's language is as despicable as scratching your crotch in public. Jude said he was glad his mother had forced him to go to Dawson College, even though at the time the idea sounded as appealing to him as a year in a dentist's chair. In the tone of voice adopted by people who have survived the unthinkable, Jude listed the many traumatic experiences he had suffered in an Anglo environment. The awful food, the repetitive insults, the cold shoulders, the snarls. However, he recognized it had been worth the many humiliations.

"Most decent dealers in Montreal are Anglos. And I sell hashish in large quantities."

He said this with neutrality, the way he might have confessed to collecting stamps. He looked up and smiled at the driver in the rear-view mirror. The Haitian was caught off guard. He looked away, shifting in his seat, and from then on pretended to be absorbed by the empty streets.

Jude went on. In 1970, his family had moved to Outremont, keeping him even farther away from his childhood friends. He lived with his mom, his little brother, a stepfather he called by his first name, and the stepfather's two daughters from a previous marriage. According to Jude, his stepsisters were much uglier than Cinderella's.

"And more stupid."

His little brother was okay, but at the age of eleven was still too young to be much fun. His mom was an ex-beauty queen who had turned to booze and pills to make it through her dull and predictable suburban life.

"She's a *Valley of the Dolls* character," he said without smiling.

When his mom was high, her vision became blurry, and her mirror swore she was still the prettiest of them all. His biological dad was dead, killed in a car accident the night before Jude's tenth birthday. Jude had no nice memories of him. He said the man was a Casanova who took a hike whenever his path crossed a 36+ bra. His mom remarried a couple of years later to an overweight and wealthy man who wasn't particularly fond of her boys. Between two Valiums and a Quaalude, she worked hard on her version of the American dream: a house in a posh area, a husband with a good income, clean kids, a swimming pool, and three aquariums filled with tropical fish. Jude said he was sure his mother suspected something about his *business*, but she didn't want to know. His stepfather couldn't possibly have noticed, drowned as he was in his corporate meetings and countless business trips.

Like most fascinating people, Jude manifested little interest in the interlocutor facing him, incidentally me at that moment. He was too engrossed in his own incarnation to dwell on an ant like me. I didn't mind. In fact, I accepted it with grace. He was right actually—he wasn't missing much. My family history was boring. My mom and dad were still together after a zillion years of marriage. My father was an accountant, my mother a housewife. Her idea of getting high was dropping an aspirin whenever she felt the symptoms of a migraine (usually a persistent twitch on her left eyelid), while my dad drank his two weekly beers watching the hockey game on Saturday nights. I had a deadly obnoxious younger sister and an older brother whom I adored for no particular reason. I had never owned a purebred animal in my life, let alone creatures from the Seven Seas. Jude would have been bored enough to commit suicide. I was grateful he didn't ask.

He was funny, clever, and I desperately wanted him to kiss

me. How could this be happening with Jean-Luc and the 2.3 kids to come? In typical teenager fashion, it took only about six hours for Jean-Luc to become a memory from another lifetime. The day before, close to seventeen, I'd almost been engaged. Twenty-four hours later, I was dreaming about making out with a stranger. Go figure. Something powerful deep inside me had taken place in that kitchen corner. I had found the crowd I had always wanted to belong to, and I was positive that soon I would spend my every weekend in their company. Jude would be back on Sherbrooke Street. So would Milou and Tintin. Hugo would hang in the doorway smoking joints. Marie, Grace, Camille, and Claude would have a good laugh. I just had to be there too. I wouldn't have missed it for the world.

Jude put his arm around my shoulders as if it were the most natural thing in the world. Then, to my horror, he said he did not visit his friends' place often. He cared about them, he said, but he became bored after a while because all they ever did was hang out and get stoned. *Well, what else is there to do?* I wondered, but didn't ask. I pictured Jude having secret appointments in downtown parking lots, dealing with shady characters and addressing each other by code names. He said he rarely mixed his French world with his English world.

"It's a good strategy," he explained.

To top it all off, he was attending a CEGEP *downtown.* This was so—I don't know—mature. Jude said he didn't see the point in being stoned all the time. He tried to keep a low profile and didn't indulge in more than what was necessary to his "profession." He went to the Sherbrooke Street apartment from time to time to drop off some hashish for Hugo, one of his "associates."

"But I'd rather go out downtown."

Downtown. An area he pretended to know well enough to venture into. *Downtown.* Sure, we went downtown, sometimes. For shopping, for a movie, for a show. But we didn't exactly hang out downtown. Ever. In Old Montreal by the Old Port? Sometimes. But not downtown. *Downtown.* Where the mods hung out.[1] Where it's common to speak English and get a piece of fresh fruit in your drink. Downtown, where anything can happen. *Downtown.* The Great Wild Unknown. *Jude. Downtown.* Now my head was spinning. But I liked it. Downtown was introduced into my fairy tale (along with the ugly stepsisters). Suddenly my newfound Sherbrooke Street paradise looked as exciting as a flat tire.

Jude explained that Hugo and Alex sold hashish *au détail* (retail) to their circle of friends. One gram for seven or eight bucks. Jude himself did not sell retail. Not anymore, anyway.

"You never had problems with the police?" I asked.

"Nope. I'm very careful. Everybody will tell you. I'm real paranoid when it comes to my safety."

I was hypnotized, falling harder and harder for this golden boy. I was so grateful he was giving *me* the time of day. He probably knew dozens of prettier girls he could easily seduce. Then again, I was fresh meat in this crowd where new women were as rare as a hair on a stripper's leg. Marie, Camille, and Grace owned the territory, and if new boys were always welcome, girls were shunned.

Jude and I talked and talked. We were really hitting it off. Listening to him and contemplating the next few hours, I began to think the prospect of landing in my bed with my sister snoring in her sleep next to me was too much of an anticlimax to stand. Walking the distance from my home to my brother's place seemed a better plan. Carl had his own apartment three blocks away from my parents' house, and I

---

1. Not to be mistaken with the British phenomenon of the same name, though there are some similarities. British mods, mainly teenage boys, were a '60s thing. They dressed up fancily, popped amphetamines, and devoured pop rock or so-called art rock. By contrast, Québec mods, teenage boys and girls, arrived later in the '70s, prompted by the early disco music. They also dressed up in fancy clothes with linen shirts and platform shoes, but speed was not their only pleasure. A Québec mods was willing to get high on just about anything he could put his jewelled hands on. And whether there was one or ten of them, the word was mods, never used in the singular form.

often went there to sleep on weekends. It was the first place my mother would call late at night if she didn't find me in bed. And this being Friday night, the place might be empty, since my brother often spent his weekends at his girlfriend's place up north in Les Laurentides. I prayed he wouldn't be home. I needed to be by myself to digest the images of my unforgettable evening. There would surely be some pot lying around, which meant I could smoke a last joint before going to bed and dream with eyes wide open about my new friends.

The taxi stopped in front of my parents' house. Inspired by Jude's daring ways, I asked the driver if he would mind dropping me off a little farther along—the kind of thing I was usually much too shy to do. He complied, stopping in front of Carl's place, clearly impatient to get on with his destiny, anywhere far away from us. Jude said goodbye, surprising me by asking if I had a sister I could introduce him to. I had been honest enough to tell him I was involved with "some kind of a boyfriend," mainly because I didn't want to appear undesirable. I detected a disappointment in Jude's basset-hound eyes when I told him about Jean-Luc, something that made me feel akin to Raquel Welch.

At that point of my life, I superstitiously indulged in no more than one lie a day, and I had already exhausted my daily allowance with my haute couture blathering. I had also shamelessly lied about the nature of my relationship with Jean-Luc. I told Jude I loved Jean-Luc, then cowardly added that *I used to love him.* "Jean-Luc and I are childhood friends. Puppy love, you know, someone I think about, here and there." I'd tried hard to make it sound as though he was almost dead or about to be drafted to Vietnam. To answer Jude's only question about my family—yeah, I did have a baby sister (rolling eyes with disgust), but she was a gross fourteen-year-old and "kind of mentally ill." Killed the bird in the egg but did nothing to my lying score of the day. Jude made a sound like "too bad." Two lies. No, three, actually, because my sister was not mentally deficient. Three lies in a single day. Very bad omen.

The driver was now threatening to step on the gas with the back door open if he had to. I stepped out, but not before timidly inviting Jude in to smoke a last joint. This was crazy because 1) I wasn't even sure whether my brother was home, 2) I didn't know whether there was anything to smoke, and 3) if there was, that pot was most likely to be stale and dry as sawdust. I suddenly feared Jude would laugh as if I was offering him to join a cookie exchange held by an old ladies' knitting club. I wasn't sure about much anymore, but I knew I didn't want that night to end. To my relief, Jude accepted with no hesitation. The taxi driver, who had already pocketed the five bucks for the longer ride to Outremont, was quickly dismissed. Jude didn't ask for a cash return of any kind even though we were no more than halfway to the negotiated fare.

Really, what a guy.

Chapter 5

Listening to Carey (not Mariah, but Joni's)

*T*HE GODS WERE ON my side. My brother was nowhere in sight. Hallelujah!

I had yet to inform Jude that we were in an adult-free zone. He was tiptoeing, probably nervous at the idea of triggering parental intervention. Then he realized how small the place was and that there was no way this was my parents'. He relaxed a bit, asked if we were allowed in.

"Of course," I said. "What do you think? That I break into strangers' apartments?"

He obviously knew people who did exactly that because he didn't answer.

I told him where we were, adding that my brother was most probably up north and explaining that I had a key to Carl's place because I was in charge of feeding his cat whenever he was away. I went into the kitchen with Jude trailing behind me. I picked up the cat's dish from the floor and poured fresh water into it. I was nervous, my hands wouldn't stop shaking, and I kept babbling nonsense while Jude took his jacket off. He leaned against the wall and tucked his T-shirt methodically into his pants. He stood there with a big grin, his hands in his pockets. I felt my face turning crimson. I was in a full blah-blah mode by then.

"You see, Suzanne, that's her name, my brother's girl-friend, well she's from Ste-Adèle. This girl really hates the city and …"

I reached for a can of cat food below the sink, talking and talking as if Jude was begging me to go on. The cat was nowhere to be seen.

"You know, the pollution and the noise. She runs to her folks' place the second she gets out of school …" I said a couple more senseless things about the unpredictable weather in Les Laurentides. I didn't look at Jude once, just minded the cat food. "God knows why she likes it so much up there. Even in the summer. You know with all the black flies! Those bastards fly away with small pieces of skin, you know. And the fucking mosquitoes! Well, you probably know how bad it is up north …"

Say something, Jude. I'm drowning here.

Jude followed me on my way to the living room. I must have added, "Gentlemen, start your engines," because before I had a moment to put a record on the turntable or squeeze the grass out from the hiding space under the couch, Jude was all over me. Of course, I couldn't have been more cooperative.

The waterbed in my brother's bedroom was empty and available, but Jude never suggested that we should borrow it. As for me, when a moment is perfect, I don't like to jinx my luck by moving things or people around too much.

Instead, we made love on my brother's living room carpet. The whole affair was simple but enormously satisfying. Jude was experienced compared with Jean-Luc, my bible boy, and sole point of reference, and I experienced immense sensual pleasure in his arms. At that age, bodies are pink, breath is fresh no matter what was previously ingested, and hands are trembling with intensity. Words are scarce and those that are uttered have the romantic authenticity of sentiments seldom (if ever) expressed before.

The only drawback was the size of his penis. At first, I thought it only looked bigger because of Jude's modest frame, something like an optical illusion. But my hand came back from its investigation reporting that this thing was much larger than anatomically fathomable. Mind you, besides Jean-Luc's and the occasional accidental peek at my dad's and brother's, I had not seen many penises. I don't remember if *Playgirl* magazine even existed at the time. My instincts told me the item might be too much for me to handle, and sure enough, I felt a little pain in the pelvic area.

I don't care what some women say about it, I don't see the appeal of a monster penis. I mean, get real. What can you possibly do with all this? Jude seemed aware of his handicap and was as gentle as a seventeen-year-old boy with a serious hard-on can be. I took that pain as my first scar from Jude's love. He was my prince, and I would never let him go. We made love twice and fell asleep, a couple of interlaced angels rolled in a chequered blanket on a cloud of green shag carpeting.

My mother called. I told her I'd be back the next day around noon. Of course, I didn't mention a word about Jude. Minutes later, I was back on the carpet, spooning my new love.

I woke up at ten. I got up quietly, took a shower, made some coffee, and put on Joni Mitchell's *Blue* album. Her crystalline voice praised California. My soul was as full of sunshine as the Western state, and I too on this Saturday morning felt like buying myself a piano and strewing flowers throughout the room. Life was simply glorious.

Jude was still fast asleep. The cat, Syphilis (she was no beauty), finally deigned to grace the room with her presence. She sat next to Jude's hip, examining with great interest his uncovered, limp penis, appearing to debate whether she should attack it or not. *Friend or foe?*

Syphilis came from the local SPCA, and her claws had been removed by her previous owner. Still, I was certain she believed that she, the cat of the house, was expected to do something about this *thing*.

Friend or foe?

For Pete's sake, she had seen rats smaller than that!

Friend or foe?

Jude turned toward her in his sleep. The one-eyed creature sprang forward suddenly, inches from Syphilis's inquisitive nostrils. She jumped backward, but curiosity took over when she couldn't detect a trace of aggressive behaviour from the reptile. A skin tube ready to jump at her throat? She doubted it. For several minutes, she cautiously inspected the area through the dense pubic hair.

Friend or foe?

Hell, she had no idea. I could tell the suspense was driving her nuts. Syphilis sat back, annoyed and possibly looking for a fight. She stared at me. Her inquiries were simple enough. (What's the story here? What's this? A toy? A joke? An insect?)

"None of that, silly cat."

I kissed Jude's hip. Syphilis looked stunned. She licked her front paw, putting some distance between herself and the crisis at hand. Unable to identify an imminent threat, she decided to ignore the potential danger and instead, in a sisterhood gesture, she lay down by Jude's side and put a soft paw on the monster. She half closed her eyes, purring softly.

Friend.

Chapter 6

Listening to Jackson Brown wondering if love needs
his heart

THOUGH I SHOULD HAVE known better, if not by experience at least by mere logic, I ended up being brutally honest with Jean-Luc. Explaining in graphic detail why I was leaving him for Jude was definitely not the smartest move of my life. I had demonstrated far more savvy years before when at the precocious age of five I had informed my kindergarten boyfriend of the week, Michel, himself five and a half, that our relationship was going nowhere and that I had an irrepressible crush on the new boy in class. I didn't explain to Michel why I preferred the other boy, but any fool could see that my heart's new contender wore funky clothes and could draw absolutely divine cats and dogs with a basic box of Crayolas. I did not discuss the details with Michel (he was already pulling on some other girl's hair anyway). I just made my message clear by saying something in the neighbourhood of "If you try holding my hand again, I'll scream." Not that saying this to Jean-Luc would have been smart, but compared with what I did, it would have been pure wisdom.

While I was frolicking on the fibres of my brother's carpet with Jude, my still-very-official boyfriend Jean-Luc, mysteriously alerted by some radar, was placing frantic calls to my parents' house. "At least ten times," according to my mom, who tended to exaggerate whenever she was exasperated. Jude left Carl's place around two in the afternoon, and I went home. He said he would not be able to see me before the next day, and I should know that he often *worked* on weekend nights. Business to attend to. I didn't absorb this most disturbing information about his availability on Saturday nights. Instead, what I saw was a perfect opportunity to break up with Jean-Luc.

Jude didn't ask me to dump Jean-Luc, but I was sure there was no doubt in his mind that I would. I wished it could be as simple as snuffing a cigarette. *Poof.* Gone. I admit with lingering shame that the way I handled myself that evening was despicable. Believe me, I never intended to be cruel. I've tried to piece together the events of that unfortunate evening on numerous occasions, looking for a rational explanation for my behaviour (and I imagine Jean-Luc did too), but to no avail. I was just so stupid.

Jean-Luc's repeated calls made me nervous. Was he suspecting something? *Damn.* It was remarkably easy for me to convince myself that this separation was for the best. No doubt about it, Jean-Luc would land on his feet in no time. He would marry a smart, nice, plump girl with hips wide enough to carry the many children he wished to raise.

"Seven kids would be better, don't you think, Geneviève? One for each colour of the rainbow," he used to say with watery eyes.

Cute, I know. But that Sherbrooke Street smoke-filled kitchen made me realize that having children and staying home were the last things I wanted to do with my life.

After a vague explanation to my mother concerning my whereabouts the previous evening, I phoned Jean-Luc. He answered after the first ring, muttering a small hello. His tone somehow irritated me, and I made sure mine was neutral. "Hi," I said with as much calm as I could muster.

"Oh, hi Geneviève."

He sounded as if he was afraid of something. Or maybe it was just my imagination.

"So what's new?" I asked. The moment I said this, I cursed myself because, of course, this would open the door for—

"Oh, nothing much. What about you?"

"Nothing," I blurted.

Whoops. There went my daily lie. I couldn't afford that. "Well, actually, yes, something—hmm—I would really like to see you."

It sounded as if I *needed* to see him. As if I couldn't wait to be in his arms. *Shit.* The conversation was not going the way I wanted. I should have called my friend Véronique first to rehearse. I was flying solo like a dumb-ass with no net to protect myself from my failing inspiration. I knew I had to call her and tell her about Jude. After all, she was my best friend, though we didn't get to see each other that much anymore. Of course, she wouldn't approve.

"Jean-Luc is such a catch," she'd whine.

I was already picturing myself telling her about the facts of life and all the things she would never understand as long as she didn't let her virginity take a hike. She'd never had a crush on anybody. Except perhaps on Jean-Luc. Well, she could have him now if she wanted. However, she should probably wait a few months in the name of etiquette. I was mentally throwing Jean-Luc into Véronique's arms, something odd considering that a couple of weeks before I had snapped at her for dancing too close to him at her birthday party.

Jean-Luc, unaware of the inner dialogue between crazy me and my evil self, was ardently responsive to my plea. Of course. He always was. With a nudge-nudge-wink-wink inflection in his voice, he said, "Sure! Anytime you want—what about tonight? It's special, after all."

Am I missing something here?

Jean-Luc chuckled nervously.

And then I remembered. *Oh! How could I have forgotten? Of course!*

"I was thinking, today being our tenth-month anniversary, I'd like to take you out for a romantic candlelit dinner downtown. What do you say?"

Honest to God, I had totally forgotten about the anniversary. *Has it already been ten months? Sorry, Jean-Luc, but we won't make it to the eleventh.* It was sad to think that on the same date the following month, Jean-Luc would be celebrating the one-month anniversary of our breakup, instead of our eleventh together. *Bummer.* But I couldn't help it.

This reminded me of my mother's sister, Aunt Cécile. She had dumped her husband—Uncle René—on the occasion of their twenty-fifth wedding anniversary. She "fired" him at the reception, a party she had paid for and organized all by herself since Uncle René was unable to chip in. He had spent most of his adult life "between jobs." His full-time mission consisted of ignoring Aunt Cécile and the bills to be paid. After twenty-five long years of marriage juggling a lazy husband, two children, a sloppy dog, a lousy job, and endless domestic drudgery, Aunt Cécile felt ready to devote the rest of her days on earth to taking care of herself. She had carefully planned her exit and she could think of no other way to do it. Uncle René didn't see it coming. Nobody did.

It happened at Ruby Foo's, a big red-and-black Chinese restaurant on Décarie Boulevard. I remember the party, the toasts, the jolly atmosphere, the guests kissing, the yellow ribbons around the cupcakes, the sparkling white wine ready to be popped. And all of a sudden, Aunt Cécile's speech at the microphone.

"Hush, hush, everyone. Please—can I have your attention for a moment?"

Guests gathered around her, all smiles.

"Sorry you came all this way to hear this, but I want to avoid unnecessary gossip."

People chuckled, anticipating a good joke. Turning to Uncle René, Aunt Cécile sighed, her large breasts covered in a floral print.

"I've had enough of you, René. I'm leaving you. You've never been a good husband to me. You've never cared to find a job to help me pay the bills. You've never tried to make my life easier. You've never lifted a finger to help me at home. You sit on your fat ass in front of the TV all day while I work like a slave. The kids are grown up now, René, and I want my life back. There's no use trying to make me change my mind. I'm all set to go. I have my own place, my own bank account, everything. I'll be out of the house by Monday."

You could hear a fly fart.

"In other words, René, I want a divorce."

I remember the glasses raised, ready to toast, the awkward silence, the strangled laughs, and the open jaws awaiting the punch line. Aunt Cécile turned to the crowd.

"For the record, he has never been violent, and it's not because he drinks too much or anything of the kind. And I'm not having an affair. I just don't love this man anymore, and I haven't for a long, long time." Aunt Cécile shook her head slowly from side to side, a resigned expression on her face.

Several seconds passed and suddenly the reception hall resembled the *Titanic* after it hit the iceberg. Chairs were shoved out of the way, people looked around in disbelief. Fingers pointed in all directions. Outstretched arms reached for Uncle René. A scandal. Aunt Cécile grabbed the microphone again.

"I'm sorry, really sorry. Maybe it's better for everyone to go home. Thanks for coming."

And then she walked out, ignoring the collective outrage. Cécile's oldest sister, my mom, caught up with her on the street. My mother later told me they didn't utter a word to each other as they walked. Aunt Cécile hurried on as if her life was waiting for her somewhere up that street. My mom led her sister toward a delicatessen nearby. Aunt Cécile didn't object. They sat in a booth and each ordered a double shot of St. Léger scotch. My mom took Cécile's hand, the one with the wedding band still on.

"Why did you have to do it today, Cécile? Why today, on your twenty-fifth wedding anniversary?"

"That was my last gift to him, sister—two events and only one date to remember. René's so lazy. Men like him pray for this kind of simplification."

"Hello? Hello? So? What do you say? What time should I pick you up?" Jean-Luc was almost screaming on the line.

Scene for a breakup: a candlelit dinner. Take one. "Where would you like to go?" I mumbled.

"A little French restaurant downtown called Fanny. My mom says it's *very* romantic."

Great, just what I need. A romantic restaurant chosen by his mother who would most likely pick us up afterward as she usually did on the rare occasions we went downtown. *No way, José.* Of course, I had the option of postponing the breakup, but I knew I couldn't go through a romantic evening with Jean-Luc. Cancelling the anniversary dinner was also out of the question. I was trapped. I realized that up to that moment my voice had been free of any speck of excitement. I tried harder.

"Well, wow! That sounds nice! But you know what? This time I'd really like for us to take the subway back and forth. We should give your mom the night off. I'd rather be alone with you tonight."

Unaware of the elephant about to sit on his face, Jean-Luc was delighted. "But she doesn't mind, you know."

"Sure, but I'd like to do it this way—I mean, if it's okay with you, of course."

"Sure, why not?"

He was so easy to convince. It was too bad this conversation was almost over, just as I was finally getting the hang of it.

"Great. It's all set, then. Do you mind if I pick you up a little early, like at around five?"

Shit, that's in less than two hours.

"I'd like to stop at l'Alternatif on our way to the restaurant. I want to get the new Uriah Heep album. Man, I heard it last night at Gilles's place and it blew my mind. His parents were out for the evening. We smoked a few joints and checked out new records. Cool album. You'll love it too, I'm sure. So? Five is good?"

Notice anything? Jean-Luc made no attempt to know where *I* had been the night before. He willingly admitted he had spent it at Gilles's, but he didn't end with "What about you? What did *you* do last night?"

"I'll make a reservation for seven, okay, *chérie*?"

Though I had always enjoyed hearing Jean-Luc call me *chérie*, that day it was unpleasant, like chewing on aluminum foil. One thing was sure—I was done with him. "Fine, Jean-Luc. See you then."

How could a smart girl like me have fallen out of love so quickly with the most perfect catch? I didn't know. Maybe the only reason I had ever pictured myself spending the rest of my days with him was because it was the "normal" thing to do. Our families expected it and approved of it.

As I hung up on his enthusiastic "See ya!" I felt the sour taste of bile gushing from the pit of my stomach up my throat. This was the first breakup I had initiated since my kindergarten experience. You could say I was out of practice. But first things first: what do you wear for such an occasion?

With no time to spare, I skipped phoning Véronique, praying I'd reach her the next day before she heard the big news from a sobbing Jean-Luc. I rushed to my room, looking for something appropriate to wear. Heaven knows I rarely shopped with this type of event in mind. Jean skirts, jeans, jean dress—those were all I owned. My closet was an ocean of indigo blue. *Crisis, crisis.*

Simone, my kid sister, was sitting on her bed in the room we shared. She was concentrating intensely on her long nails (two things were long on her otherwise petite body—her thick black hair and her razor-sharp, witchy nails). She glanced briefly in my direction, a bottle of red Cutex in her hand. Her bed was covered with blood-red cotton balls. It was gross, as if she had accidentally severed one of her fingers. Or someone else's. I hated the smell of nail polish, and she knew it, but did she give a damn? I was far too upset to even bother mentioning it to her, let alone fighting about it. It was her lucky fuckin' day.

I rushed to the wall and tore off every idol picture from my past—Bobby Sherman, David Cassidy, the Jackson 5— signalling my little-girl life was completely over. Simone raised her eyes, absently blowing on her nails. She made no remark. She had never cared for teenybopper idols anyway. (As a matter of fact, she'd quit listening to the Partridge Family and the Osmonds the day she put her hands on a James Taylor album. Then she turned to Bruce Cockburn, Elton John, Crosby, Stills, Nash & Young, Jackson Browne, Joni Mitchell, and others—as far as I was concerned, the girl had impeccable taste in music.)

Her indifference shifted to a lower gear—in fact, it evap- orated—when I opened the door of her closet. I slid the hangers from side to side, casually removing a few items. She squeaked like a mouse and jumped up. I pushed her away with one hand. Predictably, she rushed to the kitchen, urging Mom to intervene. I heard her say something about me invading her privacy. *Man, I can't believe it—what a brat.* While Simone was pleading for assistance, I put together the perfect outfit to impersonate my own version of the Princess of Darkness. A black skirt of mine plain as a rainy day and my sister's black woollen turtleneck. *Black is good. It makes a mourning statement, and as a bonus my perspiration will go unnoticed.* Mom made her entrance, my hysterical sister trailing behind her. When Simone recognized her sweater in my hands, she flipped out like a lady catching a maid snooping in her jewellery box.

Mom grabbed her in time. She was aiming for my throat with her painted nails, something that would have made a mess of the both of us considering the polish wasn't dry yet. I explained to my mother that all I wanted was to borrow the sweater for one evening. One evening. That was all. No big deal. That alone sent my sister into a fit suitable for a straitjacket. Mom scolded us gently. Why couldn't we share our things nicely between sisters?

"Why can't we?" Simone bellowed. "I'll tell you why! Because she never ever lends me anything of hers."

Well, she had a point. If she wanted anything that was mine she had to pay with crisp one-dollar bills or a back massage. But on that day, I was willing to yield in order to gain. As if I were addressing myself to the most fortunate soul on earth, I said I would gladly exchange the sweater for (I caught my breath) my entire Beatles collection. For one evening only and not a minute more. I made the conditions clear: should she scratch any of my records with her stupid claws, I'd cut her entire wardrobe into pieces so small she'd never be able to put them back together, no matter how good she was at sewing.

"All the Beatles plus Deep Purple in Rock," she whined.

The little rodent had balls. She sensed I was as helpless as a cornered coyote, and she viciously took advantage of the situation. I stayed cool, instead playing the mature one. After all, I was older. "Fine," I said, "but then I also want your black belt and your black tights." (Disdain here, as if I were asking for one of those bloody cotton balls on her bed.)

I figured the deal was fair enough. A win-win situation, as we say today. I was in for a big surprise.

Still hiding behind my mother, the little nuisance barked, "You get the belt and the tights if I can borrow the T-shirt you bought at Dapper Dan last week. For one day only."

Bitch! I had gone to a great deal of trouble to hide this new acquisition from her. I'd gone as far as keeping it in my schoolbag and putting it on only once at school. How naïve of me! Nothing escaped that viper. And I was the one invading her privacy? *God, give me strength, or I'll strangle her.*

"Don't act as if you don't know what I'm talking about," she snarled. "I saw it in your schoolbag. You want me to show it to you?"

I could have started a second round of arguments just by asking what the hell she was doing with her creepy little paws in my bag, but Mom gave me her sad, begging-for-closure look. The poor woman had to get back to her kitchen. I could distinctly perceive something burning on the stove. Custard, from the smell of it. I gave up, not because I wanted to please my sister but because I adored my mother. I was also running out of time, as well as of patience, and I needed to remain focused. Reluctantly, I extended my hand to shake Simone's in a white-flag gesture, but she mistook my intention for a slap aimed at her cheek. She screeched and jumped back. I raised my eyes at the ceiling as if I wished for them to roll to the back of my head.

"Okay. You win."

Simone ran to my record box and grabbed the albums she had fought for. Then the smart-ass followed Mom all the way back to the kitchen. She didn't know that this time she didn't have to leave the room to avoid further confrontation. True, on any other occasion, I would have quietly waited for Mom to get back to the kitchen before I pulled Simone's hair, which would have sent her into a screaming fit alarming enough for my mother to run back to our room. Then, and only then, would I have meticulously calculated my move and leaped on my bed—in a smooth motion, a magazine in hand—at the precise moment my mom would have pushed the door open and witnessed Simone running around and howling like a wolverine. Mom would have looked at me and I at her. The expression on my face would have said, "What the hell is wrong with her now?" as if Simone was suffering from some rare type of neurological disorder, just as I had told Jude.

Despite my behaviour, I occasionally felt sorry for my little sister. I mean, my older brother teased me to madness sometimes, so I turned to Simone and gave her the same treatment. But who did she have to drive nuts? She often begged our parents to have a little brother or sister (with a strong preference for a sister, of course—much easier to control). She too wanted her own special someone to abuse.

"Then again," my dad would say to her, "the next child would also want a younger brother or sister. This one would want one too. And so on. So tell me dear, who would be the last lucky one?"

"Yeah, Dad, right. Gotta be me."

Poor Simone.

Chapter 7

Listening to Elton John urging us to set the mission on fire

I WAS FINALLY LEFT TO myself with everything I needed to make it through a date I anticipated with dread. I dressed in my black attire and faced the mirror. I looked cute in a morbid way. Like a straight-haired version of Edith Piaf, though my features had little in common with the French singer's. Edith was pale and always seemed as if she were about to faint. And I wasn't that skinny. My thick auburn hair covered my shoulders like a cheap fur collar. I hated it, along with the stupid birthmark like a bull's eye in the middle of my forehead. If it weren't for that, I wouldn't have had to wear bangs. And I hated my bangs. I can't remember being thrilled about any aspect of my body at that age. I was often told that my eyes were beautiful, but it seemed as if people said this to anybody with non-brown eyes. Mine were grey, grey as a stormy day. Watching life through those couldn't possibly lead me to happiness. I paid little attention to compliments. To me, they were lies, something meant to make me feel good, nothing more.

I put on some baby-blue eye shadow and thick mid-night-blue mascara (a common fashion faux pas of the '70s), and finished up with a touch of pink, glistening Mary Quant lip gloss. The mirror reflected signs of the transformation taking place in me. I felt it was obvious. Weren't my eyes shinier than usual? Wasn't my posture more womanly? It was plain to see how I had matured in the past twenty-four hours.

I walked to the kitchen. My sister made a nasty comment about me looking like Alice Cooper, but I ignored her. My mom glanced up from the chicken she was stuffing and said, "*Mon Dieu*, Geneviève, you look like you're on your way to the slaughterhouse."

It was there. Written all over my face. All of sudden, I felt a hundred years old. Dear Mom. I could never hide anything from her. She knew my insides as thoroughly as those of the chicken in her hands. I was embarrassed by my emotional nudity, as if she could see what I was about to do.

"Everything's fine." I said nervously. "Why do you say that?"

"I don't know, baby. Something about the way you're holding yourself."

I immediately straightened my spine, in the process shedding a bit of the world from my shoulders.

My sister was a lot more helpful. "You look fat—that's what it is. Black makes people look fat. Everybody knows that."

Oh man, she is playing with the handles of her own casket. My mom threw an angry look at her, harsh enough to turn Simone into a salt statue. My sister got the drift and silently returned to the pile of records in front of her. I decided to ignore her comment once again. She would pay for all of this, of course, but later. Mom's tired eyes gave me a million thanks. One less battle to squelch.

The doorbell rang. I jumped like the villain that I was. My mom wiped her hands on her apron and ran to the door the way she always did. She embraced my tall ex-to-be in her tiny arms. I knew how Jean-Luc appreciated my mom and how she considered him almost as her second son. After all, he had been around forever. Jean-Luc and I had always been close friends, long before we had started dating, and I knew my folks would be devastated by our breakup. Especially my mom. But she would respect my choice. For the duration of her brief stay on this planet, this woman never, ever let me down.

I had the greatest mom in the world. Nothing shocked her. Over the years, I dragged home some alarming characters: guys with long greasy hair, tangled beards, glassy eyes. Or girls covered with beads and patchouli, not to mention cats, dogs, a snake, and six rats (I have a thing for animals). My mom never judged anything at face value. She had a way of making you feel like you could change things in this hopeless world. There was no point in lying to her because the truth never made her angry. If you went wrong, she was convinced that she and God had no choice but to forgive you. This was her precept, and she religiously lived by it. I tried hard to treat my parents with contempt—it's a mission at that age—but I found this as painful as my mother did. She truly was an angel, and I felt blessed to have her for a mom.

Jean-Luc was coming my way, arm in arm with my mother. Winking at me while hugging him, she said she'd bake not one but two chocolate pies if he cared to join us for dinner the following week. I frowned. How could she extend this invitation without asking me first? Then again, why should she? Shouldn't I have been delighted that they got along so well? Jean-Luc took one glance at me and smiled so hand-somely that for a moment I thought I was about to make a huge mistake. He placed a chaste kiss on my mouth. And another one. I did not feel a thing. I mean, it was as if I had been kissed by a box of unsalted crackers. It did not make me shiver one bit. Jean-Luc didn't notice, and he smacked his lips with pleasure. He complimented my outfit.

My mother beamed. "You see? You do look great!"

She said this as if my sister's opinion carried any weight with me. *Not.*

"Ready?" he asked.

He showed no sign of distress. He wouldn't have been so impatient had he known what was in store for him. I knew he'd had to save money to be able to afford this expensive meal. Once again, I considered putting the whole thing off. But eggs were broken, and a messy omelette was on its way.

To make things harder, Jean-Luc looked better than ever. He was wearing my favourite sweater, as blue as his eyes. If it weren't for the skin between eyes and wool you'd never have known where one ended and the other began. His curly blond hair fell smoothly on his shoulders. His pants were perfectly cut. He looked like an advertisement for Le Chateau, Montreal's chic boutique for teenagers and anybody thin enough to fit into their fashionable clothes. He would have taken the breath away from any girl. And I was about to let him go.

I grabbed my coat, and we left. In the subway, I paid little attention to what Jean-Luc was saying, nodding here and there. At sixteen, good looks are more important than almost anything else, and Jean-Luc was a feast for the eyes.

His presence was comforting. With him I could be myself. He liked me any way I was. He smelled of bills being paid on time, refrigerators full of food, and vacations in remote camping grounds. His skin was flawless and smooth, free of facial hair, something that made him a smooth kisser at any time of the day. I stared at his reflection in the window. I felt worse and worse by the minute. *C'mon girl, toughen up a bit here. Concentrate on Jude's face.* This image instantly pulled my scattered brain back together. *I have to tell Jean-Luc about Jude before we make it to the restaurant.*

Chapter 8
Listening to Black Sabbath and a creature made of iron
who gets no loving

IT WAS ALREADY DARK when we got off at the Berri-De Montigny station. As we walked up St. Denis Street, the city lampposts ignited themselves one after the other as if to indicate the path to hell. We entered l'Alternatif, the record store where French Canadians bought the same records the Anglos got for themselves at Phantasmagoria in the west side of town. Babe Ruth's "The Mexican" was blasting from large speakers on the walls, and customers flipped through the albums in the bins, moving their asses to the rhythm. Jean-Luc found the Uriah Heep LP he was looking for. Titled *Look at Yourself* and with the fake mirror on the sleeve, it was an inescapable invitation. My soon-to-be ex said he also wanted to get Rare Earth's single "Get Ready," and we had a heated discussion about that. Rare Earth was a mods band. We despised mods, their platform boots, their shiny nylon shirts, their bubble-gum music. I gave him an impatient look, and we walked out, en route to our farewell dinner.

I have to tell him before we get to the restaurant.

Just then, Jean-Luc met a friend of his from school. They

talked on a street corner for what felt like an eternity. My blood pressure was rising. Finally, they said goodbye. The clock at Birks showed six forty.

"You want to go for a beer first?" I tried.

"No, let's have a drink at Fanny instead. It beats a brasserie, no?"

"Sure."

We can talk as we walk. But the Saturday evening crowd was swelling, and we had to zigzag our way through St. Catherine Street. The restaurant was a lot closer than I had anticipated, and before I knew it we were in front of Fanny. I hadn't had a chance to talk. *What does it matter where I tell him? Just a drink.* I didn't want him wasting his hard-earned money on dinner.

Jean-Luc's mother was right—Fanny was romantic indeed. Each table was nested in a lovely alcove designed for two. A perfect place to propose. That thought almost made me faint in the arms of the charming *maître d'*, but I quickly regained my composure. Jean-Luc could not possibly expect us to get married at this point of our relationship. Not before we were both out of school, for one thing.

We were led to our table at once. I felt increasingly anxious. We took a seat on the velvet chairs and felt awkward and out of place the way teenagers do when they're by themselves in a grown-up restaurant. We were given heavy, bulky menus bound in a jacket of copper leaves with Fanny in big letters embossed on both sides. *Like Moses's stones. The Ten Commandments. Do unto others …*

Oh help me, God.

Nobody asked if we wanted a drink. You know, an *aperitif.* They probably thought we couldn't afford a drink *and* a meal. Too shy to ask for drinks, we read the menu. Before I could open my mouth about Jude, a snobbish fake-French-from-France waiter stepped in our alcove. Some waiters look at you when you place your order, others don't. This one didn't.

His attention was captivated by the kitchen door as if he feared the chef would catch fire at any moment in a rare case of spontaneous combustion. After describing *la carte du jour* in terms you'd normally reserve for a thesis on the essence of surrealist painting, our waiter left us to our oversized menus. I chose the Wolfe Chicken, named after a valiant British general who, in 1759, whipped the ass of a French army on Québec's soil. Jean-Luc, who looked even more intimidated than I was by the restaurant's austere atmosphere, auspiciously opted for the rack of lamb. To wash down this prophetic meal, my ex-to-be, horrified at the prices in *la carte des vins,* ordered the cheapest wine on it, a bottle of Mateus Rosé, a choice that made our waiter wince ferociously. I didn't care since I didn't like wine much or any other type of alcohol. *I'll tell him after dinner. Just before dessert.*

The wine was promptly served. An accordionist playing "La Vie en Rose" showed up out of nowhere. Jean-Luc raised his glass to him. I took a sip. Jean-Luc emptied his glass in one gulp—not the way he usually drank alcohol. I supposed he felt a little out of place in this elegant setting. For that matter, so did I. After an extended version of "Sous les Ponts de Paris" followed by "Ma P'tite Folie," the accordionist finally moved to another couple. Jean-Luc poured himself some more wine. I was still working on my first glass.

"Jean-Luc—"

The waiter suddenly showed up with our hot plates. I hardly touched my food while Jean-Luc devoured the ribs of the world's softest creature. He drank the rest of the Mateus. He didn't talk much, but he smiled an awful lot. He must have been famished because once he was done with his dish, he finished my bird.

"Good stuff, eh?"

He was drunk, grinning like an idiot. I had never seen him this way. Why was he drinking so fast?

Is he about to propose?

Time was running out. I felt out of breath, like a swimmer crossing the English Channel.

"Jean-Luc ... we have to talk."

The tone of my voice must have been misleading because he smiled beatifically, as if he were expecting *me* to propose.

"Jean-Luc. I'm leaving you. I'm in love with somebody else."

His mouth twitched on one side. "What?" He was just about to fall face first into the bread basket. "Wha—what, baby?" He moved toward me over the table, knocking off the salt and pepper shakers in the process. People stared. He leaned back, giggling to himself. He bent forward to pick up his napkin on the floor.

We have to get out of here. And fast.

I thought about Simone sitting on my bed at that moment, listening to the Beatles, my brand-new T-shirt over her pyjamas. *Help* or *Rubber Soul*. Perhaps it was *Magical Mystery Tour*. Or *Revolver*. The "For No One" track, the one about the things a girl will do when she doesn't need her lover anymore.

Jean-Luc emerged from his napkin expedition, waving it around as if it were a winning lottery ticket.

"I'm serious, Jean-Luc. Last night I met this wonderful guy. I'm in love with him, and I think you and I should stop seeing each other."

It seemed as if my words had finally penetrated—or maybe not. He looked stunned, like a moose facing headlights on an isolated Canadian highway. He stared at the empty bottle of wine. Perhaps he felt he was hearing things. He was way too drunk and I was way too sober for this situation. This is the moment when my judgement took the rest of the day off.

Possessed by God knows what, I went on. "I was with him last night and we made love. Not once but twice. This morning too. I didn't know making love could be so intense, so ..."

Over-the-top stupid, I know. His glazed eyes continued to

stare at the drained Mateus bottle.

"It's sad for us," I babbled on. "Especially today being our tenth-month anniversary, but I couldn't hold it in anymore. You and I, we've always been more friends than lovers, haven't we? I'm in love with him, Jean-Luc. I really think this guy could be the man of my life." Then I added timidly, "I hope we can stay friends."

To my surprise, I felt my eyes water. Jean-Luc was smiling no more. He reached for the empty bottle and grabbed it, then his hand stopped halfway, paralyzed in mid-air. Was he considering smashing it on my head?

"You what?"

He was livid, I'd say fully awake, for a moment. I was a parachutist relying on a broken umbrella for a safe landing. I dove into the heart of the issue, resuming rather matter-of-factly, "I made love with him more than once. That alone shows you how serious it is."

But Jean-Luc was much too drunk to comprehend something like this. Hell, I just wanted him to get it, and get it fast. This relationship was over, and there would be no coming back, no reconciliation, no further discussion. In other words, no hope.

"It's terrible to have to tell you this. But you have to know. You deserve all my honesty. You know how much I care for you, but this guy made me realize how you and I are like family. More like brother and sister. His name is Jude, and he …" I was handling this drunken boy like a car with no brakes on a steep hill.

"You mean you're leaving me *because some asshole fucked you twice?*"

The waiter, who had just walked in, eager to share his enthusiastic poetry about the marvellous desserts awaiting us should we be refined enough to order some, made an instant U-turn. I had never heard Jean-Luc curse that way before. Cheap Portuguese wine certainly didn't agree with him.

He was completely out of it. Insulting me. Insulting Jude. Nuclear disaster was in the making.

I was dismayed to hear him refer to Jude as an asshole. There was also this accusation, this revolting *lie*, implying Jude and I had *fucked* together. We had done none of that. We had *made love*, yes, I was ready to admit that much. But *fuck? No sir.* In my temporary insane state of mind I felt Jean-Luc was asking for it. Before I could think twice, I blurted out, "The size of your dick may have something to do with it too. But that's not why I love him. I love him because he's exciting, he's worldly, and he knows about stuff you don't know shit about."

I know, I know, I deserved death by strangulation with a rope, Sicilian style, like they did in *The Godfather* to Connie's husband, the one who betrayed Sonny. The one who did it all wrong. Nothing I said was right. I didn't know how to dump a perfectly nice—if somewhat boring—boyfriend. I didn't know the right lines, the classic "It's not you, it's me" or the noble "You have nothing to do with this" or the humble "It's not your fault, I have personal issues to deal with before I can get involved in a serious relationship." And, of course, I was unaware of the reassuring "No, I swear there's no one else."

I had also grossly underestimated Jean-Luc's drunkenness. He leaped up to grab my arm over the table, but lost his balance and ended up with his belly flat on the floor. I rose, put my coat on, and headed for the door. I heard the *maître d'* yelling, "*Mademoiselle!*"

Desperate to escape the scene, I ran out without a backward glance. Poor Jean-Luc.

Chapter 9

Listening to King Crimson chatting with the wind

IT WAS SNOWING, THE first snowfall of the winter. I ran and ran, sobbing and hiccupping. My lungs were exploding, I was out of breath and distressed. At first I couldn't locate the subway, but I finally spotted the familiar sign two blocks away. As I waited for the traffic to clear on the avenue separating me from what I thought would be my salvation, I heard a plaintive scream from behind. I turned around and saw Jean-Luc.

He was nearing a corner a block away. He was trying to run but he was limping, God knows why. Have you seen *The Shining*, when Jack Nicholson runs like a lunatic in a frozen maze? Same thing. I saw he had left the Uriah Heep record at the restaurant—I don't know why I noticed because I really couldn't have cared less at the moment. Suddenly, Jean-Luc howled, a sound that froze me, like the one I heard the summer our neighbour's dog was hit by a truck right in front of our house.

I was terrified and nearly peed in my borrowed black tights. I didn't recognize this clumsy monster coming at me, and I wanted my mama badly. Running down the subway's staircase, I waited for the train, hiding as best as I could among the handful of passengers on the platform. I spotted Jean-Luc coming down, completely dishevelled and yelling my name. Man, it was a scary sight. The train appeared, and he saw me getting in. He jumped in too.

Six stations to go, six long stops. I leaned on the back window. Meanwhile, Jean-Luc was getting closer to me, hopping from one car to the other, station after station. Suddenly, I heard a brief stunned shriek from the woman sitting in front of me. Jean-Luc was right behind me in the next car. He was banging his head repeatedly on the window. He looked insane. Then he began hitting the glass with his closed fists. The skin on his joints broke open, and before long blood was spattered all over the window. He shouted my name, staring at my face. This boy I knew so well, this boy who could not have hurt a fly when in his right mind, was threatening to kill anyone who would attempt to approach him.

At the next stop, he managed to make his way into my car. I avoided his bloody hands by a hair and breathlessly slipped out on the platform. The gods clearly had every intention of making me pay for my previous lack of table manners because Jean-Luc managed to step out too. I ran toward the exit, glancing back sporadically to evaluate the distance separating us, but Jean-Luc had vanished. I couldn't see him, but I could clearly hear him cursing, using a large array of words from the Bitch Dictionary. I was just about to run up the stairs when I realized that the voice was coming from down the tracks. I cautiously walked toward the far edge of the platform to take a look.

Jean-Luc was walking between the rails. The platform was deserted, not a soul in sight. No passengers, no guards, no city employees. I pleaded with him to climb back onto the platform, an offer he flatly refused. "My life isn't worth shit without you!" he screamed.

"Tell that to my sister!" I yelled.

I walked back and forth above him. "Jean-Luc, stop this! Don't be silly—this is dangerous!"

He began to cry. He cried as angry people do, rage coming out in tears. This only served to aggravate him to a higher degree. He said he wanted to get rid of the pain right under my eyes. By this time I was in tears too. I felt the vibration of a train coming in the distance. Almost hysterical, I begged him to climb back onto the platform. Walking directly below me, he extended his arms sideways, as if awaiting crucifixion. Then he turned, silently making his way back to the staircase at the far end of the ramp and sitting on the lowest step. He wouldn't climb up, he said, not unless I swore I loved him more than anything. The train was getting closer. I yelled it over and over again, that I loved him, that I adored him, that he was all I had ever cared for.

He turned to look toward the tunnel and shouted, "*Liar!*"

And he climbed up, his arms reaching for me. I held on to him. The train slowed down as it pulled into the station, and I didn't let go of Jean-Luc until it was stopped.

We got on and took a seat, saying nothing, almost ignoring each other. Jean-Luc rocked himself softly, holding my arm tightly. I watched his reflection in the window. *Look at him. What a contrast.* His hair and clothes were stained with blood. His hands were bleeding. His lips were caked with dried saliva. The other passengers tried hard not to stare at us. I wanted to make a sign for help, but I was paralyzed with fear. And I didn't want Jean-Luc to get into a fight.

He followed me out of the Jean-Talon station. On the sidewalk, he released my arm and grabbed my hand firmly. There were about five blocks between us and my mother's warm kitchen. How would I explain the sight of him to my family? I could only imagine the scene. My worried mother, my angry father, and my taunting, nagging sister.

Jean-Luc caught a glimpse of himself in a shop window,

and he stopped dead in his tracks. He dropped my hand and immediately applied himself to straightening up the unfamiliar face staring at him.

And that was it. He didn't reclaim my hand ever again. Jean-Luc was pulling himself together. He licked his fingers and rubbed the blood from his face. He stood there making little disapproving noises with his tongue. His black plastic pocket comb in hand, he worked on an image that would need no less than eight hours of sleep and a cold shower before it returned to its usual handsome state. I walked away, quietly at first, but soon I hurried my pace.

There was no need for me to hide anymore, but I didn't know it at the time, so I watched Jean-Luc, peering from a receded doorway. Once he was done with his grooming, he proceeded to make his way in the direction of home, a couple of miles away from that shop window and me. I followed surreptitiously. He had a lot to do. There were so many things to be fixed, to be put in perspective. Things to be examined from a safe distance.

Dragging his feet in the first snow of the year, Jean-Luc walked on with peaceful resignation, like a wounded soldier. I continued to watch him, slipping into doorways and alcoves to remain out of sight. But not once did he turn back to look for me. My ex-boyfriend was finally taking his leave, his exit far from gracious, his pride shattered to pieces. The black prints of his steps on the sidewalk vanished almost immediately in the now heavy snow.

I WAS SO UPSET when I announced our breakup the next morning that my parents assumed Jean-Luc had dumped *me*. Even my sister kept quiet. It was clear that something awful had taken place, but I never found the courage to tell them what Jean-Luc (and I) had done. I had driven that boy to madness, and the result was mostly my fault.

A couple of weeks later, I showed up in my mother's kitchen with Jude. My parents were relieved to see me happy again. Around that time, I decided to abandon my commitment to one lie a day. I had learned the hard way that in some situations, a blunt lie is much more compassionate than a disturbing truth.

Chapter 10

Listening to Genesis observing creeping creatures on a rug

$\mathcal{J}$ANUARY 1974. I BECAME a familiar face at the exclusive Sherbrooke Street kitchen table, with or without Jude rolling joints by my side. My weekends revolved around my new crowd. As one of the new regulars, I was promoted to sit at the table, laughing with everybody and ignoring whoever sat in the corner I had once occupied. Even Grace was showing genuine kindness toward me. I said the right things and came up with the right questions. My new friends asked for my opinion, told Milou to shut up whenever I said something funny, and waited for me before they went anywhere. I was respected. I was perfect. I was rolling.

Then one evening, stoned out of his skull on green-barrel acid, Frankie said, "Hey man, is it true what Alain says? Did you actually go to high school in a college run by nuns? Like a convent? A Catholic convent?"

Cold sweat beaded between my shoulder blades. Bewildered faces turned to look at me. This question was as dangerous as a swarm of locusts over a corn field. *If I lie on this one, my past will catch up with me and haunt me forever. Shit.* Going to a convent was as uncool as shaving your head to join the army, I knew that. But I told the truth—it seemed the lesser of two evils.

Everybody in the kitchen burst out laughing. How could have I done something so "straight," so Julie Andrewsy? My friends clicked their tongues and shook their heads. I could tell they disapproved. For the first time, I was losing ground. *Shit.*

The boring truth was that when I was about to begin high school, my circle of friends, all of them girls, were ritzy enough to attend private school, and I wanted to be with them. My parents couldn't afford it, but every year the nuns at the posh Notre Dame de la Trinité Convent took poorer students here and there at a fire-sale fee. I applied, and they took me because my grades were good. The nuns taught Latin and ancient Greek, two mostly useless languages, but the combination of both looked darn good on a CEGEP application form. Yes, I had been in a convent.

Without flinching, I told my new crowd, "I was a little bad ... well, actually, the truth is I was so bad that my parents forced me to go."

Eyes opened wide. I could easily read their minds. *Whoa! I wonder what she could have possibly done to deserve that. She looks so harmless.* That lie made me look tough. I liked that. A tiger in antelope skin.

Most of my new friends had spent their high school years at Collège Aimé-Renaud. In this institution, English and French students of both sexes were kept dangerously close to one another. Riots occurred on a weekly basis. Kids set fire to the cafeteria garbage cans at least twice a year. They wrote graffiti on teachers' clothes. Those were the kinds of pranks my friends had grown accustomed to. As far as they were concerned, being trapped in a blazing building surrounded by adults with smileys on their clothes was like a day at the beach compared with being subjected to the daily scrutiny of a bunch of nuns. To free myself from the irreversible, embarrassing stamp of my past, I tried hard to keep their attention on the tiger and as far away as possible from Julie Antelope Andrews.

I had indeed indulged in my fair share of venial sins within the walls of the Notre Dame de la Trinité Convent. In the privacy of my own thoughts, I was rather proud of the offended expressions my bad-girl behaviour had occasionally painted on the congregation faces. I have to admit that setting fire to the place had never crossed my mind, though. Destroying God's real estate can't possibly be a good idea.

The Notre Dame de la Trinité Convent consisted of an ancient four-story building erected in the dead centre of a flowery garden. Facing the garden was a small white chapel with a broken window on the side, caused by a pigeon that had once flown right through it and died on the spot during a service, freaking the nuns out. The sisters decided to leave the window broken to make sure other birds would take the hint.

Protected by the mighty St. Lawrence River on one side and a wrought-iron fence as high as giraffes on all others, the nuns kept flawless vigilance over their flock of virgins. If a passionate lover had planned to ravish a girl from the main building, he would have had no other alternative but to sneak in from the river. Tragically for him, the river-watching nun was always on duty, ready—no, eager—to give the alert. Even if he managed to escape her, creepy gargoyles all over the fence and the main building would scare the shit out of him and destroy his last shred of courage.

A pretty cage, it was. Pale old wrinkled nuns, retired teachers, and missionaries alike, minded the large garden, still awed by the sight of a budding stem. Apple trees, plum trees, and massive oaks led to the small white chapel. Despite the tall, blackened stone walls, the main building felt more like a house than an educational institution. The interior was welcoming with the floors, walls, ceilings, and staircases all made of solid oak. Every morning at ten, the wood-polishing nun made sure everything shone as if the Holy Family was expected for lunch. The persistent smell of lemon oil mixed with vinegar invaded our nostrils the moment we stepped inside the building.

There were also the scrub-the-washrooms nun, the sweeping nun, the clean-the-snowy-boots nun, the pray-all-the-time nun, the very pretty nun, the don't-miss-your-bus nun, and an alarming number of too-old nuns. Those crones were mainly nameless to us. The nuns we knew well were the teaching nuns. These ones had names. Sister Gertrude, Sister Marie, Sister Audette, Sister Louise. They weren't all nice but they were good people. I always felt comfortable there. Protected. From what? I have no idea. Perhaps from my own self.

My favourite prank—and the one I chose to tell my new crowd that night in the hope of saving my fierce wildcat image from extinction—indeed saved my ass. And not because it was that daring. It was stupid, really. But it was funny (especially if you were stoned, something I knew I could count on with the Sherbrooke Street kitchen table attendees). It was a true story. I didn't have to make it up.

After two years at Notre Dame de la Trinité Convent, I had set my mind on becoming a journalist. From what I had gathered, this job had a lot to do with exposing information otherwise unavailable to the public. My best friend at the time was Anne-Marie-des-Anges. We were both thirteen. She too came from the "poor" section of town. It hadn't taken long for my richer friends to find new rich friends to mingle with, and they had been avoiding me since. I didn't care—I had new friends too, both rich and poor. Anne-Marie-des-Anges and I agreed on practically everything. Together we achieved a deliriously wild level of imagination, and we nourished each other's ambitious minds relentlessly.

Anne-Marie-des-Anges was only four foot ten inches in

height. She insisted on being called by her full name, her only solace next to the skyscraper-tall Catherines and Isabelles surrounding us. When we met, she said she would call me Jenny. Nobody ever called me Jenny then, but I accepted with no hesitation. I figured Anne-Marie-des-Anges wouldn't consider being friends with someone whose name held more than two syllables. I might have been taller than her, but she had the longest name. I had no problem with that.

Anne-Marie-des-Anges and I managed to create the first—and last—newspaper ever published in the congregation's history. She approached her role of assistant to the editor (me) with initiative and fearlessness. The nuns were enormously excited by our venture, and they put a small room at our disposal on the second floor. They also supplied a desk, two chairs, a rusty typewriter, and an old printing machine, uttering an awful lot of sighs and oh-sweet-Jesuses in the process. Anne-Marie-des-Anges and I spent most of our recess time working on the newspaper. Every day right after lunch, we rushed to our "office" the second we were allowed to leave the table. We were "excused," as they used to say. Thrilled by our fervour, the nuns smiled at one another with devilish connivance.

But convent life proved to be a cruelly sterile environment for two hungry investigators on the lookout for exciting news to splash over a front page. Weekly mass sermons and old, tanned, wrinkled sisters returning from India, Rwanda, or Nicaragua didn't exactly represent the kind of juicy scoops we were craving, though we suspected the missionaries shamelessly spent their days and the parishioners' hard-earned money in fancy tropical resorts on beaches in faraway lands, smearing their semi-holy bodies with *monoi* lotion, a sweaty drink by their side. This alone was a subject riveting enough for a good piece of liberal journalism, but we didn't have the means to investigate on site. No funds, no pictures. No pictures, no story. A nun never confesses even if you poke her with a bayonet.

In fact, we had no idea what we were looking for, and our initial enthusiasm quickly melted into liquid boredom the way most juvenile dreams do when there's nothing around to fuel them. Just as we were considering leaving journalism to the dogs and drowning ourselves in Latin for the rest of our school days, an extraordinary opportunity shoved its warm snout into our open palms.

During recess on an otherwise uneventful morning, Josée, a girl who had gained a considerable reputation for the disgusting habit she had of eating her own scabs, mentioned that she had been told by a *reliable* source that nuns bathed with all their clothes on, the complete nun outfit, head gear and all, and slept naked. There were half a dozen students surrounding Josée at the time, including Anne-Marie-des-Anges and me.

"Come *on*," Anne-Marie-des-Anges said, skeptical.

"Come *on*," another girl echoed.

"That's impossible," the others chimed in.

But our cannibal insisted. She said she had heard her uncle, himself a priest, talking about it to her parents. Liliane, the girl with parents so rich she was driven to school in a limousine, rolled her eyes and shrugged.

"Really? All dressed up?"

Her best friend, Chantal, the girl who could not talk without saying the word *ass* at one point or another, wanted details. "Really? How do they wash up their ass? And how can they get their hair wet with that piece of cardboard stapled to their heads? No, c'mon, that's horseshit."

Josée sighed. "You're a bunch of Catholic idiots in denial."

That was quite an attack coming from a girl whose main nourishment consisted of dried blood and pus. The other girls frowned. They stuck out their tongues.

"Liar, liar, pants on fire."

This attack put Josée in the rather delicate situation of

coming across as a raging maniac twice in the same school year. First for eating her scabs and now for her outrageous story about the nuns' bathing attire. Jeanne, the older one who had guts, a.k.a. the no-more-pimples one, a.k.a. the one who takes no more shit from anybody anymore, reminded her that to be in denial, "whatever the fuck that means," was surely far better than being a freaky vampire who fed on herself.

"Up your ass, Josée!" echoed Chantal.

The girls scattered. My assistant and I lingered a little longer.

"Your uncle, the priest, did he actually *see* them bathe all dressed up?" I asked seriously. "Did he peek at them in their baths with all their clothes on?"

"I'm afraid I can't answer that," Josée whispered.

The implication of a priest spying on bathing or sleeping nuns was far more disturbing than what they were or were not wearing. But we had to let this one go. We had to stick to the nuns' clothing, or the absence of it, and keep her priest uncle out of it if we didn't want to have blood on our hands (though we could certainly bet that Josée would be grateful for some giant scab to pick on). Anne-Marie-des-Anges turned her back to Josée, and her eyes met mine. We had a Dragnet moment. Our prayers were finally answered—after all, God never wanders far away from convents. The man has to keep an eye on his harem of devoted wives. The Big Guy, the one Sister Gertrude talked about in our religion course, had just slipped under our fingertips a hot story begging for media attention.

But first we had to investigate. We agreed regretfully that Josée's story smelled like a pile of stinking bullshit. We were running a respectable paper, not some tabloid crap. But what if she was right? We were salivating in advance, picturing the front page of our next edition: *Bathing Nuns, Naked or—? Read Our Exclusive Report.* We couldn't wait.

Later that day, we questioned Josée in private, concerned as we were about the reliability of her uncle's claims.

Josée was semi-cooperative. "He knows very important priests."

"Who?"

"My uncle."

"No," I said. "I mean, who does he know?"

"I can't tell you that."

"Why?" I said mockingly. "Your life's in danger?"

She didn't answer right away but looked around as if her neck was indeed on the line.

"Officials. Important people. I can't tell you more."

Our Notre Dame de la Trinité Convent's Deep Throat ignored us for a second to snack on a fresh scab on her knee. She always seemed to have a crust conveniently located on a part of her body that was easy for her to reach. I pulled Anne-Marie-des-Anges to the side. The sight of Josée feeding on dried pieces of skin made me queasy. That was a major eating disorder if I had ever seen one. But a good story, she had. Anne-Marie-des-Anges wasn't so sure. She suggested we write an article on Josée's diet instead.

"That's a great idea, Jenny! We could subject her to lengthy interviews with a cast of psychiatrists and have her explain why the hell she eats herself up like that."

I disagreed. Josée's habit grossed everybody out, and since our newspaper was mostly read at lunchtime or recess, in other words, at moments when food was involved, I strongly objected to the idea.

"I don't want to touch Josée with a ten-foot pole. I mean it. Literally."

The nuns' bathing and sleeping clothes, now that was a subject everybody would want to read about. The thought that the sisters would go ape shit if we covered a story about their private lives never crossed our minds. After all, hadn't Anne-Marie-des-Anges and I sworn to each other in a messy blood pact over the typewriter that we would never, ever spread false rumours or step back in front of danger? The truth and only the truth would be delivered to our readers.

After recess we exchanged many notes during Sister Audette's geography class. Within an hour we had developed the skeleton of a plan. That same evening I told my mom I'd be sleeping at Anne-Marie-des-Anges's place the following Thursday, and Anne-Marie-des-Anges told her parents she'd be at mine. This remarkably easy task accomplished, we worked out the details of our expedition.

The next Thursday afternoon, when the last bell rang, students rushed to the school buses as they always did. Girls teased one another and slammed their locker doors. Anne-Marie-des-Anges and I waited until the last minute of that daily chaos, and when the coast became clear, we escaped to the convent's basement where the biology classes took place. The sisters had isolated the convent "laboratory" in this creepy, damp, and musty room right next to what was rumoured to be an ancient nun cemetery. (We could have made a story about that too, but we were much too scared to talk about it, let alone spend a night looking for the ghosts of dead nuns rumoured to be haunting the piano lesson rooms on the third floor.) This was also where the sisters kept the rats for the yearly dissection. We knew that the nuns wanted no contact whatsoever with them.

Anne-Marie-des-Anges and I were in charge of the rodents, and we treated them like royalty. They quickly grew in number because no one besides the two of us was allowed to touch one hair on their albino backs. It was the longest war in the convent's chronicles and, I'm rather proud to say, one we won. There was no dissection performed on rats at Notre Dame de la Trinité Convent as long as Anne-Marie-des-Anges and I were around. We flew into fits whenever Sister Germaine, the biology teacher, attempted to persuade us to put the rodents to sleep with ether so we could mutilate them later with the brand-new scalpel each of us was given before class started.

The only concession we made was to separate males from females here and there to restrict reproduction. The nuns gave up after a while because Anne-Marie-des-Anges was incredibly good at faking an asthma attack when she was upset about something, and they didn't want her death on their immaculate conscience. The rest of the girls didn't complain. None of them were eager to defend the sisters' taste for blood. Anyway, they didn't like the idea of handling a rat, dead or alive. Instead, the nuns made them capture frogs from the riverbank, and these poor creatures sacrificed their rubbery bodies to science at the hands of barbarously inexperienced surgeons. I always hated the idea of inflicting pain on animals, and I got my mother to write a note to Mère Supérieure excusing me from this revolting practice.

At exactly 5:00 p.m., Anne-Marie-des-Anges and I were sitting in the narrow, windowless closet next to the biology classroom where the rat cages were kept. Our babies were sleeping soundly, well fed, comfy, and clean. Anne-Marie-des-Anges held the camera she had "borrowed" from her sister. She took a few pictures of the cages to test it. We didn't talk, and we hardly moved. We heard the last stragglers hurrying out the main door above us, shrieking like bats under the late afternoon sun. One of the bus drivers honked briefly.

"Always the same late ones," muttered Anne-Marie-des-Anges.

I motioned for her to shut up and stay quiet.

"Shhh!" I commanded. Sound detection is a nun's innate talent. We couldn't be too careful.

We returned our attention to the noises upstairs. Doors were shut, flat-heel shoes hammered the front steps, and giggles died away. We heard the sound of crushed gravel under the tires of the eight school buses taking the students back home for the evening.

And suddenly, silence.

Someone closed a door. More silence. An authoritarian foot echoed on the wooden floor. Then that heavy silence again.

We were safe. No nun in her right mind would have considered climbing down the shaky staircase leading to the condemned closet packed with rats.

Hours passed before we both agreed it was time for action. At nine, we moved out from our hiding place, and soundlessly we made our way slowly up the stairs.

And there it was. A few steps before us, the fourth and last floor, where students were not allowed. The nuns' living quarters.

We retraced our steps down to the third floor and waited a little more. We didn't like the third floor. Many students had reported seeing the ghosts of dead nuns in the corridor. Suddenly, it dawned on us that we had overlooked the essential. What if the nuns bathed in the morning and not at night? We cursed ourselves in the dark.

The lack of noise was remarkable, not even the faintest snore. In a whisper, I asked Anne-Marie-des-Anges to write down on her notepad something about the snore-free silence. She whispered back that snoring was a sin, therefore a nun would never dare to do it with all the other sisters around. I leaned closer and told her she was mistaking snoring for masturbation.

"I can't recall reading anywhere that snoring is on the list of the capital no-nos," I muttered.

Now it was her turn to tell me to shut the fuck up. Anne-Marie-des-Anges swore to have once heard her sister-in-law mention that snoring was a sin. She looked willing to discuss the matter ad nauseam, if she had to. I ignored her. This was neither the time nor the place for a debate.

We waited and waited, eager to catch a glimpse of a naked sister on her way in or out of the bathroom. But nothing happened. Not a sound, not a move. Nothing. Not one single picture taken yet. Bummer.

Anne-Marie-des-Anges had an idea. A deadly idea, that is. She motioned for me to come down to the third floor again. The stairs squeaked under our feet, and we cringed with each step. Once at a safe distance from the sisters' zone, Anne-Marie-des-Anges reminded me that the nuns were terrified of rats. Saying that, she raised her eyebrows as if what she was getting at was so obvious I just had to read it on the wall behind her.

I mumbled slowly, "You want to release rats on the fourth floor and—oh—"

I couldn't finish my sentence. I feared the words might annoy God's dead wives frolicking in the piano lesson rooms next to us. Anne-Marie-des-Anges sounded like a boxing coach.

"If you want to become a *real* journalist Jenny, you have to be willing to take dangerous risks. If you can't go through this now, well, *maybe*, I repeat, *maybe*, you're not cut out for this kind of job after all."

She insisted on *maybe* as if what she really wanted to say was *surely*. She was right. I knew it in my heart. *But man, that's a crazy idea.* Anne-Marie-des-Anges reminded me of a piece we had once read in a *Marie Claire* magazine about an undercover female journalist who had posed as a whore for months in order to write a story on a prostitute's daily life. We had marvelled at her guts.

"How do you think Dorothée Manseau would feel about setting a few rats free in a nun's dormitory, if it meant exposing the truth?"

I nodded.

Anne-Marie-des-Anges answered herself. "She would just do it Jenny and you know that."

"Okay, okay," I heard myself saying.

She was already storming downstairs, sliding down the banister. I followed her.

We chose our rats carefully. All males, of course, our females being either pregnant or way too impressionable for wild outings after dark. We eliminated babies and teens and ended up with eight big healthy boys with fearless red eyes. Nothing could frighten these macho lovers. They fought each other viciously anytime one of the ladies couldn't make up her mind about which one of them should father her next litter. But nowadays the girls were in no mood for lovemaking, and the bullying boys appeared buddies enough to join forces on this confidential mission. We put them all in the same cage and went back upstairs using every precaution to keep ourselves and the rats quiet. A good hour had passed since the idea had sprung into Anne-Marie-des-Anges's head. It was time to put this plan B to work.

What happened next was quite predictable, as you'd expect. The rats, with no information about what precisely was expected of them, just did their rat thing. Once the cage was unlocked and the door flipped open, they extended their necks and whiskers toward the great wide-open space in front of them. It probably reminded them of the mazes we sometimes put together to keep them smart and in shape. A short consensus unfolded, and our rats apparently agreed to investigate. Suspecting a piece of cheese hidden somewhere, they dispersed to add to their efficiency. Anne-Marie-des-Anges set her camera, ready for action. We held our breath.

Though some of the nuns were fast asleep, others weren't, and the sight of these creatures invading their spartan cells was enough to make the sisters go berserk. Screaming, they flew from their beds, scattering all over the fourth floor. Well, not all of them—a few nuns from the missions who were used to the presence of rodents slept through most of the ordeal. But the ensuing chaos from the others was as if we had set fire to the walls the way it was done in other schools in town, where idle teens were left to the uncaring hands of heretic laymen and God-unworthy women.

But we had unmasked the truth. Well, part of it anyway. Nuns might have bathed fully dressed—this part was still uncertain—but they didn't go to bed naked. It was right in front of us. Running around and shrieking like there was no tomorrow, were nuns, not in their nun clothes or in negligees, no sir, but in striped flannel pyjamas. *Snap, snap, snap.* Anne-Marie-des-Anges, undeterred, took as many pictures as she could, the flash of her camera blinding the hysterical nuns. But I could tell my friend was just as disappointed as I was.

Damn Josée.

Of course we were caught, still sitting on the stairs, arguing over whether to abandon our rats and run for our lives. We tried to pretend we had lost our way to the school bus six hours earlier. We were ordered by a communal shrill to gather our rats. The poor things were extremely agitated by then and threatened to bite anyone in sight, including Anne-Marie-des-Anges and me. Mère Supérieure, along with a couple of the younger sisters, was leaning against a dresser. She sounded awfully pissed off at us when she repeatedly moaned, "God, oh dear God," in between something about Anne-Marie-des-Anges and I being expelled, not only from school, but from heaven as well.

"So much for freedom of the press!" Anne-Marie-des-Anges yelled when they dragged us away.

They placed an angry phone call to our mothers and spilled the beans. We were harangued and punished, and we were expelled. Anne-Marie-des-Anges and I were not allowed to talk to each other for weeks after the event. But it took only three days for the nuns to absolve us in their infinite mercy and take us back at school. To make up for lost time, they religiously applied the same rigorous discipline their organization had once used to convert pagans. Of course, our article never made it to the press, and our humble print shop was dismantled the next Monday morning. The urge to become a journalist abandoned me for good, and I concentrated harder than ever on Latin and ancient Greek. To the acute satisfaction of all the nuns involved directly or not in my reform, I finished the year with ninety-eight percent in both disciplines.

I had to repeat this story over and over on Sherbrooke Street, getting into all the nitty-gritty details. With time, the eight rats changed to a hundred, and nuns went sleeping naked with each other. So what? Whatever it took to make me look wild and crazy and gain the admiration of my friends.

Chapter 11

Listening to the Beatles mending a hole in the ceiling

I FELT READY TO TRY hallucinogenic drugs. Everybody was doing them except me. Jude agreed to monitor what I would swallow and when. According to him, dropping acid with strangers was as reckless as diving off a cliff into a wild ocean on a dark night. A most foolish move.

On the night of my seventeenth birthday, snuggly wrapped in the safe blanket of my new crowd, I tried mescaline for the first time. Like a priest distributing wafers, Jude dropped a red plastic pill in every willing mouth around the Sherbrooke Street kitchen table. Shortly after, he left.

"Business to attend to," he said, promising to be back within an hour. He winked at me. "When the pill kicks in."

Three hours later, he returned. By then, everybody was tripping out. That is everybody, but me. I was concentrating, but zilch—a Midol had more effect on my brain. Jude was flabbergasted. The other ones were too out of it to give a damn. They lay in the living room listening to Gentle Giant's *Octopus*, putting the needle back over and over on "Raconteur Troubadour." Camille and Claude were locked in their room. We could hear them laughing hysterically, as if George

Carlin was giving them a private performance. Every once in a while, someone in the living room burst out laughing, echoing Camille's bellow. Then the noise from the bedroom stopped abruptly, and the moaning began. Someone cranked up the volume to cover the copulating sounds, and within a minute all my friends seemed to be floating in what I imagined was a wavy sea of vibrant colours. Was I so out of touch with reality when sober that I couldn't differentiate reality from a mescaline trip? Did I perceive these two mental states as being one and the same? Was my reality someone else's mescaline trip? Or vice versa?

Jude did not accept my obvious sobriety. He said I must have dropped the damn pill on the floor somewhere. Or perhaps Jeff, the McGill University chemist who provided him with the mescaline—at high price on account of its purity—had thrown a placebo in the bag just to see if it was possible for a human being to experience self-induced hallucinations. God knows he was weird enough to come up with something of the kind.

Jude bought his chemical candies exclusively from Jeff because the man could be trusted. After all, he was a certified chemist. Jeff often charged twice as much as the other dealers in town, but Jude was a faithful customer regardless of the price. He believed that paying a higher price to keep your marbles in line was a sound principle. We didn't argue.

I had been introduced to Jeff a couple of weeks before. Jude and I were walking out from the Seville Theatre on St. Catherine Street after seeing Roman Polanski's *Chinatown*. Jude said he had to go somewhere not far and only for a few minutes. I was still haunted by Faye Dunaway's declaration about her sister also being her daughter, so I welcomed the distraction.

We entered a Victorian building by the side door in the chic area of Westmount. We could clearly hear Frank Zappa's *Fillmore East* album in the hallway. Jude knocked on the first door next to the elevator. A strong male voice was singing along with Frank and the Mothers. When the door opened, the man facing us nodded his head, inviting us to step in. He did not interrupt his singing. We stood in the entrance. Jude looked bored, and I was wondering if we were at the right place. The chemist wore baggy corduroy pants and an overcoat splattered with stains. His hair was thick, almost white, though he couldn't have been older than thirty. He kept it parted neatly from the centre of his skull, like an open book on his head. A badge on his shirt collar read Reality Is for People Who Can't Handle Drugs.

He shut the door behind us. The *papapapapapa* choir at the end of the song kicked in, and Jeff knelt in front of us, one hand in his overcoat pocket, the other up in the air imploring God knows what to Lord knows whom. When the live crowd cheered, Jeff stood, bowing left and right and saying "Thank you, thank you, we love you all" to an invisible audience. Only then did he say hello. With no warning he grabbed my hand, kissed it, and clicked his heels together the way army officers do in front of a superior. Or a lady. Jude was apparently used to Jeff's erratic behaviour because he didn't flinch.

The chemist's apartment had been transformed into an untidy laboratory, and judging by the dirt accumulated in the corners, the place had not seen a vacuum cleaner in years. In the living room, I noticed the fading traces of a woman's touch. A crystal vase with dried flowers (covered with dust), a David Hamilton framed picture (hanging sideways), delicate things all out of place amid the phenomenal mess. The apartment in itself was quite nice, with a spacious balcony overlooking downtown. But Jeff's total lack of commitment to any concept of decor combined with the volume of junk spread all over the floor made the place look like an attic screaming for a garage sale. His dedication to science had nothing to do with curing liver cancer or genital herpes. His endless hours of research were all converging toward his one unique goal: to synthesize any psychedelic substance available on earth and metamorphose it in such a way that it would guarantee a meeting with God—or any of his official representatives. Jeff was obviously getting high on his own stash. A conversation with him was like trying to catch a grasshopper; it required a strong hold on the leash of the subject at hand. According to Jude, he was a "chemistry artist." Jeff claimed his pills could take anyone "way out there" in a matter of forty-five minutes.

"Say it, Jude, my man! Ain't I the greatest travel agent in the city?" he'd roar.

Among his pompous colleagues at McGill University, Jeff was known as one of the most promising (though eccentric) chemists in his department, if not in the whole city. Of course, nobody suspected that he was a closet devil's apprentice. You'd think that the complete collection of Timothy Leary's books on his office shelves would have given someone a hint. Jeff was immensely proud of his brainchild. He enthusiastically reassured people who cared enough to ask that nobody would ever get sick on his stuff.

"Of course, there's the slight possibility of a bad trip. Very slight but nevertheless present. Paranoid companions, bad weather, upset stomach, flatulence, these things can spoil a magic moment and ruin your trip. Of course, there's nothing I can do about that. It all depends on how you're feeling at the time." He said he could easily list a hundred more detractors. "A violent crowd is the worst of all. However, try it on a broken heart, and you'll feel a spectacular healing. You have to understand *before* you drop mescaline or acid that your journey could turn into a bad memory. But I personally can assure you that with my babies your boat will not sink, no matter how rotten you may feel. You'll never need to alert the Coast Guards. Understand?"

Well, if I got that right, you might go ape shit but not enough to rush to the nearest psychiatric bin. *Got it.*

But Doctor Jeff's medicine was not producing its famous effect on me. Jude phoned the chemist to check his placebo theory. Jeff pleaded he would never, ever, do something so "unprofessional." The conversation was cut short. Jude said the chemist sounded awfully offended by the accusation. He had to hang up on him because Jeff wouldn't calm down.

"For Christ's sake! You'd think I was asking him if he was a narc."

Staring at the others, I found it hard to doubt Jeff's claim. Everybody was sporting the beatific expression you'd expect to see on a loved one in a casket. Serene, still Mona Lisa smiles. I was desperate to join them, wherever they were. It was still early for this birthday girl, so Jude suggested I drop another pill. He dropped one too. This time he would keep an eye on me. He made sure the red plastic dissolved on my tongue. An hour went by. Watching Jude's eyes, I could tell the pill was doing its trick on him, but nothing was happening to me.

For a time, I wondered if they weren't all victims of an overactive imagination. Jude was in great spirits now, trying hard not to laugh at my depressed expression. He thought I was pulling his leg. Shouldn't I at least have been a little stunned? He went to the kitchen and rolled me a joint the size of a church beam but declined when I offered him a drag. Nobody wanted a drag. I walked straight to the turntable to change the damn Gentle Giant record. I picked Jethro Tull's *Aqualung*. Alex jumped up from his stupor and gently asked me to move away from the turntable. For the next fifteen minutes, he fought his hallucinations, trying to choose a suitable record. The others, rolling from side to side like a bunch of beached belugas, complained about the absence of music. What was wrong with them? Since when was *Aqualung* not good enough? Alex was gazing at the cow on the album cover of Pink Floyd's *Atom Heart Mother.* Quite a cow, considering the analysis he was putting her through. You'd think he was expecting her to step out of the picture and take a crap on the living room floor. To put an end to the whining, Alex finally put the record on, and everybody went back to heaven with *ahhhhhs* of deep satisfaction. Jude joined them. I sat there with nothing to do and nobody to talk to. I grabbed a comic book and went back to the kitchen.

"Happy birthday to me, my ass!"

Everybody was enjoying my birthday but me. I toyed with the idea of dropping another pill but got bored with the probable outcome before even reaching for the vial. I sat in the kitchen by myself until two in the morning. I had told my mom I would sleep at a friend's place and didn't have to go home. She'd said it would be fine as long as I promised to be a good girl. Was I ever, sitting at a kitchen table by myself eating cookies and reading the latest *Asterix*.

The corpses in the living room slowly returned to life. Jude called me. I showed up, my mouth stretched by too many Ritz crackers shoved in at once.

"No need for the Coast Guards. I'm just suffering from a serious attack of the munchies."

"Hungry?" he asked.

"Well, duh. What do you think, Sherlock?" I was pissed off, profoundly disappointed, and planning to wear a major pout until hell froze over. Jude giggled. "I don't know anybody who can take two of these and not feel stoned! Man, you're something else!" he yelled.

After a while, everybody gathered in the kitchen for a smoke. Even Camille and Claude showed up, greeting us enthusiastically as if they had just come back from a trip to Europe. Soon everybody was told about my "condition," and for a moment I feared that once again I was about to lose my friends' respect. However, to my surprise, I became a living legend. I heard many expressions of awe coated with disbelief. Everyone came closer to take a good look at me as if there were a set of Siamese twins joined at the hips standing on the kitchen floor. I instantly became the benchmark for mescaline intake. Hugo suggested I gulp the entire contents of the vial to see what would happen. Jude was against the idea. As he said, "I see no benefit in wasting good dope in a bottomless well."

Chapter 12

*Listening to John Lennon reminding us that you can't
conceal being emotionally impaired*

A COUPLE OF WEEKS LATER, we went to see Strawbs
in concert at the Place des Arts. For the occasion,
Jude thought it would be okay for me to drop four red
pills. This would be his last attempt to make me take off
on mescaline. If this didn't work we definitely would have
to subject my non-cooperative brain to more powerful
substances. LSD, for example.

I washed the pills down with orange juice. *Amen.*
Everybody expected me to convulse in profound delirium
but the whole show went on, and nothing happened. My
fame would be eternal. Alex told me I was *the* acid queen the
Who were singing about. I blushed with pride.

After the show, we went out for a bite at the pizzeria close
to the apartment. The restaurant was named Cozy, but this
was a dirty lie. It was a diner with neon lights, plastic plates,
and plastic tablecloths.

We ordered an extra-large pepperoni pizza. Claude flipped
the pages of the mini jukebox in the booth. He put a quarter
in the machine, and we agreed on three selections. By the

time the pizza was served, everyone was playing air guitar to the Allman Brothers. I didn't play along, I was pouting. Jude said he would get me some real acid. Soon.

Hugo pointed out that up to that point, I had swallowed six red pills altogether. He smiled wickedly. "Know what? One of these days, could be a year from now, you'll be smoking a joint quietly somewhere and bang! All six pills will kick in at once."

This perspective made Frankie drool with envy, but it scared the shit out of me.

Marie pinched Hugo's arm. "Hugo, don't be an asshole!"

Milou and Hugo were laughing, discussing the effect of six mescaline pills on a mortal's grey matter. When they started imitating the little girl in *The Exorcist*, I turned the other way and asked Grace where she'd gotten the lovely new gold chain around her neck. It turned out to be a gift from a grateful lover. *Well, of course.* Hugo was talking louder to get my attention despite Marie's attempt to calm him down. He grabbed his throat with both hands, whispering in a dry voice, "Your mother sucks cocks in hell," while Milou held his tongue out, spitting pieces of green pepper all over the table. I didn't think it was funny. Any reference to that movie gave me the willies, and every single one of my friends was aware of the traumatic effect it'd had on me. Something like bad radiation on my system. I had destroyed Hugo's *Tubular Bells* record the day I discovered it in one of the record boxes. Luckily for me he never noticed. The sound of the very first bars of that record made me shiver, inundating my mind with the most disturbing scenes from the movie. I hated that flick.

The waitress positioned herself as far as possible from Hugo and Milou and threw the bill on the table. Jude picked it up, declaring with a certain hauteur that he would take care of it. Of course, no one argued. We were used to an occasional treat from him. Nobody, including me, had any idea of how rich Jude actually was, but he could afford an extra-large pepperoni pizza on any given day of the week. That alone was proof that he wasn't faking his financial ease.

On the way back to the apartment, Jude said he was in the mood to go out for a drink. Alex suggested we go to Le Petit Salon, the neighbourhood bar. The cold was reasonably bearable on that March evening, so we turned around and headed toward it.

At a time when the sight of ten hippies walking into their premises was annoying to the vast majority of bar owners in town (who understandingly preferred the patronage of hard-core drinkers versus pot smokers hugging the same glass of beer all night), we were always welcomed at Le Petit Salon. We knew other places far more exciting on St. Denis Street and in Old Montreal, but it seemed that no matter where we went, we found more and more bikers everywhere.

As far as we were concerned, the Hell's Angels were a con-temporary version of the British and the Dutch of the fifteenth century. They came to your place with no invitation, and if they liked what they saw they took it over and threw you out. The Hells tolerated us hippies more than they accepted the mods, who were, let's face it, extremely annoying. Still, we walked on eggshells around them.

Billy the barman was happy to see us. The owner, Daniel, waved from a table in the back. Billy was an Anglo who spoke Québécois flawlessly while Daniel was a Québécois who pre-tended to be an Anglo. He worshipped England because he had once been in love with a girl from Southampton who he swore looked just like Twiggy, but with tits. Daniel adored everything about Great Britain, particularly the clothes and the accent. He exhibited both with the hope of fooling people about his roots, daring behaviour in the east part of Montreal. I guess we admired him for that. Love can make people do the most unpatriotic things.

Le Petit Salon was the only brasserie in our neighbourhood.

The standard menu in this type of place was frighteningly rustic. A huge plate of spaghetti with meatballs or a greasy pig-knuckle stew with a beer, the whole deal for ninety-nine cents. These former taverns had once been reserved exclusively for men, but recently most had been renovated into pub-like bars, henceforth called brasseries, where women were *admitted.* Only a few brave females accepted the invitation on the pink neon sign reading *Bienvenue aux dames.* It took time and nerve before they actually pushed that tavern door open to enter and order a draft beer. But the times, they were a-changin'.

Billy the barman was a nice guy. He was in his thirties, married, with a five-year-old daughter. We got along pretty well with him, his wife Linda, and little Annie. In the summertime, we'd often cram into Billy's and Frankie's cars and drive to Rawdon Falls for a picnic. Billy never accepted any tips from us, and we no longer tried to push an extra quarter on him. Instead, we let him know whenever we went outside to smoke a joint.

"That's my tip," he'd say, inhaling.

Some of us—including me—were under age, making it illegal for us to be in a bar. But if we weren't eighteen yet, we were close enough. Anyway, the cops were much too busy with the bikers downtown to bother with a quiet brasserie in the middle of nowhere.

We pushed three tables together and ordered two pitchers of beer. René Lecavalier, the voice of hockey in those days, was commentating the game on TV in the back room. Beer bellies were screaming and swearing each time Les Canadiens de Montréal skated near the adversary net. We asked Daniel to crank up the music a little to cover the grunts of the large mammals watching the game. Daniel obliged—he didn't mind. He preferred hippies to hockey fans (the only sports he fancied, of course, were rugby and snooker). Billy stood behind Jude's chair, a bar towel tucked in his jeans, listening to Alex's colourful rendition of the Strawbs show. This barman was an unconditional Chicago fan. Sometimes Alex put one of their records on the turntable behind the bar, and we'd all get up to look at Billy shaking his derrière to "25 or 6 to 4" as he waited tables.

THAT SPRING, CAMILLE AND Claude got married and moved in their own place. Alex, Hugo, Grace, and Marie rented an apartment a block away from the newlyweds—we could not imagine being separated from them by streets, let alone by neighbourhoods. I was still living with my parents at the time, but home was wherever my friends lived. The new apartment was on Jarry Street, and it was a much nicer place with a large bay window overlooking a quiet street corner. Quite a change from the dark basement they'd left behind.

Nevertheless, the transition was difficult for everyone. We felt like a bunch of bats trapped under the Sahara sun. Too much light. Too much exposure. It killed the out-of-time atmosphere that had automatically engulfed us the moment we stepped in the apartment on Sherbrooke Street. No one could afford (or cared) to buy curtains for the bay window. I noticed cracks in the walls, lines I had never seen in my friends' faces, the sorry state of the living room couch. Too much reality, I suppose. But on the bright side, there were no more leaks or mildew in the bathroom, and there was a handle on the fridge door.

"I hate this place." Marie said over and over again.

Chapter 13

Listening to Bob Dylan complaining about a pail of tears
leaking out of his ears

JUNE 1974. THE KITCHEN table remained spotless and empty for days on end. Marie kept complaining about the apartment. She hated everything about it. The tidy bedrooms, the decor, Grace's potted plant with leaves that looked like pink elephant ears, Hugo's new chequered bed cover. Marie had no need for any of that. Where had our gypsy souls gone? She begged Hugo to run away with her to California, something he didn't want to do. Marie threatened to hitchhike all the way south by herself. Hugo didn't believe she'd ever find the guts to leave him because she always said she loved him more than her own self.

Then one day, Daniel told us he was closing Le Petit Salon for eight weeks. He was investing in renovations with the hope of attracting new customers. This left us with no place to hang out for a while. After much discussion we agreed to head for Old Montreal—to hell with the Angels.

At the Iroquois Bar on La Place Jacques Cartier, Marie befriended a biker with pumped up arms and an American accent. She invited him to sit with us and introduced him as

"Don from California." Her eyes were sparkling. Before long she was sitting on the big man's lap, laughing and hiding her face in his thick neck. Hugo was swallowing his pride. He was hurting like hell, we could tell, but Marie ignored him. This was so unlike her that everyone assumed she'd had too much to drink. That's what we told Hugo as he watched her whisper something in the American's ear.

Grace tried to make him smile. "She'll be *soooo* fucking sorry tomorrow!"

What we didn't know was that Marie had finally landed her hand on a ticket to California, and she had no intention of loosening her grip.

The next morning, she didn't look sorry one bit. She sang in the shower. Hugo acted as though he didn't give a damn while Marie packed some of her belongings, which consisted of nothing more than a couple of beaded skirts and three bottles of essential oils stuffed in a small duffel bag. Don-from-California had told her she would have to be invisible and as light as possible if she expected him to take her along.

She kissed us goodbye one by one, keeping Hugo for last. He let her tongue dart into his mouth as he hugged her tight. She brushed her lips on his forehead before letting him go. Then she rushed out the front door as if chased by a rabid dog. From the bay window, we watched her take a seat behind the fat biker. She waved goodbye. There was no trace of tears on her cheeks or remorse in her eyes.

"I'll be back soon! Promise!" she screamed as the bike took off.

"She'll be back," we told Hugo.

He didn't believe she would.

To lighten the atmosphere, Alex grabbed *Magical Mystery Tour* from the record box. While George Harrison sang the chorus of his song about a street with a bluebird name, Hugo left the kitchen and locked himself in his room.

He was devastated, but he made feeble, rather pathetic

efforts to hide it, like a fly trying to conceal an ox with its shadow. For weeks everyone avoided the subject of love, women, and Marie, of course. He isolated himself in his room most of the time but was abnormally inquisitive whenever the phone rang. He spent hours in bed reading science-fiction novels and rarely joined us when we went out. While Hugo anesthetized his pain by smoking joint after joint and reading Isaac Asimov's *Foundation* series and Frank Herbert's *Dune*, Marie's image slowly faded away to be upstaged by a full cast of cosmic babes.

A few weeks later, Grace's bones had replaced Marie's curvaceous body in Hugo's bed, and there she remained in her eagerness to soothe his soul every morning with a fresh smile. Everyone was gossiping. Grace was falling in love with him, and everyone noticed that Hugo was using her to forget Marie.

We never heard from Marie again.

Chapter 14

Listening to Yes wondering if they really counted
up to one hundred

MY MOM AND DAD weren't happy with me. They complained that I was home for no more than a few hours a week. Later, when I was much older, they told me they had worried that Jude was taking over my life. And of course, they were right. They were always right—especially my mom.

Except on the rare occasions when Jude's parents took the kids out of town for a couple of days or whenever Carl left for the weekend, I came home to sleep every night, but I rarely spent time with my family since meeting Jude. When I was home, I was either waiting for a call or placing one myself. I hardly shared a meal with them anymore.

My friends were baffled by my parents. They thought my folks were either too loose or that they didn't care for me. True, I could do almost everything I wanted (though they wouldn't allow me to move in with my friends until I had reached my age of majority). What my friends couldn't understand was that my parents had a different vision of education and child-rearing. Mom and Dad believed that children needed serious and constant guidance until the age of ten. After that, they accepted the fact that it was impossible to protect us for the duration of our lives, and with increasing freedom, we kids were allowed to experiment and make our own mistakes.

My brother and sister weren't wild the way I was. They were "straight," as we used to say then. I was a lot more adventurous and curious. My parents let us three live our lives while letting us know they would always be there for us, no matter what. They didn't believe that tying me down would fix whatever was wrong with me—if indeed there was something wrong with me. Most of the teenagers I knew who had strict parents turned out badly at one point or another because nothing is sexier to teenagers than disobeying their parents. But mine were usually the first people I'd confide in when I had a problem, whatever it was. It had always worked perfectly, but since I'd been with Jude, I found myself more secretive. More irritable too. Deep down inside, I must have known Jude was probably not the man of my life, one of the reasons being I didn't know how to make sense of him to my parents. Of course Mom and Dad noticed and offered to have a chat with me many times, but I avoided them because being Jude's girlfriend was a mission more than a love affair.

For one thing, he was turning into an increasingly high-maintenance boyfriend. His expectations of unconditional devotion were becoming outrageous. He expected me to guess what would make him happy, and when and where it would make him happy. I had to dress the way he wanted, say the things he wanted me to say, remember the things he wanted me to remember, and relate them with the words he favoured. A year and a half into our relationship, I was convinced that the kind of girl Jude was looking for was a cross between Cheryl Tiegs and a golden retriever. He wanted beauty and total dedication, but I was no supermodel, and my eyes didn't water every time he tapped gently on my head. Where were we heading?

He was also terribly jealous. I had slept with Jude on the first night we met and had not hesitated to ditch my boyfriend of ten months to be with him. How could he ever trust a person like me, he'd ask? The twisted logic of his jealous mind angered the shit out of me.

And that lie about my embroidery artistry crept back to haunt me. I couldn't even draw a monkey's tail on his jacket. As far as Jude was concerned, I was carrying the Queen of Deception's every gene. Where would I stop? He said *I* was the one to blame for his suspicion. His emotional insecurity? All my fault. If I just hadn't been *that* easy! I made him feel insecure, something he repeated every time I became furious at him for assuming I was on my way to sleep with half the planet and conspiring to lie to the other half about it. I began to seriously question my feelings for him.

In retrospect, our first year together felt like a fast drive in a convertible on the Autobahn with duct tape over my mouth. Jude took me to trendy bars and fancy restaurants. He met with his "partners" to talk about dope deals while I silently sipped a glass of expensive wine. These meetings were typically brief but at times they dragged on for hours. Of course, nobody ever asked me the time of day. When I was motioned to get ready to leave, I did so, obediently, compliantly, and enthusiastically, but not too much so, otherwise people would have guessed how bored I was. My presence must have been quite unremarkable because nobody seemed to mind that I could hear everything that was discussed. I was like an extra pocket in Jude's unembroidered jean jacket. This lack of attention didn't upset me. Not for a while, anyway, because everything was so new. I ate it all up, my mind in a permanent state of bedazzlement.

I accompanied Jude on his business meetings because I wanted to spend more time with him and be part of his world. I figured that if I got involved a bit it would change things between us, and he would learn to trust me more. But despite my best intentions, the novelty wore off, and I grew bored of following him around. Bored enough to dare to say no and go back to my friends on Jarry Street while my boyfriend ran around town doing business deals.

♧

AUGUST CAME AND BEFORE long, Jude was driving me insane with his ridiculous suspicions and demands. He would order me to put a jacket on in the heat of summer because he figured everybody, including cats and dogs, was looking at my small tits. At first his behaviour flattered me the way it does when you're young and naïve enough to associate possessiveness with passionate love, but I quickly grew tired of it. Back on Jarry Street, everybody else did too.

Hugo enjoyed provoking Jude by grabbing my waist and pinching my ass. This drove Jude up the wall, but he was too embarrassed to make a scene. Nonetheless, he forbade me to talk to Hugo, and when I told him to, in polite terms, go have sex with himself, he became livid and disappeared for two days.

When he came back, Camille and Grace begged him to leave me alone but he couldn't, he said. It was beyond his control. If I stayed at Le Petit Salon while he was out dealing, he'd grill Billy afterward, asking him about every little thing I had done and everyone I had spoken to. Billy hated it as much as the rest of us.

The only occasions we still enjoyed each other's company were when we were alone. In these rare happy moments, Jude and I loved to discuss all kinds of things: life after death, the relevancy of gurus, how fucked up the adults were, the stupid government, and, of course, music. However, these moments were few and far between. Having Jude all to myself eventually became almost impossible.

94

Following my total failure at raising a decent buzz for myself with mescaline, I was introduced to LSD. At last, the door that had appeared to be stuck flew wide open, allowing a fresh breeze on my brain cells, sweeping away dust and cobwebs in the process. I always figured that I would never forget the first time I tried LSD. It's a momentous event, classified along with other life-altering occurrences such as the first time you set foot on a plane, or where you were when you heard John Lennon had been shot to death. The incident that took place on the night of my first LSD experience still resonates in my memories with more accuracy than the actual meeting with the drug. How can I forget? A girl never fails to recall the first time she performed oral sex. A blow job. You know, the kind that doesn't involve a joint.

Chapter 15

It's a Beautiful Day

$\mathcal{J}$UDE HAD INVITED ME to come over to his place. His parents and siblings were away for a long weekend. We had the house all to ourselves for three full days. When I arrived, we went straight to his room. We sat on his bed, and as was the custom when we were alone for more than ten minutes, we kissed, my thin mouth locked on his Jagger lips. We started making out, clothes flying all over the place.

Jude's penis was still a challenge for me, but in certain positions I could manage it without feeling too much pain. On this particular day, my boyfriend was in the mood for something different—as far as I was concerned, anyway. He hugged me and kissed my neck sweetly. I really thought he was about to say "I love you," but the words that came out from his mouth were,

"I'd like you to blow me, my love."

For me, a "blow" implied a joint. The word for oral sex in French is *pipe.* He had explicitly said "blow." This took me by surprise, and I was mystified that he'd want to smoke a joint while negotiating a full erection. I asked in a whisper, "Can't you wait until we're finished?"

He laughed softly. "Well, actually, that's how I'd like to finish it this time."

I didn't understand. *Oh well. Whatever turns you on.*

I got up and grabbed the chunk of hashish and a rolling paper from his desk. When I turned back to look at him, Jude had positioned himself right in the middle of the bed with two pillows under his head and all the covers thrown to the side, his phallus reaching fantastically for the ceiling. His eyes were closed. A smile of anticipation was drawn on his face. I sat on the tip of the bed and rolled a joint. On the radio, the band It's a Beautiful Day was singing "White Bird." I sang along. Jude opened one eye and leaned on his elbows asking what the hell I was doing. My answer made him laugh out loud. He took the hash and paper away from my hands, dropped them on the floor and made a graphic attempt to explain what he was expecting from me.

"Oh," I said, "you mean—*oh.*"

Well, I had never done *that* before. To tell the truth, I was not even sure whether this was not a practice normally reserved for brief encounters in a whorehouse. The way I looked at it you should pay hard cash money if you wanted *that* from a girl. I mean who in her right mind would want to do *that* if no money or mansion in Tuscany was involved? Whenever my brother Carl saw a young girl driving a fancy car he always made the same gesture of screwing his hands sideways while pushing his tongue into his cheek. I understood that if your dad was not a millionaire, and you were young, female, and rich, it meant you were performing *that* on somebody on a regular basis. Considering the matter at hand, a car seemed like a fair deal. Now, my boyfriend was asking for *that,* and presumably this one had to be performed for free and in the name of love. That was exactly what he said when I mumbled my hesitation.

"Come on—if you love me."

It would be much later in life before I would discover that

men use these words for any sexual act they know will upset you. Love has as much to do with it as begging for a new car. But I didn't know better then, and the implication that I might not love him enough was unbearable. I answered sheepishly, "Of course I love you."

Okay. No need to panic. I knelt in front of him, consumed with all the delight of a prisoner approaching the guillotine. Jude gently pushed my head toward the anaconda. The snake was pulsating with blood, ready to explode—or so it seemed from that angle—if the treatment were not applied at once. I carefully let the giant slide into my mouth, terrified I would bite it accidentally because Jude kept moving his hips from side to side.

Time passed as the rhythm grew more intense. It was all I could do to keep from gagging, and I focused on that. At the point where ecstasy captured the best part of Jude's grey matter, he pushed my head way too hard down on the reptile. To make an embarrassing story as short as possible, I did more than gag—I barfed all over his stomach. He kept his eyes closed, amazed at the amount of warm liquid on his stomach. I realized he had no idea what had just happened. He lay there in bliss, thinking it was only semen on his stomach, but soon enough the stench gave him a hint.

"White Bird" wasn't even over yet.

Jude opened his eyes and looked down on himself. He screeched. I ran to the bathroom to rinse my mouth and get a towel. We cleaned up the mess, not voicing a word to each other. I finally said something in the line of, "You shouldn't have pushed my head down."

"I see," was all he uttered.

Once we were done with the cleaning, Jude lit some incense to get rid of the rancid smell. We dressed and sat back on the bed. He grabbed my hand, gave me a kiss on the cheek as if nothing that bad had happened, and said the magic words, "Wanna try some LSD?"

The mood changed instantly from awkward to electrifying, and I was sucking on half a blotter of LSD, for a change. We sat down comfortably, listening to music. Forty-five minutes or so passed.

I suddenly felt a shiver in my brain. John McLaughlin's *Apocalypse* album was playing, and my mind began racing with the guitar. Colourful visions popped into my head, escorting each instrument and every note. I was immediately filled with immense happiness and a profound serenity. I looked around. Jude was talking to me. I could hear the words he was saying, but it was as if he was speaking Russian. His lips moved, but I could not make sense of what he was saying. My mind was much too busy. Jude shoved the McLaughlin album cover in my hands. I only meant to glance at it, but it instantly became my whole universe. On it, the silhouette of a flutist stood in the middle of a lake surrounded by a bushy green forest, a rainbow at his feet and a bolt of light shooting through his head. I had never seen anything so perfect or so inspiring (though I had seen this album cover a hundred times before). I amazed myself with the cleverness of my own mind. Every detail of my life, of the room, of the music, had a spiritual significance. My role in the cosmos was pinned down. The mysticism of everything from the light to the doorknob overwhelmed me. I wanted the music to keep on coming. Jude played one record after the other. I could see he was concentrating hard to make judicious choices.

We listened to Herbie Hancock's *Head Hunters*, and when that proved to be too much for me to handle, he switched to *Sgt. Pepper's* for the entire length of the album. That suited me just fine. To lighten up the mood left by the last song on side B, Jude switched to Frank Zappa's *Apostrophe*. The song about the yellow snow cracked me up. I was laughing so hard my sides hurt. Jude was laughing too. Tears rolled down our cheeks. Then he said that we should go out for a walk. I agreed enthusiastically, as if he was asking me to be the first woman in space.

"Yes! Yes! Yes!"

The sun was going down in the Outremont sky, and the sharp colours it created made my eyes water. I don't remember seeing anybody. I felt as if we were the only human beings in the city. We held hands and made our way silently in the direction of the park where we used to smoke joints whenever Jude's parents were home. The park was nearby, but it seemed as if hours had passed before we finally felt the moist grass beneath our feet. We lay on the ground, looking at the sky. Jude said something about the secret of life. It was so clever that I wondered why I had never thought about it before. A minute later I had forgotten it. The sky was tattooed with a thousand stars, and we stayed there, motionless. I felt a spiritual peace impossible to describe. Jude and I quietly resolved every problem on earth. We even gave a shot at defining God. We walked back home, kissing and feeling in complete harmony with all and everything.

Back in his house we slipped out of our clothes, took a shower while marvelling at the shampoo bottle and the tiles on the wall, and then went back to lie in bed. Jude put on Joni Mitchell's latest album *Court and Spark*, and we made love, very tenderly this time.

Never again did Jude attempt to coax me into performing oral sex on him, and I never gave it another shot. Not with him, I mean.

Chapter 16

*Listening to Elton John bidding farewell to a road
paved in gold*

O N ONE OF THE weekends Carl was away, I invited Hugo,
Alex, and Grace to join Jude and me for dinner at
my brother's apartment. I cooked a chicken, mashed some
potatoes, and baked a chocolate cake mix.

Everybody was having a good time. The food was good,
Syphilis was purring, each of us seemed happy to be there. I
don't remember what we were talking about, but at one point
I happened to disagree with the general opinion voiced at
the table. The subject of the discussion couldn't have been of
great importance because by the time I was finished explaining my point of view, I clearly remember the sight of Grace
and Hugo wrestling with the chicken wishbone. Between two
mouthfuls of potatoes, Alex challenged my theory, but Jude
interrupted him by putting a hand on his arm and shaking
his head the way a mother would to keep her normal child
from arguing with the dumb one.

Then Jude turned to me and with a load of condescension
said, "Just get dessert, would you?"

My reaction took me more than anybody else by surprise.

Everyone but Jude felt the dry gusty wind of an incoming typhoon. I grabbed my soiled plate, walked around the table toward Jude, and hit him on the head, breaking the plate in two. The fine china Mom had offered to Carl as a housewarming gift was terribly fragile—I knew that. Otherwise I'm pretty sure I wouldn't have done it. Pretty sure.

The effect was painless, but dramatic enough. Jude remained surprisingly calm considering the affront. Our three guests were speechless. My eyes ran from the broken pieces in my hands to Jude's head and to everybody else around the table. The rest of me felt victorious and in control. Jude brushed the top of his head, apparently expecting a bump. He looked at the chicken bones resting on his plate.

"Well," he said, sighing and shaking his head.

Alex, Hugo, and Grace sat motionless, their mouths open. I made my way calmly toward the living room to change the record, hoping Jude would follow me. I was ready for a fight. But he didn't come. When I returned to the kitchen, Alex was whistling and rolling a joint while Grace and Hugo were at the sink, washing the dishes and giggling.

"Where's Jude?"

Hugo pointed to the bathroom.

So what now? Was I expected to feel bad, sorry for what I'd done? As if Jude hadn't been asking for it, time and time again? For once, he was having a taste of *my* needs and *my* demands.

You will not treat me like this, Jude. I will not apologize. Asshole. And yeah, by the way, we should break up.

When Jude came back to us, the joint was ready, and everybody tried to act as normally as possible. The cake stood in the middle of the table next to the dessert plates and forks. Jude took a seat. I leaned forward to cut the cake, holding a plate in one hand and a knife in the other. Jude was about to say something but stopped dead in his tracks. We looked at him with raised eyebrows in an attempt to encourage him to go on, but his thick lips remained tightly shut.

Hugo couldn't think straight anymore and he didn't try to hide it. First it came out like the uncontrolled giggle of a mediocre ventriloquist, then it blossomed into a full belly laugh. Before long, Alex was chuckling. Grace followed. I did too. Jude didn't. He locked himself in the bathroom once again, a move that had the unfortunate effect of making us roar even more. Grace and I urged the boys to keep quiet. Hugo and Alex reluctantly calmed down.

Minutes later, Jude returned as if everything was fine. We ate the cake and smoked the joint. Whenever Jude uttered a few words, anything at all, Hugo rushed to snatch whatever I held in my hand at the time—the ashtray, the teapot, even Syphilis the cat, for fear I would smash it on Jude's head. Grace and Alex howled on each occasion. I could smell the threat of a third world war boiling in Jude's mind—it was so plain to see. He would never forgive me for this, and I knew it. But I didn't care anymore. His prehistoric attitude was insufferable. It aggravated the shit out of me. In a way, I was proud of myself. It showed a new level of my self-respect.

The summer of '74 was the last summer I would spend as Jude's official girlfriend (and loyal subject). By then we had cultivated amazing skills at pissing each other off, and we both worked fervently at perfecting our art. At first, we argued only in private. But soon we were at each other's throats in front of everybody and at any time. Our friends were beginning to avoid us. Hugo stated on behalf of the others that they would stay away until we were both inoculated for rabies, and he wasn't joking one bit when he said it. This took its toll on me, but I was stalling to break up with Jude. We were both hanging out with the same crowd, and that alone complicated things.

When the September wind swept away another amazing summer of fun—if not of love—I found the courage to conquer my procrastination. I had to let him go. If I didn't, I was bound to become a bitter woman on the lookout for a hit man to kill my boyfriend. This time, however, I planned everything in advance to make sure I wouldn't let my emotions take over. For one thing, I would tell Jude immediately and not wait for a "perfect moment" that might never come, the way I had done with Jean-Luc. I knew Jude would become frantic. He would immediately assume there was another guy in my life. He'd probably get verbally abusive. I had to be ready for anything and not allow one single abrasive comment to escape my mouth. I was determined to roll my white gloves all the way up, and I vowed to keep them there, no matter how crazy it might get. My mind was all dressed up for the event. But it ended up with no place to go.

Chapter 17

Listening to Thijs van Leer, the lead singer of Focus,
yodelling his brains out

*I*T WAS A SUNNY autumn afternoon and the impeccable blue sky seemed like a good omen. It was the kind of blue that makes you believe you're going to have a great day.

Jude picked me up at CEGEP, and we decided to walk all the way up to Jarry Street instead of taking the bus. It was a long walk, so I had plenty of time to do *it*. To dump him.

This time I didn't postpone the news. We hadn't been walking for more than three minutes when I said, "Jude, there's something I need to talk to you about."

He smiled knowingly. "You're right, Geneviève. This can't go on anymore."

Huh?

Jude's sudden clairvoyance was stunning and completely unexpected. He'd hit the nail right on the head as precisely as I had broken a plate on his.

He went on. "I don't think there's anything left between us but friendship. Would you agree?"

I couldn't believe these words were coming from the mouth of Jude, a man who usually made me feel as if he couldn't care less about what I thought. *Friendship?* I let him talk.

He said he realized we weren't made for each other. "Of course, you want someone better for yourself. Why would you stick around someone as irritating as I am? I'm such a control freak—and don't you believe I'm not aware of it. Don't think I don't kick myself sometimes, because I do. I can be such an asshole! It's a wonder you lasted this long."

My mind became stuck between relief and anger. Where the hell had *this* Jude been hiding for the last few months? This was the Jude I remembered from the older days. He was so damn convincing that I momentarily suspected this man who could not stand for me to kiss my own brother had found himself another girl. Nevertheless, I had a strong feeling he was playing with my head, and I was right. There was no other girl. The truth was he never believed I would find the guts to leave him. And Jude being a hopeless control freak, he wanted to be the one ditching me and not the other way around. All he had to do was to hypnotize this familiar fly stuck in his web one last time.

He talked all the way to the apartment. Controlling, he was, until the end.

"Well, what can I say?" I said with clenched teeth.

"I knew you'd understand."

Man, this guy could really infuriate me! For a second, I toyed with the idea of arguing one last time with him, but I knew better. It would be like pissing in a violin, a hollow sound with no resonance. Better to forget about it. Let him have it his way. *All I want, after all, is to get out of this relationship. Fast.*

"Fine by me," I said.

So it was over. A few corners from the apartment, Jude stopped and made me plunge deeply into his puppy eyes. He kissed me on the lips, holding my chin between his index finger and thumb.

"You'll always be one of my favourite girls."

I chose not to feel like the old pair of slippers he seemed to be comparing me with.

Then, I don't know what happened, but suddenly I felt this irrepressible desire to make love with him one last time. My heart was chirping like a sparrow. We stopped on the sidewalk and kissed passionately like two bears in heat, desperately clinging to each other. We hardly noticed the school bus pulling up right beside us or the children trying to make their way around us. Some of the kids smacked their lips and roared, pointing at us. My ex-boyfriend growled, showing his teeth, and they ran away, screaming like a bunch of hyenas.

We walked hand in hand, stopping every ten steps to kiss. Though we both felt as horny as GIs on R&R, we had no place to go. We were minutes away from the apartment. I was heavily confused, my heart capsizing in a sea of doubts. Jude was in control again.

The moment we set foot in the apartment, Hugo's voice called out, yelling at us to rush to his bedroom.

"Come in! Come in! Quick!"

He was with Yvan, a friend from CEGEP. Yvan was with his constant companion, Lucy, a black Labrador. Yvan was a terribly quiet guy. You had to push a mirror under his nose to make sure he was breathing. He shared Hugo's passion for sci-fi books and—we had to take Hugo's word for this— could be as talkative as an auctioneer. To the rest of us, he never said more than what was absolutely necessary. We always acted as if he wasn't around, an attitude that seemed to suit him just fine. When it came to socializing, his black Lab was far more exuberant. Some of us weren't too crazy about Yvan, but everybody loved Lucy.

Yvan was demonstrating something he had recently discovered about his dog. Apparently Lucy had an undeniable musical ear, a quality that would not go unnoticed by us. Yvan explained with as many words as he could muster,

"Loves organ."

There was an incredulous silence, as if Yvan were saying that Lucy could play chess. Hugo said Lucy's love for organ music was so overwhelming that she couldn't help but sing along.

Jude was skeptical. "What do you mean she *sings along*?"

Hugo said he had heard her for himself. "She sings, man!"

Yvan's face was impassive, but I deciphered the shadow of a smirk.

At that moment our so-called soprano was completely absorbed in greeting Jude and me. Hugo put the first song of Elton John's *Goodbye Yellow Brick Road* album on the turntable. The intro has a synthesizer that sounds close enough to an organ. Suddenly Lucy interrupted her social duties. She raised her ears, squealed, and ran to the closest speaker. She moved her head up and down a little (off beat, but still). Then she lifted her nose up high, and there she went. *Woo-wooing* with all her heart, her eyes half closed, her lips trembling like a Maria Callas. When the organ stopped and Elton John's piano took over, Lucy snapped back to her canine reality, her eyes wet with disappointment as if God had kicked her out of heaven. Jude ran to the record boxes and took out a couple of Emerson, Lake & Palmer's albums and Rick Wakeman's *Six Wives of Henry the VIII*. Lucy sang at the top of her lungs for another thirty minutes. She appeared to be in a trance, her voice breaking up here and there but her spirit remaining intact, exalted. Lucy in the sky with an organ. God bless your soul, dear dog. The performance was spectacular enough to make two sex-craved teenagers forget about their raging hormones for a while.

Later that evening, Jude and I, still horny for each other, joined our friends around the kitchen table. Nobody knew about our breakup yet, and we still behaved like a couple. This being Wednesday, our usual spot (Carl's place) was unavailable, and we wouldn't have dreamed of borrowing a room at the apartment. Jude came up with a good idea. He leaned toward me and whispered something about Milou's place. Milou always worked on Wednesday nights, and his place was only a short taxi ride away. Jude was positive our stripper friend wouldn't mind if we used his bedroom for the evening.

He placed a call to the club. I left the kitchen and sat next to him on the living room couch.

Sure enough, Milou did not object one bit. "No problem!" he yelled to cover the sound of the music at the club. Getting into his place would be easy since he kept his key under the front door mat. Jude was about to hang up and go back at nursing his hard-on when Milou added, "Oh! Just one thing, though." I motioned to Jude to put the receiver between us. Milou's stories were never boring.

"What?" Jude was all smiles. He knew where he could get laid. He didn't need much more to be in a great mood.

"A guy I know went on a hunting trip."

Jude had no time for that. I gave him a quizzical look. "So?"

"He killed a moose."

Jude sighed. "So?"

"He skinned the animal right where he shot it."

Jude grew impatient while I was waiting for the punch line. There was always one in Milou's antics. "Good for him," Jude said. "And your point is?"

"A moose is a large animal. Where else could you skin it but right where you killed it?"

I could tell Jude cared solely about the beast roaming in his pants and not the ones grazing in the deep Canadian woods. "Would you please get to the point, man."

Milou lowered his voice and mumbled something.

"What?" Jude said.

"The moose skin."

"What about the fuckin' moose skin?"

"It's in the fridge."

There was a pause. Milou added, "Headless, of course."

Jude frowned. He pinched the flesh between his eyes with his fingers. His sexual urge appeared to be momentarily challenged by the image offered to him. This was too absurd. I was speechless. "And may I ask why you would keep a moose skin in your fridge?"

Milou explained that he was planning to use it as a bedcover. "A moose skin?"

"Well, that's exactly the point, man! Nobody has done it before! Nobody I know anyway. Man, what beautiful fur—so soft, so brown, so smooth—so—"

Jude told Milou he sounded like Michael Palin in the Monty Python parrot sketch. "You're weird, man."

"No. You're wrong. Really. You'll see—you've never touched anything like it."

"You're right. I never had the occasion to pet a moose," Jude said, sighing again.

Milou got all excited. "Well, man, tonight you can go ahead and touch one!"

Jude shook his head. He made a sign for me to get ready to leave, but I wanted to hear what was coming next.

"Did you say it's in the fridge? Milou? Are you there?"

Milou said something about a drunken woman who was trying to pinch his butt.

"Milou? Hello? Did you say you kept it in the *fridge*?"

"Well, didn't I just say that? *It's not clean yet!*"

"What do you mean, it's not clean?"

Milou sighed and dragged each word out as if he were reporting to a nagging mother. "I—mean—it—still—has—blood—left—on—it! Don't you understand? *Pervert!*"

Jude was annoyed by the insult. "Fuck you, Milou."

"Sorry, man, I wasn't talking to you, it's that crazy woman. She can't keep her fuckin' hands to herself. Yeah, you. *Pervert! Pedophile!*"

"Excuse me for insisting, Milou, but wouldn't it be better

for you to let the blood dry first?"

"What? *Get away, octopus, or I'll bite you!* What? Hell no, not really. The guy who gave it to me, well, it was his first time killing a moose, and, well, he didn't do a very good job."

"Meaning what?" Jude made a sign for me to stop laughing.

Milou exhaled noisily. "Meaning it requires a little re-fri-ge-ra-tion. I told you, it's in the fridge! Are you deaf?"

"And since when did you become a taxidermist?"

"It's no big deal, man. Anybody can clean a moose hide."

Milou's exasperation was starting to amuse Jude. He winked at me. "But isn't the thing too big to fit in your fridge?" At that point Jude had to cover the receiver with his hand because he was laughing as much as I was.

"I had to *squeeze* it in, if you need to know. It's rather *huge.* I haven't been at my place in a few days," he said, making a kind of snarling noise. "I met this chick, man, she's *wild!* I'll tell you all about her. She's from Lac St. Jean. A real nut. Anyway, I'll take care of the moose by the end of the week. I wanted you to know that's all, you know, in case you want to get yourself something cold to drink. I really have to go, man—the bitch is pulling my underwear down. *Stop it!*"

Milou threatened the drunken woman. We heard him tell her that if she didn't leave him alone, he would take off *her* underwear.

A harsh whisky voice came from the back. "Yeah, yeah, promises, promises."

Milou hung up.

We smoked a last joint because Alex wanted us to hear David Bowie's new album. I didn't like Bowie much in those days. I found his music, I don't know, ambiguous (I made up for it later). Opinions were briefly exchanged, and we left soon afterward. We were stoned *and* horny. By then, Jude and I had completely forgotten about Milou's moose.

Chapter 18

*Listening to the Beatles singing about a Western legend
and a kid who's asking whether killing is a sin*

T HE MOMENT WE OPENED the door, an unbearable stench assaulted our nostrils. The floor was wet.

"Man, I think there's been a flood in here."

Milou's place. Of course, anything could happen in there. Jude located the light switch by the door. The liquid on the floor was unidentifiable. It looked like slimy brownish water, and judging from the stink, we assumed the toilet had overflowed.

The apartment consisted of a long corridor with the bedroom at one hand and a large kitchen at the other. The bathroom was somewhere in between. We headed in the direction of the bedroom. The water had not leaked that far yet, and the waterbed in the middle of the room looked inviting enough. The sheets appeared to be somewhat clean. A fluffy baby-blue carpet hushed our steps.

We proceeded to explore the rest of the apartment, hunting for the source of the sewer smell. The bathroom looked irreproachable, with matching towels and what seemed to be a brand-new shower curtain. As we made our way toward the kitchen, the gooey stuff under our feet became thicker.

Jude blurted, "The moose!"

A big part of me had hoped the moose bit was just a joke.

His hands hunted for the switch on the kitchen wall. The intensity of the odour suggested we were dangerously close to the source of the stench. At that point, we were breathing from our mouths. Jude clicked the lights on. What surrounded us looked like the set of a slasher movie. The floor was covered with a thick coat of blood mixed with dirty water. The fridge door was spotted with bloody stains and fastened with a rope in a desperate, and useless, attempt to keep it shut. Through the gaps we could see the remains of the Canadian wildlife symbol tucked tightly in.

"Well, I'll be damned!" Jude repeated over and over again.

I felt like throwing up. I cupped my hand over my nose and got closer. Some things definitely look out of place in a Westinghouse appliance. I could hardly believe what I was seeing. The plastic shelves from the fridge lay stacked on the counter. Moose blood dripped on the floor and mixed with the melted ice from the freezer. We moved back and forth, punctuating our every step with a "Shit!" or a "Damn!"

We made it back to the bedroom and took our shoes off before stepping on the baby-blue carpet. You could say the thrill was gone. All that blood, all that stink, all that slime. Not the best preliminaries to lovemaking. Jude tried to get me in the mood, but the vision of the fridge was haunting me with every stinking breath I took. Before he had time to pull off my T-shirt, I told him I didn't feel like it anymore—this place was too wretched. Undeterred, he led me gently toward the bed. He tried to kiss me, but I pushed him away. He got the message. I'm sure he was just as dispirited as I was, but a healthy boy cannot pass up an opportunity for sex. He zipped up his pants, I grabbed my coat, and out we went.

We hailed a taxi and bargained for the ride. Jude dropped me at home with a kiss on my cheek.

"See you around!"

Finally, our breakup was official.

When Milou returned home at the end of the week, he told us his neighbours met him at the door. They complained about the smell. They pointed to the bloody prints on the floor. Something fishy was going on. Someone said they should call the police. To demonstrate he was no serial killer, Milou showed them the moose skin, by then covered with maggots and flies. The horrified neighbours threatened to call the city, the prime minister, the army, the SPCA, even the RCMP, if they had to. As a result, Milou had to give up his moose-skin bedcover project. He phoned his hunter friend, and the man came back to pick up what was left of the moose. He tossed the skin in the box of his truck, drove out to the woods and threw it in the forest where it probably scared the dickens out of every squirrel walking by.

WHAT A BEAUTY YOU must have been, Mister Moose, when this fur was still connected to your head and bones. I'll bet you were a big moose (aren't you all?), feared and respected in your part of the wild. Moose ladies probably winked at you, hoping you'd ask them out on a date sometime. You must have fathered at least a dozen bucks.

Then, one sad day, some small dick with a big gun and a questionable sense of sportsmanship came along and ruined everything for you. He hung your head on the living room wall of a chalet next to a forest you used to love while your skin rested in a stripper's fridge, miles away from your home.

What a waste.

Since that day, I've been an enthusiastic vegetarian.

Chapter 19

Listening to Cat Stevens and his first laceration

LIFE WITHOUT JUDE—AND MEAT—TURNED out to be much nicer. Our friends were openly relieved to hear about our breakup. It was a situation everyone could live with since the whole thing had been executed in a climate of mutual civility. Also, Jude became really busy around that time, and we hardly saw him anymore. That alone contributed to a smooth transition. I was back at the Jarry Street apartment spending most of my time with my friends.

On Thursdays, Camille's day off, my CEGEP classes ended at noon. I usually spent the afternoon at her place. I really liked Camille. We'd yap and laugh, listening to all the Genesis albums in chronological order, our little ritual. Then I normally helped her with dinner—I was more often than not invited to stay for the evening—and by the time Claude got home from work, the house smelled nicely of fried onions and garlic. Now that they were married, Camille and Claude had taken some distance from us, but I always tried to see Camille at least once a week, no matter what. Though I liked Grace a lot, I'd always had more affinities with Camille.

Camille hated to see me alone, as in "single" alone. She said I should consider going out with Alex.

"Oh no!" I flatly answered.

Alex was older. He looked like Eric Clapton. Also, Alain had once told me that Alex played the clarinet like a pro (not that he bragged about it in front of us, mind you. Apparently his mother had forced him to take lessons for years). He was simply out of my league. Furthermore, he was the indisputable pied piper of our crowd. Sure, he was nice to me. Nicer than the other guys, actually. Hugo, Milou, and Frankie loved to tease me, even on bad days, but not Alex. However, though he always seemed pleased to see me hanging around every weekend, I felt he kept a little distance. He had always known me as his close friend's girlfriend, and I suspected it would take a long time for him to adjust to my single status. Perhaps more time than it would take for Jude and I combined. But Camille was relentless. Every damn Thursday she began her tirade, repeating what a perfect match we'd make. There was no doubt in her mind, Alex and I were made for each other.

No matter how forcefully I rejected the idea, Camille pleaded her case with the vigour of an underdog lawyer. They had known each other since childhood and used to spend all their free time together. "That is, before it got serious between Claude and me. Alex and I were best friends and nothing more, in case you're wondering. There was no sexual electricity between us." She shook her head. "Mind you, now that I'm married, we don't speak much anymore, the way we used to. Alex isn't the kind of guy who'll talk about his feelings to people. If he did with me, it was because he knew he could trust me. So, sister, consider yourself lucky that I'm about to give you a secret peek into Alex's past life. If you tell, I'll never speak to you again."

Of course, I was curious. While Camille took a moment to evaluate whether she could trust me, my mind wandered. I liked Alex a lot. Better, I admired him. His composure, his

class, his fairness. But I was in no hurry to get involved in a
new relationship. Not right away. Also, I figured that if Alex
didn't have a girlfriend it was simply because he didn't want
one. But Camille had an explanation for that. She said Alex's
chastity was the result of a broken heart. This was news to me,
but then again I'd never had an intimate conversation with
Alex. I felt like a minion next to him. I was in awe of him, so
it was only natural he wouldn't think of me as a confidante.
He probably figured I was too immature. Then again, I had
never heard anyone discuss Alex's love life, or rather the lack of
it. I'd always assumed he was waiting for the right woman to
come along. Had it been me, I definitely would have known.
I said all this to Camille, but she assured me I didn't get it.

"It happened a few years ago. Alex was still living with
his folks at the time. A neurotic, snobbish, beautiful brunette who lived around the corner—" She broke off and lit a
cigarette. "The born-again virgin type," she added with you-
know-what-I-mean eyes. "Alex was crazy about her."

According to Camille, the prig princess had deigned to let
Alex take her out on a few occasions, but she never gave back
more than a goodnight kiss. She had expensive tastes, and
Alex spent every dime he earned on gifts to please her.

"After a few months, without a word of explanation, the
Barbie girl dropped Alex. Her heart was set on another guy.
This one drove a shiny sports car and was fat, stupid, and
ugly as a boil. For months, every time the red Mustang raced
by his door, Alex's mood went from bad to worse."

She explained that this was the main reason Alex had
decided to move away from his parents' place. (I figured
the clarinet lessons didn't help either.) He couldn't stand it
anymore. Camille pretended to push an invisible knife into
her heart.

"The first cut is—hmm, what was it again—so deep? Can't
remember the damn lyrics. Who sings that again? Donovan?
No, no—Cat Stevens. Yeah, that's it. Cat Stevens."

Camille pulled the ghost blade out. "That's where you come in. You see, what Alex needs is a nice, ordinary girl."

She meant well, but her words made me feel like an extra in the cast of *Ben-Hur*. One that cheers while the chosen ones race.

Was I attracted to him, she prodded? The idea had never crossed my mind. But Thursday after Thursday I caught myself thinking about it more than I should have. Maybe precisely *because* it was so impossible. Alex was Jude's friend, and he would never get involved with me. A universal cryptic male law forbade it. "Thou shalt not touch an ex-girlfriend of thy friend." I scrubbed the idea from my mind every time Camille tried to paint it in. Weeks later, she abdicated and quit her campaign trail. To tell the truth, I was a little sad to have won my case.

At the time, Hugo, Grace, Alex, and I spent most of our free time together. Milou, Tintin, and Frankie joined us every once in a while, but not as much as they used to. Jude became busier every day, and we often lost track of his whereabouts. But we knew he'd gotten himself a car and spent considerable time trying to get the prettiest girls he met downtown to jump in for a ride. He was ready for a little love, and he was advertising it out loud. Jude being Jude, he could not remain without a female companion for long. I had to bite my lip hard to stop from suggesting a quick visit to the local animal shelter.

We still saw him at concerts and at Le Petit Salon, where he occasionally showed up, every time with a different girl by his side. He rarely came to the apartment anymore. He told Hugo he was planning to take a trip to India and Afghanistan in search of the perfect hashish and the perfect guru. The best of both, of course, since the best of everything had always been Jude's apparent birthright.

Camille's wish for an improbable union between me and Alex was granted quite unexpectedly. It took place on the day Hugo's impossible prophecy came true. That's what made it happen. Otherwise, I doubt it would have ever taken place.

Chapter 20

*Listening to the Rolling Stones warning a dispirited
housewife about the danger of overdosing on Quaaludes*

Late one Saturday afternoon in January of 1975, Jude stopped in for a surprise visit at the apartment, a wicked grin stretched across his face. He was pleased to see we were all there, and he urged us to gather in the living room for "the experience of a lifetime."

Nobody rushed. Grace went to pee, Milou made a phone call, and Alex got up at least three times to adjust the volume of the music. Jude impatiently ordered us to sit down and shut the fuck up. From his pocket he pulled out a small glass vial filled almost to the brim with purple powder. It looked like something you'd want to blow on a Christmas tree.

"Know what that is?" Jude asked.

He turned to Alex like a magician looking for an assistant. He opened the bottle and put a few grains of the powder on the coffee table. We leaned forward to take a look. Jude was beyond himself with excitement.

"Boys and girls, *voila*—Jeff's latest achievement. Synthesized psilocybin. In other words, my friends, this is the fuckin' Holy Grail."

But there was more. Jude announced he was leaving the following week for India and Afghanistan. He pledged to come back with the ultimate hashish and the greatest guru. The hashish quest was perfectly understandable, but the guru bit sounded a little freakish. Jude had always shown a keen interest in eastern religions, swamis, meditation, chakras, Nirvana, and all that sort of thing, but nobody thought he was actually serious about it.

As far as we were concerned, Jude was much too dedicated to his business and his money to seriously consider devoting his life to spiritual matters. However, lately everybody had noticed some changes in him. He began carrying weird books in his surplus army bag. Books with titles like *Life and Teaching of the Masters of the Far East* and *Autobiography of a Yogi*. Hugo asked if *Life and Teachings of the Cowboys of the Far West* was available, and Milou wanted to know where he could lay his hands on *The Autobiography of Yogi and Boo-Boo*. Besides Alex, who loved to discuss and argue about everything under the sun, everyone else teased Jude about his guru search. He didn't seem to take offense, and if he did, he didn't show it.

We were far more fascinated by the purple dust in the vial than the absurd possibility of Jude attaining enlightenment. Jude said the powdered psilocybin was his departure gift to us all.

"We may never see each other again," he said, looking away like Max von Sydow in a Bergman movie.

Hugo rolled his eyes and said there was no need to dramatize. True, he was going to a funky part of the world, but since Jude had often dealt with people over there—directly or not—he had contacts, people, who could help him if he ever was in trouble.

Jude kept his enigmatic smile. Nobody was laughing anymore. Someone we knew personally was about to board a jumbo jet plane and propel his ass all the way to the other side of the globe. For a boy who had never ventured farther away than New York, he sure looked confident. Lost in his thoughts, Jude played with the vial of purple powder in his hand. He suddenly snapped out of his reverie. "So any volunteers for a meeting with the gods, courtesy of the best travel agent on earth?"

Jude got a toothpick from his pocket and rolled one end on the tip of his tongue. Then he inserted the toothpick in the vial. A few grains stuck on. He carefully pulled it out from the bottle.

Alex asked, "That's it?"

"Yep, man, very powerful stuff."

We all looked at each other, a little nervous.

Alex got closer. "Hit me."

He sucked on the tip of the toothpick, ingesting no more than half a dozen grains of the purple dust. Considering the amount of powder left in the vial, Jude could have left for a decade, and we would not have missed his chemist's services. Everyone but Jude imitated Alex, and we all sat back, waiting to see what would happen next. Someone put on Soft Machine's *Bundles* LP. Jude left, but I don't know who would have noticed. Everyone was sailing in deep inner contemplation. I sat between Alex and Hugo, lost in my own magical land.

Some time later—though I have no idea how long—I opened my eyes and saw the others sitting and talking at the kitchen table. I couldn't talk. No way. I had swallowed only a little of the purple powder, taking the precaution of shaking the toothpick twice before sucking on it. I could actually see myself doing it. I was transfixed, amazed at this sudden ability to relive the past. I shook my head. My mind was besieged by an army of nonsense. I felt a trap closing on me. Something like a straitjacket. I did not feel bad physically or mentally. I felt terrible *spiritually.* It's the only word I knew to describe it.

My heart was pulsating violently—it felt disconnected from the rest of my body. Alex approached, handing me a joint. I stared at him speechlessly. He went, "Uh oh. Hey guys, I think she's flipping out."

Milou appeared all smiles next to him. "No, man, c'mon! This powder is as smooth as a stroll on a pink cloud."

I hid my face in the beanbag chair. My hands were dripping with sweat. I wanted to die. My life was an accident. I had no place on this planet. My existence, this big mistake, was just about to be corrected in a most terrifying way. Grace took my hand.

Hugo's face lit up. "You know, man, when she took all that mescaline months ago?"

I understood every syllable loud and clear.

"That's impossible," I said, fighting hallucinations.

Chapter 21

*Listening to Bob Dylan inviting a girl to make herself
comfortable on a bed frame made of copper and zinc*

H UGO'S IMPLAUSIBLE EXPLANATION SOMEHOW reassured
me. If indeed this was the case, it meant it would be
over in a few hours. If not, well, God knows what would
become of me. My mind was convinced that my life didn't
mean a thing to anybody. I felt I was at the mercy of my
destiny, no matter how dreadful it would turn out to be. The
universe was demanding to get even with me.

The music stopped. Someone flicked the radio on. *Tubular
Bells* was playing on CHOM-FM. The sound of it catapulted
me into even higher paranoia. Suddenly, it became all too
clear to me. My friends were all part of a satanic cult dedicated to stealing my soul, burning me alive, and sprinkling my
ashes on a beheaded cat. Or something like that. Meanwhile,
everybody was trying to reason with me. They didn't make
the link between my discomfort and the music. Grace, who
knew me better, suddenly clicked.

"The fuckin' music. She hates that fuckin' Exorcist music!
Alex, would you please change the station? Quick, for
Christ's sake!"

He turned the dial, and I heard an innocent French song. That felt much better. But I wished Grace hadn't mentioned the word. *Exorcist.* Terrifying images cascaded in my brain. I grabbed my head with my hands. Everyone was fussing around me, trying to figure out the right thing to do or say, all the while dealing with their own altered minds. Here and there, I experienced sudden waves of sanity. Whenever it happened, I concentrated on Hugo's unlikely explanation. *This is nothing more than six red mescaline pills finally finding their way through my brain's wiring.* Unfortunately, seconds after, I was once again persuaded that my friends were evil and I (poor me) the only angel around to save the day. Man, it was weird.

The French song playing on the radio was popular at the time. I don't remember who sang it. Like a lullaby. The lyrics said, in French, "As if there was a bit of chalk in the inkpot." Bang! There I went again. I was the chalk powder lost in an ocean of evil.

"Six mescaline pills, man, that's all …" I heard everyone say.

Alex said I could probably use some fresh air, and he led me out the door. The others stayed behind.

The fresh breeze lifted my spirits instantly. Alex took my hand. I don't remember what time it was, or if I felt the cold. Like an attack of coughing, the feeling of doom crept back in and out.

We sat on the sidewalk. Alex said that as long as he was there with me, everything would be cool and nobody would try to hurt me. His own buzz was wearing off. His mouth was dry. He handed me a cigarette, but I refused it. I was still high as the stratosphere. I wasn't ready to go back to the apartment. I couldn't bear to feel walls around me. Alex sneezed and looked at his watch. According to his calculations—as well as his vast experience with hallucinogens—my trip would most certainly start to wear off in a few more hours.

I didn't know how much longer I could take it.

"You'll be fine. You can trust me on this one."

Hours later, we were sitting on a public bench in front of the neighbourhood laundromat. I knew Alex was probably tired by then, but I didn't hear him complaining once. It was dark. I had no idea what time it was, but I was beginning to feel a little better.

We noticed a man heading toward us in the parking lot facing the laundromat. He was coming our way, slowly but decisively. I didn't like this vision one bit (real or not). Alarmed by my reaction, Alex said the man was probably lost. He called out, asking if we could help him.

The man simply said, "No thanks." He stopped a few feet from us and cracked a generous smile, his head tilting sideways as if he was wondering where he'd seen our faces before.

"Actually, I was wondering if I could do something for you."

The man was about seventy years old, perhaps older. Definitely sober. His cheeks were covered with a late-day beard. Not that he looked neglected, because he didn't. Rather like a respectable man pulled out of bed because of an emergency. He wore a dark coat over his grey pants and a white shirt buttoned all the way up to his sagging neck. He looked like a nice man. There was nothing awkward about him except that he did not seem like the kind of person who would go out of his way to chat with two hippies on a deserted street after dark. He acted casually, as if there was nothing unusual about him or us being there. Tortoiseshell glasses magnified his eyes.

"No, we're fine, thank you," Alex answered.

The man smiled again and hesitated as if he wanted to add something, but instead he swivelled on his heels and walked away a few steps. A garbage truck stopped on the other side of the street and picked up the trash from a restaurant's bin. The man turned to face us.

"Sure you don't need anything?" he shouted to cover the noise.

"Really, everything's fine," Alex shouted back.

The man went on and disappeared into the night.

In a matter of seconds, I felt much better. My dark thoughts took a hike in the open sky. Just like that. I mean, it wasn't as if the old man had performed a miracle or said anything extraordinary. But somehow his words made every discrepancy in my head slip back neatly into the folder where it belonged. If Alex hadn't been there to witness it all, I would have assumed the old man was just another hallucination.

It was past one o'clock when we got back to the apartment, and everybody was sleeping. Alex said I should call my mom to tell her where I was. When I hung up he took my hand and led me to his bedroom. He told me to get in bed.

"You need to rest. It'll make you feel better."

There was no way I could do that. I was still too wired. Alex lay down next to me and held my hand for as long as I can remember.

I woke up the next morning feeling fine. At the kitchen table I found Hugo, Alex, and Grace having coffee, eggs, and toast.

"Feeling better?" Grace said, winking.

In a sleepy voice I said yes, wondering whether the wink was because of Alex and me sleeping in the same bed. I turned to him and stuttered some inadequate words to thank him, but Alex wouldn't hear a word of it.

"No, really, no sweat. These things happen."

"I swear I'll never touch that stuff again."

Alex didn't agree. "This is like riding a horse. If you fall, you have to climb back on, otherwise you'll never be able to ride again. And riding is everything. The horse has nothing to do with your fall. I don't know what kind of rider you are, but for me the notion of never riding again would be inconceivable. There's nothing new to discover under this sun if the horse is taken away. I don't need to ride often, but if I stopped completely, I'd become intellectually lazy. I'd lose perspective on things. I believe this kind of dope makes me, you, and all of us, better human beings."

He meant what he said down to the marrow of his soul, and as a result, my resolution flew out the open window. But I would certainly take an acid break for a while.

When Hugo and Grace asked us about our outing the night before, Alex told them about the old man.

Hugo laughed. "I bet the poor guy was contemplating suicide. It took the two of you to convince him that life was worth something after all. One look at your sorry asses, and he said to himself, 'If these two losers can survive in this world, there's hope for everybody else on earth.'"

Grace and Alex smiled. I shrugged and changed the subject. Whoever the old man was, I owed him.

Chapter 22

*Listening to Genesis singing about Juliette and Romeo
going to the movies*

GOING BACK TO SLEEP in Alex's bed that winter came naturally to me because it was always a drag to go back to my parents' house late at night. Sleeping on the living room floor with Milou, Tintin, and/or Frankie was not an option I would have seriously considered. I'd rather have caught the last bus heading home than crash on a beanbag chair with all my clothes on surrounded by snoring, flatulent men. If Alex and I had been able to accomplish this proximity without promiscuity once, we could surely repeat the experience no matter how odd the situation appeared to others.

It became a Saturday night routine. We left Le Petit Salon after last call, then I headed to Alex's room and slept in his bed. He never formally invited me to do so, but he always seemed pleased to find me there. We never kissed, much less slept naked next to each other. I lay underneath the covers in a T-shirt with my panties on, and Alex slept over the covers with his jeans on. Nothing happened. This strange arrangement was described in detail to our friends, and despite the initial torrent of whistles, snarls, and jokes, everybody grew used to the idea—except Camille, of course. Her expectations were much higher. Hugo told me I should spend one night with Alex and the next one with him to see who would try jumping my bones first. Grace punched him in the arm. We had all noticed that she was getting unusually possessive of him.

Back home, my mother smiled when I told her about Alex. She didn't say much. I was eighteen by then, and I could do whatever I wanted. I could share my bed with a damn python if such was my desire.

She asked if I was still taking the pill. "I mean—since your breakup with Jude."

Of course I was, I told her. She seemed relieved. I exploded. "Why do you ask?"

She took clothes out of the drier and shoved in another batch of wet laundry.

"Well, if you ask me—"

I stormed out of the room. "I did not ask for your opinion, Mom! If you must know—I will not sleep with him! What's wrong with a guy and a girl sharing the same bed without having sex? You jump to conclusions like everybody else! Know what? It makes me wanna puke!"

She followed my path, clutching a basket of warm clothes in her arms. She stopped on the staircase and let out a deep sigh. A mother sigh. The sigh you hear from women who have raised three children from birth to adulthood. She looked so tired lately.

"Take a deep breath, will you?" she said. "*Mon Dieu!* All I'm trying to say is this. Alex is a gentleman. Quite a remarkable young man. You should tell him you appreciate the way he respects you."

I picked the smell of oregano and homemade soup from her clothes.

"That's all I was trying to say. Help me with that basket, will you?"

I followed her all the way up the staircase. "Sorry, Mom—yeah, you're right. I'll do that. Hey, Mom—I love you."

"Me too, dear. But if you go on like this, you'll die of a heart attack before your time. Spare your heart—you've only got one."

The next Thursday, when I told Camille about the "sleeping arrangement" with Alex, she forgot at once her promise to "never ever again" (her words, not mine) put her nose in my business. Camille was thrilled to see Cupid's bow finally aiming in the right direction, and she had every intention to give him a push. Now that she was married, Camille's newfound mission in life was to put an end to everybody else's celibacy. As far as she was concerned, now that Jude was out of the picture thousands of miles away, running after gurus around the Taj Mahal, there was nothing else standing between Alex and me. This time I listened more closely.

Camille admitted she had never discussed the matter with Alex. When I told her she should harass him instead of me, hoping she would, she said it was useless to involve men in affairs of the heart.

"They don't know what's good for them. You have to be wise and make it happen. It's a little tricky, you see, because Alex has to believe it was *his* idea all along. Men are like that. When a guy feels smart, it releases the animal in him, and what you lose by not having the satisfaction of letting him know you have orchestrated the whole thing, you win later under the covers."

Who had educated this girl? Xaviera Hollander?

Camille seemed to know about men the way a marine biologist knows about ocean mammals. Hard facts, figures, curves, straight lines. She put her hands on my shoulders and asked what the hell was wrong with me. "I mean, let me get the picture straight here. You didn't try anything? Not once? What about him then?"

"Nothing. It never came up, that's all."

Camille smiled. "What never came up?"

"Nothing," I said, ignoring the pun.

"But you've never tried—or have you?"

She was hunting for my irises the way they do in old movies. "No, not really."

"You're a fool, Geneviève." She sat next to me. "Alex is an excellent catch. Good to the bone. You know that. You're just pretending you don't need anybody, and that, my friend, is unhealthy. You two are made—"

"Enough already! Camille, please!"

Camille's eyes widened, and her mouth disappeared. Her lips looked as if they were sewn shut from the inside. She made a noticeable effort to keep them that way, possibly fearing too many bilious words might break free and cause irreversible damage. She was determined not to spill a single drop of an unpleasant comment on her kitchen floor. She took a deep breath and kept the air in for a moment. After a long exhalation, she graciously swallowed her mouthful of profanities. Camille hated to be contradicted. She never stated something she wasn't dead sure about. If you disagreed with her, she was liable to erupt like a volcano. I was in no mood for that.

If this exchange had taken place in a World War II movie, I would have been the French rebel and Camille the German Kommandant. She would have slapped my face many times with her black kid glove to make me pay for my insolence and my stiff refusal to cooperate by revealing the Resistance members' identities. I would have collapsed on a chair, my lips tight, a stream of blood running from my nose. We would have spited each other, believing without a shadow of a doubt that the other was losing ground. But the Kommandant was mightier.

I've always attributed Camille's spirited personality to her flammable genes—half Sicilian, half Irish. She told me her story one quiet evening at Le Petit Salon. She said she was the result of a short but extremely passionate—and extramarital—affair between her father and an Irish woman. Apparently the woman had flown back to Ireland shortly after giving birth to Camille, leaving the baby behind, with the promise of returning to Montreal within a month or two. But she never came back. Gone for good. Not even a postcard. Her name was Abigail Cantwell. Abbie, we guessed, to Camille's father.

Before leaving for Ireland, Abigail had arranged for a neighbour to take care of her daughter until her return. Spring came and passed. The late summer wind turned the leaves around, and there was still no news from her. Abigail's silent message was clear. She had no intention of returning. Or maybe she was dead. There were no calls, no letters, and no address or telephone number where she could be reached. She had told Camille's father that she'd be in Belfast and nothing more. He hadn't asked for details because he was sure she would be back in no time. To his Sicilian way of thinking, a mother would never abandon her children. He could have tried to locate her, or taken a plane to find her, but he had nothing to say to make her want to come back and nothing to offer her. He was a married man. A married Sicilian man. Camille said a Sicilian husband might kill his wife, but he would never divorce her.

Camille's dad decided to face his responsibilities and begged his own wife, also a Sicilian, to take Camille in and give her a home. Despite her initial disgust, his wife accepted. She had been praying to God for a child every night since her wedding day and had already gone through three miscarriages. Camille awkwardly filled the empty hole in this woman's heart the way a piece of plastic covers a broken window, something meant to stop the draft until the real thing is put in place. But that baby was to be her only child. Camille became part of the household, sharing the family home with her dad, her new mom, and a Sicilian grandmother who crossed herself every time Camille walked by.

Camille was fourteen when she learned the truth about her biological mother. Though she had suspected it all along, by sheer logic, really, she needed to hear it, loud and clear. Every single Sunday her family used to go out for lunch at Le Temple des Parfums, a small Chinese restaurant in Montreal, in the east part of town. On that fateful Sunday, while her father was busy ordering the usual dishes, Camille asked about the circumstances of her birth and why she didn't look anything like her mom, with her strawberry blond hair and her large green eyes. The rush of blood tainting her grandmother's face confirmed she was on to something. There was an awkward silence at the table. Her mom started sobbing. Her grandmother crossed herself over and over. Her father looked as if he was stuck between hell and somewhere even worse. This thing had to come out. Though not ideal, this was at least a good enough occasion to set things straight. There was no such thing as a perfect timing for this kind of confession.

The first part of the answer came from her dad's mouth, full of wonton soup at the time. Sighs and words like "Yeah— had an affair—stupid—you came along—she left and never came back—we kept you."

"What?" Camille gasped.

Her dad nodded absently. Her mother and grandmother minded their plates, nose down. Camille's initial shock gave way to only partial surprise. She certainly shared a lot of physical traits with her dad, notably her chin and her gapped teeth, but she looked nothing like her mom. She had never dared to ask why, but now that she had, she was ready for the truth. A truth she'd instinctively known ever since she was old enough to count.

"But you're my real dad, right?"

"Of course, darling. Now eat, or it will get cold."

Camille didn't feel emotional about the revelation. It was

as if they were talking about someone else's life. Knowing that her so-called mother had abandoned her instantly destroyed any thread of affection for her. Camille had only one mother, and this one was sitting right next to her. Her father tried to change the conversation.

"How was she?" Camille interrupted.

She heard more chopped-up phrases like "Irish—I was wrong—she abandoned you—somewhere in Ireland—don't remember much about her" (this last one was repeated again and again). And finally, "I'm so sorry." Camille didn't grasp it all, but her father was done with the subject before the chicken chow mein had made its round on the lazy Susan on the table.

She tried again. "But why didn't she—"

The waiter showed up with the sweet-and-sour shrimp, Camille's favourite dish, and her thoughts were disorganized for a moment. When her father sent the pork chop suey back to the kitchen because there was no pork in it, Camille tried to shift the conversation back to the Irish woman. Her father asked her to shut up because he was explaining to the Chinese man what was wrong with the dish. Minutes later, the topic was abruptly and irreversibly put to death by the nonna's lethal gaze in her grandchild's direction. Before Camille knew it, the meal was over, and the fortune cookies were passed around. She didn't find the nerve to bring the subject up again that day. But at least now she knew. She thought maybe one day her dad would be willing to tell her a little more—that is, if she could find a way to be alone with him. But that rarely happened, and her father passed away before she could learn one more thing about Abigail Cantwell. What she had really wanted to ask him was why her mother hadn't taken her baby with her. And yet Camille already knew the answer.

"I can only guess she didn't love me enough to take me along."

Her father hadn't had to spell it out to her.

Three rivers ran in Camille's blood. The fiery nature of her biological mother, the uncontrollable urges of her father, and the repressed fury of the two women who had raised her as their own. A great recipe for a Molotov cocktail. After that conversation at Le Petit Salon, I looked at Camille in a different way. This poor girl had no choice but to cope with this menagerie fighting in her veins. All things considered, she was managing remarkably well.

Back in Camille's kitchen, I went to the sink to get myself a glass of water. I looked out the window into the yard next door, where the neighbour was hanging laundry out to dry. White, yellow, and blue bed sheets flapped joyously in the wind like large Tibetan prayer flags. Or sails. I thought of the upcoming weekend, and everything we'd do. Alex and I, with Hugo and Grace.

"I'm not his type. We're friends, Alex and me, that's all. If he wanted me, he would have made a move by now, wouldn't he?"

"Oh, you're so mistaken, my dear. He doesn't know he wants you. Otherwise, do you really believe he'd let you in his bed? Get real!" She filed a broken nail on her left index finger. "You and him get along just fine. What's *soooo* different between Alex and, let's say, Jude? What? You tell me—I'm all ears."

When I didn't reply, she paused, then continued. "Oh yeah. The size of his dick. What else? Maybe Alex's not half as obnoxious. What else? What is so scary about Alex? Too worldly? Jude was *soooo* worldly, remember? I didn't see that stop you!"

She had to pee, but she didn't want to lose her momentum so she left the bathroom door ajar. "Listen closely, my friend. I'll tell you what you should do."

She came out, zipping up her jeans. She had peed. She had my attention. She was on top of things. Between the two of us, she was the one who knew about men. I was at her mercy.

"For one thing, you can't jump on him. Alex is a prude, *and* he's Greek, which means he has to initiate the call. You have to help him a little."

"How?" Alex or not, it might serve me one day to know about these things.

"Well, you know, like a woman does when she wants to seduce a man—discreetly."

"And may I ask how a woman does this sort of thing?"

Camille held her doctorate in the language of love while I struggled with the basic alphabet. She sure sounded as if she knew her stuff. Wasn't she already married to a good man? Maybe her knowledge came from those romance novels she was reading all the time.

"It's *soooo* easy. You just have to think of Maude."

Camille could play Maude in *Harold and Maude* better than Ruth Gordon herself. Remember the scene where Maude invites Harold into her home and shows him all the things that make her feel happy, like her musical instruments and that machine with all kinds of smells such as "Snowfall on 42nd Street"? Camille could recreate the entire scene, word for word. She smiled at me, shoved a tablecloth over her shoulders as if it were a feather boa, and waltzed around the room. I almost peed my pants laughing. After a few minutes she crashed on a chair, trying to catch her breath. Asthma. She looked for the pump in her purse and inhaled deeply.

The illness came from her mother's side. At least, that's what Camille had been told. It was one of the reasons she had always suspected something was fishy. The Sicilians in her family did not recognize asthma as a disease of their own. Asthma was transmitted by unhealthy people who had never felt the Palermo sun on their skin. Nobody on the Italian island contracted asthma, and if they did they called it something else.

After Camille had been told about her biological mother, *la nonna* felt it was her duty to let her granddaughter know about the many shortcomings of her Irish genes. "Ireland is wet all the time. No sun, only rain. A crazy place, full of untrustworthy women. A poor and dirty country. People there eat potatoes and nothing else. They only drink beer. A diet for farm animals!" she would tell Camille. "That's why Irish music is so depressing and Irish people so pale. A wet land nesting dangerous germs and bad women!"

On every single occasion Camille felt physical pain, whether it was from asthma, a tummy ache, a scorched knee, or a broken heart, *la nonna* blamed Ireland. She'd slam her fist on the marble of her kitchen counter, cursing St. Patrick's land in a dialect nobody understood. As far as the *nonna* was concerned, Ireland was responsible for everything wrong in this world. The high cost of stamps, the hurricanes on the east coast, and the mad horse that had trampled her husband to death back in 1948.

"An Irish horse!" she'd say, spitting in the bathroom sink.

I listened to Genesis while Camille caught her breath. I rolled a joint, stroking Zoé-the-cat with my foot, humming the song.

"So will you do it?" Camille was breathing normally now.

"Do what?"

"Get him to make a move, that's what!"

"If you promise on Claude's head to drop the subject once I've humiliated myself and prove you wrong, yes I will."

"Good!"

We sang with the record. Very loud.

Once a man—

My favourite part in *Harold and Maude* is when they're both sitting by a pond somewhere near a dump, and Harold chooses that moment to offer Maude a cheap ring he'd won at the fair. Maude takes the ring and marvels at it. She gives Harold a peck on the cheek and throws the piece of jewellery in the water. Harold is shocked. Maude smiles at him and says, "Now I will always know where it is."

Chapter 23

*Listening to Michel Rivard singing a heartbreaking song
about Cervantes's hero*

IN APRIL, I WAS getting close to being finished with CEGEP, and I informed my parents I was thinking of taking a year off school before heading to university. I wanted to work for a while and get a feel for adult life before I'd have to dive into it for good. I'd always had good grades. This indicated to my parents that I was capable of discipline and not out of control. Of course, Mom and Dad were not overly happy with my decision, but true to form, they were supportive.

I found a job working in a bookshop called La Librairie du Perroquet Vert. It was located in a mall, not too far from the apartment. I was thrilled. I could leave work and head for my friends' place to smoke a joint before going home for dinner. I remember feeling very lucky about that.

It was hard for me to believe I was getting paid for doing something I enjoyed so much. I had always loved bookshops. The quiet readers, the smell of printed words, the alphabetical order of authors, and the idealistic assumption that if you were to read everything within the walls you'd be incredibly smart. Perhaps too smart for your own good. A bookshop is a holy space, like a monastery. I buried my nose in books—literally—and inhaled deeply as if knowledge and pleasure could be snorted from a piece of paper.

A movie is seen in a matter of a couple of hours, but a good book stays with you for a lifetime. Reading is a simply fabulous way to spend time. Sitting alone in a park on a quiet day, I could be catapulted into the Civil War or find myself drinking jasmine tea in Shanghai. I might be on a bus on the way to work when I find myself identifying with a noble medieval hero. Or a despotic felon. I could be someone else for hundreds of pages. Books never failed to provide the precise words to explain my inner thoughts. *Les mots pour le dire.* The words to express them.

Contrary to popular belief, working in a bookstore doesn't mean you get paid to read. People would tell me, "You work in a bookshop? Lucky you, you can read all day!"

No, I couldn't. There were books to be put on shelves, phone calls to be answered, and impatient customers to be served. It was a job, not a pastime.

Some customers came up with the craziest requests. One day I was asked to find a book with "bright colours on the covers—a love story." When pressed for more details, the woman looked at me strangely. Her expression asked, What else could you possibly need to know to find a book like this in such a small place? On another occasion a man had me run up and down the ladder for an hour in search of the perfect book to fit the last vacant space in his new redwood wall unit. This man was buying books the same way he bought underwear. It had to fit just right. The content didn't matter. My favourite request of all time came from a middle-aged suburban mother.

"I need a book for my daughter's French literature class," she said. "It's called *The Stranger* by Camus." As I led her down the aisle, she added, "I can't remember the name of the author, though—sorry for that."

One of the girls I worked with was named Dominique. She was a painter studying art at the Université de Montréal. We got along pretty well. I met her in the back of the store on my first day at work. Sitting on a wooden crate, she was eating a ham sandwich and reading a booklet entitled *Le lien entre le nez et l'orgasme féminin* (The link between the nose and the feminine orgasm). She said hello and introduced herself. She had the habit of talking from the side of her mouth, liberating her thoughts sparingly as if every word she uttered was let out on parole. It wasn't long before we were having lunch together every day. Had I met her anywhere else, I'm sure we would have become close friends outside of work. But at the apartment we did not easily fraternize with people we worked with. Too close for the comfort of our dope-dealing friends.

Dominique was best friends with the store's cashier, Charles. Half French, half Québécois, Charles was low key, cute, and melancholic. His spleen was aching for a *raison de vivre* and a muse who looked like Jane Birkin. He spent his life listening to blues music while reading French porn comic books. Dominique called him Charlie Brown. They went out together sometimes to a movie or for a coffee. Dominique was married and too much in love with her husband to ever consider having an affair with Charles, but I always suspected he was in love with her.

There was also Delphine, flown in from Paris to add some class to La Librairie du Perroquet Vert. She worked on weekends only. Delphine was twenty-five years old and incredibly French. Her crimson lips were drawn on creamy skin that had never seen a pimple. I always pictured her wearing naughty lingerie under her fancy clothes. Black or red bras and panties, depending on her mood of the day, her ass and tits as smooth as her face. Delphine could afford the latest fashion, she smelled of Chanel No. 5, and she invariably ended every sentence with "*Et bien, voila!*" Male customers were charmed and bought anything she suggested.

In Canada, if you sport a French-from-France accent—and no doubt it's the same in a lot of other countries—people will immediately assume you know everything about literature, paintings, wine, and cheese. Sadly, our Delphine was an unconditional fan of Harlequin novels, and she couldn't differentiate a Monet from a Picasso, a Bourgogne Aligoté from a Pouilly-Fuissé, or a Gouda from a camembert. She had a hard time making friends in the city, handicapped as she was with her French-from-France attitude. Dominique and I used to make fun of her. I think we were a little jealous because Delphine embodied what we perceived as feminine perfection. The kind of girl who sounded classy even when she swore. Girls will hate you for that.

Delphine came to Montreal in February, a time of the year that made her hate the city instantly and for eternity. The cold was particularly brutal that winter. On her first day out, she fell on the icy pavement. Then it snowed all night long. The next morning it took her half an hour to scrape the ice from her car windshield. Montrealers around her hurried from one heated place to another, their noses down, studying the ground and negotiating their way around patches of ice.

"*Pays de merde!*" she told herself, close to tears. Nothing would change her mind that, indeed, the entirety of Canada was a shitty country, as was everything in it.

The food Delphine bought at the Metro Richelieu supermarket was pronounced tasteless. The coffee served in most restaurants was appallingly disgusting. She was miserable and remained that way for weeks. She missed her country of birth like a dog misses a freshly cut tail. She could almost feel it there, inches away from her. But no matter how much she hated the weather and the locals, Canada was a door open wide for European dreams, and her mind was set to stay. She figured that with her French accent from France and her good looks, she'd be able to land any job she wanted in "this *putain de pays*" ("fuckin' country" this time). In France, she sounded like everybody else, and with her far from impressive curriculum vitae, her chances of making it—as in making lots of money—in Paris or Lyon were at best slim. But in Québec she sounded like Mireille Mathieu, and that alone was bound to assure her a fat meal ticket for the rest of her days.

She was infatuated with Didier Marnie, the bookshop owner, also from Paris. Didier's family was indecently rich and owned a chain of bookshops spread all around the world. Unfortunately for Delphine, Didier didn't display the slightest interest in her. She may have looked like a Degas painting to us, but to Didier she was just an ordinary girl. This heir was probably used to ladies dressed in Ralph Lauren riding suits who owned purebred horses and spent their days sipping kir in medieval châteaux near Bordeaux. He was the type of man who believed he was born with a great destiny. In the aboriginal land of maple syrup, he had no time for a castaway like Delphine. Dominique believed that Delphine had a crush on Didier mainly because she missed home. Delphine was secretly convinced that Québec was a land of losers, nothing more than a nation of French-from-France wannabes.

I had never seen a picture of Christian Dior, but I imagined he looked like Didier. Blond, tall, and exquisitely dressed, he nevertheless looked geeky to us at the time. On the finger where you might have expected to see a wedding band, he wore a thick gold ring displaying his family crest inlaid with diamonds and rubies. His nuptial finger was dedicated to his family.

While Delphine missed Paris, Didier was inconsolable. He looked like a bespectacled walrus in his ridiculous fur coat. His teeth chattered, his face was red, his eyebrows frosted. "*Putain de pays,*" he said through his teeth. "*Putain de putain de pays de merde!*"

In other words, he, just like Delphine, hated Montreal and the rest of Canada with a passion. All this being said, Didier was good to us. In a sad attempt at being friendly, he complimented us whenever he could. We could tell he was outraged by the way we dressed, the way we talked, the crude jokes we made, the junk food we ate. Delphine and Didier worked at La Librairie du Perroquet Vert throughout the longest and coldest winter I can remember. At last, Didier went back to Paris. Delphine quit the bookshop for a job in a poorly heated art gallery in downtown Montreal. Two pneumonias later, she switched to a little French bistro in Old Montreal where she served tables next to a large fireplace. Books, paintings, wine, and cheese. She'd done them all.

French citizens rarely look forward to a life outside of France, especially if the destination is Canada—that was how things were in those days anyway. Canada wasn't America. America was New York, LA, Miami, or Chicago. Their motivation had little to do with their love of snow or the Canadian beaver. They came for the money or, as was the case for Delphine, with the hope of getting some sort of public recognition for the sole achievement of being so perfectly French. In Québec, they suffered in silence, lost in a nation populated by beings they saw as uneducated peasants who should be grateful for the French manners and *savoir vivre* their European cousins were willing to share. It's hard to get attached to people coming to you on these terms. *Maudit Français*—damned Frenchies from France—is a Québécois expression, one every Québécois knows, has used, and will use again at one time or another.

To annoy Delphine, Dominique told her that according to a recent study, we Québécois spoke the purest French on the planet. Delphine choked on her *chocolatine* and almost fell off her four-inch heels.

"*C'est impossible!*"

It was like telling Shakespeare the latest linguistic research showed that the English language's roots were found in a dialect once used by a pigmy tribe in Nigeria. Delphine was shocked, and I'm guessing that to this day she still hasn't recovered.

When my day at the bookshop was done, I walked to my friends' place for a welcome interlude before heading home. I was happy. I had a little money of my own and could open a savings account at the bank. Hugo, Alex, and Grace got used to my presence on weekdays. When I got there, Alex was usually home and Hugo and Grace were on their way back from work. It wasn't long after settling into this routine that I noticed Hugo was getting tired of Grace's constant physical presence next to him, whether it was at the kitchen table or in his bed. Though we never discussed it at that time, Alex had also noticed. Grace had to be blindly in love not to see it.

Chapter 24

*Listening to CSN, who remind us to persevere because
love is on its way*

"I'T's GONNA BE A great party, man! You know, wild! Lots of chicks and great dope!" Late for class, the boy excused himself. Hugo hardly knew him.

He looked at the scribbling on the paper. An address in Oka in the Laurentides region. A summerhouse by the water. Saturday was underlined twice. It was to take place on June 21, the first day of summer.

At Le Petit Salon that same evening, Hugo told us about the invitation, but nobody felt like going. Our friend pleaded and whined. Camille and Claude said they might have considered it, but they were attending a wedding that day. Billy the barman was willing to go. He was off that night, and his wife was in Florida visiting her mother with the kid. One by one we caved in. No big deal, just a party.

When Saturday came, Hugo made Milou promise he wouldn't strip no matter how wasted he got. Milou turned to Tintin and told him he would hold *him* responsible if he ever did. This formality completed, we split in Frankie's and Billy's cars and headed for Oka.

The house was isolated somewhere on an endless dirt road. No neighbours. No parents. No police. An ideal setup for teenagers eager to go to extremes. The sun had not given up on its day shift yet, but the party was already running wild with Bachman-Turner Overdrive, the sound loud enough to make ears bleed. Ridiculously huge speakers buzzed with feedback. Naked people swam in the Lake of Deux Montagnes. A couple was making out on a garden chair. Joints, pipes, and chillums travelled freely from one mouth to another. As I stepped out of the car, I saw a guy with a syringe behind a tree. *Oh well.*

At least fifty people milled about on the lawn, partying and dancing. A barefoot thirtyish man with long, tangled hair and patched jeans hanging off his skinny hips came over to greet us. His face was stamped with an I-started-drinking-at-seven-this-morning grin. His bare chest was red, burned to a crisp by the sun. His name was Jean. Hugo's friend from school was nowhere around.

"Welcome, man, welcome!" he said, gesturing wildly. "*Woohoo!* Want some beer, man? Wanna smoke something, man? Wanna go inside the house, man? *Outside* the house? In the lake, man? *Whatever* you want, man!" He lifted his face toward the sky, his hands reaching up. "We're gonna have a blast tonight! *A blast! Yahoooo!*" He grabbed Alex's arm. "Yeah, man, lots more people are on their way. *Lots more, man!*"

We glanced at each other. Jean looked deadly serious about his prediction.

"Oh yeah, at least another hundred people! Last night I counted *a hundred*—yeah—*a hundred* and, huh—*a hundred* and—huh—*three*—yeah, that's it! *Three!*"

Jean pursed his lips, evaluating his claim. He screamed another "*Yahoooo*," his face twitching as if he were about to have a seizure. His expression melted into a vacant gaze. "Yeah, a lot more, man. How many? Maybe you want to know?" He looked suspiciously at a speechless Alex, then he hugged him like a long-gone brother. "Have fun, man!"

He walked back toward the house. Hugo, Milou, Tintin, Frankie, and Billy followed him, while Alex, Grace, and I stayed behind and headed toward the lake.

We sat on the grass with a bottle of beer fished from a tub on the porch. I wished I'd stayed home. I could tell Alex and Grace felt the same way. People around us were loaded, as in barf-in-the-lake loaded. It was easy to imagine what they'd look like in a few hours. Alex pointed to a guy disguised as Merlin who was distributing acid blotters. Acid, booze, and strangers. A legendary bad combination. The three of us decided to stick around a little, smoke a few joints, and wait for Billy or Frankie to take us home. Grace went hunting for Hugo. This was not his trip either.

"Yeah," she said, returning without him, "let's have a few laughs and get the fuck out of here."

Someone told us the party had officially started the morning before. There were corpses lying here and there on the beach (some of them might be dead, for all we knew), and carloads of fresh newcomers arriving from the dusty road. A typical teenager processing line. Hugo and the rest of the boys remained invisible for a full hour. Grace kept glancing around surreptitiously, looking for him.

"Fuck it. Let's go home," she said.

At that very moment, Milou, Tintin, and Hugo erupted on the porch with two girls. They didn't see us in the shade, and none of us three made a move to signal our presence. We watched silently, unsure about what to do next. Grace's expression turned sombre. Hugo was holding one of the girls by the waist. The prettiest one. For a moment—make that a dog year for Grace—the girl leaned on Hugo, pressing her large-enough-to-alarm tits on his chest. A really good-looking girl. A flower child, pretty and juvenile. A lot like Marie. A bright lilac Indian sari hugged her lean body. Turquoise and silver jewellery sparkled rhythmically whenever she laughed. A line of dark coal surrounded her big eyes. If I ever decided to wear something other than jeans and T-shirts one day, I thought that's how I'd like to look. Comfortably sexy.

Hugo was acting like a man with a message, and the message was: "I'm free to do as I wish." We were close enough to confirm the girl's beauty but a little too far to hear what they were all talking about. Hugo whispered something in the girl's ear, and she put her hand on his cheek. Grace gasped. The girl's eyes looked peculiarly large for her face, even from that distance. So big, in fact, that they surely needed the coal to keep them from spilling all over her cheeks, like sandbags stacked by a river to avoid a flood. She asked something of Milou, he made a face at Hugo, and they all laughed again. The girl's mouth gleamed with red lipstick, white teeth, and endless oohs and ahhs. She was listening to Hugo intensely, her eyes riveted to his mouth. Both Grace and I knew what that meant. The girl was trying to imagine what it would be like to be kissed by him.

Hugo and Grace had never been an official item, it was true. However, since Marie's exit, Hugo had shared his bed with Grace and only Grace. But tonight he was hunting openly with the clean conscience of an honest man. In his defense, I have to admit that the girl in front of him could have tempted the pope himself. I took Grace by the arm and led her away from this torture chamber. Alex followed us toward the lake. Somebody somewhere was playing acoustic guitar. The moon shone, a wedge of lemon in a blueberry sky. Alex got busy rolling a joint. He smiled at Grace.

"Big joint," he promised.

"Better be," she said sadly.

She looked at the ground, fighting her tears, while Alex fought the sand on his rolling paper. As for me, I was fighting the urge to find Billy or Frankie myself and get out of this place. I heard a plaintive bark coming from the house. Then, shortly after, another pleading bark.

"What are they doing to that dog?" I said.

Grace shrugged. I got up. "I'll go see. You know me and animals, I can't help it. I'll look for Frankie and Billy while I'm at it."

I entered the house from the side door. Another bark. The dog sounded not so much in pain but in distress. Little shrieks. I hurried my pace toward the living room. Cushions were scattered all over the floor, and the furniture had been stacked on the back wall in the hope of salvaging it. In a corner, half a dozen people were passing a giant water pipe around. I could hardly make out faces with the density of the smoke, but I spotted everything I was looking for. Frankie and Billy to start with, and a puppy lost in a Turkish bath of hashish smoke and body odour. A terrier, black and white with long hair like the ones on the cover of the notebooks I used to buy when I was in Grade 2. I asked Frankie to hand it to me.

A voice said, "This is my dog."

The guy was drunk, and he looked filthy. I figured he was the one smelling like a dead carcass.

"What's her name?" I asked after checking the dog's genitals.

"It doesn't have a name. But mine is Denis." The man chuckled as he tried to sit up straight on a cushion. "I found it on the street on my way here, no collar or anything. I thought my little girl might like it."

I felt outraged, as if he were introducing a whale in a tennis court. "This is no place for a puppy."

The girl next to him said, "Well, it's better than leaving it in the trunk of his car!" She punched Denis on the shoulder. "This crazy asshole was afraid the dog would shit in his car," she bellowed, "so he put it in the trunk on his way here."

My eyes opened so wide I must have looked as if I had just noticed an army of centipedes crawling over Denis's face.

He looked back at me, grinning. "It's just a dog."

I felt my anger growing. I hated when people said that. I still do.

"Lighten up," he said. "Here, take some acid. Everybody's tripping out tonight. Drop one of these, and in an hour you won't give a damn about the bitch."

Everybody laughed.

"Nah, thanks."

Between two puffs, Billy said he would take us home. Denis turned around to talk to a girl behind him. I chose this opportunity to walk away with the dog. I figured Denis wouldn't notice or mind one way or the other. He had said it himself—after taking that pill he didn't care about the dog anymore. He'd taken the pill, I hadn't. He didn't care, I did.

I found Grace and Alex lying on the sand with four dented beer cans next to them. Hugo Casanova was still at large. The beach was almost deserted now. I saw some people gathering wood for a bonfire. Grace was sobbing in brief little gulps, her pain resonating uselessly in the night like a repeated Morse code message lost on an empty ocean. Trapped in his masculine inadequacies, Alex was pretending to sleep. The dog barked, startling both of them. I said she was probably hungry, and Alex immediately offered to get her something to eat from the house.

"Bring a bowl of water too, if you can."

"Got it."

Nice guy. Really.

The little dog drank and peed at the same time. Along with the bowl of water, Alex had found some grilled chicken in the fridge. The dog eagerly ate every piece I gave her. The moment she was done, she climbed on my lap, curled up in a little ball, and went to sleep. She was mine from that moment on. I swore to myself I'd keep her until death parted us. Billy showed up, his car keys in his hand. Alex returned to the house to find Hugo, Milou, Tintin, and Frankie, but he came back saying they didn't want to leave just yet. Grace got up and walked to the lawn where the cars were parked. I thought I might manage to convince Hugo to come home so I asked Alex where he'd seen him. I handed him the dog and asked him to mind her for a moment.

Hugo was in the kitchen. He was sharing a chair with the beauty from the porch. He motioned for me to get closer and whispered in my ear that there was no way in hell he'd leave before this girl did what she promised to do to him if he stayed until sunrise. He would hitchhike home on his knees if he had to.

It took Billy half an hour to find his car on the front lawn. Alex slid into the passenger's seat, and Grace threw herself on the back seat as if shoved in by the police. I squeezed in beside her, the dog on my lap. She gazed absently out the window, biting her lips. Her rage and tears confirmed something we had all suspected for a long time—Grace was madly in love with Hugo. He was not just another fuck friend, as she'd always claimed. I put my arm around her. Billy and Alex sighed in unison as we made our way from the lawn and on the dirt road. I let Grace hold the dog most of the way. Billy dropped us home and headed back to the party.

Grace locked herself up in Hugo's bedroom. Alex said she was better left alone. "She needs time to calm down."

We made peanut butter sandwiches and played with the dog.

"What's her name?" Alex asked.

"No idea yet. You think this guy will want her back?"

"Maybe. But if you ask me, it's Hugo you should be concerned about. He likes dogs, but not in his place." He yawned. "Better go to bed. I have to go downtown in the morning."

"Why?"

"The Eagles. I want to get their new album. It's called One of These Nights."

"I'll go with you."

The terrier was sleeping on her back, her tongue hanging out.

"Cute little thing," Alex said.

"Adorable."

Then he turned and kissed me. Just like that. I kissed him back, quite passionately. But it didn't go one inch further. Camille wouldn't have been proud of me.

Chapter 25

Listening to Pink Floyd talking about you, me,
and the others

HUGO WALKED IN AROUND five in the morning. I heard him because the noise startled the dog. Alex was fast asleep. I tiptoed out of the room with the puppy in my arms. Luckily Hugo was alone. He waved at me.

"Hello there!" He looked happy with himself. That is, until he saw the dog. "Tell me I'm not seeing what I'm seeing."

"Lower your voice! Everybody's sleeping! And no, you're not seeing what you're seeing."

"I don't want a dog in here, like in *staying here*—clear?"

"Deal! Now shut the fuck up and go to bed! Grace is waiting for you." I said to get his mind off the dog. Hugo pretended he didn't hear me. I lowered my voice. "So, what about the girl?"

He was trying with much difficulty to take his shoes off. I didn't offer to help.

"Great piece of ass. But too crazy for me." He took all his clothes off except for his underwear. "Can it sing?" he blurted.

"What?"

"The dog!"

"Sure. But only to Electric Light Orchestra."

He didn't smile. He said he needed to sleep and headed toward his bedroom.

Grace was still awake. She yelled something at him. Hugo's voice overcame hers.

"I don't owe you shit, girl! If you're not happy, you just have to get the hell out of here. I'm tired, and I want to get some sleep. Get out or shut up and go to bed!"

I heard some commotion. Maybe she was beating the hell out of him. God knows he deserved it. I drew closer. The door flew open, and Grace stormed out. She kissed the dog in my arms, mumbled a goodbye to me, and disappeared out the front door. Hugo turned off the light. I heard him crawl into his waterbed. I checked on Alex, but he was still sleeping soundly. I took the dog out for a pee. I was too busy with my own thoughts to go chasing after Grace.

The streets were wet, and a light drizzle thickened the air, coating everything in a veil of steam. Light dripped here and there through the thick clouds. I saw Grace's footprints in the mud patch in front of the door.

"I know what I'll tell her to make her feel better," I said to the dog. "I'll say, 'My friend, tits and ass are nothing more than tits and ass, but most men feel like they've discovered the wheel anytime they put their hands on a new set.' I'll bet it'll make her laugh."

The puppy danced around, her muzzle up in the air, yapping playfully. Then she rose up on her two rear paws, balancing carefully, and she jumped a few times. It was quite remarkable, and I clapped. "Maybe you can't sing, but you sure can dance! I'll call you Boogie."

The smell of coffee woke Alex. Camille later took all the credit for what happened next, but she honestly had nothing to do with it. It was simply written in the stars—she had said it herself. Alex came to me in the kitchen and kissed me again. As if we were a couple. *Wow.* I told him about Hugo's return, Grace's departure, and the dog's name. He did not comment on Hugo or Grace, but he loved the dog's name, and that won me another kiss. I couldn't leave the puppy alone with Hugo so Alex headed downtown by himself. Staying with Boogie turned out to be a wise decision.

When Hugo emerged from his bedroom, his skull gripped in a gigantic hangover, it was safer—to say the least—to keep the dog away from him. This man had never been big on dogs. Small dogs were "rats" or "insects" to him. I don't think he would have gone so far as to hurt Boogie, but I doubt he would have minded if someone else had.

He sat at the kitchen table, his hair defying gravity. I pushed a cup of coffee in front of him. He drank silently. "Good coffee."

The caffeine might have fuelled life into his neurons, but it did nothing for his appearance. The girl last night might have thought he was irresistible, but one glance in his direction that morning, and she would have run away. In this state he couldn't attract a fly. Not even a Spanish one.

"It's the orange juice that got to me last night. I hate orange juice," he said rubbing his neck.

"The orange juice or the vodka?"

"Please don't mention that word."

"What? Vodka?"

"Shut up, would you, please?"

He said he felt like a large animal was rotting in his guts. Or in his brain. I poured him a second cup of coffee. He put one hand on his forehead and with the other rearranged the male unit in his underwear. He attempted to smile, but it came out all wrong, as if he was disgusted about something. He looked at me. "So, gorgeous, what's new?" he mumbled.

"I wish I could say the same about you, Hugo, but honestly, it would be totally uncalled for."

He coughed.

"That bad, eh?"

"Worse."

"Oh well. Maybe I need a shower."

"Try a fire hose."

I refrained from asking about Grace. *Not yet.* Of course, I didn't mention a thing about Alex and me, even though the urge was strong to tell someone—anyone.

Hugo took a long shower, shaved, and put on some cologne. When he came back to the kitchen, he looked almost human. He got on his knees to pet Boogie.

"Hi, little rat! You're cute, but you're just passing through. Did your saviour tell you that? Very soon, it's back to the streets! Bye bye, insect!"

I tried to ignore him, but he raised his voice. "Ciao, cucaracha!"

Aggravating someone who's dealing with a major hangover is never a good idea. But I figured sprinkling a bit of Grace in the conversation couldn't hurt my cause. I followed Hugo into the living room and threw myself into the beanbag chair next to him. He was pretending to read an old *Rolling Stone.*

I pulled my hair nonchalantly into a ponytail. "So what're you gonna do about Grace?"

Hugo shook his head as if I had pronounced the unmentionable. "Vodka" and "Grace" were two words he didn't want to hear that morning. "Fuck her," he said.

If he was looking for sympathy, he was using the wrong set of words.

"So that's it? Fuck her?" I said. "That's all you have to say? Don't tell me you didn't know she was falling in love with you! Everybody knew!"

He shrugged.

"Hugo, you're a real asshole."

"Really? Am I?"

He went to his room. He didn't close the door. I took the gesture as an invitation to follow him.

"So what are you gonna do about Grace?" I repeated.

"I don't know! Fuck! Will you leave me alone? What do you want me to do?"

I hate it when people destroy something and later whine that there's nothing they can do about it. When you've acted like a weasel, there are a million things you can do to redeem yourself.

"Do you plan to see the girl from the party again?"

He curled his lips. "Nah, I don't think so. Too crazy for me!"

"And you plan to avoid Grace for the rest of your life?"

I saw him considering this unlikely possibility, wishing he would never have to deal with her again. But this was impossible, and I told him so. Grace was our friend.

"All right, all right! I'll talk to her."

"When?"

"Next time she's here."

"She won't come back, Hugo! Not unless you take the first steps, and you know it! You've been an asshole—we both agree on that. The least you can do is ask for her forgiveness. You humiliated her, and it's just fair that you drag your ass in the mud a little and let her regain some of her dignity. She's your friend, no? We'll all be friends for life, you say it all the time. Tell her you've been an asshole. You don't have to sleep with her afterward, she'll understand. *We'll* make her understand. But man, tell her you're sorry for what you did and how you did it!"

"Okay. I'll call her. Now get out of here."

"When? She must be at her parents' place. You can reach her there. If not, they'll certainly know where she is." I could tell my voice irritated him like a bad case of eczema.

"This afternoon."

"Okay. But you better do it."

"Now fuck off, Geneviève, will you?"

I got up and hurried to the bathroom to take a shower,

dragging Boogie with me. I wanted to be clean and cute for Alex's return.

Alex came back, pleased as a mouse in a cheese hole. Hugo remained in his room, getting mentally ready—my guess—for his confrontation with Grace. Alex took the record out from the bag so carefully you'd have thought he was handling a newborn baby. There it was: *One of these nights*. We went to his room with Boogie. Alex closed the door, petted the dog, and put the record on the turntable he kept in his room.

The album cover showed a Georgia O'Keeffe's kind of painting depicting a cow's skull. From the first notes, Don Henley's voice filled the air. We analyzed everything, dissecting track after track. I loved the first track best. Alex asked if I'd be in the mood for psilocybin later that night. Yeah, why not. Two months had already passed since my bad trip.

"We'll stick together?" I said.

"You bet. Don't worry."

And he kissed me.

"You know," he said, "I guess Grace will move out now, and Hugo and I can't afford the place by ourselves. Why don't you move in with us? Would you like that?"

He kissed me again. Big kisser, this guy. I couldn't believe my ears or my hungry mouth. We attacked each other like wolves. Not enough skin to rub. Not enough mouth to cover. We didn't want Hugo to hear us, so we made love soundlessly, with cautious dedication. I cannot say that I had strong feelings for Alex. Not at that point anyway. But he was so nice, so good, that I was positive I'd fall in love with him sooner or later. Alex was tall, good-looking, and strong. I was definitely attracted to him physically. He wasn't mischievous and unpredictable the way Hugo was. Unlike Frankie, Tintin, and Milou, he was reliable at all times, day or night. I felt I could trust him with my own life and never have to worry about a thing as long as he was around. Resting on his chest, I pictured Camille's congratulations, her famous pineapple cake rising up in the oven and a bottle of bubbly wine shoved in the freezer to celebrate the event. I couldn't wait to tell her. She'd be so proud of me.

There was a knock on the bedroom door. Alex and I sprang out of bed. We giggled and crawled back under the covers. "Come in!"

Hugo. "Hi guys."

He wanted to know about the Eagles album.

"Sounds a little different than the last one. But very good. Surprisingly satisfying actually." Alex said, his hand on mine.

I blushed. Hugo took a step in. His face jumped backward as if the room had been completely rearranged.

"You guys are naked?"

"Yep."

"Well, I'll be darned. You made it!"

"Yep."

A typical male exchange of basic facts. Hugo addressed himself to Alex—and Alex alone—as if I were sitting in another country. "Will she be moving in?"

Alex was all smiles and strangely at ease, considering he was butt naked. "Yep."

"Cool. Good. So it's settled then. You're in."

I was a little disappointed by his lack of enthusiasm. "What about Grace?" I asked.

Did I have to spoil this as-good-as-it-gets moment? Hugo frowned, probably revising his latest comment. Was he ready to live with someone terminally obsessed with vodka and the G-word? I could tell he was having second thoughts. Alex said there was enough room for everybody. Hugo came over and stroked my hair a little more firmly than he should.

"You're in. I'm happy about this. Let's keep it that way, okay?"

"Sure—"

And he stepped out.

Another knock. Hugo again. "What about the rat?"

Alex looked annoyed. "What about it?"

"You know the rule, man. No dogs in this house."

"Yeah, we talked about it. As soon as we find a good home, the dog's gone." Alex squeezed my arm under the blanket.

"Sooner than later, then?"

"Yep."

"It's a deal, then?"

"Well, I suppose so."

"Cool," Hugo said, turning and heading back to his room. I protested vehemently. Alex said I shouldn't worry. In fact, he said, I should forget all about it.

"Time will go by, and Hugo will get attached to her. You'll see. No problem. Promise."

I cut the kissing short and made him swear he would never agree to get rid of Boogie. Alex crossed his heart.

When we got up, Hugo was sitting in the living room, wrestling with the twisted telephone cord. He was getting set for The Phone Call. He didn't seem to mind our presence. In fact, he looked as if he could use the company. Grace answered, and he said "Hi, Grace." She hung up on him. He turned toward us with a did-you-hear-that face. Sitting next to my new love, I lifted my eyes from the newspaper.

"Try and try again, Hugo. Don't give up until she listens."

Alex told him to do as I said. He said girls knew best about these things. Three attempts later, Hugo had graduated from "Hi, Grace" to "Hi, Grace, it's me." We were getting somewhere. The ninth time, she listened. Hugo was inspired now and determined to tell her his true feelings and thoughts. He wasn't in love with her, and he told her so. Grace probably accused him of lying because Hugo became defensive. "I've never told you," he said emphatically, "not once, no matter how horny, no matter how stoned, that I was in love with you!"

True. We'd have known for sure if he had. Grace wouldn't have been able to keep this one to herself. Hugo raised his voice again. They were fuck friends, he said, and had never been anything more than that. He said he enjoyed the sex, the conversations. And her company. "Well, most of the time," he added with contempt.

Grace screamed—we could hear her clearly by then. "Hugo, you're a fuckin' liar! You've never said the words, but your actions spoke for themselves. You *do* love me, for Christ's sake!"

"*No, I don't!* I'm a free man, Grace, and I want to be by myself for a while. Nothing personal and—"

She regained her calm because we couldn't hear her anymore.

"Now that's a lie, Grace. Don't say things like that. You know I like you—I what? Man, I refuse to get into this! No, I've told you a million times, there's nothing wrong with you! It's me. No, there's nobody else! I don't feel—I don't know, man, you know, it's not the first time we've talked about this! *Colice de tabarnac!*" Hugo had lost what was left of his equanimity and was swearing like a one-eyed pirate. "Can you be reasonable for a moment? *Saint-Ciboire!* Yeah, damn right. Reasonable. Why don't you look at this like, I don't know—like a great opportunity to meet new people? Grace, please, don't do this to me!"

I wasn't sure he deserved her forgiveness. *Don't do this to me.* What a lousy thing to say. I was sure Grace was choking with tears.

In a last attempt to save their friendship, Hugo said, "Come over. We'll smoke a joint and play a game of Risk."

She said something and Hugo hung up.

"So?" Alex and I asked in unison.

"She's fine. I bet she's already on her way here."

Hugo stretched like a cat recovering from a fight. "She'll be all right. She'll be over in no time, begging me to let her stay for the night. You'll see."

Less than an hour later, there was a knock at the door.

Hugo mouthed, "I told you so."

But it wasn't Grace. It was Denis coming to get his dog.

Chapter 26

*Listening to the Beatles singing about a large
marine mammal with tusks*

"OKAY, GUYS, THE JOKE's over. Where's the dog? I'm kind of in a hurry."

Boogie was still in Alex's bedroom, door shut. She must have been asleep because we couldn't hear her.

"We want to keep the dog," Alex said to Denis.

We want to keep the dog. I liked that.

Hugo went nuts. "Say that again? No way, man. We are *not* keeping that dog. A deal is a deal. Give it back to him!"

Alex made a sign for Hugo to join him in the kitchen, but Hugo chose to ignore him. He preferred to stand there and twist the dishrag in his hands as if it were the dog's neck.

Denis repeated that he had to go. He turned to Alex. "I don't think you understand, man. This is my dog, you know, like *tuk*-nically speaking, I mean."

The vast land of four-syllable words had yet to be conquered by Denis. Was it because it was too early in the day or already too late in his life?

"I promised the dog to my daughter on the phone last night, man, and fuck—uh—if you have to know everything,

I got real wasted, and I couldn't make it home. I woke up on the beach this morning. I looked everywhere for the fucking dog. More than an hour, man! You should have told me you took it away! If it wasn't for your friend the barman, I'd still be looking for the damn thing. You stole my dog, man. That's not real cool, is it? I mean, that's totally uncool, no?"

Denis's eyes scanned the room. "Where is it anyway?" He was getting edgy. He still stank like road kill baking under a mid-afternoon sun.

I looked first at Alex, then Hugo. Nobody said a word.

"I'm so late, man," he went on. "So *fuckin'* late. Enough already—I need that dog. You don't know my wife, man. She'll be really pissed off at me, you know, like totally pissed off at me—" He lit a cigarette. "If I walk in with the dog, my little girl will be happy, and my ol' lady might forget about last night. Domestic pressure, man, got it? Need the dog. No way out of it."

Alex asked him to reconsider.

"You don't understand, man. I already told my kid about the dog. If I don't show up with it, this will be my last day on earth. My wife can be really mean. She used to date bikers, get it? She takes no shit from anybody. Especially not from me!"

He sure looked terrified. Alex insisted again. Hugo's disgusted stare shifted in my direction. He hated me at that moment, I could tell. Denis remained categorical (a word he wouldn't have tried to pronounce himself for fear of permanent brain damage). Three simple words, *Need the dog.*

Hugo clapped his hands loudly. "Well, that settles it, then. Nothing will make our friend Denis change his mind."

Well, maybe one thing.

Alex disappeared for a moment and returned, not with Boogie as Hugo clearly expected, but with a big chunk of Kashmir hashish, a birthday gift from Milou. "I'll exchange this for the rat," he said.

Hugo smacked his palm on his forehead with a loud thump. "Man, are you losing your mind or what?"

Denis's face said it all. He pressed the chunk with his fingers. "Well, I could drive to the pound and get a similar dog." He was laughing like a moron now. A stinking moron.

"Now that's an excellent idea!" Alex said. "Your kid will never see the difference, your wife will be delighted, *and* one more dog will be saved from the pound. You also get yourself a nice chunk of great smoke! Excellent deal, isn't it?" He reached out to shake Denis's hand. The stinker hesitated for a minute. "You look like a reasonable man, Denis. Please don't do this to me."

Alex winked at Hugo. I'm pretty sure that's when I fell in love with him.

Denis left with a smile and five grams of heavenly hash in his pocket.

Hugo was fuming. "That was your stash, man! Are you out of your mind? And the fuckin' dog. What about this fuckin' dog? *No* dogs in here. You promised, man! You want me to call Camille and let *her* refresh your memory? She'll tell you. She was there when we agreed on this light years ago. What is it with you people changing house rules without discussing it with me? What is this shit? You're both ganging up against me now?"

Hugo's day felt like wet soap—he had no grip on anything. He was mad at Alex, at me, at Grace, at the vodka, at his headache, and above all, at the fucking dog.

"*You* said no dogs in here," Alex replied. "Yeah I remember very well! *You* repeated it time and time again, Hugo. You made that law! You see, I happen to love dogs, and I've always wished I had one. This one's here now, and it will stay, so you'd better get a grip on yourself and learn to live with it. End of the discussion."

Whoa. But Hugo wasn't done just yet "I can't believe it. The dog stays, and the hash's gone! Why, man? Fuck, man, why?"

I swallowed my breath. Alex sat next to me and kissed my forehead. "Why? Because I'm sure it's the right thing to do, and when I feel that good about something, nice things happen to me. A crazy thing, Hugo, difficult to explain, actually. And by the way, it's only a fuckin' piece of hash!"

Hugo was livid. "Crazy fucker. Dumb shit!"

The bell rang.

"Now that's Grace!" Alex said. We were relieved. Hugo would have to take his mind somewhere else for a few hours.

He opened the door, his shoulders hunched, ready for another round of calamity. "Oh!"

If it was Grace, she was holding a gun. Or she was naked and covered in maple syrup. Hugo took two steps back and turned toward us, his mouth wide open.

And in walked Jude.

Chapter 27

*Listening to James Taylor being greeted by his dog David
after a long trip abroad*

*H*E HUGGED HUGO FOR a long time. Then he saw Alex and me. "Hey! How are you guys?"

Tanned and dressed in funky clothes, Jude was stepping back into our lives. The air around him carried scents from another world. Jude was back. Six months had passed since we had last seen him. *Holy Ghost.* He didn't look all that different, but he glowed. And he was much thinner.

"Never mind us, man!" Alex said. "What about you? How was Asia? How was your trip? Come on in, have a seat."

Jude was wearing a beautiful grey woollen coat. I reached out to touch it. He caressed the collar. "Wool from Kashmir. The best."

Of course. "It's beautiful."

He peered at me intently for a few beats longer than necessary, then at Alex sitting next to me. He took a plastic bag out of his pocket. From it, he pulled a piece of hash the size of an extra-large egg. "With love from Afghanistan!" he yelled.

The dust in India had certainly not dimmed the power of his voice. Alex had been right. The hash given away was back.

Almost instantly. The proof was right there on the table. Hugo was flabbergasted.

"That's fuckin' weird—"

"I'm also right about the dog, Hugo."

Jude turned to Alex. "What dog?"

"That dog over there. A long story. Forget about it for now, and tell us about your trip."

Assisted by half a dozen joints and a box of Oreo cookies, Jude took us from Kabul to Delhi and all the way up to Kathmandu. He told us tales of snake charmers, luscious palaces built in the middle of lakes, goats riding on motorcycles, mountains so high they bruise the sky, and colours so bright you need sunglasses to look at them. He had witnessed a cremation by the Ganges River in the sacred city of Benares and had chanted with the mourners. He told us about the fading beauty of the Taj Mahal and the elegance of the floating houses in Kashmir. He said he had smoked his brains out, paying little and getting much. Camels, elephants, rhinos, tigers, fakirs, and monks—he had seen it all. Gurus had welcomed him in their ashrams as if he were a close relative. He had found the best hashish in this part of Asia, and a large quantity was on its way to Montreal.

"That was the easy part," Jude said, crumbling a piece of Afghani. "The hard part was to put my hand on the perfect guru. Very difficult. Quite a challenge actually."

Showing no pain, Jude sat on the floor in lotus position. He said he had located the best middleman between us and the Big Boss in Heaven. "I cut the red tape!" he laughed.

He said this guru had introduced him to God. Literally. For a moment, Jude seemed to be in a trance. He closed his eyes and turned his head up. His lips parted. Boogie came sniffing at him. Jude didn't move. He looked like a crippled pilgrim in a Renaissance painting. The dog chose this moment to pee on his Kashmiri coat. Damn yak smell, I suppose.

Chapter 28

Listening to the Beatles praising a lunatic on a mountain

AFTER HIS RETURN, JUDE's life revolved around his master. He grew a moustache, dressed entirely in white, and spent hours meditating in his bedroom.

His mother had welcomed him home like a prodigal son. He seemed more mature to her, and she told him so. He had hugged her for the longest time ever at the airport. "You haven't done this since you were a little boy," she told Jude on their way home.

"You're growing into a fine young man, my son," she rejoiced, pouring herself a drink while Jude searched through his luggage on the living room floor. He found what he was looking for and approached her with the most beautiful silk shawl she had ever seen.

The son Mother India had sent back to Mrs. P pleased her. She had spent the last few months worrying herself sick about her son's safety. But there he was. Jude had valiantly survived India, her personal version of hell. She hoped he might even be inspired enough to get a good job now. Maybe even go back to school!

"Wouldn't that be nice?" she told him. "You're such a smart

boy. It's a pity to see all that potential going to waste."

Between two pills and a gin and tonic, she waited for the tie-dyed T-shirts and the hash pipes to disappear. But they didn't. Jude had no plans whatsoever to change his career. He was a successful businessman, and he considered his activities to be neither more nor less commendable than the ones conducted by other entrepreneurs. He had no intention of giving it up. And, glorious luck, his guru didn't think his trade was immoral. Better, the Indian man offered him absolute protection in exchange for ten percent of Jude's earnings. This would have cooled most people off, but as far as Jude was concerned it was a fair deal.

Jude said his master didn't actually *need* the money. That was not what the ten percent donation was all about. The idea was for the disciple to manifest detachment from the material world. Jude figured that ten percent of his earnings was a small price to pay for a divine shield of protection, a fireproof wall erected by God himself. He believed it was smarter to offer that dough to God than to throw it at the mob. Jude's affairs were prospering. That alone indicated God's approval. This master of his was mightier than La Cosa Nostra and the Hell's Angels combined. With this guru by his side, the mob and the bikers had no choice but to leave him alone. And they did exactly that. Jude had never felt so safe.

His Indian master could operate this kind of miracle. Magical wonders. Jude's shipments of dope from Asia were periodically searched by customs agents, but nothing was ever found. Dogs barked but ran in the wrong direction. Officers' hands fondled but missed their target by an inch. Impossible situations became manageable, often at the last minute. Pure magic. Jude had always been paranoid enough to avoid any kind of risks. Nevertheless, the divine power at work here was undisputable.

His guru did not expect Jude to sell all his belongings

and move to India to live at his master's feet. But from a guru's point of view, this new disciple did the next best thing. Jude made sure his god in flesh had access to everything he wanted, needed, or admired from the Western world. Jude sent packages of all sizes to the ashram gate up in the northern mountains of Uttar Pradesh, where a wooden crate served as a mailbox. Radios, watches, books, stationery, speakers, microphones, amps, all arrived there for the guru—a gift almost every day. Like Christmas four times a week. Magic.

His name was Holiji. Dropped into my Canadian ear, *Guru Holiji* sounded decidedly mystical. He was a Sikh. Sikhism is a very old religion with its roots in the province of Punjab in India. It teaches belief in one God and repudiates the caste system, one of the things that differentiate it from Hinduism and Islam. Jude showed us a book written by his guru. The face on the cover was inspiring. The man looked fifty years old, maybe younger—it's always hard to say with Asians. His hair was tucked into a white turban. His moustache ran down to his chest, where it drowned in a silver beard. The skin was smooth and stretched evenly on rosy, plump cheeks. The eyes were a deep shade of brown. They stared at the camera like a seagull aiming for a fish. He was handsome in a Santa Claus way. Jude pulled a few snapshots from his pocket. In one, Holiji stood next to him in front of a temple. Like a proud father, the Indian man was holding Jude by the shoulder. Our friend's eyes were shut, his face bathed in gratitude.

Each year in November, as soon as the monsoon was over, Holiji toured India in a minibus for a few months searching for vagrant souls to swell up his congregation. Jude had met him on such a trip. Holiji was preaching to a crowd accompanied by a dozen devotees, Indians and Westerners alike. Smitten to pieces by what he heard, Jude decided to tag along and check the man out. On every picture he passed around, the guru was dressed in white from head to toe, his clothes impeccable and crisp. Blinding white. By contrast, the Westerners surrounding him looked like garbage collectors. Faces unshaven, dirty, wrinkled clothes covered with amber dust. They looked tired and in a great need of a bath. But the master glowed—starched, immaculate, and eager to change one more destiny. A snowman in a coalmine. Dirt did not stick on this exceptional human being.

"This man is pure like a dove!" Jude boasted. "I've met so many gurus in India, man, and this one is *the* one. But let me tell you about the others. I met some fuckin' insane bastards over there."

One of those was Sai Baba. Jude said he had found him appealing at first but soon discovered he had no taste for the guru's Disneyland type of magic. He was also disturbed by the rumour circulating about Sai Baba's inclination for little boys whenever the urge to explore the marvellous world of sex became too overwhelming to be subdued. Farther along the way, not too far from Bombay in a town called Pune Bhagwan Rajneesh's disciples, the sannyasins, stroked Jude the wrong way with their guaranteed-germ-free environment and severe hygiene rules. Their moronic surnames and their military regime alienated him even more. These annoyances aside, Jude was profoundly moved by their seminars on tantric yoga. Having experimental sex with different women for hours on end, all in the name of enlightenment, was definitely the kind of doctrine Jude could go for. However, he said, he realized that there was something wrong with that kind of sexual encounter (we looked at one another incredulously). He also spent some time with the Krishnas, but, according to Jude, they turned out to be a little too sedated to be attractive to anyone but junkies. Furthermore, Jude had no talent for dancing and singing, he hated to hang around airports, and that's where you found Krishnas in the 1970s.

Farther away, in Darjeeling, a distant Indian town up in the mountains close to the Nepali border, Jude stumbled by coincidence on Guru Holiji. This holy man was the successor of Sant Baba Ram Singh, a most respected semi-god renowned for his legendary *darshan*—a vision of the divine experienced by a devotee just by being in the presence of a guru, or by looking into his eyes—his meeting with John F. Kennedy sometime in the early '60s, and his indisputable wisdom. Jude showed us a black and white picture of his master's master. At first glance, he looked very much like Holiji. Same stature, definitely the same clothes, same Indian features, but older. Like father and son. I took Holiji's book to compare both faces. Holiji's expression was all kindness and goodness, but his spiritual father inspired something else. Something other than respect or fear. I scrutinized every little detail of Sant Baba Ram Singh's face, and what struck me was neither the small scar above his left eyebrow nor his stony, solemn visage. It was much more subtle than that. I finally put my finger on it. Whereas his right eye displayed total compassionate love, the other betrayed defiance. It created the most fantastic expression. I wanted to hear more about him. Jude obliged.

"Sant Baba Ram Singh passed away in 1973. Weeks before his death, he told his disciples in India that Holiji would be the next one in charge at the ashram. It was a delicate matter because Sant Baba Ram Singh had a biological son, very devoted, and about the same age as Holiji. People at the ashram reported that the son showed no signs of disappointment or frustration whatsoever at the announcement. Like everybody else, he bowed to Holiji and asked for his blessings. On the evening of Sant Baba Ram Singh's cremation, Holiji moved into his new quarters with his wife. He said that he needed to remain as close as possible to the holy man's last breath. The next day he blessed everyone around—disciples, villagers, visitors, everyone crossing his path. The people at the ashram waited impatiently to see whether they would recognize the old master's eyes in Holiji's. You know, his *darshan*. And they did! Isn't that great?"

Wow.

Afterward, Jude said, Holiji sat still in his old master's house for seven days, meditating in the dark with no food or water. On the eighth day, he told his disciples that Sant Baba Ram Singh had successfully completed the Divine Wisdom Transfer. A new anointed God was walking on earth.

Jude said people in India did not approach death the way we did. "To them, death is a life event as ordinary as a walk down the road. Nothing to fear or resent. Nothing to die for." He laughed. "That's if you're ready, of course."

"What do you mean?" I asked fervently.

"Well, if no one shows you the path to follow, you can waste a long time wandering between spiritual planes. Only meditation can prepare you for death. And not just any kind of meditation." Jude dug his finger rather unceremoniously up his nose. "Holiji is the one who knows the way. I'm not saying he's the only one. I'm saying he's the best one."

"He showed you how to meditate? Stop that! It's disgusting."

Jude reluctantly disengaged his index finger from his nostril. "Better. He gave me a mantra to align my soul with God. It's called the *simran*."

I was fascinated. So was Alex. But not Hugo. I could tell he wasn't buying it. Not for a second.

I asked Jude if I could borrow Holiji's book.

BACK AT THE APARTMENT, Alex and I went right to our room, lay on the bed, and opened the dog-eared book. Jude had taken a lot of notes in it, most of them impossible to decipher. We ignored them and started to read Holiji's words. The more we read, the more the feeling grew in us that our lives were about to change profoundly.

Chapter 29

Listening to George Harrison pleading for love, hope,
and peace on earth

HOLIJI'S DISCIPLES WERE REQUESTED to live by a few simple precepts, one of them being the complete abstinence from meat. Holiji himself had never chewed a piece of flesh in his life, and this restricted diet was mandatory if you wished to be part of his flock. Apparently, it was impossible to reach heaven's high planes if you happened to cooperate—directly or not—to the slaughter of animals. I was already a vegetarian, so this rule presented no problems for me. *Good.*

The second rule was the practice of meditation. This one had to be performed every day by sitting still for no less than thirty minutes, repeating mentally a divine sequence of five words, the *simran*, a meditation tool divulged by Holiji himself on the holy day of initiation. No problem there either. Sitting on my butt for half an hour a day didn't sound like an insurmountable deed. With dedication and will, I figured it would be fun to squeeze into my busy schedule large chunks of time to find the meaning of life. I might even find tremendous happiness in the practice of daily contemplation. I could turn out to be a gifted disciple. *Who knows?*

I pictured myself an older devotee assisting young pursuers of truth. I envisioned my serenity while listening to their moral struggles. From that moment, in my heart, almost everything about Holiji was promoted from small to capital letters.

Holiji's third rule was a little trickier. It said we should gather in his name once a week for group meditation. Needless to say, Jude took it on himself to organize these reunions, the *satsangs*. Every Sunday morning, devotees were asked to meet at Sean's house—he was one of Jude's Anglo friends. It was the only space available to us at the time. Jude invited every soul he knew, from his dope-dealing partners to his mother's friends. Some got hooked.

After each of us had read Holiji's book cover to cover, Milou, Tintin, Frankie, Alex, and I went to the *satsangs* together. We went no more than twice a month at the beginning. The *satsangs* took place on Sunday mornings, which were the inevitable groggy conclusion to Saturday-night excesses, and we loved to spend them in bed, especially in wintertime.

Sean was a part-time grass dealer. His bungalow was in Notre-Dame-de-Grace (referred to as NDG by Montreal's Anglophones mainly because saying the actual French name makes them sound as stupid as we Frenchies do when we encounter highway road signs with names like Ottenburn Park or Beaconsfield). In a tiny and damp carpeted room in the basement of Sean's house, we assembled in Holiji's name. That way, we didn't disturb his girlfriend, who didn't exactly see eye to eye with Sean when it came to our Indian wonder man. To her, he was all right but nothing worth kicking her almost religious ceremony of a ham and sausage dinner on Wednesdays. Pining on her ass waiting for God to manifest himself was not her idea of an appropriate way to spend a single hour of her life. The more Sean became wrapped up in Holiji's doctrine, the more she hated the guru. She went out of her way to stack Maple Leaf bacon in the freezer. She didn't want to have anything to do with Holiji—or us, for that matter. Sean said her girlfriend referred to us as his "sect of friends."

We rang the doorbell at 9:00 a.m. and Sean rushed us to the basement like pregnant daughters he was ashamed of. His girlfriend peeked at us with disgust from the kitchen as if something slimy was making its way inside her bungalow. She never said hello. Jude said we shouldn't take it personally—he was the one she hated most.

In the basement, we sat in silence on the dusty wall-to-wall imitation grass carpet. Perched on individual cushions, we twisted our lower bodies in an attempt to master the lotus position. Some, including me, didn't even bother to give it a try. Instead, I contemplated the scene—this mixture of specimens from Jude's diverse social circles. A petri dish of his past, present, and future relationships.

We meditated with ecstatic smiles to the sound of audio-tapes featuring Holiji. We had to concentrate hard to get what he was saying. He spoke with a thick Indian accent, and the poor quality of the tape made his voice almost inaudible. However, we got the essentials. Come to think of it, we had always known the essentials. Peace, love, be kind and gener-ous, don't do to others what you don't want done to yourself. You would have thought we were hearing it for the first time.

After a few sessions, we fell into a routine. Meditation was usually over by noon, and we happily climbed upstairs toward the light and the dry wooden floor. That was the moment when Sean's girlfriend invariably grabbed her purse and went out for a drive, or, weather permitting, sat in the sandbox at the playground next to the house, waiting for us to get the hell out of her place. With cups of spiced Indian tea in hand, we sat in her kitchen, whispering about Holiji's infinite power. Nobody but Jude was initiated. We couldn't wait for our day in the sun.

Chapter 30

*Listening to Elton John singing that love is the reason
we are on earth*

Unconditional love is difficult to master on a day-to-day basis.

It didn't take long for me to realize that the bug travelling up most devotees' asses made me feel really uncomfortable. No matter how hard I attempted to rationalize their behaviour, some disciples irritated the hell out of me, something I was terribly ashamed of. How could I despise people from my own spiritual clan? I loathed their docile behaviour and their opinions on what was good or evil. They rarely, if ever, laughed heartily. Holier-than-thou apostles in drab attire. The Sunday assembly reminded me of morning mass at my old convent. Joyful as a cemetery.

I concluded that spiritual growth is a personal venture, and that I didn't have to agree with everybody on the subject of my religious beliefs, not even within my own circle, and nobody needed to agree with me. I could love Holiji and still take the liberty of disliking some of his disciples. I didn't have to follow anyone but my master. I had to show compassion, yes, even tolerance—that's what it was all about—but I didn't have to love every one of my brothers and sisters as though they were family. Of course not.

I wanted to be Holiji's disciple because I wanted the world to see what I was capable of. Everybody had personal reasons for getting involved, and for me, it was that I wanted to be judged for what I really was and not only for the bits and pieces I was letting others see. I considered myself to be a peaceful, life-loving individual, and if I became scarlet with rage and hatred at times, I could not hurt a fly that had not bugged me in the first place. I wanted people to know that above all I was a follower of Guru Holiji, The-Only-Master-Worth-Talking-About. I wanted to exude this feature that would make me respectable at all times. Something that would make people talk differently about me.

"Did she really say that? Nah, it couldn't be. Don't you know she's a disciple of Holiji?" or "She's not [________]." (Fill in blank with something like selfish, vicious, or vengeful.) "That's impossible. She's with Guru Holiji!"

And each time they'd pronounce his name they would cross themselves the Holiji Way (not defined at the time of fantasy) and think of me.

There were more rules in Holiji's book, but they weren't regarded by anyone (including Holiji himself) as anything more than strong suggestions, which, if repeatedly ignored, were more liable to occasionally raise an eyebrow than to get you in real trouble with the Big Man. For example, the rule stating we should only have sex to procreate.

That was plainly absurd. Especially coming from Jude's mouth on a Sunday morning. Reading aloud a passage from Holiji's book about sexual relationships, Jude sounded like a six-year-old Cantonese boy struggling with a French edition of *War and Peace*. "No Sex." "Abstinence." "Chaste." These words gave him jaw cramps. When it came to sex, Jude was still the weakest among all men, no matter how hard he tried to make people believe he wasn't the same person anymore.

The Anglo faction among us appeared to believe that life with no recreational sex was feasible, but for us Frenchies it meant denying our hormonal heritage. We needed to take just one glance at each other to silently agree: this law had to go. But Jude said Holiji advised us to slow down on the occurrences, keeping in mind that the goal was the total elimination of the act unless we meant to have a child. *Yeah, sure. Call me when I'm sixty.* We were free birds in the love mood of the '70s. The intellectual conflict between spiritual attainment and sexual bliss sent our brains on a spectacular roller-coaster ride, just as it had for millions of people before us. No more thoughts about sex? No more craving for skin-to-skin contact? A frightening concept, to say the least. We bitched about this rule whenever Jude wasn't around.

"Enlightenment's great, man, but if it means living like a monk, sorry, but I'm out."

"How do you ever find out how to cope with the temptations of life if you don't measure yourself against them, again and again and again?"

"Yeah, and all that free fun lost in the gutter!"

Alex, Milou, Tintin (even though he was the only one of us who rarely had sex), Frankie, and I agreed on the spot no signature on paper required—to a treaty stipulating that *we* didn't have to stick to the "no sex" bit. We weren't about to let this detail stand between us and self-realization. We Frenchies had to discard this rule on account of our condition, our physical urges, which called for something like a note from the family doctor excusing us from gym class. We promised to somehow work on the concept, but it was useless. It's hard to get rid of the nasty habit of having orgasms. So we all went back to fucking our brains out. At this point of my life, I was just getting the hang of it. There was no way in hell I was going to push my meagre gain back under a rock.

"Slowly but surely," we agreed. One less orgasm at a time.

Milou couldn't get over it. "How can we be expected to live without sex? Sorry, man, but if a Farrah Fawcett lookalike showed up in my Las Vegas suite longing to blow on my nipples and telling me I'm her big daddy, I don't think I'd ever be spiritual enough to find the inner strength to kick her out."

Solid arguments.

The last rule was about money. It was *recommended*, but—and the words were underlined—only if we *really* wanted to do it, to give a percentage of our monthly earnings to the Holiji fund. Ten percent was suggested in case we didn't know what to start with. This money would allow our master to travel across the world, delighting his children with his presence and acquiring new disciples along the way. Wouldn't it be nice to know we worked a few hours every week to bring eternal glory to total strangers? Like ten percent of our time? Sadly, the contribution to the travel fund also happened to be a problem with most devotees, Anglos and Frenchies alike. Not many takers. We cleaned our consciences by asserting rightly that Jude's contribution was probably more than enough to make up for the rest of us. Sex and money we'd keep.

"It will make life that much easier with Hugo," Alex said to Jude, although he knew it was a weak excuse.

To our delight, Holiji was cool on the question of mind-altering substances. No rules for or against it. We didn't dare to question why, fearing any curiosity on our part would trigger a review of this God-inspired policy.

Chapter 31

Listening to George Harrison praising a saccharine god

IN THE 1970S, GURUS popped out of India like hot *chapatis* from a tandoori oven. There was nothing odd or unusual about following a spiritual master. People valued gurus the same way they fancy therapists today, as someone who could guide your steps simply because the familiar path of your own life could no longer be approached the way it had always been. For the average young seeker in the '70s, choosing a master was difficult and often deceptive. Who was the best god in flesh? We all agreed about the Dalai Lama, Yogananda, Meher Baba, or Sri Aurobindo, but what about all the others? Most spiritual leaders' campaigns were fierce and aggressive, but in an infinitely compassionate way ("Find God Now! Don't Let Your Own Life Kill You! Are You Afraid of Being Happy *and* Healthy?") If only there had been enough time to check them all out, one master after the other, one religion at a time, one ritual at a time, one sacred book at a time. This crucial decision was meant to be done instinctively, and that was in fact the catch-22. It was impossible to test every concept, every religion, and every master. Not enough time in a lifetime to draw a solid conclusion. How could we recognize the right guru from the many nice but nevertheless misleading imposters? Wouldn't a bad choice have an impact on all our future incarnations?

Then again, maybe not. Maybe what was ludicrous in the first place was the need to look for someone or something specific to "fix" us. Every given day, humans, animals, and even trees have something to teach us. Everything and everyone coming our way is saying something about us and our relationship to the world. In other words, everything that isn't me has something to teach me.

What did we know about God in the 1970s anyway? In those carefree days, we relied on our "feel good" radar to get closer to him. But that was like relying on a rectal thermometer to determine the direction of the wind. Luckily for us, our Holiji had been singled out by a wise old man who looked scary enough to be taken seriously, the holy Sant Baba Ram Singh. A man who definitely knew more about God than all of us disciples put together.

By October, Jude still didn't know about Alex and me. He had been back for more than three months already, but the right moment hadn't come yet. Alex wanted to talk with him alone, man to man, and explain to his friend how we had fallen in love. Around Jude, Alex and I acted like the buddies we'd been before Jude left for Asia, and our friends played along.

Then, one afternoon when Alex was alone at the apartment, Jude dropped in to smoke a joint. Alex figured it was an appropriate moment to tell him the truth, and he did so as concisely as possible. Jude smiled as if he knew already. "I sensed something going wrong—uh—I mean, going on."

Forked tongue. And bullshit if you asked me. He didn't want to look surprised, that was all. He told Alex it was quite all right but, he added, he had always assumed that his closest friends would never dare to jump his exes. No matter what the circumstances.

"It just happened, man." Alex told me he felt ashamed. Jude was like a brother to him. What if he had fatally severed the trust between them?

Jude apparently didn't want him to think so because he said, "Hey, don't misunderstand me here. It's no problem." He put his hand on Alex's shoulder. "Really man, I mean it. In fact, I *forgive* you."

Alex was dumbfounded but grateful.

When he related the episode to me that evening, I was livid. "Forgive? Forgive what? Before leaving for India, Jude slept with at least a dozen girls, and only God knows how many pilgrims he fucked along the dirt roads of India. For Holiji's sake, Alex! Wake up and smell the Valium he's pushing down your throat. You've done nothing that needs Jude's forgiveness."

I was furious. I took a deep yogi breath, concentrating on my master. *Peace and compassion, Geneviève. Jude is upset, and he's trying to protect himself.* Another deep inhalation. *God loves Jude even when I'm angry at him. This anger will soon pass like the clouds above.* Wise girl. I congratulated myself. I was in control, relaxed. *Shanti.* It was so easy to be good. Holiji was already shaping a new and better me.

Jude got busy organizing a North and South American tour for Holiji. He came to the apartment several times to discuss our upcoming meeting with the human being we were calling Master. The news had every one of us (except Hugo) supremely excited. We would get to judge the man for ourselves. Did we realize the incredible opportunity facing us, Jude wondered, the journey about to begin? He said we should invite our friends and the friends of our friends, our families, our neighbours, and anybody with enough marbles to appreciate the good piece of luck God was throwing their way.

To show his commitment to Holiji, Jude did something odd and risky, another weird-shaped stone on the wall of his numerous commitments to his guru. He told his business partners that during Holiji's visit, they had to receive initiation before he'd agree to close new deals with them. An initiated person would certainly never consider screwing a brother or a sister. Surprisingly, most of them went for it. Some even became devoted to Holiji. This was just another way for Jude to bring a little more of the Lord's mercy on himself and his business.

We spent hours discussing Initiation Day. In Holiji's hands, everything in our lives would be changed forever. Not only would we be safer here on earth, but everything would also be taken care of in the hereafter. Holiji promised to be there. Here, there, and all over the place, just like the Beatles' song. Always by our side with an easy-to-follow afterlife itinerary. They'd be no need for St. Peter.

We were also informed of another miracle. Once initiated, we would never have to reincarnate again. Initiated disciples were instructed to do their best to resume their ongoing existence in the most noble possible way, but Jude reminded us, "When you die, your karma won't matter anymore. After initiation, you will own an express passage to Nirvana and a seat next to the greatest masters. It's all taken care of. You will live in heaven forever and ever."

We didn't know what to make of that. Milou for one was skeptical.

"I don't know, man," he asked Jude one Sunday. "What if I'm destined to be another Hugh Hefner in my next incarnation? Or another Mozart? Or Mother Theresa?"

Jane Fonda came into my mind. Beauty, fame, fortune, values. What if I could be like her and live her life?

Jude said we were missing the point. "You really think these people are happier than you are? Forget about them, man! Your life is also meaningful in its own, you know, small way. I want you to think about the implications of reincarnating as a cockroach, a Bee Gees brother, or a political refugee!

Of course, if you don't *really* believe in reincarnation you're fucked right there. No big incentive to prevent something you don't even believe in."

Of course, we believed in reincarnation. What was so strange about reincarnation anyway? It was too much of a romantic concept to be brushed off. It was *so* mystic to us, *so* spooky. Being exempted from life's endless spiral also meant we would never have to go through the hardships of youthful angst again. That alone was a bargain. With Holiji's help, the repetitive process of decay would stop for good. Sant Baba Ram Singh talked about it too in his book. No more hardships. He promised.

As a Caucasian kid from Montreal born in the 1950s, my idea of life's hardships had little to do with surviving typhoons or making my way through the desert without the assistance of a loyal camel. I couldn't conceive such a level of despair, and consequently, I couldn't compare my lot to it. There are degrees of distress one can't make sense of, whenever they are far too great or far too small.

I rubbed Holiji's promise on the microscopic tissue of my pains. No more reincarnations also meant that once this life was done with, there would be no more tortured nights lying awake and wondering what the hell I was supposed to do with my life. No more contradictions or unanswered questions. No more zits. A permanent high, knowing my happiness was secured no matter how badly I fucked up here on earth. We were so lucky, really. I felt like a bum who finds a pile of one-hundred-dollar bills in a garbage bag. In heaven with Holiji, I'd be where I wanted to be forever, never, ever feeling bored or restless. Never, ever missing anything or anybody and rejoicing in the endless celebration thrown in honour of us, the Chosen Ones. All I needed was that darn backstage pass. That secret mantra. The *simran*.

Hugo was unconvinced, to say the least.

"Why don't you give it a shot, Hugo? What do you have

to lose?" Jude asked.

"Meat, sex, and time."

"Man, that's stupid. C'mon, we're talking important stuff here. Look at it as an investment in the quality of your afterlife."

Hugo yawned. "I don't believe in insurance."

"Okay then, what about spiritual growth? Shouldn't you be a little concerned about that?"

Hugo walked away.

"Give me two good reasons why you always avoid this conversation, man?" Jude pleaded following him.

"Steak and fuck."

You'd think Jude was getting some remuneration for every new head he was dragging toward Holiji, when in fact he was the one paying for each new devotee not contributing to the holy fund. But Hugo was immovable, like the stubborn Iroquois populating his family tree. Every day, we bombarded him with our personal version of what was wrong with him. We trapped him in endless arguments. We tried many times to persuade him to join us at the next *satsang*. If only once.

"I'd rather eat squirrel shit."

Hugo ate meat and laughed at us, but he still managed to remain Jude's most trusted business partner. That was because Jude thought he understood the man—after all, Hugo was a childhood friend. Jude absolved his arrogance because he figured the problem was that Hugo wasn't ready just yet. A late bloomer.

Had we been the Beatles, Hugo would have been referred to as "the skeptical one." In his eyes, good things were always less promising than what they appeared to be. Over the next months, Jude did everything he could to change his friend's disposition toward Holiji, but Hugo didn't flinch once. He smiled vacantly and passed the joint.

Chapter 32

*Listening to The Who singing about the hardship
of looking at life through blue eyes*

NOVEMBER 1975. WHEN WE weren't on Hugo's case, we spent hours telling one another how Holiji's teachings had changed our lives for the better. We made sure Hugo was close enough to hear every detail. He became terribly bored with us and started going out on weekend nights, spending a lot of his time at Le Petit Salon whereas the rest of us hardly visited the place anymore. Some nights he came home with new friends. Sometimes girls. Sometimes only one girl.

We had all but given up on Grace. She rarely returned our calls, and when she did she always came up with a hundred excuses to stay away. She had recently moved into a tiny studio on Plateau Mont-Royal and found a new job working in an office downtown. For months, we had pictured her lost in a sea of grief and sorrow.

Then, one day, she came for a visit. She had called in advance to make sure Hugo wouldn't be around. We were thrilled to see her again. We assumed this would be the perfect opportunity to introduce her to Holiji. To our surprise, she wasn't keen on the idea.

"Are you morons all out of your minds? Seriously? A fuckin' *guru*? Are you crazy? You're fucking with me, right?"

Alex handed her Holiji's book. She glanced at it for a second and dropped it on the beanbag chair next to her. "Man, what's going on? Are you all mentally deranged? What the hell is wrong with you guys?"

Frankie wanted to explain. I did too. "Grace, if you'd only—" I began.

"You *are* fucking serious! I come back after months, and this is what you morons have to tell me? You have a guru? You spend your evenings *meditating*? What else should I be aware of? Who got a sex change? Who joined the army? Man! Fuck! I can't take this shit."

And out the door she went. We looked at each other, disappointed.

Camille was always overjoyed at the sight of Alex and me holding hands, but she too snarled at Holiji. "A guru? You are so passé! No meat? Are you crazy or something? You'll both catch your death of scurvy, for Christ's sake! What's wrong with you two? Forget about your stupid guru. I've been cooking all day and I don't want to lose my appetite for it."

The word *stupid* coupled with *guru* sounded blasphemous to our soon-to-be-initiated ears, like swearing in a cathedral. I was fidgeting on my chair. Alex didn't like it either. Hesitantly, he asked Camille if she could be a little more respectful.

She sighed. "What the hell are you trying to prove anyway?"

We didn't know precisely. Something to do with peace on earth and a smooth transition into the other world.

Camille wasn't buying it. "My father will be long gone by the time I croak. He'll take care of me when I get there."

"What if you die before him? Or what if he doesn't show up?" I tried.

"Easy. I'll grab the first person I recognize. Might be you, you never know." She was so agitated that she was about to have a coughing spell. "A sect! You guys are in a sect—*tabarnac!* This is so dangerous. This Holiji could be nothing more than just another insane asshole, like Charles Manson, and you're throwing your lives at him?"

Alex and I looked at each other, speechless.

After dinner, Claude asked a few polite questions about our holy man. I guess we explained everything wrong because after a few minutes, he said he had enough, adding that he'd get back to us if he ever felt the need to hear more. He looked satisfied the way people do when you confirm to them something they've suspected all along. In short, he wasn't impressed. Like Christians or Jews before us, we resigned ourselves to practicing our faith in secret to avoid the wrath it was creating.

Camille didn't want to talk about it anymore. She went to the bathroom and came back with a plastic bottle. She said it was a new miracle product, a spray that erased red wine stains on delicate fabrics. The conversation shifted from Holiji to stain remover—same thing, if you think about it.

Every day, Alex and I secluded ourselves and meditated hour after hour in preparation for our imminent Initiation Day. We read Holiji's book to each other. We filled up our spiritual journal with a minute account of our daily actions, missives we were invited to copy out and mail to the ashram once a month. Hanging out with our friends was no longer considered a priority. I cherished these quiet evenings at home with Alex.

During this time, Hugo was cruising downtown in his newly acquired second-hand blue Rambler. His automobile and his sex life were his only gurus. When he wasn't talking about one, he was bragging about the other. Alex and I listened to Hugo surf his waterbed with girls he didn't care to introduce us to.

A month later, Grace came back again, and she stayed put even when Hugo was around. He didn't seem surprised in the least.

"She can't live without us, no matter how fucked up you guys are."

Chapter 33

Listening to James Taylor singing about an inebriated
captain who's nostalgic for an island

GRACE DIDN'T KNOW WHAT she hated the most, the sight of Hugo with a new girl every week or the sound of Jude's robotic sermon about a turbaned clown from India.

"Fuck! Damn! Fuck!" she repeated.

By January 1976, there was no more late-night partying at Le Petit Salon—although we still went there occasionally—and no more evenings doing nothing but being silly. No more pepperoni on pizzas and no more *Bugs Bunny/Road Runner Hour* on Sunday mornings with the fattest joint of the week.

"Fuck! Fuck! Fuck! Fun has been officially replaced by Master—Master mas-fucking-ter Holiji."

She whined to Hugo. She told him she wished she were dead, but not before killing every single one of us for the crime of being such bores. Grace wasn't the guru type. She was the guy type—make that the Hugo type. Worshipping Hugo was her thing. Getting closer to God was not a concept she entertained. To her, religion was a purifying bath in which you had to dip a week or so before you were scheduled to drop dead. A matter of being sufficiently fervent at the right moment. As far as Grace was concerned, *now* was not the right moment. There was plenty of time to get ready to die. Decades. Whenever Grace heard about a funeral, she expected the words "very old" to be part of the story.

Hugo could have been her ally on that. They could have laughed together at us. But, of course, this was out of the question. Hugo was far from Grace's reach, even farther away than he was from ours. She missed the old days. Hugo welcoming her with a wet kiss, Steely Dan blaring from the speakers, everybody delighted to see her. She wished Jude would leave again, this time for "goddamn Timbuktu," a city Grace didn't believe really existed.

"Let him die in the desert. That's all he deserves, the bastard. He's turned you all into fuckin' vegetables."

Poor Grace. Week after week, she found us in the kitchen talking about redemption and contrition. Hugo made matters even worse by displaying his sexual trophies. She had to listen to our nonsense while he was kissing Louise, Nicole, or some "fuck-breath Michelle."

She decided she couldn't take it anymore. One Friday evening, she hopped on the metro heading downtown, and returned with her own fuck buddy. After that, every weekend she came back from her excursion with a different date. Things were almost back to normal.

Grace and Hugo never hung on to their dates for more than a few days. Every Friday night, each was accompanied by a lover who looked out of place. It was plain to see that their fuck buddies were more in a hurry to have sex than to socialize. The introductions were typically brief, and we saw no point in memorizing names.

It soon became clear that Hugo and Grace were no longer meeting at the apartment by accident. They calculated their entrances meticulously, flanked by their respective catch of the day. If Grace showed up too late to run into Hugo, the next day they'd both lie to each other about their fish. They seemed to thrive on trying to outdo each other. Grace wanted Hugo to hurt, and Hugo did everything he could to show he didn't care. She never believed he didn't. She couldn't accept it. God knows why, because it was clear to us that he really didn't give a damn.

Hugo's determination to remain aloof made Grace act like a madwoman at times. One evening, a group of musicians we were friends with were playing at Le Petit Salon, and we all agreed to meet there for the event. It took place on a Friday, Catch Day. Unfortunately for her, Grace was fishless that night. She figured there was nothing left for her to do but get drunk.

Two sets and four rum and cokes later, Grace stood up from her seat at the bar. With the clear intention of insulting Hugo's date, who happened to be sitting a few feet from her, she stumbled in the girl's direction. The word *offended* came to her lips. She didn't feel insulted or shocked, but excruciatingly offended. She waited for Hugo to go to the john. As she approached her prey, Grace showed the kind of condescension nobles from the seventeenth century displayed toward serfs in the novels she sometimes borrowed from her mother. She grabbed the empty chair in front of the girl, made a deplorable attempt to throw her leg over it, missed, and landed on her butt, a situation that aggravated the shit out of her.

Hugo's fish laughed nervously and leaned over to investigate. "Are you okay?"

Grace took one long look at her. "Fuck off, bitch."

In her advanced state of inebriety, Grace realized that her legs were somewhere else in the room and not below her waist, where any sober person would assume they should be. She stayed on the floor for a moment, catching her breath. Hugo's date was wide-eyed with an unmistakable I'm-pretty-sure-I-heard-you-right-so-you-better-say-you're-sorry expression. Grace's eyes travelled from the girl's shoes to her face.

"You stink. That shitty perfume of yours, it makes me sick. What is it called? Eau de Fuck Face? Vomit de Guerlain? Couldn't you wash yourself instead of smearing that shit on you?"

The blond fish blinked several times, which made Grace chuckle. The girl finally said, "Yeah, well—uh—fuck you too, okay?"

Grace didn't fire back. She stood and walked to the bar, pushing chairs aside like so many unwanted dance partners. Hugo came back from the restroom, looking at his watch. The fish told him about Grace, and Hugo glanced at the bar. He laughed. He didn't retaliate. He enjoyed the game. He waited for Grace to look his way, then he kissed the girl, his mouth wide open, his hands all over her butt. Grace scanned the people around the bar. Our eyes met, and she motioned for me to join her.

She was busy peeling the label from her bottle of beer. She considered working on mine but I told her she couldn't have it before I was done with it. She gathered the shredded pieces on the sticky counter and flattened them one by one in a futile attempt to put the label back together. She peered furtively in Hugo's direction. "He can screw that cunt as many times as he wants. See if I care."

"You should be careful, Grace. You're bound to hurt yourself one of these days."

She laughed. "Man, did I ever tell her off!"

Grace and Hugo kept the Friday fish market going on strong. But our two fishermen became progressively bored out of their wits with their dates, so they smoked joint after joint with us in the kitchen, ignoring their companions. Meanwhile their catch grew restless, gazing out the living room window, their scales fading in shades of blue like those of tuna caught in a net.

As most war stories end, one party defeated the other. It was Hugo the Conqueror who won the battle. Our boy fell or rather stumbled in love. Nothing major but enough to send him into googoo-gaga land for a while. His biggest fish in months. He treated her the way you might treat a lost kitten when you want it to come back for a little milk every day. This girl was bathing in Hugo's excessive attention. She was a goldfish, the kind who's there strictly for a good time, an inclination that made her a perfect match for him. He wanted her to stick around a little, but not forever.

She too reminded me of Marie. Of course, Grace despised her. We expected her to. We wanted her to. When Hugo was out of the room, we cheered her up by referring to the girl as "the ugly toad" or some insult along that line. We should have applied Holiji's teachings, of course, by remaining neutral and nice to everyone involved. But Grace needed us on her side and bitching about Hugo's new girlfriend seemed to be the most compassionate thing to do. Actually, the girl happened to be rather nice, and we told Hugo she was really cool. I guess we were only trying to make Hugo and Grace happy with us.

Grace came back day after day, demonstrating the same masochism she was known to exhibit whenever her world went from bad to rotten. She analyzed Hugo and his Ugly Bitch's every move as if they were laboratory subjects under observation. She sat on a kitchen chair, a little too quiet, pretending to feel something other than what was really there but fooling nobody. She joked with a sad smile and played Risk with Frankie.

However, when she heard Hugo talking about his plan to take the Worm for a week's vacation in the Bahamas, Grace was so appalled that she saw no alternative but to seek revenge at once. If she intended to survive this one, she had to reply with force. Hugo was asking for it.

She disappeared for two weeks. True to Hugo's recurring prediction, she came back, this time with a glittering new fish carrying her shopping bags. He was a nice fish. He asked Grace to beam her perfect smile, and when she did he smacked his mouth on hers. Cute. Grace was proud to tell us her date could do all kinds of magic tricks with a ball. Alex and I named him Flipper.

Flipper and the goldfish became regular Friday evening fixtures. Hugo saw straight through Grace's scheme, and to push her aggravation a little deeper, he invited the two lovebirds to join him and his girl in the Bahamas. Grace's fish wiggled with exuberant joy like any porpoise glimpsing the possibility of going back to the sea. Of course, the plan never came to fruition. The goldfish was out of the picture soon afterward, and Flipper followed a week later. They were both released into the wild. Too small for keeps.

Hugo and Grace were about to resume their weekly fishing competition when the big news was dropped on us. It was now official—Holiji was scheduled to arrive in Montreal on the first day of August. That left us with a little less than eight months to get ready.

Chapter 34

Listening to Bob Marley confessing he killed a policeman
in self-defence

As far as Grace was concerned, Holiji's arrival meant the beginning of the end. Depressed, she barely managed to go through the motions of her life, avoiding obstacles like a clumsy funambulist. She fell time and time again, licking her wounds only once she was out of our sight. Day after day, Grace's spirit plummeted a little more. We could only stand by, watching helplessly.

Then one morning she was awakened by a cool breeze blowing on her upper body. She said later she was surprised to find the window shut and the covers tucked tightly around her. She got out of bed and went to work.

By nine o'clock sharp her hands were resting on her typewriter. Like professional ballet dancers, her fingers obediently adopted their correct position over the *A, S, D,* and *F* on left side and the *J, K, L,* and *;* on the right, patiently awaiting instructions. An anonymous hand tossed a letter in front of her, and she began to type in a regular cadence. The mechanical symphony of the machine was comforting to her. *Tap, tap, tap, tap, tap.* Smart, irreproachable letters appearing in rigorously straight lines, the luxurious built-in facility correcting smudges and errors, the firm pull to disengage the paper. Movements she had repeated more often than any other in her life. But her mind was somewhere else that morning.

"What was I thinking about again?" she said to herself. She drew a complete blank. "I can't remember typing a single word, yet it's all there."

She shrugged and looked at the clock. It was already twenty past nine. Twenty minutes she couldn't account for. And she hadn't smoked a single joint yet.

"What was I thinking about again?"

The answer slipped away, like a word on the tip of her tongue, like an impression or the faint silhouette of an emotion. "What's wrong with me?"

"Fuckin' gas," she answered herself. "Must be my mother's damn pea soup."

But her mother's soup usually agreed with her. If not the pea soup, then what? If she'd had to show a doctor where she felt cold air blowing through, Grace would have pointed to her chest. With every breath, the rush of oxygen stung her lungs like icy water on her sensitive teeth. Or an extra-strong cough drop melting in the back of her throat. She went on typing, her mind drifting again in a dreamlike trance. She looked at the clock again, it was ten thirty. Coffee break.

The warm liquid tickled her tongue. Finishing it, she threw the Styrofoam cup in the bin and walked to the bathroom. There she washed her hands and observed her face carefully in the mirror. Her reflection seemed to be aware of something she was just about to realize herself. A simple sentence.

"I don't love Hugo anymore."

Hugo had left the building. He had escaped. No—even better, he had been thrown out, no longer confined in her heart, where he had spent far too much time and energy destroying everything around him, like an elephant in a glass house. She stared at her chest, then her gut. Gone, gone, gone. The area between her legs. Nothing there either. Gone. *Where is he?* Not on her mind, that was for sure. *False alert?* She scanned her heart and head again. Nothing. It seemed Hugo had mysteriously been exorcized from her.

Love is weird. You think you'll never get over a broken heart, and then *wham!* It happens out of nowhere. Like a cancer patient who has been told his brain tumour has miraculously dissolved, Grace felt deeply happy for the first time in many moons. It seemed as though her future was full of promises. For no better reasons than the ones she already had, she was done with Hugo. He had vacated the premises of her heart like a weasel running for his life, and this landlady was delighted—but shocked to witness the mess he had left behind.

Now that Hugo had been relegated to the attic of her mind, she had to clean up her heart for future rentals. "Out, out, out you go. You go, Hugo. Hugo, you go." She said it in a rhyming, singsong voice.

She laughed aloud. She was not passing gas after all. She was having a brand-new day.

Later on when Grace told me about this epiphanic day of hers, she said that on that night, she fell asleep yearning for love with a capital *L*. The next day, her thoughts were clear. She had to reorganize her priorities and refine her aim, and she knew she would need some practice before being able to claim victory. To achieve this, Grace rowed her fishing boat back to the shore, determined to hunt herself some real mammal.

Hugo and Grace's dates had provided Jude, the incorrigible proselytizer, with the virgin audience he was preying on, and this disciple of Holiji's kept every fish he caught, no matter how small. His sermons moved few of them, but every once in a while he succeeded in reeling in a fresh devotee from these unlikely waters. Whenever the individual displayed the slightest interest in spirituality, he or she was in for a complete tour of the New Age literature. The Tibetan *and* the Egyptian *Book of the Dead*, Madame Blavatsky, the birth of Buddha, the death of Jesus in Kashmir, the Bhagavad Gita, the Dalai Lama, and unavoidably, Holiji.

Grace had heard "Jude's bullshit" a hundred times already. However, I could tell she was now listening more closely but didn't want anybody to notice. She questioned Jude casually about God and death as if she was asking for directions around town. "Serious" boyfriends came and went, and I felt she was using them as a shield between Jude and her growing interest in Holiji. The Indian man was sounding more and more like a reliable tenant to her.

One rainy Sunday morning, she rang the bell at Sean's place. She came in dripping and weeping. She said she had become obsessed with the image of Holiji offering her his hand like those angels on church ceilings. She felt she needed his guidance too. We were delighted.

The way I saw it, Hugo had brought Grace to Holiji, as if this accidental offering could make up for his lack of interest in the guru's teachings. Grace became the most zealous of us all. And Hugo was finally a free man.

Life glided smoothly between work, Holiji, Alex, Holiji, friends, and Holiji again. Grace practiced yoga twice a week with us. Alex and I read the *Mahabharata*. Frankie, Milou, and Tintin came over every Wednesday night for meditation followed by a few joints. Jude introduced us to classical music, and we listened to Mozart, Mahler, and Beethoven before going to sleep.

It was during this period of quiet bliss that Fiona walked into our lives.

Chapter 35

*Listening to Emerson, Lake & Palmer singing about
a really fortunate guy who owns white horses*

SHE CAME FROM VANCOUVER with a bunch of destitute
artists in need of money. Her name, Fiona, sounded like
a snake slithering on snow. She spoke little French herself,
but her entourage was almost exclusively formed of French
Québécois who had chosen to move to Vancouver on Canada's
West Coast in the mid-1960s. Though she couldn't have been
aware of it at the time, in her bags, stashed amid her clothes,
her cosmetics, and a cast-iron pan ("invaluable for cooking and
self-protection," she explained), Fiona was carrying work for
Milou, love for Jude, money for Hugo, and a business for me.

Her wealthy grandfather was from England, and she
claimed to be some kind of baroness. She sure acted like
royalty. Fiona was twenty-four years old, tall, strikingly pretty,
with red hair and skin spotted with freckles. Even her green
eyes were stained with orange dots. She had a thin mouth,
a little pinched, which gave her an air of assertiveness, the
self-assurance some people parade when they know they are
incredibly smart *and* beautiful at the same time. Feathers
that seemed to have been plucked from an unlikely leopard

hung from her bracelets, softening the continuous tingling of her silver jewellery. She was a natural redhead. We all knew that for a fact because we saw her stark naked the night we went to Le Chaton Rose to see Milou's new show.

Milou never spoke much about his job (mainly because we never asked), but one day he tickled our imaginations when he got stoned enough to talk about his latest production. He said the new girls sharing the stage with him were *real* professionals. "I'm sick of clumsy debutantes, man."

He seemed so proud of himself. Of course, Tintin shared his enthusiasm. From what I understood, Tintin was now Milou's sound man, light man, dresser, chauffeur, nurse, shrink, and any other servant indispensable to a true star.

Milou said he owed his new solo show to a really nice girl, Fiona, a fellow stripper. She had managed to persuade the owner of Le Chaton Rose to allow Milou a chance to perform a twenty-minute "sextravaganza," a work of art that would clearly demonstrate our friend's talents.

His show was based on an obscure concept we never managed to grasp. Something about the link between *men's* sexual liberation, animal rights, Graceland, and the world's general lack of respect for nature. As we listened to him, foreheads frowned. Eyes narrowed. To illustrate what we non-strippers didn't get, Milou unrolled the poster promoting his show. He watched our faces with anticipation, his eyes wide. The image revealed itself in full length. The others' expressions, and I'm sure mine too, changed to what was later referred to by Milou as "facial diarrhea." Jaws dropped, eyebrows reached for hairlines. Eyes widened.

On glossy pale blue paper was a black and white picture of him with a crown on his head. A limp fake-fur cape hung from his naked shoulders, and a tiny G-string with the word King printed in purple concealed his manhood. A faceless naked black girl lay at his feet like a slave, her curly platinum wig covering Milou's feet like a thousand albino eels.

Milou held a shovel close to the girl's butt as if he meant to pick her up and, one had to conclude, throw her away. Like snow. Or dirt. Milou le Roi du Strip was written in psychedelic letters at the bottom of the poster.

None of us was surprised or horrified. After all, this was Milou, and we all knew his imagination rarely reflected the nature of his inner self. He loved women—even more, he respected them. He was merely attempting to capture his audience's attention by resorting to one of the oldest tricks in the trade: shock 'em and they'll listen.

Nobody had the heart to say anything, good or bad. Not even Hugo, who never missed an opportunity to ridicule Milou. Disappointed, Le Roi du Strip pursed his lips. He put the poster back in his bag and looked at his watch as if he had an appointment. The doorbell rang, Boogie barked, and Camille walked in with Claude. Zoé-the-cat had been diagnosed with cancer. Camille was devastated. Priorities shifted. No one raised the topic of the poster again that night, least of all Milou. I felt bad for him. What the hell, why not go to the club and see it with our very own eyes, just this one time? Would it kill us to encourage him a little? Wouldn't it please Holiji to know we were spreading joy in our own small way?

Had I not insisted a few days later on paying a visit to Le Chaton Rose to see Milou's show, had I not dared to conceive of an inconceivable notion—"Let's go out for a drink and watch our friend wiggle his willy" (something I was myself a little apprehensive about)—had I not been so irrational, we might have never met Fiona, and the destinies of most of us sitting around that kitchen table that night would have turned out quite differently, for better or for worse.

Grace refused to join us, raising the argument that Holiji would definitely not approve. Camille and Claude were married, and as a newlywed couple you don't do that kind of thing. Jude was busy as usual but, like the rest of us, he was curious. He tagged along.

Chapter 36

Listening to Bob Dylan pounding on the gates of paradise

LE CHATON ROSE WAS on St. Lawrence Street, Montreal's main street. La rue St. Laurent, as we say. *La main.* An unusually polite doorman asked us if we were over eighteen years old. Yeah, sure, we told him. He didn't ask to see IDs.

Milou was on stage, talking to Tintin. They had their clothes on. *Good.*

Indeed, everybody in the club had clothes on except for the waitresses, who were topless. I had never been in a strip club before. These girls walked around, balancing their tits carefully over large pitchers of beer.

Tintin saw us first, and he opened his arms, cracking a wide smile. Milou screamed in delight as if the Rolling Stones had just walked in to see *his* show. He gave each of us a sweaty hug and asked a busboy to set a table close to the stage.

Besides sweating, Milou was also alarmingly out of breath. "Sorry guys, but I have to get backstage now. I'm on right after the first part. I'm the main star tonight!" He beamed and left us, waving. "I'll see you after the show."

We ordered beer from a bare-breasted waitress and silently waited, chain-smoking cigarettes and glancing around nonchalantly as if we were used to this type of setting. I doubt we fooled the regulars. Finally, the lights dimmed. We heard the sweet voice of Marvin Gay.

And there she was. Fiona the Fabulous, read the banner behind her. We expected a worn-out creature with sad, empty eyes. But no. She was absolutely stunning. She took her clothes off painfully slowly, her body undulating to the rhythm of the music. The feathers on her bracelets caught threads of lights here and there. More skin was exposed, and before long her last garment fell to the stage floor.

I gazed around the room. The audience—mostly males— was hypnotized. I looked at our table. Hugo was smiling vacantly, like an idiot who can't find his village. Frankie was pensive, as if he'd just had the theory of relativity explained to him. Alex was glancing nervously at his glass of beer. I could tell he was not comfortable.

"Grace was probably right," he whispered. "Holiji would not approve."

Jude was almost levitating. His eyes looked as they did on Sunday mornings after meditation. Fiona-the-Fabulous bowed gracefully. The clientele gave her a standing ovation. Drops of sweat rolled down her pinkish body and made their way to her manicured feet. The customers clapped and whistled.

Jude's reaction was most startling of all. He stood on his chair, shouting and clapping like a trained seal. "*Bravo! Bravo!*"

Fiona-the-Fabulous made a *pas de deux* toward our table and blew a kiss in his direction. Jude lost his balance and fell off his chair. She laughed and waved again.

Jude was in love. As usual, he had the right connections to get what he wanted. But he would have to be patient. Milou's show was about to start, and Jude needed Milou to get to Fiona-the-Fabulous. You could tell he welcomed the distraction. He was much too flustered to meet her face to face right away.

When Milou erupted on stage with his cape and his crown, we forgot all about Fiona—except for Jude. An Elvis song rang in the air. Milou slid on the floor, moving his hips sideways, his cape flying around his torso. He mouthed the song while taking his clothes off—or rather, two girls, who were also busy undressing each other, helped him strip off his crown and cape. Then the girls put a collar and a leash on him. We heard the first bars of Elvis singing about a hunting dog. Milou jumped on all fours. The girls walked him around the stage, smacking his bare butt with their open palms while he attempted to bite their asses. He lifted his leg and with the help of a prop hidden in his armpit spurted water on the girls as if he was peeing on them. You get the idea. That was just the beginning. We got more Elvis songs. Then Hawaiian shirts, leather pants, a white jumpsuit with a humongous collar, a kimono—you name it, he threw it all at the crowd, one song after the other. While he was busy changing outfits backstage, his two "lovely assistants" danced and played together to the sounds of the Beach Boys. The clientele was laughing and seemed to enjoy the show.

We knew Milou was not the creep he appeared to be on stage. The spectators probably thought of him as a monkey with no brain, none of them suspecting how decent this naked guy was. Milou was a good soul, he had a huge heart. The nicest people come in all clothes (or in this case in no clothes at all). In the same way, Fiona-the-Fabulous would turn out to be anything but weak, out of control, uneducated, or on hard drugs. Not even close.

At the end of his act, Milou also received a standing ovation. Truck drivers, bikers, car salesmen, middle-aged women—they all loved Elvis or were drunk enough to love him that night. Jude disappeared the moment Milou's show was over.

♣

What happened next wasn't clarified until much later on. Milou related what happened backstage after Jude left us. Later that week, Jude, who was eager to brag about his date with Fiona, told us bits and pieces of their first evening together. However, Jude being a guy, the order of events was rather blurry, and not really accurate according to what Fiona told me later during a trip we took together to New York. Like any girl bitten by love, she remembered every detail about this evening. She even recalled what cologne Jude was wearing that night—Eau Sauvage by Christian Dior. As far as I'm concerned, I always prefer hearing stories from a woman's mouth. Guys can be so sloppy when it comes to details.

The bouncer at the stage door allowed just enough space for Jude to squeeze in. After taking a moment to comb his hair with his fingers, Jude approached Milou to congratulate him. Like a fox in a henhouse with only one chicken in mind, Jude tried to catch a glimpse of Fiona-the-So-Incredibly-Fabulous. He had little time or patience to wait while Milou carried on with an analysis of his performance. He cut Milou short and demanded to be introduced at once to the "first-part girl."

Milou opened his eyes wide. "Fiona? Really?"

"Keep your voice down," Jude hissed, drawing a laugh from Milou. "Shut the fuck up!"

In the male world, three or four words are often equivalent to a hundred between women. Milou winked at Jude and led him down a narrow spiral staircase buzzing with naked girls climbing up and down. These girls didn't look half as good as they did from afar on stage. Jude slowed his pace for a second. Shit. A bit of a downer for him. What if Fiona-the-Fabulous was not so fabulous after all? He looked down the stairs and hurried, almost running. He had to put an end—or a beginning—to this, and fast, or his head would explode.

He landed on a cement floor covered with sawdust, Milou on his heels. Milou greeted and kissed everyone as they

slalomed through beer crates, which drove Jude crazy. Our
boy was in a hurry. They ended up in a dead-end corridor
pierced with three doors covered with graffiti. A naked yellow
bulb danced two inches above their heads. The air smelled of
hot wax and stale beer. Behind one door, they could hear
girlish giggles muffled by the sound of a blender crushing
something. Ice, by the sound of it. Milou knocked briefly on
the first door on the left.

"Come in!"

And there she was, dressed in white, sitting on a loveseat
covered with a white sheet. A flickering neon lamp on a
vanity and a dozen perfumed candles lit the room. But Jude
could tell that, despite the poor light—hallelujah!—Fiona
was indeed even more fabulous up close. It was time to get
down to business.

She wasn't alone. Facing her in a metallic chair, a garden
chair really, was a slim black girl who had obviously suffered
the cruel misfortune of coming into this world as a boy. (In
those days, we inappropriately said words like "transvestite"
or "transsexual" for lack of a better term such as "transgen-
der person", which came up much later. Using one of the
two meant you didn't judge. I don't have to list here what
words were otherwise used. Luckily most people know better
nowadays).

Fiona-the-Fabulous and the girl were laughing and kissing
each other's hands. The red-haired beauty was a little surprised
to see Jude behind Milou. One more man expressing his
excessive appreciation after seeing her on stage. An admirer
hoping to have his way with her. Fiona-the-Fabulous was
disappointed at Milou for wheeling one of those into her
dressing room. "Oh, hi Milou." She made a point of ignoring
Jude. "Remember Julia?" Milou smiled at the girl who smiled
back. The girl resumed her conversation with Fiona. Jude
looked around nervously.

Thank God for the dim light. Jude was counting on it so

the redheaded goddess wouldn't notice how much younger he was—there must have been five years' difference in their ages. Boys probably didn't have the balls to venture backstage, so he hoped his audacity would make him seem more mature.

Fiona abruptly ended her conversation, interrupting Julia in mid-sentence. The slender girl seemed to understand she was expected to shut up. She stopped talking, crystallizing in her chair, hanging on her thoughts, her mouth still full of gossip.

Jude's eyes met Fiona's and, yeah, for a minute time did stop, just like it does in movies. Milou stood in front of the mirror, wiping lipstick marks from his thighs. Fiona turned toward her friend and said she'd see her again the next day. The girl straightened up her long frame, leaning on the armrests of the small chair. The metal bent slightly, releasing exasperated squeaks. She was taller than Jude, muscular and skinny as a famished cat. All legs really. She kissed Fiona fondly on the forehead, nodded at Milou, ignored Jude, and left the room.

Milou made the introductions, telling Fiona Jude was his best friend, a fact that startled both Fiona and Jude. She had never heard about Jude before and had always assumed Tintin was his closest pal. As for Jude, he had never suspected his friend held him in such high esteem.

Fiona was happy to see that the fellow came with some kind of reference. She invited Jude to make himself comfortable on the chair abandoned by her previous guest. She sat higher up on the loveseat, making him feel as if he'd been granted an audience with her. The chair cracked plaintively every time Jude made the slightest move. He wondered how Fiona's friend had managed to keep it silent. He couldn't even breathe without provoking squeaky laments. Fiona offered them slices of papaya sprinkled with fresh lime and a glass of Perrier water with a splash of lemon. She told Milou she was delighted to give only one performance a night for the rest of the month.

"It's a great arrangement," she said, smiling. "I need the time off to attend to my other obligations, and it gives you a chance to demonstrate what you can do to entertain an audience."

Milou figured it was time to leave. He felt he wasn't needed anymore to fill up the occasional awkward silence between the two love birds. He was pleased to help Jude get closer to his stripper friend. Milou really liked Fiona and looked up to her. She was friendly, smart and insanely pretty if you liked the red-haired type. Milou excused himself and joined us back in the club.

"Jude and Fiona," he said as he rubbed his index fingers together. "I think he's crazy about her." He said he had never seen Jude looking so smitten by a woman. I asked him what kind of girl Fiona was.

On his first day at Le Chaton Rose, Fiona was the one who'd explained to Milou everything he needed to know about the owner and the other girls. She was a born leader, he told us. He was pretty sure she wasn't the type who'd mind having a busy dope dealer as a boyfriend. On countless occasions, he had heard her complain that she had too much to do and not enough time to do it all. She took dance and literature classes. She also owned some kind of business back on the West Coast. A girl in command of her own life. One who was not waiting for others to shape her future.

Whenever Fiona discussed the strippers' schedules with them—who should go on stage first, who should be last, who should have a week night off, and so on—she reminded Milou of a devoted teacher dealing with rowdy teens. Her tone was always kind, reassuring, her arguments right to the point, and her concentration unaltered no matter how unruly the other strippers acted.

Fiona disposed of her time meticulously. She didn't seem to spend much time just having fun. One evening, she told

Milou she believed most people were dreaming their life away. She was fancy and educated. A high-maintenance woman surely, but the overall package would most likely be irresistible to Jude. The more he looked at them, Milou said, the more he asked himself how it was that he had never thought about it before. It was so obvious. They were perfect for each other. "Isn't Jude a wee bit too jealous to date a stripper?" I laughed. Nobody answered. Frankie was drunk, leaning on his folded arms, Hugo was considering spending five bucks on a private dance, and Alex couldn't wait to get out of there.

Milou didn't actually know much about Fabulous Fiona. He knew she had once been married to a sculptor. He had overheard her mention it to the girls. As far as he could tell, Fiona was no bimbo, and she was not the type who would welcome a one-night stand. If Jude was looking for a fuck-and-go kind of evening, he had the wrong fowl in front of him.

Back in Fiona's dressing room, Jude felt he was the luckiest man in the world. Fiona was a dream on two legs. She spoke English with an upper-class accent. When she laughed, she threw her head back, and every time she did Jude was aroused by the sight of her neck. Her laugh sounded very sexy to him. It was more like a giggle, really. Jude had never heard anything so sensual in his life. He felt the twitch of an erection and attempted to change his position on the screaming chair. Fiona glanced at his crotch as if she knew why he was fidgeting. Jude felt himself blushing for the very first time in his life. He reached for his glass on the floor in a cacophony of rusty sounds and talked with her about her performance, Vancouver, and George Benson's concert the week before at the former Playboy Club on Aylmer Street in Montreal.

At last Jude got up his nerve and asked Fiona to go out for a drink. She accepted, but not before making him promise he wouldn't try anything funny with her. She wasn't just imploring him to do so, she was demanding it. Jude swore he wouldn't, his fingers crossed behind his back.

Chapter 37

*Listening to the Beatles talking about a guy coming from
nowhere who has the world at his feet*

JUDE AND FIONA LEFT the club, and he took her to
the Witchy Moon bar in Old Montreal. Milou once
said he had seen Ron Wood and Rod Stewart having a
drink there. With Fiona by his side, Jude wouldn't have
noticed Jimmy Page if he had smashed his red double-neck
Gibson over his head. All he could see, smell, and hear was
Fiona-the-Increasingly-Fabulous.

They took a quiet booth far away from the dance floor.
Fiona noticed someone she knew on the other side of the
room and waved in that direction. She excused herself and
promised to be back in a minute. She negotiated her way
across the dance floor toward an older man and his girlfriend.
They talked for a minute, and Fiona turned and pointed in
Jude's direction. The trio smiled at him. Jude hoped the
couple wouldn't join them. Luckily, Fiona came back by
herself.

Every hair on Jude's body stood up. He was troubled. He
didn't feel in control the way he usually did. Fiona, on the
other hand, was clearly used to men being intimidated by

her beauty. She seemed to enjoy Jude's company, enough to give him the idea of kissing her. In the same situation with any other girl on earth, Jude would have tried that something "funny" he had promised not to initiate, but he didn't have the balls, after all. Not with her. He wasn't in control. He couldn't find his markers. For the first time ever, Jude felt a strong desire to be influenced by a woman. To be guided by her, to be told what to do, to let her lead. Fiona inspired something new in him. A feeling between love and fear. She simply blew his mind. She took a sip of her drink and started to talk about herself. He did not miss a word. The more she opened up, the more he was astounded.

To start with, Fiona had been a disciple of Sant Baba Ram Singh. The coincidence was truly astounding. She was mildly intrigued when Jude exclaimed in delight that he was a disciple of Holiji. Jude was amazed by this incredible twist of fate. Fiona, on the other hand, apparently accepted extreme, bizarre fortuities as part of her everyday life. She told Jude she had received initiation in Vancouver from the man himself. What were the chances? Incredible as it was, Fiona didn't seem to think it was so unusual. She said she was accustomed to seeing her master manifest himself when she least expected it. Things like this happened to her all the time. She didn't know Milou was about to receive initiation, but that didn't seem to impress her either. He had never mentioned a word about it to her or to anyone else at the club, for that matter.

"Well, a strip joint isn't exactly the kind of place where you'd feel like talking about your spiritual orientation, is it? Actually, it's the last place you'd want to talk about it. Like discussing business in a church or something," Jude ventured.

Fiona agreed. She had never told anyone about Sant Baba Ram Singh at the club either. "People who find it normal that you take your clothes off in front of them, total strangers, would be shocked to find out you actually lead a spiritual life. I'm guessing it would make me less desirable in their eyes."

Jude didn't answer, but he had never heard anything so silly in his life. How could any man not be attracted to this woman?

Then she asked Jude about Sadhu Das.

"Who?"

"Sadhu Das."

"Who is he?"

"The other guru. S-A-D-H-U-D-A-S," she spelled, assuming he was confused by her poor pronunciation.

Jude had never heard the name.

"Of course you know about him. He claims to be Sant Baba Ram Singh's successor."

Jude didn't know anything about that, but the fabulous stripper did. Fiona added that she and everybody living around Holiji's ashram had heard about Sadhu Das. She proceeded to recount Sadhu Das's story. Fiona and Jude told me slightly different version of this tale, so I'll tell it here in my own words. Over time, Sadhu Das's story became a legend, one every devotee of Holiji was familiar with, so I hope my account is not too disrespectful of Sadhu Das's devotees.

Apparently, one monsoon day, this wise man ran down from his cave in the mountains in the north of India, yelling that he had received a direct instruction from God. He claimed to have heard the words loud and clear on the thirty-third day of his biennial fast. The Lord had ordered him to move his ass (the exact words have been lost) and rush to the dying Sant Baba Ram Singh's ashram to inform the people there that he was officially the next one in charge. But when he asked God where the ashram was located, and if he could repeat the name of the guru once again, God was already gone.

The old man initiated the long journey down the Himalayan mountain calmly enough, but soon he was seen putting his life at risk running like a maniac through villages and bushes. Just like anybody else in his situation, he expected the civilized world to welcome him as the Messiah or at the very least as a mini Messiah (he was short, and over the years a hunch on his back had robbed him of another six inches). He was ready to feel the moisture of rose petals under his calloused feet. He figured everything would go smoothly. Relying on his instinct, he thought he'd find the ashram rapidly, and after a few words with Sant-Baba-Something, he'd be proclaimed his official successor in no time.

When he bolted through the village of his birth, screaming that he was the spiritual son of a guru named Sant-Baba-Something, he got the treatment reserved for mentally deranged hobos. The villagers shook their heads in disgust and pity. The long-gone man had returned a madman.

"I'm not mad! You, you are the ones who are mad to ignore me! God has spoken!"

No one had ever heard of a Sant-Baba-Something. This news was a great disappointment for our guru wannabe. He fell down on his knees, crying. People tried to console him.

If the villagers were kind to him, it was simply because this man, whom they used to call Rajeev Moorthy, had once been a respected doctor in their small community. For thirty-odd years, actually. Then one morning he'd hung a sign on his office door reading Closed for God and for Good. An auspicious dream had persuaded him to quit his practice and embrace the sadhu path. He had left the village that day as destitute and naked as he was on the morning of his return.

The old man said that if he couldn't count on anybody to help him, he would have to leave the village for good—once again. He told them it was his spiritual duty to pursue this most holy quest. The villagers escorted him down the road from a distance. Most didn't care—they had believed him dead and gone for years already. Rajeev reluctantly left, his back to the sun, not knowing where he was heading. Wherever it was, he didn't want the light to blind him on the way.

He walked and walked. Every now and then, a superstitious bus driver offered him a ride. Everywhere he went, he asked about Sant-Baba-Something. He was told by people who had better things to do that there were as many gurus in India as there were birds. "A lot of them you'll never see but they're out there all the same, thousands of them," they'd tell him.

When some villagers asked him his own name, Rajeev blurted, "Sadhu Das."

The two words flew out of his mouth like those birds the villagers were talking about. Surely anyone in his sandals would have reached the same conclusion: this was his God-given name. Another revelation. God was manifesting himself a second time. The Creator must have been rather uninspired because Sadhu Das is quite a common moniker for a holy man in India.

Ignited by this new manifestation, Sadhu Das implored everyone he met to become involved. They had to help him in his mission or else they'd be damned. Villagers everywhere told him they didn't believe so. This Sant-Baba-Something he was talking about, who was he anyway? What did he look like? Well, hell, Sadhu Das had no idea. When the villagers lost interest, he claimed the man was also known as The Only One. The villagers told him there were as few Only Ones as there were tigers in the Indian forests. Close to extinction and, like tigers, they tended to be shy. They hid in the most remote parts of the wild. But they did exist.

"Nothing is impossible," they told him, hoping he'd fuck off for good and let them get back to work.

Day after day, the small man wandered. Nobody anywhere had the time or the inner calling to lend him a hand. He really thought he was going mad, and the truth is, he was. He repeated his litany to every soul he met—to cows crossing the roads, to children minding their own business, to women returning from the river with clay jars on their heads.

"On the thirty-third morning of my fast ..." He blath-
ered on. People and cows avoided him as politely as they
could. He was advised to look farther on. He headed north,
zigzagging from one village to another. Sadhu Das followed
the wind.

Then one morning, in a small hamlet close to Godsara in
Uttar Pradesh, his perseverance finally paid off. The name
Sant-Baba-Something was familiar to some. The saint they
knew was called Sant Baba Ram Singh.

Rajeev hit his forehead three times with his open palm.
"That's it! That's his name!"

He was given precise directions on how to get to the holy
domicile. What Sadhu Das didn't know yet was that he was
already too late to see his predecessor alive.

By the time he reached Sant Baba Ram Singh's ashram,
he was a much madder man than he had been three months
before, which is saying a lot. The ashram lay there, a hundred
feet away from him. At first he believed he was once again
the victim of a mirage. He had endured his share of hallucinations in the past few weeks. Sadhu Das collapsed in the
dry cow dung at his feet and prostrated himself one hundred
times. The dung felt real, the grass around it felt real, the
people giving him shit for messing up their cow dung felt
real.

"Therefore, the ashram must be real!"

Sadhu Das got up and stormed through the pink gates.
As he passed the doors he heard God's voice singing to him.

You are my son.

You are my pride and joy.

Or something along those lines. People at the ashram
interrupted their activities. They did not approve of lunatics,
but it was not in their hearts to laugh at their misfortune.
Compassion dictated a respectful attitude in all circumstances. They put up with Sadhu Das and others like him the same
way they tolerated drought, unwanted pregnancies, religious

wars, and earthquakes. Events where they had no choice but to go along with the flow.

Sadhu Das coughed to get their attention. He improvised an authoritarian pose and demanded to be led to the master in charge. Holiji was already the indisputable new boss by then. It took the small man some time to understand what was going on. Then he lost it completely. Throwing his fists into the open sky, his eyes on fire, he swore Holiji was an imposter. He yelled that sooner or later, every single one of them would see the truth and bow to him and only him. Sadhu Das ordered the people at the ashram to come over and pay respects to their new father. Everybody obliged before returning to their chores. Word spread rapidly through the small community, and before long, everywhere Sadhu Das turned people bowed to him respectfully. Real guru or not, crazy or not, the man deserved the admiration bestowed on anybody willing to spend weeks isolated in a cavern just to hear a word from God, a fact no rural Indian would argue with. But everyone agreed that this alone did not make Sadhu Das the chosen son of Sant Baba Ram Singh. He was nobody's father either. Still, he was welcomed as everybody always was. Even Holiji bent over to greet him. Sadhu Das fumed and ran out of the ashram.

He prayed every day for Sant Baba Ram Singh's followers to recognize their mistake. They should have been waiting for him! God had to send another message soon because Sadhu Das had never felt so uninspired. This time he swore he would listen closely. In the meantime, he had to think of a way to reach his children with the help of a sensible speech he had yet to write.

For a few days he became so engrossed in the preparation of his comeback that he failed to hear the next holy revelation from his boss. It was a pity, because God had a thing or two he wanted to clarify with the little man. But Sadhu Das was too busy with the rehearsing of his speech to lend an ear. God grew tired of watching another one of his children fuck up, so he shut up for good. Sadhu Das now owned two revelations, and he would get no more.

He was becoming loonier by the minute, roaming through the villages neighbouring the ashram. Nobody listened to him. He told people he was going insane precisely because nobody was listening to him. The problem was, nothing he said made sense. Every soul around was acquainted with someone who had been present the day Sant Baba Ram Singh had appointed Holiji as his successor.

Fiona told Jude that Sadhu Das was still seen prowling around the ashram, stopping pilgrims and tourists to tell them his story.

"As you know, India is full of vengeful gurus," she said. "When a master dies, it's not unusual for outsiders to fight for succession."

Jude didn't know. In fact, he was speechless.

Chapter 38

*Listening to Lou Reed singing about a girl who remained
focused even when she had a dick in her mouth*

*J*UDE HAD NOT INTERRUPTED Fiona once. He was upset.
Holiji had never mentioned a word about Sadhu Das.
Why?

Perhaps he had avoided the subject, knowing the problem
was under control. Jude was outraged that someone other
than Holiji would dare to claim to be the new master. Who
would be foolish enough to defy God himself?

Jude began to speak with so much passion and so loudly
that drops of saliva flew out with his words. Fiona discreetly
covered her glass with her hand. Jude told her the cavern
man couldn't possibly be Sant Baba Ram Singh's successor.

Nodding, she said she was aware of that. "I saw Holiji's
face in a dream the day I was told about Sant Baba Ram
Singh's death."

"Really?" Jude was hypnotized again.

"Well, I'm pretty sure."

The problem was that she remembered seeing the new
beloved one's face in a dream, but the next morning the
picture had faded drastically. It could have been anybody.

Nevertheless, with her fuzzy memory as her only compass, Fiona had left for India in search of her holy father's successor. Sadhu Das had something in common with her, Fiona added, giggling. They had both embraced a path with no road signs to guide them.

"I guess I was luckier than him—that is, if one believes in luck."

She told Jude that following her dream, she too had met Holiji on a dirt road in India. Totally by coincidence, of course. Her spirit was attracted to him immediately. Holiji told her who he was. His face seemed vaguely familiar, but a far cry from the third-eye thunderbolt she had been expecting. By then, the dream was already a few weeks old. Was this man *the* man?

"I was disoriented. I didn't know for sure."

A little later she was told about Sadhu Das, and she didn't know what to believe anymore. "I realized Sadhu Das was an eccentric sadhu, but by the time I made it to India, he had already acquired quite a large group of followers. There were rumours about him performing small miracles such as throwing himself in bonfires or pulling water from a dry well."

That impressed the hell out of Jude.

Fiona said that in India such manifestations were not considered that odd. "India is a spiritual supermarket where endless aisles lead you from one miracle to another."

Jude hadn't seen anything like that during his journey. Not even at Sai Baba's place. Fiona added that ever since her guru's death, she had prayed every single day for him to guide her toward his successor's feet. Toward the one she was expected to serve and follow. Her daily meditations had been quite intense for a while. And now, finally, Jude was sitting in front of her telling her about Holiji. She squeaked like a rubber duck. Jude laughed, feeling lust dripping from his face.

Fiona became serious again. She was getting a bit drunk, and she apologized, saying she always drank too fast when she was happy. Booze had never been her thing. Nor drugs. Her body was her temple, she said. And a pristine one it was. By then, Fiona had noticed Jude was falling for her and though she still was not sure about the nature of her own feelings, she knew exactly how to keep him aroused and dazzled until she found out.

She whispered wetly in Jude's ear. "Tonight there's no more doubt in my mind. It *was* Holiji's face that I saw in my dream."

Though she persisted in acting casually for someone who had just been splashed with bright light after months of painful darkness, Fiona was pleased. "It's so nice to be able to talk about these things with someone who's also been initiated," she said. "I want to go on serving my master forever."

"And how are you serving him?"

"Well, I'm able to help the ashram in many, many ways."

Really? To Jude, she didn't look the type who would scrub an Indian latrine chanting Shiva's name. Did she tend to other domestic chores? Or maybe she plowed the large garden behind the ashram? Or did she care for the sick? Feed the beggars?

He mentioned a few of these things and she simply answered, "No."

She dug for something in her purse. A Polaroid of herself with Sant Baba Ram Singh. The saint was gripping her arm as if he feared she was about to fly away. She wore a vaporous orange sari. Jude thought Fiona should have held on tighter to the old man. With her by his side, he might have chosen not to die.

Fiona kissed the picture and, holding it with both her hands, she brushed it against her forehead. "I own a little business in Vancouver, and I gave ten percent of its profits to Sant Baba Ram Singh's ashram." She paused. "I sent every penny up to the day I learned about his death."

Fuelled by jealousy, an irrational fear leaped into Jude's mind that her "little business in Vancouver" might be a prostitution ring. No, he reasoned, that couldn't be. Sant Baba Ram Singh would never accept that kind of money. Dope money, yes. Casual sex money, no.

"So you've been to the ashram?" he asked.

"A couple of times only."

"And you say you've never seen Holiji at Sant Baba Ram Singh's side?"

Fiona shook her head the way Indians do—an affirmative nod yes accompanied by the shaking motion of a no. "Like I said, I wasn't there often. Sant Baba used to meet me in Delhi or in a quiet resort in the south of India where he could relax and get away from it all. I paid for all his expenses, of course, and he always came alone. He never mentioned a word about a successor, and I never asked. I couldn't imagine he'd die without letting me know."

She was on the brink of tears. She went on. "He just died, that's all. Like the Cheyenne chief in *Little Big Man*. He woke up one morning, and for no physical reason whatsoever he decided that it was a good day to make his passage to the other world. I was very busy the weeks prior to his death and had no contact with him at all. Something I deeply regret, believe me—"

Jude tried to console her. "Sant Baba Ram Singh announced the name of his successor on January 17th, right after the morning *satsang*. His own son was present. Dozens of people were at his side. He designated Holiji. I talked to devotees who witnessed the whole thing for themselves."

Fiona said she had spent a few days with her master in Delhi no more than a week before that date. Why hadn't he told her about Holiji?

"Holiji's coming to Montreal in August," Jude said in another attempt to brighten her gloomy mood.

Her eyes widened. "He's coming to town? Really? In three months?" She bounced up and down on her chair, cheering. "That's not a coincidence. It's a sign, isn't it?"

She raised her glass to Holiji's visit. Holiji or Sant Baba Ram Singh—they were both one and the same, and she was delighted to know she was about to see her master again.

"Sant Baba always treated me like his own daughter. Since he died, I've been aching for guidance, and I suppose that's why you and I met today. You're the messenger. I've always believed he would point me in the right direction. You and I met at Le Chaton Rose—just the kind of pranks he likes to play on me." She looked away, melancholy again. "Do you happen to have a picture of Holiji with you?" she asked.

Jude pulled one out of his wallet. She took a good look at it and lifted it to her forehead. When she gave it back to Jude, he told her she could keep it. For good luck, he said.

"No, no, you keep it. It's yours," she insisted.

He told her not to worry, that he had other ones. The truth was, he didn't. Not one that could fit in his wallet anyway. As a matter of fact, it had taken Jude quite a long time to find a picture of Holiji small enough to do the trick. But he didn't mind. He knew the picture would remain close to Fiona's heart, and that's precisely where he was planning to hang his hat for the next hundred years.

It was getting late, close to last call at the Witchy Moon. "Do you smoke pot?" he asked her tentatively.

Fiona looked at her glass. "Well, no, not really," she said with a little hesitation. "But I know where to find good hashish in India."

Jude pretended to be mildly interested. "Really? You mean for a few joints?"

"Well, no, dear. I mean large volumes, really large volumes."

Chapter 39

Listening to Joni Mitchell asking for help

$\mathcal{J}$UDE FELT THE HONEY of a perfect moment sliding down his throat. He kissed Fiona's palm gently and laughed out loud as he customarily did when something good was coming his way. He asked the waiter for two glasses of their best champagne. He didn't let go of Fiona's hand. He meant to say something incredibly poetic, something she would later repeat to their grandchildren on the rainy afternoon of his funeral. Sadly, the words coming to him consisted mainly of moronic one-syllable grunts, many pages away from his literary ambition.

It would soon become plain to all of us that these two would either be together until death did them part, or—if I may say so—until their respective egos put an end to it.

But on that first date at the Witchy Moon, a little tipsy and gazing silently at a picture of their children hanging somewhere on the party wall of their minds, Fiona and Jude had what they would describe later as "an unforgettable moment of togetherness." To add to their contentment, they agreed all that rejoicing was a gift from their gurus. They sincerely wanted to make all the right moves, say all the right things, and avoid any unsalvageable faux pas toward each other. They felt blessed as people do when they've just been introduced to the person they're certain they'll spend the rest of their life with.

To regain a modicum of his composure, Jude engaged his brain in business gear. He prayed his voice wouldn't tremble. "I'm always looking for big quantities of hashish."

The truth was, he didn't need Fiona's connections. He didn't need her money either, nor did he need a road map to the best crops of grass in northern India. But he was ready to yield to Fiona in every way—spiritually, physically, emotionally, and yeah, even financially. That's how much in love our boy was. If Sant Baba Ram Singh and Holiji had brought Fiona to him, it was for a celestial, a karmic purpose, and his duty was to keep her attracted to him.

As for Fiona, she was elated as a baby bird dipping in a summer fountain. Business and love in the same package on the same day. She swallowed a mouthful of champagne with all the grace a Dom Perignon deserves. She too wanted to say something meaningful, something sweet, words in the same line as the ones Jude wished he could tell her.

The deejay played Boz Scaggs' "Lowdown." Fiona instantly got up to dance next to their table. She restrained herself, as if she wanted to show Jude that she could enjoy a song without having to take her clothes off. Jude was in love—there was no way around it. Fiona would soon be his. His to pet, to dare, to test, to shower with gifts, to play with her mind, to lie to—all the things he associated with being in love. She extended her right arm, inviting him to join her. He declined politely. She coiled her body slowly. Her lips parted. Jude stared at the neck that had given him a hard-on a few hours before. It dawned on him that there was no way in hell he could consider this woman as the grandmother of his grandchildren. Not if she carried on shaking her naked butt in front of drooling assholes.

Jealous Jude. The mere contemplation of the anonymous army of men who had so far seen Fiona-the-Fabulous naked sent him into a labyrinth of mental torments. How many hard-ons did she actually provoke in a week? A month? A year? How many men made love to their wives fantasizing about Fiona-the-Fabulous-Redhead from Le Chaton Rose? Fiona spreading her wings, her magic wand pointing at their swelling dicks.

He got up to go to the restroom. Fiona let out a little cry of delight, and Jude danced with her for a few seconds. He pointed to the john. He didn't have to go, but he desperately needed to be alone for a moment. When he returned, Fiona was still dancing. Though the place was half empty by then, every man in the place was looking at her. Maybe some of them recognized the stripper. Jude asked her kindly to sit down. Fiona complied docilely, brushing wet locks from her forehead.

She looked at her empty glass and pouted. The barman announced the last call. Jude ordered more champagne—a whole bottle this time. The waiter told him they would have to drink it within the next thirty minutes. Jude shrugged. "Just bring the bottle, will you?"

Fiona put her head on his shoulder. She probably didn't notice his lips coming from behind because she uncurled her spine and rolled her head around before Jude got to kiss any reachable part of her skin. She was whispering again because she wanted him to get closer. She was talking dope deals, her head close to his mouth. He could feel her lips sporadically touching his earlobe.

"I use runners. The best runners I know are Québécois I met on the West Coast. For years, they've been telling me that in Québec there are a lot more reliable folks like them looking for this kind of opportunity. I persuaded a couple of them to come back here to help me find more runners. You know, good people. People I can count on."

She was waiting for Jude to digest it all.

So that was the kind of business she ran? He was relieved to hear this. After all, this was much better than a whorehouse. Fiona-the-Fabulous was a small-time dope dealer. As far as Jude was concerned, and all of us had heard him say it countless times, runners were insanely risky. It was much easier—not to mention more lucrative—to work with boats. Human beings could be so unpredictable. Runners could turn out to be weak when confronted by the police. You also needed to know the individuals working for you. The most reliable ones often ended up as friends, and these friends could end up in prison—in the worst case, in India or in Pakistan. Runners were too hazardous. Too complicated to organize, too karmically loaded.

"And how do you bring your stuff in?" Fiona asked. "Or do you do it yourself?"

"I use boats."

For a millisecond, but it didn't escape Jude, Fiona's eyes widened. She massaged her throat with her hand. This was better than what she had anticipated, judging by Jude's young age. That boy was certainly full of surprises.

"So you have contacts with people working in Asian ports?"

He nodded.

"Are you sure you can trust them?"

"With my own life."

This time her irises popped wide and remained that way. Jude was careful with his choice of words. "Personally, I'm not fond of runners. I prefer less traffic and bigger profits."

Fiona felt a shiver running up her spine. She thought that was the sexiest line she had heard in a long time. Her instinct told her this boy was not to be treated like a subaltern. When Jude moistened his lower lip with his tongue, had it not been for the irrevocable law stipulating a girl should never kiss first, Fiona would have thrown herself at him. She didn't, she couldn't. Not just yet. Instead she went back to business.

The opportunities were dancing in her head. She handed him her empty glass for a refill.

"I don't believe boats are better or worse than runners," she said with conviction. "No matter how lucky you are, you win some, you lose some. It's unavoidable. But we could do both. My runners are very good, and they have all my trust. I've worked with them for years."

She wanted him to understand that she too knew people willing to walk barefoot on broken glass for her, if they had to. Jude kept cool. He didn't want to look patronizing, though that's how he always felt when small dealers talked shop with him. He absolutely didn't want to offend Fiona, so he kept quiet until he could think of something to say that wouldn't kill this perfect moment.

"Runners could smuggle hash, and boats could wheel in grass," she went on. "We could alternate suppliers. We'll split fifty-fifty. You take care of your part of the distribution on the East Coast, and I'll take care of mine on the West Coast, including part of the United States."

Whoa. She was telling Jude how to split his hard-earned money with her. Had she been anybody else, he would have been amused by her arrogance. A stripper from a cheap downtown club telling him how *she* planned to secure *him* a buck. I'll bet he didn't know whether to laugh at her or fall on his knees and praise the Lord for his good luck. Fiona needed him. That alone lessened the outrage. He was pleasantly drunk, as much from the champagne as from the beautiful future ahead of him with Fiona by his side. Smart, beautiful, spiritual, vegetarian dope dealer—Fabulous Fiona.

"I know good people who can move the stuff on the West Coast. So, what do you say?"

Fiona reminded Jude of Faye Dunaway in the movie *Network.* In one scene Dunaway, who portrays a TV network executive, is having sex with a colleague. Throughout the whole act, she keeps discussing the details of a business deal, never giving up on the subject, no matter how hard her lover tries to make her forget about it.

Jude wasn't sure where to begin. To start with, he was already supplying parts of the Canadian West Coast. But hadn't she mentioned the States? A little piece of the US West Coast would be nice. On the other hand, if she had something big going on, why had he never heard of her? Poor baby. She had no idea who she was dealing with. Obviously Fiona was a small potato. For the second time that evening, Jude felt a wave of doubt sinking his soul. First, when he thought Fiona might not be as pretty up close as he had imagined from a distance, and now. Was Fiona nothing more than a small-time dope dealer? He touched her necklace. A silver heart on a gold chain. She unlocked it. Inside was a black and white oval picture of Sant Baba Ram Singh.

Jude didn't answer Fiona. A man's silence can send a woman into a sea of suppositions. Fiona figured she was probably too pushy for a first date, and it might be a good idea to change the topic of conversation. But no matter how hard she tried to avoid it, she remained inches from the subject of their financial association. It was impossible for her to forget about it. She had prayed for this for so long. Not the falling in love part, but the making real money part. She was still under the impression that she could control her feelings for Jude.

She talked about Milou and the girls back at the club. She said she was stripping to pay for "the basics." Apart from the club and her classes, all her spare time was dedicated to briefing potential runners and minding her business in Vancouver. She said she needed a partner because she couldn't take care of everything alone anymore. Especially not if the new runners were as good as the ones she already had. "In Québec, customs are easier to cope with than in Vancouver."

She was talking shop again.

By the time Jude took her home, it was past 4:00 a.m.

Fiona invited him in for a drink, but Jude refused, saying he was too tired. That was another lie. He couldn't have slept if his life had depended on it. He felt like driving around town thinking about her. The fact was, he was too shaken to be able to perform competently in bed. Besides, it didn't hurt to appear a little aloof—he knew women, and that would only make her want him more. Fiona didn't insist, but she pouted again. By then, she was attracted to him enough to let him make love to her. Despite his impediment, Jude did want her to know how much he liked her, so he kissed her lips dramatically, as if it were the last kiss on earth. Before taking his leave, Jude felt a sudden rush of paranoia. What if Fiona thought he didn't want to have sex with that perfect body of hers because he was embarrassed by his manhood?

"You won't be disappointed," he said, stroking her hair.

"And you weren't disappointed ... or were you?" I said to Fiona in New York when she got to that part. Fiona giggled. Then she said, "You know, Geneviève, I was crazy about him, I just didn't know it yet. Now, on bad days, I wish that night had never taken place. On good ones, I wonder what would have happened to me if it hadn't."

Chapter 40

Listening to CSNY singing about a really pretty house

YOU SHOULDN'T BE CALLED a prophet for predicting that making a lot of illegal money will lead you to a proportionate amount of risks. But you could be called a prophet for providing an unheard of yet religiously logical theory on why that is so. Holiji was that kind of guru.

Because they longed to believe it was their spiritual duty, Fiona and Jude became professionally and personally involved. Fiona quit her job at Le Chaton Rose a week after meeting Jude. He didn't have to insist much. Fiona had made no secret of the fact that she hated the club and its clientele. She felt that a striptease was a form of ballet, as in "classical dance," and if you meant to be competent at it you had to work hard. Really hard. Long hours of practice, research, and rehearsal. In fact, it required so much effort and discipline that in Fiona's opinion this kind of artistic performance deserved a respectful and mostly silent audience, not a bunch of rowdy, uneducated drunks.

During their first weeks together, everything ran smoothly. Runners and boats wheeled dope into Canada, and distribution was carried out rapidly and efficiently. Not a hitch, not a speck of trouble. Their love life was just as orderly. They couldn't remember being happier. Only one thing spoiled their blissful existence.

Fiona busied herself looking for a place where they both could live, a place where they'd be comfortable when the baby came. Not that she was pregnant yet, but Fiona's biological clock was ticking a little louder every day. For practical and romantic reasons, and of course spiritual ones too, she set her choice on Jude as the sperm donor.

Jude was not so enthusiastic. "A baby? Forget it, honey. Not now." End of discussion.

"You haven't heard the last of it," Fiona muttered, walking away.

They rented a cozy house in Westmount. Fiona spent hours reading books on how to attain beatitude through interior decoration. She built walls in the vast open space in the basement and added a shin high plank of wood on the floor across the doorframe, the way they do in China to protect homes from evil. She ordered a couple of miniature do-it-yourself waterfalls from California to attract good spirits. Jude delighted her with bamboo furniture and laced wood screens bought in Asia on one of his trips. Fiona's taste was as exquisite as it was exotic. Cushions from Morocco, fabrics from Borneo, *papier maché* from Radjasthan, frail puppets from Indonesia, carpets from Afghanistan, and floor tiles of blue and sand from Guatemala. A bohemian crystal chandelier, part of her great-grandmother's legacy, dangled above their queen-sized bed. Fiona carefully set every room in perfect *feng shui* harmony. She perspired and puffed, pushing furniture here and there until she attained the level of perfection she was aiming for.

Then one day, they lost a feather. And a second one soon after that. Two runners on their way back to Montreal were caught in Paris's airport, Charles de Gaulle. The two students from Chicoutimi had come with excellent references, and

Fiona had not seen the trouble coming. Guilt weighed on her conscience, and she felt it her duty to make sure their prison time was not too unpleasant. Plus, she had to act quickly if she expected the two boys to keep their mouths shut. And fast meant expensive.

Jude was furious. "Damn runners," he fumed.

Fiona made frantic long-distance calls to Europe, promising to fix everything as fast as humanly—and divinely—possible. To Jude's absolute dismay, later that month a truck loaded with hashish on its way to Toronto was busted by the RCMP—the second bust since he'd partnered with Fiona. Dreading celestial disapproval or a boycott from their masters, he feverishly checked with Holiji. Over the phone, the holy man explained that in order to remain humble and conquer ego, one had to encounter defeat.

"Defeat is there to remind you that nothing physical or material should ever be taken for granted."

He explained to Jude that one of his many missions on earth was to make sure this highly crucial lesson was understood by every one of his children. For that reason—and for that reason alone—he made sure they occasionally experienced minor material setbacks.

"You're not punished with any more harshness or more leniency than any other of my children. It's a simple karmic rule. Earnings mean occasional losses. It's only karma, my son. It has nothing to do with God's approval."

The man made so much sense. Who could argue with him?

Fiona and Jude attacked their daily activities with the renewed certainty that their master was carefully premeditating every single thing they acknowledged, from a quarter found on the sidewalk to runners getting busted in Paris. Sure, they were required to be responsible for their own destiny, but only to a certain extent.

Not long after, I heard Fiona say, "We all need a master to take over and guide us through the endless maze we call reality."

But what about the others? I sometimes wondered. What about all the good people who would never get to meet Holiji simply because they were from, say, Moose Jaw in Saskatchewan, a town that did not figure in Holiji's tour? What about them? The ones who might have followed him if they only had the chance? What was the fate of those souls?

Fiona's diagnosis was simple. Two pairs of words. "Karmic reincarnations. Cyclic deaths."

She explained that these confused and unfortunate spirits would come back to earth again and again until their karma carried them toward the ultimate ascension, their unique dwelling, their only home sweet home. In other words, at the feet of Holiji or one of his incarnations.

JUDE LOOKED FOR A strategy to work around his losses. He pondered over his calculator, adding and subtracting the same figures repeatedly, not talking much, tirelessly rearranging his priorities and the items that occupied his desk. At last, he came up with the rough draft of a plausible solution, and only then did he start to relax a bit. The plan was simple: bait the RCMP agents and feed them a medium-sized shipment of extremely low-quality dope in one port while unloading the good stuff somewhere else along the Canadian coast.

He tried not to worry too much about the busted runners in Paris. Those poor bastards were facing their own karma. What could he possibly do about that? He couldn't understand why Fiona persisted in hiring runners. Interfering with the karma of strangers could only bring her bad luck.

Jude considered it in his best interest to supply money to help Fiona get good lawyers for the two Chicoutimi boys. He was confident that she too would refine her recruitment techniques and balance the odds as conscientiously as he had. She was a smart girl; she knew the risks. She consulted astrologers. Things could only get back on track.

Chapter 41

*Listening to Neil Young stating that a man needs
a woman to clean up after him*

THE COUPLE DECIDED TO visit Holiji in India despite their busy schedule. They still had many concerns about the delicate logistics of Holiji's first North and South American tour. Sponsored by devotees, this trip would take the holy man from Lima to Montreal with no fewer than a dozen stops along the way. Some worried about his health. Was it proper to ask a holy master to get inoculated? Holiji laughed at the idea. He said he refused to be pampered. This man did not fear viruses.

When Jude showed up at the ashram with Fiona, Holiji welcomed her with a big smile and a fatherly hug. He didn't remember seeing her before and said he was grateful to be introduced to someone who had spent so much quality time with Sant Baba Ram Singh.

"My guru's children are my children," he said, beaming. "And I'm eager to meet every single one of them. I hope they will be as wise as you are, my dear child, and hurry to their father's feet. Sant Baba Ram Singh told me that all his children would come to me, every single one of them. Fiona is not the first one, and I hope not the last."

It was early June and the monsoon season was expected to hit the region in a couple of weeks. The weather was beginning to be unbearably hot, and Jude and Fiona wanted to get back to Montreal before the rain began. The way Holiji talked, Jude and Fiona felt the man had known their destiny all along—that they would meet when the time was right. After his warm greetings, Holiji looked a little uneasy. Oddly, his usual cheerful demeanour seemed clouded by something troubling.

The guru led them to the bungalow they would occupy during their stay at the ashram. Before taking his leave, Holiji told Jude and Fiona he was concerned. He asked them to meet him under the banyan tree behind the ashram right after the morning *satsang*. They rushed to him the moment they left the meditation hall. Jude was appalled to hear Holiji announce that maybe they were making too much money after all. He gently admonished them, saying too much greed could cause them to lose it all.

Jude didn't see it that way. "But aren't you happy, Master? Look at the ashram! The school, the dispensary, the railings for the handicapped? Not to mention that God is giving us the means to send you out in the world to spread your wisdom. Your children are blessed. And there are more of them every day. Shouldn't we be grateful for the abundance showered on us?"

Holiji agreed that he liked it a great deal. So much, in fact, that he wanted to keep it that way. "What's the sense of expanding your material world when you already have all that you need? To be grateful means to know when you have enough, my son." Holiji combed his beard with his fingers. He made a sweeping gesture toward the village. "Our needs were once great, but now we're on the road to a healthy and strong recovery. Everybody here can thank you for that. However, your own desires should not exceed the ones of this community. In the long run, too much money could very well bring problems to your door. Your master, your brothers, and your sisters need you free and alive, my son. Let's keep things the way they are, yes?"

Holiji was purity and compassion. Of course, he was right, but Jude was perplexed. Too much business? How could there be too much business? For him, business was like God or sex. You couldn't have too much of it.

"Too much business is the same as not enough business, my son."

It was irritating, the way he always seemed to guess Jude's most secret thoughts.

"Excess in anything is no good. It obstructs the free flow of your consciousness. I plead with you, my children. I am not warning you against an imminent disaster, but you need to fully understand the price you must pay for divine consciousness."

The holy man's gaze shifted toward the horizon. His speech slowed as if he were reading cue cards in the sky. "Please do not misunderstand me. I am very proud of you, and I will always protect you with all my power. I would never let anything or anyone hurt you or Fiona. Nevertheless, my dear ones, I'm afraid I cannot swim against your own karma in this incarnation. You should be cultivating wisdom and be content with the existence you have managed to produce so far for yourself. Be grateful every day. What you have in the here and now is all that should matter to you, remember?"

Jude was troubled. The old man was overestimating his mortal abilities. Jude didn't know how to stop making more money—it came his way almost effortlessly. To make matters even worse, every fibre of his being wished and prayed, even when he was meditating, for this medium-sized enterprise of his to inflate to empirical dimensions.

He needed to be alone for a moment with Fiona. She would surely be able to come up with a sound reason to bypass this brutal order from above.

Holiji—reading his mind again?—was stroking Fiona's shoulder. "My child, would you make sure the guest rooms are ready to receive our visitors?" A group of initiated from Hamburg was expected, and the bus from Delhi was scheduled to arrive within the hour. "They'll be tired and hungry. Old Sitara is preparing food in the communal kitchen. I'm sure she could use a little help."

Fiona obliged with all the enthusiasm she could muster. "I'll be pleased, Master." She took a few steps away and turned around. "Master, before taking my leave, may I ask for a moment alone with you later this afternoon? It could be any time after lunch, if your schedule allows it, of course."

Jude was surprised by her request.

"I would like to talk to you about my morning meditation," she added for Jude's benefit. She bowed, awaiting a reply.

Holiji was enchanted. "You do deserve special attention, my delightful child! You are a blessed star, a lost lamb sent by Sant Baba Ram Singh himself! Through me, he speaks to you. It would be my most agreeable duty to give you advice whenever you need it. Let us see ..." Holiji turned pensive for a moment, studying a notebook filled with his daily obligations. "You can come to my bungalow half an hour before the evening *satsang*."

Fiona brought her hands in prayer to her forehead and leaned to kiss Jude's cheek. Holiji said something funny. Fiona's girlish giggles flew over the thick canopy of leaves and resonated through the ashram's thin walls. Jude noticed she never missed an opportunity to let the others know how she enjoyed a unique complicity with her master.

Her heavenly duty in mind, Fiona pulled her silk scarf over her flaming hair. Waving back at Holiji and Jude, the only true loves of her life, she made her way toward the dog-shit yellow cottage next to the kitchen where they kept rooms for visitors. She marvelled at the beauty of her life. Her true love for Jude, her spiritual devotion to Holiji, the serenity they both inspired in her. The guru's presence empowered her. His vibrancy connected her to Sant Baba Ram Singh. She felt chosen once again. Saved and safe for good. She progressed slowly under the torrid Indian sun. A sudden gust of dust assaulted her and everything else on its path. She drew the scarf up to cover her eyes. For a moment she disappeared in a swirl of sand. Her mind stumbled. A strong premonition erupted in her gut like a sudden attack of fever. A dark cloud interrupted its course right between her ears. She stood there motionless, alert for a warning or a prophecy. Or rain. But nothing happened. Cloud and dust vanished in a snap. She walked on. Sitara waved at her from the kitchen porch.

Under the banyan tree, Jude was listening to Holiji's warnings. The minibus from Delhi pulled in. The Germans climbed out, red-eyed and jetlagged.

"Now go and meditate on this," Holiji said, getting up. He left Jude and greeted his exhausted children with open arms.

Jude did meditate on the subject, for hours on end. But nothing much came out of it.

Chapter 42

Listening to America singing about a nameless equine

After the long flight to New Delhi followed by a deep sleep in their comfy hotel room, Fiona's runners usually jumped on a tourist bus to visit the Red Fort or planned a longer excursion to the Taj Mahal, in Agra. On their way back from the Taj, some made a beeline for Keoladeo Bird Park to enjoy a bicycle ride among superb migrating birds. Back in Delhi, they took pictures of the marvellously organized chaos of Indian life. Every morning they were tempted by a mango *lassi* but didn't give in, afraid it might make them sick. At dinner they splurged—spicy *byriani*, sweet chutney, and, to cool their tongues, cucumber *raita*.

They tried to forget that this was not a free vacation, that they had willingly put their freedom at stake for a few thousand dollars. Back home, they had been instructed by Fiona to empty the contents of their luggage the moment they'd set foot in their hotel room in Delhi and wait for "Amit" who'd pick them up later that same day. A few days before their trip back to Montreal, the suitcases were returned by Amit, heavier, and ready to be filled with smelly clothes and colourful souvenirs. Only then did reality kick in and they began to see why they were being paid for having so much fun. The airport, the customs officials, the waiting, the neon lights, the fear, the sweat. The same motions they had gone through on their way to India, this time heading back home with luggage loaded with hashish.

Who were they? Birds of all feathers. A songwriter in need of money for his big break in the music industry, two young teachers with a baby on the way, a bored Air Canada stewardess, and countless others. There was also a seventy-nine-year-old grandmother who made a run or two every year. Good runners were odd people. Their normal lives kept their minds operating in the right mode, just like the law-abiding citizens they wanted to look like to a customs agent. They didn't have to invent respectable lives, they led them. They held regular jobs and paid taxes. Most did it only once. Others made it a habit.

The grandmother's name was Dora. Her smuggling career had started when she was seventy-two, and by the time she died at the age of eighty-three, she had completed thirteen runs between Montreal and New Delhi. A little old lady coming in with kilos of hashish in her luggage. Well dressed and innocent looking, she disembarked from the plane in Montreal on a wheelchair pushed by an airline attendant. Dora always paid for a porter to bring her precious luggage from the carousel to the other side of the arrival gate. From the moment she was delivered to Fiona, Dora's suitcases were rushed inside a van parked right outside the airport door, and Fiona drove the old woman home herself in her own car. On the way, they talked about her trip. Dora enjoyed the attention, and she was also becoming filthy rich. She went on cruises in the Caribbean, to Alaska, or through the fjords of Norway whenever she felt like it. She spoiled her grandchildren, and she played roulette at the casino twice a week with girlfriends from her tai chi class. She told her family the money came from a forgotten bond purchased decades before by her late husband. Dora never encountered a problem at the airport, and the difficult conditions in India didn't bother her. She made it look so easy that every single one of us considered boarding that plane to Delhi or Bombay. Only Milou went all the way. But I'll get to that story later.

To her credit, Fiona's small army of smugglers grew more competent, and the turnover was low. Occasionally, she was plagued by con artists, but the majority of her "employees" lived up to their promises. She cautiously chose the dates of their return according to intricate astrological charts. That alone seemed to be of a great help, and Jude was satisfied with the results. Though their passion for each other had cooled off after the Chicoutimi boy was busted, the couple resumed their lovemaking with the ardour of their first nights together.

When I asked Jude how things were between his mother and Fiona, he assured me his mother adored his girlfriend, and the fact that she had once been a stripper only added to her admiration. Fiona was everything Mrs. P had secretly wished to become before her unfortunate encounter with Jude's father. Fiona was independent and financially at ease. Her former career as an exotic dancer was proof of how determined she was to live her life her way. Fiona had done what had to be done to be in charge of her own destiny, and Mrs. P could only admire her for that. Of course, Jude's mother had no idea her oldest boy's new squeeze was also a drug dealer.

In fact, Mrs. P was pleased that finally a girl she admired was in love with her son (she had never been crazy about me). Fiona would most likely succeed in making Jude give up his "reprehensible activities." Mrs. P wasn't blind. She knew what her son was doing. I'll bet she understood a lot more about Jude than she had ever led him to believe. A son can't fool his mother forever. Jude always had a lot of money on him, thick piles of cash in his pockets. He bought himself clothes whenever he felt like it, and he ate out almost every night. He and his mother had many fights about this. Screams, curses, insults, threats, and spite. Later on, a repentant Jude would offer her a small gift to earn her forgiveness. Like his father had probably done before him. No matter how angry he had made her, Mrs. P always seemed helpless to do anything but forgive him because, like any mother, it sent her into raptures to picture her son thinking about her long enough to buy her a guilt-ridden trinket.

Did she worry about whether Fiona knew about Jude's business? I don't think so—she must have concluded that Fiona knew. Her son's new girlfriend was too smart not to have drawn the obvious conclusion, and surely she would put a stop to it soon. When she did, Mrs. P would cheer for her all the way.

"It's not that he's a bad boy," Jude heard her say one day to her friend Becky, who came over for coffee. "But I really believe he deserves a lesson. That girl might just be the answer to my prayers. There's nothing wrong with leading a normal family life. He should get a real job and raise a family, no? I had to make many sacrifices to offer my sons the luxury I felt they deserved. Why can't he be a little more grateful?" Jude vaguely wondered whether his mother would one day find a way to be happy with him.

With Fiona there to take over, Mrs. P must have felt she could finally rest a little. Jude said he changed his way and behaved extremely well with his mother whenever Fiona was around, and he began to behave just as well even when she wasn't. He really meant for his mother to love Fiona as the daughter she felt she should have had. I'm sure she loved to see Jude docilely obeying his new girlfriend. From what he had been told about his biological father, Jude knew the man would have despised him for it.

One day when we were still dating, I was at Jude's house

waiting for him, and Mrs. P, who had once been Mrs. C before her divorce with Jude's father, was ironing in the kitchen. She had probably started to drink a little too early that day because she broke the silence by telling me she believed a good side was hiding somewhere in her oldest son. *Her* part in him. I didn't say a word—I was too stunned by this sudden intimacy. She said she knew better than anyone the coward who was responsible for that poisonous gene in her son's mind. The result of this bad man's foul liquid mixed with her own purest and highest expectations was still growing in front of her eyes nearly twenty years later. It was plain to see that Mrs. P had never been a happy woman.

But finally the wind was turning, and her oldest boy was changing for the better, thanks to Fiona. It's not hard to imagine how relieved she must have felt at the time.

As far as Jude's mother was concerned, the man in India, the one Jude called Master, was a fake. This so-called magician had surely not even scratched the surface of her son's criminal mind. But Fiona was smarter. She had charm, wit, and money. Of course, that master, he didn't have any of that. "A fakir performing tricks and nothing more," she told Jude when he first told her about Holiji. The only thing she questioned regarding Fiona was her devotion to the Indian man, but she kept that to herself, believing both Jude and Fiona would eventually realize their gullibility.

Fiona came from a good family, she had impeccable manners, she cooked good food (even though it was scrupulously vegetarian), she talked like a real lady, and she knew her place in a kitchen, unlike most of the airheads Jude had brought in so far (I repeat: she never was crazy about me). Mrs. P must have been pleased indeed. Jude noticed she even stopped mixing her martinis with Valiums for a while. She couldn't believe her luck. Then again, when Jude was still a toddler, had someone told Mrs. P that one day her cherished boy would end up as a dope dealer shacking up with a stripper she would have spit at this joker. She'd have rubbed Jude's pink body with generous splashes of Eau de Floride as if it was holy water. However, nowadays, Mrs. P could find happiness in notions that would have once driven her to madness.

We had never seen Jude more serene. The affinities naturally uniting the two women made his life that much easier. In those happy days, the couple showed up at the Outremont home almost every Sunday night for dinner. Fiona was always in charge of dessert, and every time she baked sweets from scratch. Better, she wore her desserts. For instance, with an apple crust, she'd put on cinnamon essential oil. With a chocolate cake, she'd splash her shoulders with orange water. With something fruity like strawberry shortcake, there was the unmistakable smell of wet green grass in her hair. Jude's mom surely noticed every detail of Fiona's flair for seduction, which was too subtle to even compliment. How do you praise the sacred, delightful aroma of an answered prayer, that divine fragrance they talk about in the Bible?

I pictured Mrs. P presiding over the dinner table with no fewer than four kinds of salad in those pretty crystal bowls she had never used for fear of breaking them whenever I'd had dinner at their place. The suffocating air in that house must have turned to pure oxygen.

Each Sunday there were small miracles. Jude would fuss to lend a hand in the kitchen, or he'd spent time helping his stepsisters with their homework. He would even discuss politics with his stepfather. At least once a month—I'll bet she had calculated the frequency with precision, the way only a mother would—Jude brought her a gigantic bouquet of colourful flowers that invariably stained his white clothes. Time after time, the pistils left their powder all over him. Mrs. P always laughed aloud. Fiona scolded him affectionately. Jude promised to do better next time, but he never did. He was doing it on purpose, suit after suit, just to make sure they started the evening on a good note. These were undeniable signs of Fiona's power over her son.

In reality, Jude was subjecting his mind to something that not less than a year before he would have himself characterized as severe frostbite on his brain. A wound liable to leave him with deadly lesions and (in the most extreme case) might even require immediate amputation. Strangely, and almost magically since it actually took place overnight, Jude was yielding control. He had never done this before. When people commented on how he had changed, he didn't explode in his usual roar. Instead he laughed shyly, another curious transformation. All this to please Fiona, really. Just to please her to death. He loved her but he had already figured out that life with Fiona wouldn't be simple. He'd had a taste of it with the bust in Paris. That baby she pestered him with was also a pain in the neck. Nevertheless, since Holiji had told him about their karmic destinies together, Jude was henceforth convinced that Fiona was the only woman he could and would ever love for the rest of his life. He didn't have to work hard at it because he had never been so infatuated before. Alex and Hugo told me Jude had never shared much about the women he was dating, but for a while Fiona was his sole subject of conversation. They were both convinced Jude's transformation was genuine, though neither believed it would last.

Fiona sang and cooked breakfast after the Sunday *satsang*. Now that they had their own place, Jude had moved the spiritual gatherings to their new basement. Sean's wife must have been profoundly relieved. Now the group was welcome to hang around as long as anyone wished, sometimes well into the afternoon. Mrs. P showed up every once in a while. With her soon-to-be daughter-in-law present, she felt safe among the Weird Ones. She discreetly watched Fiona's every move. I felt she wanted to be there to decipher the slightest shift in her precious oyster's mood.

Hours were spent painting and decorating the guest room that would receive Holiji's sacred body. Fiona meticulously scrutinized the basement where initiation would take place. Holiji was on his way to Montreal! Initiation and the yearned-for *simran* were just days away. Jude said he would interrupt all dope deals for the duration of the master's stay. Instead, he saintly stated, he planned to spend his days meditating and elevating his soul. He was like a kid on Christmas morning. He couldn't wait to see our reaction to meeting Holiji in person.

"*Vous allez capoter!*" he said, almost salivating.

In other words, you can't imagine what's about to hit you.

Chapter 43

*Listening to Leonard Cohen and a sweet girl living
close to a river*

THE DAY OF HOLIJI's arrival was intensely sunny.

"Of course!" said Jude in the car to the airport, winking.

Had it been raining, I'm pretty sure he would have said something about the water cleansing the streets as well as our souls. Fiona sat next to him, her face free of makeup. She talked about the sun in her heart. Jude kissed her hand, laughing like a madman. Grace, Alex, and I sat in the back, smiling at each other. Frankie followed in his own car with Milou and Tintin.

Holiji emerged from the arrival gate, his face expressionless, dressed in white the way he was in the pictures. Jude yelled his name, and the man turned on his heels and waved. Jude joined his hands in prayer.

"*Namaste,* Master!"

Behind him, we *namasted* too. There were at least twenty of us at the airport. Friends of Fiona's we didn't know, some Sant Baba Ram Singh's initiates from the West Coast, a couple of Jude's business partners, even Mrs. P. Fiona stepped forward. Holiji greeted her with a long hug. She was red all over. There they were, Jude and Fiona together with him, surrounded by a flock of new devotees. A big happy family reunion.

Each one of us was introduced. He touched our foreheads and our cheeks. His English was funny, but he was easier to understand in person than on the cassettes. I remember feeling transported with delight just looking at him. We eagerly received his *darshan*. Holiji sat in Jude's car with Fiona and an American girl I heard Fiona call Suzanne who travelled with Holiji as his personal assistant. Up close, he didn't look so old. I caught myself thinking he was quite handsome. We followed in Frankie's car, spellbound.

Back at Jude's place, we sat in the kitchen for a light lunch. Holiji seemed to be particularly close to Suzanne, who followed him wherever his feet dictated. In the mayhem at the airport, I had hardly noticed her. Suzanne was a new addition to the ashram family, assisting our master with his daily tasks. Holiji was obviously fond of her; "my priceless angel," we heard him say on many occasions. Nevertheless, he seemed more at ease when addressing Fiona. I guessed Suzanne was all about schedules and obligations whereas Fiona was all about spiritual exchanges and good food. I learned that among her many responsibilities, Suzanne managed the ashram with Sitara and gave food and clothing to the beggars at the ashram door. She also supervised the large inventory of Sant Baba Ram Singh's and Holiji's books as well as audiotapes, and she minded the accounting. As a result, she often had to press Holiji into making decisions concerning earthly matters such as electricity bills and leaking roofs. Perhaps the American girl resented Fiona. Or maybe she didn't give a damn as long as she could spend her whole life in Holiji's shadow. Suzanne had abandoned a promising career in a New York marketing firm to live at the ashram with her master. She never wandered far away from him, making sure his food wasn't too hot and his chai not too sweet, her hands constantly busy catering to Holiji's well-being. She was a little chunky and a little clumsy, but the moment Holiji spoke to her, her face glowed and her eyes shone, and that shameless vulnerability made her attractive. Our master seemed accustomed to the way she was spoiling him.

After lunch, Holiji said he needed to take a nap. We hurried out of the house to let him rest. Back at the apartment, we talked about him until the small hours of the morning.

Chapter 44

*Listening to Led Zeppelin singing about a staircase
leading to paradise*

Around eight in the morning on Initiation Day, Frankie parked the car in front of Jude and Fiona's place. It was pouring rain. We were all surprisingly quiet. The air was heavy with the useless weight of futile concerns. We should have been overjoyed and in an advanced state of grateful bliss—after all, we, sinners, were about to receive the answer to the secret of life—but a sudden feeling of inadequacy overshadowed our joy. Nervous as grooms and brides on a wedding day, we approached the house. Boogie was shivering in my arms. I think she felt uneasy too.

A middle-aged woman opened the door. She was an initiated friend of Fiona's from Vancouver. She smiled blandly, almost painfully, as good people do when they don't really mean it. Not uttering a word and sparing us from a second bored grin, she led us to the living room.

Sitting on the couch with Fiona at his feet, Holiji was enjoying a cup of tea. The vision was picture perfect. Fiona rose slowly, concentrating on the precision of her movements, the way she probably did when she danced at the strip club.

She came toward us, her freckled arms reaching out. There was a trace of arrogance in her smile. She was her master's favourite daughter, no doubt about it, and she wanted us to notice. Holiji's eyes followed her. His expression was a reflection of the way I felt at that very same moment—trusting and vulnerable. Outside the living room's bay window, a darting ray of sunshine overcame the rain for a minute.

We heard noises coming from the kitchen down the hall, and Fiona sprinted in that direction. Holiji invited us to get closer to him, and we pushed each other nervously. We crowded in and waited for him to tell us what we should do next—and while he was at it, what we should do with the rest of our lives. He sat in a perfect lotus position, caressing the top of his golden feet.

"Now it is time for you, my children, to have a meeting with God."

He stretched out and yawned. Pointing at the basement, he motioned for us to follow him.

We moved downstairs, soundless as Navajos on a hunting ground. Nobody wanted to be the one disturbing the tranquility. However, and to everyone's astonishment, not long after sitting down in silent meditation, someone took the unconceivable liberty of letting out a loud fart. It made everybody laugh, and my dog barked, then we ascended into a peaceful state again. Boogie, the sleeping toddlers, and the babies lying around were guaranteed a better afterlife just like the rest of us. Their mere physical presence during initiation would alter their karmic future. Master didn't mind the presence of children. Pets didn't bother him either. The smelly fart didn't bother him. In fact, nothing of this world seemed to ever upset him.

After all the months of planning, everything was set and everyone was ready. Fiona and Jude, who were still on the top floor, came to join us all. Holiji began to talk. What he said was simply beautiful and true. Sandalwood incense overcame the fart smell. The thin swirl of smoke floated like an aureole around his words. He got up and walked among the limbs, children, and toys scattered on the floor. He told us about peace, love, death, birth, and forgiveness. He talked about the five planes we would have to travel before we could enjoy eternal life and a lot of other fantastic stuff I can't remember today but appreciated thoroughly at the time. Now seated on a thick cushion from India, he shone. Even Boogie was entranced. She ran out of my arms to curl down at his feet, and to my amazement, the master petted my dog. I remember thinking I would never wash her again.

Then he divulged the secret mantra, the *simran*, the five Sanskrit words we were so keen to learn, the divine words that would change our lives forever if we devoted hours to meditating on them. One Sanskrit term for each spiritual plane. We were instructed to say the five words in our minds repeatedly, all the time, no matter what we were doing.

The mantra, we were told, would keep our spirits on higher planes, allowing a direct connection with the will of God. A hand on our heart, we pledged to never mention the words out loud, unless it was to refresh the memory of another initiated (given the fact that the words were quite complicated to pronounce and consequently difficult to remember). We chanted the *simran* aloud—struggling with the Indian phonetics—for this one and only time. After twenty minutes, the words came to my mind easily, like air to my lungs. I breathed the words. I could repeat them effortlessly.

Next, our master instructed us to meditate on the *simran* with our eyes closed and an open heart. We were asked to visualize a white dot in the centre of our third eye and keep staring at it until an image appeared. I squinted, concentrating hard, but nothing happened. After a while, he asked us to describe our experience. I was amazed to hear what most people had to say. Someone claimed to have seen a smiling angel. Another, a green laser-like light. One heard trumpets and choirs.

Fiona waited until everybody was done. Master asked if there was something she wished to share with us. She smiled, and after pausing, she said she had seen Sant Baba Ram Singh's turban adorned with a huge diamond. "Like a sparkling third eye," she specified. She giggled.

I wanted to puke. Even if she was telling the truth, which for some reason I doubted, I thought she was showing off. Maybe I was jealous of the attention she was getting from him. That smile he had for her.

Fiona went on describing her vision. She said the diamond melted away. "And then I saw your face, my beloved Master."

Holiji gazed at her with all the goodness left on earth and told her how great that was, how great she was. "In fact," he said, raising his left eyebrow and looking at the rest of us, "this is a very rare experience."

So now she was our Bernadette Soubirous, the venerated Catholic mystic from nineteenth-century France who claimed to have chatted seventeen times with Mary. Fiona was now Bernadette-the-Fabulous. Fiona Soubirous.

"Oh, Master, why am I so blessed?"

I couldn't get rid of that jealous sting in my sides. For once in her life, she could have stepped off the stage and yielded the spotlight to others. I wanted to believe that I wasn't alone, that most people in that basement hated her that morning. She thought herself the most special one among us, as if she knew a shortcut to enlightenment. As if he liked her better than us. But of course he didn't, I told myself—I was only imagining that.

Following this exercise, Master talked about vegetarianism, anger management, jealousy, greed, bad influences, and of course, the bit about sexual abstinence. One guy sitting in the back shyly admitted to masturbating too much. Holiji told him not to worry about it. For the rest of the day, every time I looked at this guy, I could only picture him shaking his thing up and down, his eyes turned up white. This poor soul was forever referred to as "the guy who yanks his doodle too much." I mean, there's only so much I need to know about people I share a guru with. Why would anybody worry about masturbating too much anyway? It doesn't hurt anyone. Woody Allen said it: "Don't knock masturbation. It's sex with someone I love." Now, that's funny. But this initiated guy wasn't.

One middle-aged woman with too much makeup and patchouli oil on her clothes talked about her husband dying of cancer and her wavering faith since she had been confronted with the fatal diagnosis. Master had a soothing word and a solution for her and for everyone else who felt the need to whine about something, even the guy who yanked his doodle too much. He said the right thing with the right words in his Indian-spiced English. Tears streamed down cheeks, grateful hands touched his feet, velvet prayers were whispered. The little congregation we formed that day felt united as it never would again. I even forgot why Fiona had annoyed me so much a few minutes earlier. We smiled and encouraged one another. We were good people who wanted to go on being good and maybe even get better in the process. At least, we hoped, a little better than those who weren't initiated.

It was almost dark when we finally got home. I didn't talk much. I was too busy dissecting my insides. From what I gathered, everybody felt the same way. I don't know what I expected. Bolts of lightning, dead people materializing in front of me? Nothing of the sort took place. It took me a while to fall asleep.

When I woke up the next day, I felt profoundly disappointed. I repeated the mantra in my head for a long time. Where was that amazing, fuzzy warmth that had filled my soul just the day before?

A little more than two weeks after Initiation Day, Holiji left Montreal on a rainy afternoon. Without him around anymore, things began to deteriorate.

Chapter 45

*Listening to the Who wondering whether they should
leave a kid alone with their uncle*

After Holiji's departure, Milou convinced Jude to let him make a run. His destination, the valley of Kashmir, awoke in him an otherwise dormant craving for adventure. He said that when he became rich and was living in LA or New York, he would travel to Shanghai, Kabul, Cairo, and other places that made him feel like Captain Nemo.

Fiona brought two "special" suitcases to his apartment. To Milou, they looked like any other luggage. Fiona told him that an Indian man named Swarook had put them together. Each suitcase was lined with a hidden compartment designed to conceal hashish. Fiona told Milou that when she'd first seen Swarook's work she was impressed enough to place an order on the spot. Milou would be the first runner to use them. It was safest this way. Our stripper friend inspected them closely. Swarook's work was really well done. Milou saw nothing that would attract attention.

He admitted to us that he was a little scared. Not a lot, mind you, but each time he imagined himself all the way over there, in India, he had to stop for a minute and take a deep breath. He had a motive: he needed money to produce his next show. This new production would be a "theatre piece in three acts." In reality, it was a porn remake of *The Sound of Music* with a lesbian nun pursued by a Von Trapp family deeply involved in S&M, all of them sharing a castle with virgin twin nurses with uncommonly large breasts.

"With the right budget, this production could end up in Nevada in no time," he told everyone.

Jude knew the Kashmiri who was coordinating the deal—he had met him on one of his numerous trips to India. The man had been working for Fiona for a while, and she trusted him. That was the sole reason Jude allowed Milou to make the run. Mohammed, Jude told Milou, had eyes as green as string beans and was a very honest man.

"He's like a brother to Fiona."

Mohammed lived in a small village ten miles south of Srinagar, Kashmir's capital. Before Fiona walked into his life, he was a poor father relying on good luck and odd jobs to feed his six children. Now he was the father of eight, he wasn't poor anymore, and he didn't have much to do to become an even richer man. With Fiona's help, Mohammed built a house for himself and another for his brother and his own family, all thanks to the Red Lady. The fact that Mohammed happened to be the cousin of a hashish dealer living in the mountains nearby didn't hurt. Every one of his children and his brother's children worshipped Fiona and knew they owed her everything they owned. Mohammed could even afford school and uniforms for every one of them. These kids would receive the kind of education their fathers could only have dreamed of.

When we told Jude we were concerned about Milou's safety, he couldn't have been more reassuring. "Mohammed would gladly die for Fiona. Or me, or Milou, or your grandmother if Fiona asked him to."

On his way home, he was scheduled to stop in Madrid for a three-hour layover before boarding the plane taking him to Montreal. Dope dealers knew that most European airports were not a concern, least of all Madrid's. At the Spanish airport, Milou was expected to pick up the suitcases from the carousel and get them to the Air Canada counter for the second leg of his journey.

Jude had been generous with advice. "Act natural, pick your nose, do crosswords. Most of all, relax. It'll be over before you know it."

Milou could be cool enough, he assured us. If he had enough guts to take his clothes off in front of total strangers, he certainly could look a customs agent right in the eyes and lie about the contents of his luggage. Experience had shown Jude that a good-quality suit was the best attire to wear on such occasions, and he ordered Milou to have a dark blue suit specially tailored for him upon his arrival in Delhi and to wear it on his way back. He should also get a haircut. Jude explained that customs officers usually approved of a well-dressed traveller even though they ought to know better. He instructed Milou to tell the agents that after graduating from law school, his desire was to travel the world before getting a real job. He was also told to make a stop at Janpath Market in New Delhi and buy large quantities of Indian trinkets to fill up his suitcases. Fiona asked him to get her a dozen tubes of Ayurvedic toothpaste, Alex asked for some incense, Grace and I wanted black kohl, Camille wanted a blue sari. He promised to get it all as well as everything else his other friends asked him to bring home. He wouldn't alter any part of the plan for fear of jinxing his luck.

While Milou was getting ready for his big trip, I noticed Hugo was taking more and more distance from us. Every night of the week, he prowled Montreal's streets in search of spirited girls willing to laugh at his jokes, ride in his car, and have sex with him. If he had once been amused by our holy aspirations, he wasn't anymore. He began to despise us, no longer able to suffer our initiated asses.

Deep inside, I knew Hugo was no different than the rest of us. He, too, was looking for some peace of mind, for making some sense of his life. Had there been a smaller, less complicated package in Holiji's line of services, Hugo might have joined in, but this one and only offer was definitely too demanding for him. However, Hugo was grateful for the money coming in from the dope deals protected by Holiji. He had developed a solid partnership with Jude, who no longer pressured him to join our group of devotees. Hugo turned out to be a precious associate, and his partner was convinced that sooner or later he would succeed in guiding our Don Juan, slowly but surely, toward The Path.

Chapter 46

Listening to Neil Young singing about burning palaces

IN INDIA, MILOU SPENT little time at the ashram. It was September, and Holiji was away, touring in the province of West Bengal, so there was no reason for Milou to hang around. The next day he got himself a train ticket to Srinagar. Afterward, he paid a visit to a tailor in Chandni Chowk market and ordered a suit he would pick up once back in Delhi, before heading to Spain. If he picked it up the day before he was scheduled to fly, his suit would look impeccable. He figured Jude would agree.

The old locomotive made its way around the valley like a steel cobra looking for something to eat. Surrounded by Himalayan wonders, Milou was mesmerized by Kashmir. The cozy houseboat rented for him, the *Pearl of the Orient*, was spacious enough to accommodate six people comfortably. He told himself it was just too good to be true.

He missed us, but he missed Tintin more. He couldn't remember having been separated from his friend for so long. He thought those Indian kids on the train would have had a good laugh at Tintin and his fat belly. To his delight, Indians loved him, especially children. They followed him everywhere he went. Milou's genuine good heart was irresistible. With a decent suntan, he was easily mistaken for the brother of one of the men surrounding him. Indians addressed him in Hindi and were noisily stunned when Milou confessed he didn't speak a word of their language. He did everything he could to blend in. He bought himself a scarf and a rough Kashmiri wool coat, even though both were insanely itchy. He didn't care. He enjoyed the anonymity.

Three days after his arrival in Srinagar, Mohammed, the man with string-bean eyes, showed up at the *Pearl of the Orient* to pick up the suitcases. He said he would bring them back a couple of days before Milou was scheduled to return to Delhi. Mohammed looked like a nice person, but he was in too much of a hurry to leave a lasting impression on Milou. The Indian man loaded the luggage in his rusted flatbed truck, sighing like a tired deliveryman at the end of a double shift. The brand-new luggage shared the back of the truck with two goats and at least one chicken—Milou could see only one but could hear many more.

Mohammed's accent was as unsteady as Holiji's. His vocabulary, on the other hand, was far more basic. It was like having a conversation with Tonto.

"Until you back home, you enjoy you. This is beautiful country. You have servants, hashish, all you need. You need something, *verree simpul*, you send *peepul* to fetch me."

"To what?"

"To fetch me."

Following the confusion brought upon Milou, who thought *fetching* meant some kind of corporal punishment—he actually believed it was a synonym for *stoning*—Mohammed shook hands with him, saying he had to be on his way. Milou petted the goats while Mohammed fought with a stubborn starter. It was still early, not noon yet. Milou had all the time in the world. Once Mohammed was out of the way, he planned to take a ride through the canals on his own *shikara*, Kashmir's lovely gondola-like boats, and stop somewhere for a bite. The truck finally agreed to cooperate. The motor purred, and Mohammed's loud *ahhhhs* echoed Milou's silent relief. Our friend wasn't in the mood for socializing that day, especially not if it meant repeating the same thing three times and still being misunderstood. They parted with one more handshake, and Milou walked toward Dhal Lake, anticipating a day of leisure.

He spent the rest of his stay strolling around Srinagar. He joined other tourists on excursions across the purple mountains surrounding the lake. He worked on his suntan, rode ponies, played soccer with runny-nosed kids, and paid a daily visit to his favourite teahouse. His body was healthy, his mind alert, and with Holiji protecting his every move, he understandably felt confident.

One late afternoon, two days before his departure for Delhi, Milou came back to the houseboat to find his suitcases in the middle of his Victorian bedroom. Mohammed wasn't around.

"He probably didn't have time to wait," Milou concluded.

It was then that he realized he had not once asked for *peepul* to *fetch* the Indian man. Fraternizing with Fiona and Jude's business contact would have been a smart move. The couple would have appreciated the gesture. But it was too late for regrets now. Milou figured that Mohammed was too involved with his children, his houses, his goats, his chickens, and his dope deals to waste precious time sipping chai with a male stripper.

The suitcases still appeared normal to him. He lifted each carefully. The weight felt uneven. He shook his head. Was his perception impaired because he knew what was in there? He filled them up with new clothes and what was left of his old stuff. He carefully evaluated the space, mentally reserving enough room to fit in the items he had to buy in Delhi— Fiona's toothpaste, Alex's incense, Camille's sari, and kohl for

Grace and me. With the clothes added, the suitcases' weight felt a little more normal but still too heavy for what was in them. Milou thought it wise to buy some gifts and souvenirs right away to add to the bulk.

He stepped on his *shikara*. With the sun going down, it was getting a little chilly. Snuggled under a blanket with a small basket of burning coal to keep his hands warm, he waved at the children on the shore. The *shikara* man took his position behind the boat, and they floated on the calm waters of the Dahl Lake. Milou asked to be taken for a long ride, longer than the ones he usually took. He wanted to take as many pictures as he had left on his last film and, of course, to buy stuff to shove in his luggage. Along the quiet canals, merchants in their own *shikaras* approached to sell him everything imaginable, from ladies' underwear to heroin. He bought a few woollen shawls, boxes and plates made of *papier maché*, mittens, and scarves for the girls at the strip club, a beautiful blanket for his mother, and turquoise earrings for Grace, who drooled with envy whenever Fiona wore hers.

Back on the houseboat, he realized there was no way in hell he could fit everything in the two suitcases. And there was all that other stuff to get in Delhi. He resigned himself to giving away some of his old clothes.

He separated his new acquisitions in two piles and placed them evenly in the suitcases. He put the shawls on top to protect the fragile items. The Kashmiri coat would have to stay behind. He didn't see how he could take it back unless he wore it, but the coat would make him stand out from the crowd, and Jude would kill him for that. A suit. He had to wear a suit.

"I'll give it to the *shikara* man. I'm sure he can use it. I didn't like it that much anyway. Too itchy."

He made another pile with the stuff he was leaving behind and shoved it in a plastic bag. One of the suitcases was a little difficult to close. He sat on it lightly. The hash bricks remained stable under his butt. Good. With that settled, he followed the dusty road to town and gave a plastic bag full of smelly clothes to the kids he'd played soccer with. The *shikara* man was thrilled by the coat. He *namasted* again and again and even kissed Milou's hand.

"Oh, Mister Milou, thank you!"

"It's nothing. You've been very good to me."

He'd had no real conversation with his *shikara* man, nothing besides the essentials.

"Oh, Mister Milou! Thank you! Thank you from the heart of my bottom!"

The man looked so genuinely grateful that Milou had to pinch himself not to explode laughing. He didn't correct him either. This was a gem—he couldn't wait to repeat it to us. He knew we would get a kick out of it.

Four days later, Milou landed in Madrid. Dressed in his brand-new suit, he waited patiently by the belt to pick up his luggage. One of the suitcases appeared almost immediately. He smiled with satisfaction before noticing that some passengers seemed to be pointing at it. The suitcase fell from the conveyor belt to the carousel. As it passed him, Milou aimed to grab it but withdrew his hand as if bitten by a rat. Bricks of hashish were bursting through the side seams. Milou stood there like a lost child. He thought about running away, out of the airport, but an agent had already spotted him, and that was pretty much the end of it.

Milou was sentenced to three years in a Spanish prison. As a strict vegetarian, he lived on rice, potatoes, polenta, and milk. It didn't take long for him to lose his boyish, muscular figure and most of his hair. Jude's lawyers couldn't do shit to help. The Spanish judge wasn't sympathetic. A gogo boy passing that much dope through Madrid?

"Guilty, guilty, guilty," said the judge.

Milou would have to make the time.

The news of his incarceration created havoc at the apartment. We were devastated. Milou's parents went crazy, calling every ten minutes. Tintin was mad with grief. It took weeks for everybody to accept that this one was not going to go away.

Chapter 47

*Listening to a Beatles' song that meant way too much
to Charles Manson*

"DAMN RUNNERS," JUDE REPEATED to Fiona ten times a day.

Milou's terrible ordeal affected Jude profoundly. He couldn't face Milou's mother, whom he knew almost as well as his own mom. He didn't answer Mrs. T's repeated calls. He didn't know about the ripped suitcases yet, and neither did Fiona.

Following Milou's call from Madrid, Jude rushed to the airport and boarded the first flight to Spain. In his business-class seat, watching Montreal fade away, Jude began to blame Fiona. This tragedy was all her fault. She'd screwed up on a detail—he could feel it.

In the depressing visitors' room, Milou told Jude what had happened. Jude would have strangled Fiona on the spot had she been unlucky enough to be standing next to him. His friend told him to cool down. He said Fiona shouldn't be chastised for his karma. He himself was the only one to blame, he insisted. He should have phoned from Kashmir the moment he realized the suitcases felt weird. He should have delayed his return and waited for further instructions.

Milou looked sincere. He kept repeating that it was nobody's fault. Karma was nobody's fault. He said he was certain that it was part of his destiny to board that plane to India and land in a Spanish prison a month and a half later.

"You know what they say—the Lord works in mysterious ways. No need to dramatize. It's only time, you know. It's only fuckin' time." But Milou's eyes shone with tears, betraying his words. He seemed too helpless, too unhappy, and too terrified to really mean what he was saying.

Three years! Jude couldn't think straight, witnessing the damage already done to his friend. Guilt replaced pity. He swore to himself that Fiona would pay for this, but he told Milou he would forgive her. "If just for this one time," he said through his teeth, not meaning it for a second.

Fiona was waiting for him at the terminal gate when he returned to Montreal. Jude didn't wait to get in the car to give her shit. She became furious and defensive, they insulted each other's mothers, and he slapped her face. She slapped him back. Just like that. He apologized, she forgave him, and from that day on, they began beating each other up on a regular basis.

Jude thought he'd never be able to forgive Fiona for Milou's bust. He realized the horrifying truth that Fiona was dented, that maybe she wasn't that smart after all. Not as smart as he was, for one thing. Could he accept that Fiona was not the perfect human being he had always assumed she was? He took a few deep yogic breaths to help him deal with this most disturbing possibility. He felt cheated. She should have told him she was the kind of person who trusted strangers who didn't deserve it, like that jerk of a Swarook. What a fucking asshole!

Swarook, the second culprit, was the one who had worked on the suitcases. Mohammed was not to blame. It was not his job to inspect luggage to make sure it was safe—he could only assume it was safe. It was Fiona who was to blame. It was her second fuck up. First the boys in France, now Milou. Where would she screw up next?

Jude stepped on the gas of the new Mercedes Fiona had offered him as a make-up gift a week after Milou's arrest. This present was an obvious attempt to accelerate his forgiveness, but it was also an obvious admission of her culpability. He wished she'd have kept the money to hire a better lawyer for his friend. He would have to take care of that too if she didn't see to it. However, he kept the car and his opinion to himself.

WE COULD HARDLY RECOGNIZE Milou in the pictures he sent two months later. To cheer him up, Jude promised to finance the production of Milou's show in Vegas. From his cell in the Soto del Real prison, Milou wrote back, saying he would no longer be able to pursue his stripper dream. His expression in every picture confirmed he was dead serious about that. There was a strange shot in the stack that looked like an aerial view of a dry forest with a large lake in the middle. Way up north, judging by the winter light. Or maybe a landing strip in the middle of nowhere. According to Milou's letter, it was a bird's-eye view of his head. Barren as the Siberian tundra. He wrote that his hair had started to fall out the week following his arrest. The other shots showed him fat and sad. His lower lip sagged, his shoulders hung low. A miserable Friar Tuck.

Camille, Grace, and I shipped him boxes of food. Peanut butter, granola bars, maple syrup. Christmas was just a couple of weeks away, and I remember Grace adding some home-made gingerbread to the provisions. That's about all I can remember from that period. Life stood still at the apartment. Milou was on everyone's mind. Why had Holiji chosen to abandon him?

"Who are we to judge Milou's karmic destiny?" Jude said as feeble words of consolation.

I suspected it puzzled him too. Why Milou?

Chapter 48

Listening to Neil Young, who wants to know why

A YEAR PASSED. WE HEARD from Milou less and less during 1977, but each of us made a point of writing to him at least once a month. We still sent packages of food though we had no idea whether he received what we sent, letters included. We were getting used to his absence but not to the feeling of guilt every time someone mentioned his name. Luckily for us, we had Holiji's books and teachings to keep us strong.

One *satsang* morning, Fiona asked if I would agree to become her cleaning lady. "Only for a while," she added.

I accepted, not because I found the idea appealing—far from it, actually—but I didn't want my name on Fiona's black list. I could easily squeeze in an hour, maybe two, once a week for her.

"We'll pay you for your trouble, of course."

It sounded like a warning.

We were in her kitchen, getting breakfast ready for our brothers and sisters. Fiona was trying to read my mind. I felt self-conscious the way I usually did when she was on my case for something. She listed in great detail her daily responsibilities, reaching a conclusion I'm sure she hoped I had already figured out for myself: there was simply too much for her to do and not enough time to do it all. She needed "space and time" for more important matters than housework. She said it was not that she despised domestic chores, or that she considered herself to be above earthly duties such as scrubbing a kitchen floor or doing the laundry (laundry?—no way I was doing the laundry!), but there were holy duties to fulfill and these were a priority.

"I'm sure we can both agree on that!" she said, giggling. Fiona always assumed everyone else agreed with her ideas, no matter what the topic.

She added that she had no other solution but to let go of certain "humble assignments." With the wink of someone leading me to a pot of gold, Fiona said she'd also give me some clothes of hers as a bonus. "You know—things I don't want anymore, but that are still very good. Items that are a little out of date, but I'm sure you won't mind."

I watched her sternly, concealing my disbelief at her condescension. Fiona was re-enacting her own version of a blue blood's charitable deed in some pre-Revolution era. The rich being patronizingly kind to the poor, her irrefutable British heritage vibrating in the presence of a born French Canadian.

"You'll have to eat here—anything you want from the fridge, actually, because it will take you a whole day to clean up this place. You don't work at the bookshop on weekends, do you? Of course, you can come two evenings a week if that suits you better."

What? "Fiona, I don't know if I can find the time—"

"Whatever you say," she said. "I'll bend to your schedule."

She grabbed my hand and took me around the house, pointing at walls, closets, and fingerprints on windows. Cracks in the wooden floor needed vigorous vacuuming, miniature Burmese figurines of amber and jade required delicate dusting, beds had to be changed twice a week.

And those yellowish stains behind the toilet bowl.

"You know—guys," she said, laughing nervously.

"Hmm—they're not always very—uh—careful."

She looked uneasy. "You know men—they—well—they have a tendency sometimes to— you know ..." And then she laughed like Snow White in the Disney movie. A crystalline, rippling, totally-out-of-place-in-a-toilet laugh. Everybody knows Snow White would never talk to her prince, her dwarves, or even to her maids about urine stains behind the toilet bowl. She would just have to laugh at this absurd possibility. Snow White didn't even own a toilet bowl. She didn't need one, she never peed or shit because those princes—"guys, you know"—they'd never go out of their way to look for her if they knew she experienced bowel movements.

"Now let's see the garage."

What? The garage? I had to clean up the garage? Next she was going to ask me to peel potatoes! I was fuming.

"In the corner there, potatoes. You see, in the brown bag? I buy them in large quantities. You know, for a bargain." She giggled.

"I would appreciate it if you could peel some potatoes and put them in cold water before you leave. Not today, of course. I mean when you're here to work. This way they'll be ready to fry for breakfast after the *satsang*."

Jude didn't seem to mind one bit that I'd be the one in charge of washing his underwear. He seemed amused that Fiona had managed to convince me. As their official cleaning lady, I saw a different view of the couple we so often admired for their spiritual harmony. I witnessed them snapping at each other for the most insignificant of reasons. Arguments and angry repartees far outnumbered agreements and affectionate nicknames.

In retrospect, I realize this was the beginning of their decline. Love was all but gone. Fear was what kept them together. Fear of God, really. At times, it seemed that their relationship was salvageable. She would put on a sexy dress or prepare a candlelit dinner. Or he would take her to the movies. Sometimes they stopped at the apartment for a cup of tea, holding hands and winking at each other affectionately. But disenchantment returned like so many harsh winters.

The problem was simple. They couldn't walk out on this relationship the way they had done before, whenever a love affair had turned sour. They were meant to share this incarnation together. It was God's will. They acknowledged the sacredness of their union the way Christians approach marriage vows. They had no choice but to endure their intertwined fates for eternity.

Jude and Fiona had every reason in the world to want to see this dark cloud roll by and get back to the love and caring they had once felt for each other. Otherwise life could become dangerously unbearable.

Chapter 49

*Listening to Jethro Tull singing about a girl
with strabismus*

IN FEBRUARY OF 1978, Fiona convinced Jude to open a
business, a legal one. A cover-up for their operations. She
had in mind a noble occupation, a project they could both
be proud of, something that would elevate their spirits and
glue them back together. At the apartment, we figured Fiona
finally had the good sense to set her heart on something more
realistic than having a child, which was surprisingly humble
of her considering she was letting Jude have the last word.

They set their minds on a New Age centre, a haven for the
city's truth seekers, a space large enough to accommodate
life-altering activities such as meditation, yoga, astrology
readings, and vegetarian cooking classes. Fiona planned to
devote a large space to a bookshop selling New Age literature of all kinds. Customers would be offered a wide variety
of books dealing with every mystical discipline known to
man from Buddhism to Sufism, Christianity to Paganism,
Numerology to Palmistry, Tarot to Jung, but advertising a
clear preference for the teachings of Holiji. Every discipline
would be welcomed on the shelves as long as it didn't preach

hate or violence. They talked about creating a meditation room, a place they would paint in a dark shade of purple and simply throw some cushions on the floor. In a corner painted sky blue, they could lay a table for therapeutic massages. And eventually, when the centre showed some profits, a restaurant, chic and strictly meatless, of course.

"A dining room for hip vegetarian stars visiting the city!"

Fiona was remarkably persuasive, and before long Jude was all for it. But he didn't think a restaurant was a good idea. "Too many losses with food."

Fiona pouted but agreed, just to keep him happy. But she stuck to her plan. "I'll do as I please as soon as the centre proves profitable," she said emphatically. She was not about to let him have the last word on everything.

The way Jude saw it, there were many advantages to this project. For one thing, Fiona would be off his back about starting a family, busier than with a child of her own. Also, the centre would make him look like a respectable entrepreneur. To top it all off, this kind of spiritual assistance to the Montreal population could only attract excellent karma to the both of them. Jude loved the tinkling sound of good karma, like a slot machine coughing quarters. He told Fiona to start looking for a place to rent. Nothing less than a three-floor building in a nice area of the city. Fiona was in heaven.

She found the perfect spot near Old Montreal on a large avenue mainly populated by fancy antique dealers and medical specialists of all kinds. Fiona took care of everything. She hired and fired, planned and sketched, ordered and negotiated. The renovations resulted in a lovely, serene, and subtly incensed space meant as a cover-up for a couple handling an illegal, if not immoral, business on the side.

The centre would be baptized Maya, a name that suited customers of all nationalities, as well as the city law stipulating that every outdoor sign had to be in French. The word *maya* was known to Francos and Anglos alike, and it was easy to remember. Fiona said she'd seen the name in a dream. "Clear as crystal!"

We didn't expect less. Maya means *illusion* in Sanskrit, India's ancient language, and also refers to a pre-Columbian advanced civilization. A word that evoked both intelligence and deception. It couldn't have been closer to reality.

Back at the apartment, we didn't give a damn about Maya. Milou's fate was still haunting us. Whenever we caught ourselves laughing out loud, Tintin's sad eyes put an end to it, like the accusing look of a betrayed mother.

Fiona and Jude needed help to run the centre's bookshop. After hours of deliberation, Jude suggested me as a potential candidate. Fiona hated the idea. I was an ex-girlfriend of his, and her logic dictated that while she could hire me to do menial jobs in her house, she didn't want to deal with me day in and day out as a permanent employee. Jude argued that I had some bookshop experience because I was working at La Librairie du Perroquet Vert, and neither of them knew shit about selling books. Also, I had been initiated, which meant I could be trusted blindly. Fiona didn't share his point of view. In fact, Jude was irritating the hell out of her with this stupid idea of his.

"We will hire strangers and only strangers for the centre," she ranted. "I thought we had agreed on that!" She could have strangled him. "Why do you always have to change your mind about everything, for God's sake?" she whined.

"I didn't change my mind. This is the first time we've ever discuss—"

"No, it's not! *You don't listen to me when I talk!*"

Jude asked her to stop acting like a child.

"Have it your way, dear," she said. She slammed the door on her way out, the feathers on her sleeves swarming like angry bees.

I got the job at Maya. To get even, Fiona told Jude she would also hire Leon, her ex-husband, who was still living on the West Coast at the time. She argued that Leon had once managed a small publishing house.

Jude was furious. "Your ex-husband? You have an ex-husband? I had no idea you'd ever been married!"

"And divorced, if I may add! Jude, really. Are you serious? I told you about Leon a long time ago. Everybody knows! The problem is *you never listen to me!*"

The subject was over, as far as she was concerned. But Jude ordered her to clarify the matter. She tried to walk away from him, but he grabbed her wrist. He wasn't really hurting her, but he said he would if she didn't help him refresh his memory.

"I was married to Leon when I was seventeen," she said, looking bored out of her wits. "I thought he was a talented sculptor at the time. Doesn't it ring a bell? Don't you remember me telling you all this? Our marriage fell apart less than a year later because Leon turned out to be a pagan at heart. He was drawn to witchcraft and Hermeticism. He became obsessed with Aleister Crowley. I told you all this months ago! That being said, Leon isn't a bad person. He's a pagan, not a witch."

She reminded him that neither of them understood shit about magic—white or black—tarot readings, or even astral projections. "Someone has to be knowledgeable enough to advise our customers, don't you think so?"

Jude was shocked. A pagan on the payroll?

"Save your breath on stuff about the forces of evil, Jude. Leon is a good person. He wasn't always into dark stuff. He used to follow the light, but he changed his mind along the way."

Jude threw an angry look at her. "Might as well say he's mentally deranged." Rather ironically, Jude couldn't stand the idea of this ex-husband in the proximity of a woman he was beginning to loathe most of the time.

Fiona didn't miss a beat. "You're right. I tend to be attracted to morons."

"Yeah, bitches usually are."

She served him a vicious smile. "Don't you worry, my dear. Leon can be trusted because, you see, he too was initiated by Sant Baba Ram Singh. The same day I was, actually."

Fiona justified her choice by using the same logic Jude had used on her to hire me. Jude was livid. He slapped her face with an open hand. She hit him back with a closed fist, and that was it. Leon was in, though Fiona had yet to find a way to coax the sculptor into getting on a bus to Montreal.

God knows I didn't know anything about paganism or witchcraft myself. Consequently, Leon would be a welcome addition to the staff. Jude protested some more, saying he didn't want dark forces spoiling his spiritual niche. Fiona laughed in his face.

"Is it that you're afraid of him, big guy?"

Jude shrugged and told her to fuck off.

I had never seen a pagan in flesh, at least not one I could have identified as such. They said these horned god worshippers were everywhere, all around us. Would Leon wear shoes or hooves?

Chapter 50

*Listening to Talking Heads singing about being too busy
to fool around*

BEFORE WE KNEW IT, Saturday Night Fever was raging.
We thought it would go out of fashion in no time, but it
didn't. It grew stronger. More than six months had passed since
the movie's release but in the spring of 1978, the soundtrack
was still on the charts.

An entire generation was painfully coming to grips with
the fact that the Beatles and the '60s had not changed the
world that much after all. Following a brief episode of initial
disgust, a lot of hippies couldn't keep their asses from swinging to the bouncing beat of disco music. There were few
regrets and no shame for the dreams left behind. The music
of the Bee Gees, Donna Summer, ABBA, and Barry White
ruled in bars and clubs. It was an era of white platform boots,
and hairdos that made girls look as if they had just walked
out of a dishwasher. They danced through the night, their
fake gold jewellery turning to diamonds under the disco ball.

The transformation took place almost overnight. Dancing
like John Travolta became the best way to get a girl and
spending lots of money on her, the best way to keep her.

Polyester suits, cigarette-thin ties, trimmed moustaches, and skimpy dresses bounced up and down on the floor of New York's Studio 54 while their Montreal counterparts did the same at the Limelight on Crescent Street. That snort of cocaine in the restroom enticed the reluctant ones to let go of their last hippie reservations.

Maya and the disco era brought another wind of change into our lives. That annoying, repetitive, boring, alienating, disco beat pounding on the walls of the city surely had something to do with it. *Bombadabombadabombadabom.* A herd of new faces looking for a gram of hash to smoke before hitting downtown's discos invaded the apartment. Curiosity won over wisdom and one evening, despite our morbid fear of disappointing Holiji and our profound loathing for the disco sounds, we joined Hugo for a drink at Friday's, Montreal's hottest spot at the time. It was still a thrill for me to be downtown, and despite the horrible music I had a ball. We met some nice people and danced whenever the music changed from bad to not so bad. I even considered returning to Friday's once in a while—possibly—but certainly not every week. Like going to the zoo—nobody goes to the zoo every week. At three in the morning, I thought we should call it a night and resume life where we had left it.

However, Grace, possessed by Lord knows what, went back to Friday's almost every weekend. Frankie tagged along, and soon after that it was Alex, *my* Alex, who was spending most of his Saturday nights downtown. I didn't care to follow them. Disco music, people shouting at each other over the noise, the alcohol, the peroxide hair, the polished nails—it just wasn't my scene.

Inevitably I heard that Alex was a big success at Friday's. Girls invited him to dance. They were charmed even when he said things that weren't mildly interesting, he would tell me the next day, almost bragging. This reformed hippie dressed in coordinated colours, groomed and after-shaved, realized he was a hit with the disco-girls breed. Girls who spent more than ten minutes putting their makeup on. Girls who didn't hesitate to wear pantyhose at all times, even under their jeans. They liked his funky eyes, his Greek ass, and his honest hands. It turned out Alex loved the attention. When I voiced my jealous concerns, he said he wasn't interested in girls in sexy dresses, his only wish was to spread Holiji's words. I told him that I didn't care, and that all I wanted was for him to stay home with me, the way it was before. He said we should always welcome changes in our daily routine. In fact, he added, I should go to Friday's with him and preach all I could. Grace certainly did, even though he suspected she was snorting cocaine whenever it was offered to her. She later admitted that cocaine helped her find the right words to talk about Holiji.

I didn't see the point of preaching in a disco bar. I told Alex so. We fought. I cried, I don't know for how many hours. Nevertheless, Alex went back to the club every weekend. I followed him on a few occasions, but I always ended up leaving early. Alone.

"He'll change," I reassured myself.

I was still too young to know that the three most stupid words uttered by women all over the world are these: *he will change.* They don't, and he didn't. He brought home people harpooned at the club and spent the rest of the night smoking joints and boring them to death with Holiji and the many miracles he had yet to witness for himself.

I was usually sleeping by the time Alex turned the key in the front door, but the commotion always woke me. I stayed in bed, pretending to sleep, Boogie by my side. It was easy to guess how many individuals were with Alex and, most importantly, if there were any girls in the lot. I always left the door slightly ajar and by positioning myself a certain way I could see the living room quite clearly. The narrow slit didn't allow me to see everything, but it was more than enough to make out the gender of everyone in the room. On some occasions, I joined the party, but I usually preferred to stay in bed. I had heard Alex's holy stories a million times. The same stories I had once heard from Jude.

One Friday night, Alex came back earlier than usual. I detected at least two people with him, including one girl. I heard the girl talk, but I couldn't see her clearly, only her profile. I understood she was with her boyfriend, so there was presumably no reason to be concerned. I tried to go back to sleep, but that girl's voice was riveting. I loved the way she laughed. From my bed, I could see her black hair. She reminded me a little of Isabelle Adjani, the new French actress I had seen in the movie *L'Histoire d'Adèle H.* White skin, dark hair, blue eyes, she looked as if she had come from Venus. *Too pretty for comfort*, I told myself. I got dressed and walked into the living room. That's how I met Linda. She was about to become my best friend in the world. My angel, really.

Yves, Linda's boyfriend, on the other hand, was a real asshole. This guy owed his cultural knowledge to bar conversations. His brain was the size of a soya bean. He was all wrong for her. She was sweet and low key. He was rude and vulgar. Nobody liked Yves. I guess Linda could feel that.

She came back to the apartment the next day, alone this time, and she kept coming back week after week. Always without Yves. Before long, she was part of the gang. Yves had vanished somewhere between two bar stools. She still saw him from time to time for sex—god knows why—but she never brought him back to our place. Of course, Hugo was attracted to her, but she wasn't interested, and she let him know right away. He was way too wild for Linda. This girl had a huge heart. She was generous with herself, with her time, with her attention. From that very first evening, I loved her as a sister. Today I realize she was the kind of best friend every girl should have.

It was a happy period for us all. That summer, we learned

Milou would be on his way home sooner than expected. Mrs. T, Milou's mom, called at the apartment to let us know that the Spanish prison was about to set him free a year early for good conduct. His release was scheduled for September. If Tintin had been a dog, that tail of his would have wagged nonstop.

Around that time, Alex's father offered Alex and me the opportunity to move into a small but lovely apartment in the east part of town. He had purchased the place as an investment and told Alex it was time we started living as a couple. He was right. Alex and I had grown into an old item by this time. We had worked so hard at being chaste that our sex life had become, well, limp, to say the least. I was hoping a little privacy and intimacy would rekindle the passion. Alex would have been a fool to refuse the offer since we were getting the place for free. It also happened to be a block away from a metro station, so I wouldn't have to travel much to get to work.

By then, Alex was done with his Saturday night escapades. He was having more fun hanging out with Linda and me, smoking dope and listening to the latest Steely Dan album, *Aja,* a record that remained permanently on the turntable that summer. Alex was changing, but for what? I wasn't exactly sure.

Hugo, on the other hand, had not altered his ways one bit. He would crawl into the apartment in the wee hours of the morning, regularly drunk, with Frankie and a couple of loud girls who didn't sound too sober themselves. Frankie made out in the living room while Hugo rode the waves of his waterbed. In the morning, the minute Alex and I were up, Frankie would borrow our room with his date. I hated that because it meant I had to change the sheets afterward, disgusted at the idea of sleeping in someone else's dried bodily fluids.

Frankie had been looking for a place to stay ever since his mother had kicked him out the month before. He would make a perfect roommate for Hugo. Alex and I needed peace to do our devotee stuff and Hugo needed space to live his disco bit. In other words, our lives were undeniably falling into separate worlds, and the three of us agreed it was time to split.

That was how one Saturday morning Alex and I, with the help of Hugo, Frankie, and Linda, found ourselves stacking our meagre possessions in a rental truck and moving to Alex's father's apartment. This move turned out to be beneficial for everyone, though of course it made each of us a little sad. We met with the gang here and there to party the way we used to—a period we already referred to as "the good old days"—but the majority of our free time was spent apart from them.

I began working at Maya. I was sad to leave Dominique and Charles at La Librairie du Perroquet Vert, but my karmic destiny was leading me closer to the words of Holiji in a bookshop devoted to the expansion of the soul. Alex was working for his aunt as a truck driver, and Linda was making good money as a waitress in a St. Denis Street bar. We became an inseparable trio (a quartet if you include Boogie). Linda was eager to receive initiation. She was saving money to go to India on her own to meet Holiji. That alone made her precious to me. I loved talking to her about Holiji—she made everything I said sound as pure as I meant it to be. Linda was a natural devotee. She had been nothing more than mildly happy up to that point in her life, and Holiji's message was helping her see the world through pink-tinted glasses.

One day she came over with the record of a new singer, Kate Bush. It was titled *The Kick Inside*. Linda said it was rumoured the woman was an ex-Playboy playmate. She already knew every song on the album by heart, and she loved every track, especially "The Man with the Child in His Eyes."

Linda was yearning for a good man and a baby. Her parents had perished in a car accident when she was six. She was an only child, just like her parents had been, and there were no folks to hang on to. Her destiny was therefore entrusted to a foster family and she was later adopted by a childless middle-aged couple. She didn't remember her biological parents much. By the time she was mature enough to realize what she had missed, it was too late. To her great distress, her early childhood rested like cold ashes in her memory. There was a photo album given to her after the funeral, but it didn't reveal much of her past. She remembered seeing her mother peel the thin plastic sheets to affix new snapshots into it. In one of the pictures, her father was all smiles, joking with her mom. That day, four pages had been neatly aligned with new photos. Four pages out of fifty. Linda could only assume that her mom and dad had planned to fill the other forty-six pages with many more happy moments. Fifty pages might not even have sufficed. Linda said these were her "good old days," even though her memory of them was nebulous.

There was another image, this one in Linda's mind. Her mom was braiding her daughter's thick mane. The little girl felt a teardrop falling on her forehead. Her mother was sobbing quietly, pulling a little too tightly on the braid. Linda asked her why she was sad.

"Oh, I'm not sad, pumpkin. Just a little melancholy. Don't worry, there's nothing to worry about."

Then she hugged Linda with all her might, and she didn't let go. To be able to get away, Linda told her she had homework to do, a lie she sorely regretted for years after the accident. Her eyes were wet when she told me about her parents. I held her hand.

"What if they never meant to stay with me?" she cried softly in a little girl's voice. "What if they thought dying together was better than being with me?"

"Linda, that's ridiculous. You said yourself that the photo album was proof of how happy you guys were together."

"You're right," she said, looking down. "But somehow I believed for a long time they meant to leave for good that day, but didn't want me to know. Like any child, I thought my parents were gods in the flesh, powerful and eternal. In my little head, they had abandoned me to go on by themselves without having me in the way. Because they died at the same time, I believed the accident was premeditated."

"But you know better now," I tried.

"*I* know, yes, but that little girl in me doesn't, and she never will." She sighed. "I'll tell you something, Geneviève. All I ask from life is to be able to relive that scene with my own daughter. And when she walks away the way I did that day, I want to tell her that I and her dad, who could only be the love of my life, will always be there for her. I want her to understand that I'll never leave her to fend for herself."

"But your parents didn't mean to leave you!"

"Of course not," she said as if she didn't want to offend me. "But just hearing it once must feel darn good to a child." She wiped her eyes with her palms and looked up, smiling. "I know I'm being silly. Sometimes I can't help but feel like a motherless child." She shrugged. "What about you, Geneviève?" she suddenly asked. "What are 'the good old days' for you?"

"Now, I suppose."

"Now? Why?"

"The way I see it, the good old days are nothing more than a period of your life when you seemed to have a lot of choices. Or when you had none and had to make do with what you had."

"Well, if that's true, my good old days are yet to come." Linda stretched her arms and hugged me tightly, sobbing a little more.

Though I already liked her very much, from that day on, I considered Linda as a sister. My twin. The nicer of the two.

Chapter 51

Listening to Blue Oyster Cult telling us to not be scared
of death

IT WAS SEPTEMBER OF 1978. Seven hundred and one nights had passed since Milou's imprisonment, and he was finally returning home.

At the time, Hugo was living with Frankie in their macho bachelor apartment on Jarry Street. Linda, whom Milou didn't know from Adam, and Alex and I spent our time mainly at home, at Alex's dad's place. Linda left us only when it was time to go sleep. She had just moved in a tiny studio close to the bar where she worked. For a short time, Grace's devotions simmered on the back burner while she spent all her free time downtown, making new friends at Friday's. Every once in a while, she would disappear for weeks at a time, but we still saw her at *satsang* on Sundays.

Milou didn't appreciate all these changes. He was angry at us for the excessive transformations we were imposing on him. If there was one place that had symbolized everything that was great about home and his past, it was the apartment. He wanted the place the way it used to be, with everybody there, a fat joint being passed around, food on the table, and loads of belly laughs. All the familiar things he had missed so much in his prison cell.

He tried to fit back into our lives like a swollen foot squeezing into a shoe after a long flight. Something you eventually manage to do but only with a certain amount of pain. Milou didn't want to feel pain anymore. He wanted to close his eyes and reopen them to find the world the way he had left it the night before he'd foolishly stepped aboard that flight to India.

He didn't want to discuss his prison time with us. Instead he talked about it to people he hardly knew. To us, he said he needed to forget about Spain, and he spent most of his time chewing his bitterness in a corner and asking us to leave him alone. Then later on, he would complain to outsiders that his friends had abandoned him.

Milou didn't fit into his old life any more than he fitted into his leather G-string. He couldn't shed the extra weight accumulated in Spain, and he didn't really try. Dieting was just another pain. He had no motivation whatsoever to be lean and fit again. He acted outrageously, as he used to, but he couldn't be *it* anymore. God knows he didn't look like *it* after his prison time. His career as a sex bomb never got back on track. With little enthusiasm, Milou attempted to approach his "art" from another angle by choreographing other strippers' performances. But that too proved to be useless. He couldn't put his finger on what was missing in the male strippers he was auditioning. According to his own glorified and distorted memory, not a single one of them exhibited the panache he himself had once displayed in front of an audience.

Tintin had changed a lot too. He had lived for three years out of Milou's dictatorship and had done surprisingly well for himself. For one thing, he had lost weight, and he had a steady girlfriend, a curvaceous girl from Shawinigan who was crazy about him. He also got a job as a sound man in a small theatre that produced the plays of Félix Leclerc, a poet, writer, and activist dear to French Canadians' hearts.

Now that he was having sex on a regular basis, Tintin's ambitions had blossomed. The last time he could remember getting that much skin was with a brown-haired girl when he was sixteen. But that had taken place a zillion years before, and he had slept alone courting his right wrist ever since. That is, until he met Monique. However, the girl from Shawinigan didn't appreciate the way Milou behaved with Tintin. And of course, with a girlfriend between them, things could never be the same again. This was sad because Milou and Tintin's friendship had been far greater than the simple sum of its parts.

Milou became moody, something that made him lose things and friends but, quite unfortunately for him, nothing from his waistline. He even managed to lose Tintin's friendship. Tintin had offered him an expensive watch as a welcome-home gift. To My Buddy was engraved on the back. Milou had had every intention of cherishing that present for the rest of his life, but in a fit of rage he threw the timepiece in the St. Lawrence River. That night, Tintin walked out on him. It was a stupid argument, one where Milou was a hundred percent wrong. Tintin could stomach quite a lot of shit from his best friend, but he couldn't allow Milou to despise him. Milou had always treated him like a pet, which was no longer acceptable to the grown-up man he had become in latter years. Of course, Milou never meant to do any harm, he had never hurt Tintin's feelings on purpose. But Tintin was not the same anymore. He was an adult now and no longer a groupie devoted to Milou.

That night though, by the river in Old Montreal, Milou had laughed at him with disdain and pity when Tintin tried to explain how he felt about Monique and his new life. Tintin was too hurt to understand Milou's acute need to put everyone and everything down. They both had changed so much. When Tintin told him he didn't appreciate that attitude, Milou took the watch from his wrist and threw it in the water. It was so unlike Milou to act this way and even more unlike Tintin to walk away from his best friend. Maybe Milou believed that by overpowering and disgracing others he could somehow elevate his own self-esteem from the Spanish abyss where it seemed to have been irretrievably lost. Milou's soul was drowning, and when Tintin proved willing to dive in to help him get back on track, Milou ended up choking him to death in a frenetic attempt to stay afloat. A reckless, desperate reaction to keep his head out of the water. Nothing more than a lousy reflex.

Tintin-less and spiteful, Milou stumbled under his heavy weight, two hundred and fifty pounds of lost dreams circulating beneath his skin. Like a shit magnet, he mixed with people who took advantage of him. Before we knew it, he was shooting heroin. Jude made it his personal crusade to save Milou, but his assistance wasn't required. Milou was in tears when he told Jude Holiji couldn't do much for him at this point. For two years, day after boring day, night after sleepless night, he had analyzed the subject of his spiritual faith, an exercise that had left him frustrated and without the shadow of a conclusion. He was angry. He knew exactly what he was doing when he began shooting smack. He needed to indulge himself silly. He swore he would stop soon enough. And he did.

One evening, while enjoying a perfect freebase trip with two complete strangers in the house of someone he knew even less, Milou came to the realization that he was done with the junkie scene. He felt ready for withdrawal, a feat he achieved with no sweat, literally and figuratively speaking.

He came back to Holiji and the *satsangs*. He told Tintin how sorry he was, but nothing was ever the same between the two. Milou was nevertheless happy to report that the junkie experience hadn't been a complete waste of time.

"Now I know precisely how I want to die," he'd say. "A heroin overdose. No doubt about it, man. You slide, you glide, until you never want to come back. Nirvana's got to be somewhere in that syringe."

I wonder what makes people say things like that. Who has ever come back from an overdose to tell the world how wonderful it was?

Chapter 52

*Listening to Stevie Wonder warning us against
old wives' tales*

THE RENOVATIONS TO THE building where the centre
would open seemed to take forever. Though Fiona had
hoped to open Maya earlier that year in May, it took until July
for the workers to be finished. By October, Leon still hadn't
been hired, and I was alone minding the centre's bookshop.
I complained to Fiona, who was having trouble getting hold
of Leon. She told me to hang in there because she had no
intention of hiring someone else. Jude couldn't have cared
less about the overload of work dumped on me—he would
rather see me exhausted than deal with Fiona's ex-husband.

Between wrestling matches, Jude and Fiona managed
Maya. Their office in the back room on the second floor was
soundproofed to muffle the noise of their daily discord. After
a round, they'd come out of the room and approach their
clientele with blissful smiles. Perhaps the customers wondered why they felt so odd whenever Fiona or Jude sneaked
up behind them, eager to discuss Holiji's philosophy. They
probably thought it was the high level of spirituality resonating within the centre's walls that played tricks on their

minds. The fact that they were among dope dealers prone to domestic violence wouldn't have crossed their truth-seeking minds.

An old friend of Fiona's told her that her former husband was dealing grass in Vancouver to repay the heavy debts acquired after yet another disastrous exposition of his work. Apparently, the unknown art studio located far away from the city centre had failed to bring the clientele Leon was so desperately counting on. As a result, he was crippled with debts and had no choice but to accept a clerk job in an Inuit art boutique while dealing dope on the side. Luckily, the friend also knew where to reach Leon. Fiona sighed with relief.

The stars were perfectly aligned to contact him. After she reached him, to my great surprise, Fiona took me aside and confided some details about Leon and their relationship in Vancouver. She probably did this only because she feared I might look at her differently after meeting Leon. Jude wouldn't have much to do with him, but I would, and I'd get to know him far better than Fiona might be comfortable with.

"Leon. Really. I don't know what was boiling in my head the day I agreed to marry him," she told me.

She recalled being moved by the nude sketches of her he proudly sprawled on the floor the first morning she'd woken up in his bed. Leon had captured the essence of her beauty, of her strength. He was well read and intensely cultivated. The kind of guy who knows George Sand's real name and can vulgarize the genius behind Rodin's masterpieces. As a wedding gift, he had made a pint-sized sculpture of Fiona in a dancing skirt with her hair in a bun, her arms reaching for the sky. She had wept with joy the morning she found it on her pillow.

But to her great dismay, she soon discovered that the man she had promised to love forever was nothing more than an incorrigible loser. To top it off, he didn't shave, he wore dirty clothes, and his breath smelled like a sewer. "Too bad, really, because he was handsome enough," she said.

He was missing a big toe, which made him lose balance at times. Fiona told me he had lost it during a pagan festival. I didn't ask how. I wondered if Satan himself hadn't snatched the smelly thing to wear it as a protective amulet around his neck, the way Romanians keep garlic cloves in their pockets to keep vampires at bay.

Besides working at the centre, Leon would surely be willing to sell a little dope for her in Montreal. Fiona figured Jude might like that. She could not consider sending Leon on a run because her ex suffered from pteromerhanophobia. In layman's terms, he was terrified of flying. On the long-distance call to Vancouver, Fiona promised loads of hashish and a good salary if he accepted her offer and came to work at the centre's bookshop for a while. Leon was rather easy to persuade. That same day he got himself a bus ticket heading east.

"You better tell the truth, Fiona. I'm in no mood for one more failure in my life. I could get pretty vicious this time around."

Fiona knew Leon was threatening her with his magical powers. Since she had no belief whatsoever in the superiority of pagan deities over Holiji, she smiled with contempt. "Of course I'm telling the truth, Leon. I would never dare to anger you." She had to focus not to laugh aloud.

"All right, then. See you in a few days."

"Go fuck yourself, Leon," I heard Fiona muttered after hanging up.

The next morning, Leon cycled to the art gallery as he usually did and carried on with his duties. At the end of the day, he informed his Inupiat employer that he had to leave for Montreal at once because of a "very serious personal problem." He said the trouble he faced was so "viciously peculiar" that he didn't think he'd ever be able to come back to Vancouver. Leon looked so uneasy, his boss assumed the French Canadian might be dying of some awful disease. He told Leon not to hesitate to give him a call if he ever needed anything. Later that evening, Leon convinced four other leftover East Coasters to hop on the Montreal bus with him. It was a West Coast thing to travel with a crowd of friends.

Fiona didn't mention a word about Leon's arrival to Jude. She wanted to see her ex-husband face to face before introducing him to her boyfriend. Luckily for her, a bad argument the week before allowed her to ignore Jude. They had been invited to a party in a Westmount mansion owned by a Colombian cocaine dealer, a man Jude wanted no problems with. Fiona got drunk and danced with a hairy Latino who held her the way an octopus would handle a hot potato, his hands all over her. On their way home, Jude gave Fiona loads of shit for humiliating him in front of a crowd.

They were still fighting when long after midnight, while she stood by the bathroom sink washing her face, Jude hit her on the shoulder with her favourite Indonesian candle-holder. The fragile souvenir exploded in a million pieces, and Fiona was left alone to clean up the mess. She even said she was sorry. The shattered bits of broken glass looked familiar, almost normal. They fought so much nowadays that she didn't know who was to blame anymore, and she didn't care to find out. She would find a way to make him pay for all this shit. Then again, maybe not. After all, what good would it do? This was their spiritual lot. God had united them, and she thought resignedly that they had to find a way to work things out.

They slapped each other even when there were no reasons to fight, if only because the ceasefire made them both edgy. Fiona concealed her bruises with skin-coloured powder and avoided Jude's mother for a few days with the easy excuse of being too busy. She didn't count the blue and black spots on her body anymore. Her heart was hardening like a piece of frozen meat. Jude didn't ignite her spark as he used to, and though she acted as if he did every now and then, the only thrill she felt in his presence was the nervous expectation of his hand aiming at her face. That and the sweet anticipation of hitting him back.

When Leon showed up at the center, Fiona rushed downstairs to meet him. After speaking with him for a little while, she took him to the office and introduced him to Jude. Jude was taken by surprise. He was very polite, even friendly. Leon was in. In a matter of days, Jude realized Leon was no threat to him and he did a great job at the bookshop.

Fiona and Jude travelled to New York, Mexico, and Europe for professional and spiritual reasons while Leon and I managed the centre. I got along rather well with Leon. I have to admit that at the beginning he scared the shit out of me—I mean this pagan thing. Devils and black magic. I had reasons to be on my guard.

Early one morning, a sugar-fuelled child was running through the aisles of the bookshop, screaming like a banshee. His mother, conveniently deaf at the time, let the boy do whatever he pleased, and the kid did everything he could to annoy customers. Leon was trying to concentrate on a pile of inventory cards. I could tell he was irritated by the boy's high-pitched voice. He glanced angrily at the child many times. A spoiled brat with a spoiled mother. Exasperated, Leon walked toward the deserted aisle, where the boy was pulling books off the shelves just to drop them on the floor. Leon stared at him. I thought he was bracing himself to get the mother to mind her little monster, but he didn't even look at her. He stayed there, gazing at the boy. Within a minute, the child ran out of the store and threw himself in front of a car. The driver braked in time, but it was a close call. The mother snapped out of her lethargy and rushed out to her son, who was hysterical by then. She hailed a cab and disappeared in the downtown traffic, her moronic offspring clutching at her breast. The other customers gathered around the front door. My eyes met Leon's. His wicked grin sent a shiver down my spine.

For a long time after that day, I was terrified of him. I never contradicted Leon. I let him choose his work schedule first and asked if he wanted tea every time I fixed myself a cup, even though he always declined my offer. However, with time, I got to know him better, and I realized he was no Lucifer.

I took it upon myself to read as many books as I could on paganism, witchcraft, and devil worshippers. I learned how stupid it was for people to be scared. It was so childish, really. The good witches, like Leon, won't bother you unless you really get on their nerves. The bad ones, well, they can only frighten you if you give them the power to do so. The more afraid you are, the more power you pass on to them. They feed on fear. When you look at it this way, it's almost a sin to be scared of black witches. Of course, a gifted witch could scare the dickens out of you by making furniture float around or by speaking Latin with a Darth Vader voice. They can also freeze your breath and skin black cats alive on a full moon night. However, besides these gross demonstrations, they can't do much harm. I concluded that the ultimate weapon against bad witches is to be aware of their spiritual inferiority. You won't find a crowd of people with a higher level of self-loathing than a coven of so-called black witches. A legion of losers who like to think they could control the world if they only wanted to. I wasn't scared of devils any more. *The Exorcist* no longer scared me. I finally understood what the trick was: there's simply no devil out there. Mind you, to this day I still hate *Tubular Bells*.

Pimpled teenaged boys came to Maya asking for *The Satanic Bible,* a sordid book, almost comical in its juvenile stupidity. They crept to the counter then defiantly demanded the "black bible" as if the very mention of the title would make the rest of the world run away and take cover. Why did they need that book, we'd ask? One boy explained that he was fed up with his parents. He wished them dead, and he wanted it to look like an accident. Preferably, before the weekend.

"I'm invited to a party on Saturday," he said sullenly, "and I'm grounded."

Leon and I looked at each other, shook our heads in disbelief, and told the boy to take a hike.

Leon was a great help. Whenever he heard me struggle to answer questions about a book I didn't know much about, he approached me, subtly offering his wisdom. He always made me look smart in front of customers by putting clever words in my mouth that I had never uttered. He never let me lift a heavy box full of books. I began to really appreciate him. In fact, in time, he would become much more than simply a coworker to me.

Chapter 53

Listening to Cat Stevens wondering where he could find children having fun

"Your birthday is near. I thought this would be a great opportunity to show you New York. I'll take you shopping! You'll love it."

I looked around. Who was Fiona talking to? I went back to my tea and my *Yoga Journal.*

"Hey, what do you say?"

"You're talking to me?" I tried not to sound like De Niro.

"Of course. Who else is here?"

I looked around again. She was right. Only Fab Fiona and me. "Why me?"

"Silly you! Because I like you—that's why. So what do you say?"

I smiled. "Wow, Fiona. That's quite an offer. Are you sure?"

"Of course, I'm sure," she giggled.

I smiled a little more. God knows she was the last person I would have chosen to go to New York with, but hey, when life offers you something nice it's rude to spit on it. I suspected she had an ulterior motive, but I couldn't refuse the invitation because I was about to turn twenty-two and I had never done anything in my life as half as "rich" as boarding an Air Canada plane and jetting to the Big Apple. I had never slept in an expensive hotel or shopped at Bloomingdale's. I had never set foot in Central Park. And it was almost Christmas—New York would be humming with festivities.

"All expenses paid, dear!"

My ears rang with Fiona's giggles. I was pleased, but I knew damn well there was something I would have to do to earn this.

Of course there was something. Fiona was planning to bring some money to New York, and she didn't want to take the risk all by herself. The dough was to be delivered to one of her new American runners who lived in Soho. I didn't mind. In those days, it was ridiculously easy to smuggle money. No customs agent would have dreamed of bothering two nice Canadian girls on their way to a shopping spree down Fifth Avenue, not unless they showed up with syringes stuck in their arms. So Fiona and I carried seventy thousand American dollars taped all over our bodies, thirty-five thousand each (I counted the piles myself), and we boarded the Air Canada plane heading for La Guardia on a cloudy, windy day in late 1978.

Upon arrival, we rushed to the hotel. Fiona placed the bills evenly in a large brown envelope. She shoved it in her huge Gucci handbag, and we left for Soho. Once in the taxi, she changed her mind. We would go to Soho later on. She ordered the driver to head for Manhattan.

"Why waste a minute of shopping?" she said with a lilting Fiona giggle.

Saks, Tiffany, Fiorucci—the neon lights spelled store names I had seen only in movies. Fiona paid for the cab and called her runner from a phone booth to let him know we would be at his place around 9:00 p.m.

At Bloomingdale's, I fell in love with a long navy-blue winter coat with a topstitched belt. Fiona said I should try it on. It was stunning, making me look like a stewardess from a Scandinavian airline. Made of luxurious Scottish wool, it was the most sumptuous piece of clothing I had ever slipped on. The straight cut made me look tall. Of course, it was far beyond my financial reach. Fiona said she wanted to offer it to me. I refused categorically, but she insisted. She really seemed to mean it, and I really loved the coat, so I capitulated. She pecked my cheek with a kiss. I couldn't find the right words to express my gratitude. I would have never suspected she could be that nice to me, the untalented initiate she hadn't even wanted in her bookstore. This was so unusual of her, though, that as much as I didn't want to be, I was once again suspicious. There were currencies of every nature in Fiona's world, and I suspected I would also have to pay for that coat sometime in one way or another.

In the linen department, I bought a couple of blue and pink striped towels that I never intended to use because the stickers on them said Made in France. I bought them as a decoration statement for my bathroom, to show my good taste. By that point in our shopping spree, my thirst for spending was quenched to a high level of satisfaction, and I had no desire for more. But Fiona's shopping mood was just kicking in. She spent the next hour and a half trying on dresses, lingerie, jeans, suits, sweaters, and every size-6 item her freckled hands could grab from the most expensive counters. I sat there in my new coat, trying to appear cheerful though I was getting bored. Fiona left her handbag with me, winking knowingly to remind me what was in it. She emerged a hundred times from the fitting room asking if she looked "okay," "fat," or "cheap." I wisely replied "beautiful," "thin," and "classy."

It was well past seven when she finally collapsed under her shopping bags. She said she was starving, and so was I. She hailed a cab and asked the driver to take us to the Village, saying she knew an excellent vegetarian restaurant over there.

"Excellent food, homey atmosphere, and fast service," she listed as if I had asked her to justify her choice.

It began to rain, and we had to run from the cab to the restaurant's door. The place was a typical wholesome food restaurant of that era with wooden floors, an open kitchen smelling of seven-grain bread, and stir-fried vegetables you could only assume were organic. The walls were covered with pictures of Sri Chinmoy and Satchidananda, indicating the owners' predilection for gurus.

Without asking what I wished to eat, Fiona ordered a plate of fresh veggies in tamari sauce and a couple of tofu dishes. That was fine by me, but I would have favoured the black bean enchilada. Never mind that. Fiona looked happier than I had seen her in months. She seemed delighted to spend some time with her favourite slave. And the truth was, I was so happy to be in New York that I kept buttering her up and down with cheesy praise. Two girls, a tall black one and an obese white one, sat at a table meant for six behind Fiona. They were sharing an enormous piece of cake and a pot of steaming liquid. Their heads swivelled toward our table every time Fiona giggled aloud. I was sure she annoyed them.

After we were done with the veggies and the tofu, we ordered dessert. Apple crisp for me (which I was allowed to order for myself) and crème brûlée for Fiona. The American girls stood and left swiftly. Either they had forgotten an important appointment, or they couldn't stand Fiona's giggles anymore. With much difficulty, the fat one squeezed out from behind Fiona's chair, excusing herself repeatedly. They hurried to the door and disappeared into the night. By the time we had swallowed the last mouthful of peppermint tea, it was past nine. Fiona asked for the bill impatiently, and I headed for the washroom.

When I came back five minutes later, Fiona was frantic, running back and forth from the front door to the table. The restaurant staff was gathered around her. Even the cook was there. It turned out that the fat girl who had pleaded with Fiona not to move an inch to ease her way out had taken the liberty of snatching my boss's handbag from where It hung on the back of her chair at the same time. Major bummer. Seventy thousand American dollars gone up in smoke. *Ouch.* Fiona looked like she was about to pass out. None of the staff recalled ever having seen the two girls before.

Someone called the police, and before we knew it two cops walked in. The moment they laid eyes on the victim, they melted. All of a sudden, Fiona spoke English with a vaguely French accent. She reported the robbery, declaring to have had a little more than a thousand bucks in her lost wallet.

The younger police officer was shocked. "How come a smart girl like you walks around in New York City with a thousand dollars cash in her purse?"

"Canadian dollars, Officer." She didn't want to look *that* dumb.

"Oh—I see," he said, as if this were a sound explanation.

Then Fiona turned pale and asked to sit down.

"What's wrong, madam? Are you okay?"

"My passport and our plane tickets were in it too. Not to mention that this was a very expensive handbag." Then she sobbed a little, just enough to alarm her knights in uniform.

The older one said, "Don't worry, ma'am."

The younger officer cleared his throat. "We'll take care of everything. Now if you'd be nice enough to come with us to the station, we'll take a description of the suspects and with a little luck, we might find your bag—"

A ray of hope—or fear—passed through Fiona's eyes.

"—empty, of course, but if you say it was such a pretty bag, it will be worth getting it back."

She cried louder. She didn't care for the purse. Losing the seventy thousand bucks owed to a runner, now that would bring tears to anyone's eyes.

Chapter 54

*Listening to Eric Clapton whining about
George Harrison's girlfriend*

OWN AT THE POLICE station, I was mostly ignored. I was the dwarf sitting next to Snow White.

Fiona was presented with coffee, tea, hot chocolate, Smarties, *and* donuts. A young rookie even offered her half of his egg sandwich. She refused everything, a reaction none of the policemen anticipated in their haste to see her up close. They stood there in front of her, grinning like the morons that they were. Then they turned to me—I'm sure they were praying God I didn't want anything.

Whenever a cop came by and bent over to ask how he could possibly make our "stay" more comfortable, Fiona smiled shyly. Like a damsel in distress. Or she giggled—a sound I was definitely growing to loathe. She seemed innocent and a little shaken, the way any honest lady would be in a similar predicament and not totally freaked out as I suspected she really felt.

The place was buzzing with action. Weird-looking characters, undercover agents, tobacco-stained greenish walls, and a lot of swearing. It seemed someone like Kojak or Mannix would appear any second from one of the offices in the back and gallantly offer his help to Fiona, who would certainly giggle some more. But I wasn't in front of the TV with Alex and Linda. No, this was real. I was an extra in a surrealist B movie and hell, was I nervous. *If they ask me anything, I'll tell the truth—skipping the part about the money and the runner, of course.* We'd come to New York to celebrate my birthday. A girl weekend. A slave/master weekend. *Most white Americans ought to relate to this,* I figured, *police officer or not.*

I suddenly wondered about the runner waiting for us. He'd surely be getting angry. Or worse, maybe he would panic and assume Fiona had played a number on him. I didn't know whether the man she called Bob was a devotee, an old acquaintance, or just a passing runner. Come to think of it, I had not asked one single question concerning this Bob of hers who, after all, was the reason why we were in New York in the first place.

I stared at Fiona, waiting for her to give me a sign, but she wouldn't meet my eye, apparently concentrating on her composure. How could she remain so normal? I knew Jude would never let her hear the end of this one. He wouldn't be sorry for her. He would scream, he would punch, he would slam doors, he would break a couple of her favourite things. He was as much part of the problem as the seventy thousand American dollars stolen from her. Jude would be merciless. Fiona probably felt safer in a New York police station surrounded by cops and narcs than in front of her boyfriend. Nobody could bother her there. Not Jude, not Bob, not the RCMP, nobody. Like being in a spa when you know there's a heavy storm raging on the other side of the revolving door.

A detective finally came over and pulled us from our respective reveries. This detective was not bald like Kojak or slick like Mannix—he was hairy and old and out of shape enough to wear a belt *and* suspenders. He was a serious man, apparently in control of his male hormones, a true professional, at first sight anyway.

"Do you need to call somebody?" he asked Fiona in a kindly tone.

"Oh yes, please."

Really? Not Jude, surely? Who else, princess? Jude's mother?

Fiona stood, graciously refusing the assistance of the many hands reaching to help her. She turned back and opened her eyes wide, as if she had just discovered my presence by her side. With a subtly imperious air, she motioned with her head for me to follow her. I obeyed.

On our way to the detective's office, Fiona said she expected him to settle "this unfortunate matter" rapidly, as if the man had been commissioned by President Carter himself to fix her nightmare. He introduced himself as Sergeant Hirsh. She offered him a limp hand.

"With all this," Fiona said, gesturing and looking around, "I completely forgot that a friend is expecting us for a drink tonight."

The man invited us to step in his office. He mumbled something about promising to do everything in his power to get us nice girls on our way as fast as possible. I seriously wondered if Fiona had gone mad. Was she planning to call her runner from the police station?

The detective said she could phone home if she wished, adding that if she kept it short, they wouldn't charge her a thing for the long-distance call. This was a man who prided himself on his ability to adapt to whatever professional challenge life threw his way. Sergeant Hirsh turned to me, asking if I had also been robbed. Pointing to my purse, I told him I still had all my personal belongings in my possession, including a small amount of cash and my passport. I was still carrying all the shopping bags, Fiona's and mine. He didn't offer an opportunity for *me* to call home.

Turning back to Fiona, he suggested she should contact the Canadian embassy for her passport and Air Canada for the stolen tickets. Then he said she could also call a family member. Or her husband. Or boyfriend. She displayed a slight expression of distress, and it didn't take anything more for the serious, compassionate Sergeant Hirsh to find himself answering to his groin's sudden request to run to this fair damsel's rescue. He proudly offered to "sacrifice" his coffee break to place the calls himself.

"It might hasten things, you never know."

Fiona's charm, whatever I thought of it, was a miracle worker because at that very moment, Sergeant Hirsh was trying to put together the sexiest version of himself, a desire that seemed to be an excruciating exercise for his flabby belly muscles.

Fiona gave him a lavish smile full of sparkling teeth. "Thank you, Officer, you're very kind."

She pulled her chair a little closer. "In fact, everyone here is quite pleasant. Real gentlemen. Not exactly something one would expect from the almighty NYPD." She giggled. "You see, Officer Hirsh—" She paused. "—may I call you Officer? Or mayn't I?"

She said this last bit with a British accent, her lips forming a slight pout around that baroness mouth of hers. She didn't wait for the detective to protest or agree. The overweight sergeant sat there, bewitched or incredulous, I couldn't tell for sure. Fiona went on.

"My husband is in Europe on a business trip, and it's impossible for me to reach him at the moment," she said, quite serenely. "To tell you the truth, I'm almost grateful. How helpless he would feel, the dear man. It would only make matters worse, and there's nothing he can do for me now anyway. I'll tell him all about it when he gets back home and not a minute earlier."

Sergeant Hirsh couldn't have agreed more. Just by looking at him I could tell that if only he'd been lucky enough to marry a woman like Fiona, he too would have gone ape shit if he found out she had been abused in any way. Fiona rested her elbows on his desk, her gaze above the situation at hand, her glossy red locks spilling on the desk, her left nipple inches from Sergeant Hirsh's favourite pen. The man was all ears.

"And come to think of it," she added, "I won't call home either. It would alarm my family senselessly." She lowered her eyes, digging for inspiration, but the detective thought she was about to cry. She shook her head at the tissue he handed to her.

"You see, my parents are old. My only brother, a biologist, is on a mission in a dangerous part of South Africa. My mom and dad have enough worries as it is." She massaged her neck.

I'd ache too if I was bullshitting that much in the course of five minutes.

"Therefore, Mr. Hirsh," she purred, "there's only one thing I need to do, and I need to do it immediately."

I don't know about the sergeant, but I figured she was about to ask for the lady's room.

"It's imperative that I call my friend at this very moment," she went on. "He must be worried sick by now."

She glanced at her watch. It was eleven thirty. "Please, Officer, could you kindly lead me to a phone? By the way, you didn't answer me. *May* or *mayn't* I call you Officer, Mr. Hirsh?"

Sure. She could call him Officer or *mon adjudant* if it tickled her fancy. The detective didn't seem to care one way or the other as long as the title comforted her. Sergeant Hirsh now appeared ready to assist Fiona in something, make that anything.

"If you wish, I can also call your friend for you."

Man, was he ever proud of himself!

The offer took Fiona by surprise. "No, thank you. You're too kind. I can do it. It will only take a minute, really. I'll manage, but thank you very much for the offer. If I ever need help to sort this thing out, back in Canada, I mean, you'll be the first one I'll call, Officer Hirsh."

Sergeant Hirsh didn't feel quite ready to walk out on her and relinquish this perfect opportunity to have every cop in the department come to *him* to learn the juicy details about the redheaded Canadian beauty (and who knew, someone might even ask about her sidekick dwarf). Sergeant Hirsh's hands disappeared for a minute under the thick pile of files covering his ridiculously cluttered desk. His face brightened as he reeled in his phone.

"This once, I'll make an exception. You can use mine if you want. Unless you need privacy, of course."

"No, thank you, sir. You're very kind."

Sergeant Hirsh checked the phone for a tone, pressed a few buttons, and listened again before handing it to Fiona. She grabbed it nonchalantly, displaying no more or less emotion than was appropriate for the situation. She dialled a number she apparently knew by heart.

"Hello, Bob. Fiona. I have—well, I *had*—a big problem."

I couldn't help it—I started shivering.

"Well, I'm at the police station," she sighed.

She pushed the phone to her ear in case Bob started yelling at her. According to her expression, Bob was calm.

"No, nothing of the sort," she said. "You see, I was in a restaurant having dinner with my employee—"

Sergeant Hirsh raised his head to take a look at me. I was relegated to the level of employee, a word Fiona favoured among all to attribute to me.

"Well, dear, it turned out that some girl stole my purse—yeah, quite unfortunate—no, no, thank heaven, there was no violence. She snatched it—no, of course, I didn't see a thing—on my chair—yeah—no— actually no—from behind, dear."

Sergeant Hirsh moved a tad on his chair. The words "from behind, dear" coming from Fiona's mouth were apparently tampering with his concentration.

"Yeah, with my passport—both our plane tickets and all

my money."

A faint emphasis was placed on *all*, detectable by me but not the sergeant, who seemed to be concentrating on a document in front of him. Fiona went on with a lot of *hmmms* followed by a concerned "of course." The detective was sorting loose pages of paperwork, watching Fiona's crossed legs every second page he flipped. Fiona either didn't notice or she didn't mind, accustomed as she was to men doing exactly that when they were confronted with her tantalizing presence. Bob was surely a cool guy because she was done with him in no time.

"You too, darling—yeah, don't worry. I'll call you soon. Bye bye, now."

I was asked to give a description of the two girls at the restaurant. It turned out to be a total waste of time. I was so overwhelmed by the whole experience that I remembered little and nothing in particular.

The embassy supplied a temporary passport to Fiona, and Air Canada agreed to take us home the next day. All thanks to Sergeant Hirsh. I still had my coat and my towels made in France. Fiona had all her shopping bags. It wasn't that bad—not for me anyway. The way I saw it, Fiona and Jude made enough money to be able to brush off a seventy-thousand-dollar loss. Jude would be livid, however—that part was unavoidable.

How terribly uneasy Fiona must have felt with me there, the sole witness of her carelessness! Really, wasn't it a bit stupid of her to hang her handbag on the back of her chair where it was vulnerable to any preying hands? Jude would spend days on her case—unless she could come up with a better explanation for her mistake. Like being mugged in Central Park, for instance. The problem was, with me there, she had to tell the truth and nothing but the truth. No doubt she was considering abandoning me in a dark alley somewhere in Harlem. Holiji's favourite girl couldn't ask *me* to lie for her. Mind you, I might have considered playing along just to preserve my status of irreplaceable servant. But I didn't have the occasion to prove myself because Fiona didn't make any attempt to bribe me. She preferred to keep her almost-intact reputation of the perfect initiated devotee. A gifted initiate like Fiona couldn't possibly ask an ungifted initiate like me to make stories up just to save her ass. Her hands were tied by her own self-made halo. And no, I didn't offer to help. I had what I deserved for the service rendered, she had what she deserved for her carelessness. Karma indeed. She called Jude from the hotel and told him we would be coming back earlier than planned, but she didn't explain why.

He was waiting for us at the gate. He seemed delighted to see her. He hugged her with affection, saying he was sorry for the way he had handled himself on the night of the infamous party in Westmount. He wasn't sorry for long.

From the back seat of the Mercedes, I watched Jude's face whitening progressively as he listened to Fiona's account of the incident. He looked at me in the rear-view mirror, trying to detect in my eyes whether Fiona was lying. I had nothing to hide, and he had to get his attention back on the road if he didn't want to add one more calamity to my birthday festivities.

The next day, Fiona didn't show up at Maya. She called in sick and asked me to bring the accounting ledger to their place. When she opened the door, she had not one but two shiners. She said it was nothing. "Thank God nothing's broken! Thanks to Holiji!" she added, joining her hands in a prayer.

She said Jude had dispatched one of his contacts in New York to bring the money to Bob. She added he was terribly angry at her. She was a sorry mess, no makeup, her hair all frizzy, her cheeks blotchy and shiny with dried tears. She offered me some tea, saying she needed someone to talk to, but I found a pretext to be on my way. Jude was scum, something I wouldn't have been able to deny, but the way I saw it, they deserved each other.

On my way back to Maya, I remembered seeing Jude limp a little that morning. Fiona had probably kicked him hard. They fed on each other, they loved to hurt each other. I couldn't help her, and I wasn't sure that I cared to. My heart couldn't make up its mind about Fiona. Somehow seeing her miserable always made me feel better about myself.

Two days later, Jude came to work with his left arm in a sling tied around his neck. He said—but I didn't buy it for a second—that he had fallen down a ladder at home.

"Nothing to worry about. Thank God it's not broken!"

Chapter 55

*Listening to the Who asking us to gather before time
runs out*

THAT SUMMER, WE WERE all invited to join Jude and Fiona in California. A place called Laguna Beach. Camille, Claude, Grace, Frankie, and Milou went for three weeks. Hugo's boss allowed him six weeks off. Linda, Alex, and I, the luckiest, could stay in California for the whole summer. Linda and Alex had ditched their jobs, figuring it would be easy for them to find work in Montreal in the fall. Alex's aunt said she couldn't afford to spend the whole summer short of a driver. If he left, she told him, he would have to find another job upon his return. Alex took his chances. I too was in no rush. Maya was about to close for two months to undergo some major repairs. The decrepit plumbing was to blame. The third and second floors had been particularly affected, and Jude and Fiona wanted to avoid a disastrous flood. The repairs would be costly, not to mention the business losses with the store closed for eight weeks. Implacable as always, Fiona announced she would take advantage of the situation to change a thing here and there to make the place even more profitable.

One by one, we left for LA with a free ticket and a few piles of American one-hundred-dollar bills hidden strategically beneath our clothes, a small price to pay for a summer of fun. Among all of us, with the exception of Milou, who understandably didn't want to take any chances, we carried over half a million American dollars strapped to our thighs and backs. I didn't mind repeating the experience. All my friends were willing to do it, and since nothing that bad had happened to me in New York, I didn't raise an objection. Jude and Fiona left earlier and drove the Mercedes from Montreal to LA. They wanted to make a few stops along the way and bring their wisdom to devotees, potential runners, and drug dealers alike. None of us had any idea what that money was precisely for. Of course, Jude and Fiona always paid cash for everything, but considering the amount, there had to be something else.

Fine sand, palm trees, cool people, dogs playing Frisbee on the beach, vegetarian restaurants all over the place, incredible parties—what was there not to love about California? The beach house Fiona and Jude had rented to accommodate them and all of us was huge and chic. Eight bedrooms, six bathrooms, an outdoor kitchen, private access to the beach, and a grand piano in the living room. We had never seen anything like it before. Kids we hardly knew invited us to their parents' houses and let us use their swimming pools. That summer's soundtrack was the new Doobie Brothers album featuring "What a Fool Believes," a song we all loved.

Cocaine was everywhere, or so it seemed. It looked as if everybody in California was snorting. People walked around casually with miniature silver spoons dangling from chains around their necks, always ready for a snort.

One day we were invited to a party in Malibu by a beach bum we occasionally played volleyball with. It was still early when we drove up the hills, and if I remember correctly, we were the first ones on the premises. The house was the size of the convent of my youth, the kind of place people refer to as a mansion. The slender hostess took us around the house, pointing to paintings and rugs. On the living room table, there was a giant seashell, the size of a small sink. It was filled to the brim with coke.

"You can serve yourselves whenever you want," the woman told us.

She turned out to be the mother of the beach bum. She said her son would be there in a minute, and she went back to the door to greet more guests. We were flabbergasted.

Before long, everybody at the beach house was using coke almost daily. They talked nonsense for hours on end and stayed up until dawn. Alex and I tried it one evening. It made us pretty horny, and I don't remember having better sex with him, but I hated the way I felt the next day so I didn't want to do it again. Also, to please Holiji, Alex and I had finally agreed we would have sex only when we couldn't stand it anymore, and cocaine would make that impossible. There was enough hash and grass to keep me happy, so I kept the white powder at bay. Alex, on the other hand, didn't mind the side effects that much and told me he could easily control his sexual urge. Grace, Frankie, Milou, Camille, and Claude were also sniffing like crazy. Hugo loved the stuff, of course. It made the California babes that much hotter for him. Even Linda was going for it.

It was okay, really. At least that's how I explained it to myself at the time. I can't say it didn't bother me. I usually got up around nine in the morning to find everybody in the living room still discussing the same crap they had been talking about eight hours before, a mirror with fine white lines circulating among them. They went to sleep around noon and woke up at ten in the evening and started all over again. Alex joined them here and there. Sometimes everybody went out to a club late at night. I never did—I knew that as long as Linda was around I didn't have to worry about Alex.

He would never dare to flirt in front of her.

Of course, Fiona and Jude didn't touch cocaine. They got their kicks out of slapping each other's faces.

One morning, our two hosts went for a long walk by the beach. Fiona was restless. She told Jude she felt dead inside. She complained about the absence of joy, of excitement. She resented the constant sadness and bitter anger in her heart. All the symptoms she'd have expected from a frustrated, grumpy middle-aged woman but not from herself and certainly not at her age. She wasn't happy in California. Too many of us in the house. She needed space and another project to keep herself busy. She knew exactly what she needed.

Hadn't she been patient enough already? Fiona persuaded Jude that a baby would fix their relationship for good. A baby combined with the centre would do the trick. She promised it would. Reluctant as he had always been, Jude eventually gave in, willing to let her have her way just to get some peace. But they both agreed that Holiji would have to give His blessing before any final decision could be reached.

The next day, a radiant Fiona announced she was leaving for India. "I have to see Holiji at once to discuss something Jude and I want to do very soon."

She told us she needed an "enema" for her soul to purify it before "anything important" happened to her. We all played dumb like we didn't know what she wasn't saying. Her victorious expression was so plain to read.

That will be a sorry child, we collectively thought, looking around at one another.

Fiona was on the phone for two hours, looking for a plane ticket to Delhi. She was happy and giggling again. If Holiji agreed, Jude couldn't back out.

And so she left a couple of days later. Hugo took her to the airport in the Mercedes. Jude begged him to because, he said, he was suffering from a splitting headache. Hugo came back from the airport in time for a late breakfast. For a change, everybody was present at the table that morning—for the simple reason that the previous night nobody had managed to find the cocaine dealer. It took days before he showed up again. I welcomed that break.

Feeling reflective and a bit morose, I looked at everyone. The boys with their short hair, their gold jewellery and their Pierre Cardin shirts. The girls—including me—with too much makeup, scantily dressed, and worrying too much about their weight. We would never again gather around a cheap kitchen table, listening religiously to the latest Led Zeppelin album. We would no longer feel the urge to find out how a song could change the quality of our daily lives. It was all going to the dogs.

There were lots of things we would never see again. Things like a new Beatles record, a draft beer for twenty cents, or an Afghani winter coat. It made me really sad. Mick was right— getting old is a major drag. I was in my early twenties, and like the rest of us I was convinced, or rather hoped, I would be dead before I reached thirty. Past that point, life was all about balding heads, cellulite, mortgages, taxes, children, and other despicable by-products of the adult world.

We were aging. The signs were there. Especially for Frankie and Milou, who were dangerously close to the fatal number. Frankie had stopped taking acid every day, and this was another indication. That white line of coke was leading us all further and further away from Hippie Road. Maybe that's why our two older friends snorted like there was no tomorrow. They needed to forget that their hassle-free life was over. Old age was just around the corner.

Miles away from my nostalgic state of mind, Jude seemed invigorated by Fiona's departure. He was ebullient, talking louder than he had in months. At noon, he declared his headache gone.

Chapter 56

Listening to the Eagles singing about a weird hotel in a southwest state

AFTER BREAKFAST, LINDA AND I said we wanted to get ourselves California bikinis. Alex had reluctantly promised to borrow the Mercedes and take us downtown for a few hours of shopping. The swimsuits we had packed in our suitcases back in Montreal made us look like pinups on a calendar from 1958. To my great surprise, Jude said he would be happy to take us. "This way, the boys can finish their beach ball game."

So unusually kind of him. I didn't argue. I knew Alex would be relieved—he hated shopping.

Just as I stepped out to join Jude in the Mercedes, Linda stopped dead in her tracks and said she felt dizzy. I thought the problem might be related to all the cocaine she'd been snorting, but I didn't mention that for fear of aggravating her. She said it would be wiser for her to get back to bed. I offered to stay, but she said she didn't want me to. I asked Jude to give me a minute. After tucking her into bed, I ran out to the beach and asked Alex to keep an eye on her. I headed back to the car, where Jude pushed an Eagles' cassette into the Blaupunkt, and we left. We sang along, a fat smile cracking our faces.

He took me to a store called the Bikini Emporium, where I spent two long hours trying on bathing suits. Jude voiced his disapproval every time I came out of the fitting room. While I was busy changing, I could hear him flirting with the salesgirl, a typical California blonde. The conversation was peppered with "*fer shur*," "so totally," "tubular," "kinda like," "y'know"—all delivered in a nasally female voice. By the time I decided on my siren outfit, Jude couldn't have cared less. Had I told him I was considering getting myself a brown paper bag to cover my ass, he would have replied that it was a grand idea.

I remember thinking about Fiona, who was sitting at the airport at that moment, a boarding pass in her hand, about to embark on the long journey to India for the sole purpose of finding out whether she should have a child with this guy. I came out of the fitting room, giving Jude a dirty look. The girl moved away, clearly uneasy.

Jude reacted swiftly. "Hey, she's a friend, nothing more than a friend!"

"Are you talking to me or to her?" I asked.

He laughed. "Come on, man, I'm just a lonesome boy."

"Has it been three hours already? Time sure flies."

The salesgirl, who couldn't know what I was referring to, said she agreed with me. "That's *fer shur*, time does fly away!"

Why do I care, anyway? I just wished I didn't have to be around whenever Jude—or Fiona—fucked up, that's all.

The girl shoved my bikini in a pink bag sporting the logo of the store in bright aquamarine letters. Jude invited her to have dinner with him and "his friends from Canada." The blonde flatly refused. To illustrate his commitment to good taste, Jude insisted on paying for my bikini, flashing a thick pile of one-hundred-dollar bills. Suspecting she might not have noticed the Mercedes parked in front, Jude said something about his car. To get rid of him and also to make a point about what kind of woman she was, she told Jude that she was no Mercedes girl.

"Too old fashioned, too passé, too conservative," she said sighing. That girl's heart was set on Jaguars. "And only Jaguars," she said, beaming her California smile.

Any man in his right mind would have suggested to Blondie that she park her dream car somewhere up a narrow tunnel leading to her belly button, but our Jude was impressed. A bikini salesgirl lifting her nose at him? Despite his Mercedes and his cash? What could possibly be more attractive to him? Jude tried to sell her the many advantages of Mercedes over Jaguar. I yawned. As if being dumb was her unique passion in life, the girl replied that she didn't care for "French" cars. "Fancy or not," she added disdainfully.

Jude didn't correct her about the origin of Mercedes cars. Instead, he asked her at what time she would be off.

"Around four thirty," she answered, glancing at the clock behind her. "Uh, unless Barbara is late again. It happens all the time, it drives me so totally nuts." She rang the cash register. "But don't waste your time. You're really not my type."

You'd think Jude was trying to sell her an overripe avocado.

She handed him the receipt and went back to her seat behind the counter. "Nothing personal, really. *Fer shur.*" She thanked us and said she hoped to see us again. "Well, you know, as customers. I mean, like, you know, it would be kind of far out. Maybe we'll meet on the beach one day, you never know."

She thought about this possibility for a moment. "Now wouldn't that be, like, totally strange?"

Back in the car, I exploded. I told Jude he was an asshole. I listed everything I thought was wrong with him. The fist fights, Fiona's shiners, Milou, everything.

Jude didn't seem particularly alarmed by my accusations. I guess he switched his ears off after a while. "You don't know how difficult it is to live with her."

"You may be surprised at what I know," I dared to add.

"You don't understand. It's much more complicated than that. I just need to have fun for a change. I need a girl whose only wish is to have a good time and give me head. It's not the end of the world. The way I look at it, it's not even sex."

"If she barfs on you, it isn't."

He laughed, stepping on the gas to make a yellow light. He poked my arm with his bony fingers. "You take this too seriously. I bet you don't even like Fiona that much, so why make such a fuss? Drop it already."

He looked at himself in the rear-view mirror. "Don't you like your bikini?" His way of reminding me that he had just spent ninety-five American dollars on me.

"I plan to pay you back. I can pay you back right now, actually." I aimed for my purse on the floor.

Jude leaned over and grabbed it, tossing it on the back seat. "Don't insult me. All I'm asking for is a little gratitude."

He dropped me at the house, saying he had to get some groceries. He came back at five thirty with a British racing green Jaguar and the Bikini Emporium salesgirl. Winking at Hugo and Frankie, he said he had traded the Mercedes for a Jag. "Temporarily. To see how a Jag feels. To compare   I'm in the mood for comparisons."

The girl grinned vacantly, holding on tight to Jude's sleeve.

That evening, we all had dinner at the Green Heaven, a vegetarian restaurant in LA. The food was simply divine. Jude told us there was a party in Beverly Hills that same night, and the Bikini Emporium girl added that she knew the owner of the house and that, *fer shur,* we were all welcome. Everyone went except for Linda, Alex, and me. We took a cab back to the house and sat on the terrace, gazing at the ocean and smoking a few joints. Life could have been worse.

And it was just about to be.

Chapter 57

Listening to Frank Zappa singing fer shur, fer shur, while his daughter imitates the accent of some California girls

THE FOLLOWING MORNING, JUDE sat down at the breakfast table with the salesgirl next to him, and everybody acted as if she had been there since the beginning of time. Around eleven thirty, he drove her back to the Bikini Emporium in the Jaguar, and by one o'clock he had completely forgotten about her. He invited us for a late lunch at a nearby fancy restaurant overlooking the sea.

"Fiona took me there last week. Great food. You'll love it."

He flirted shamelessly with the waitress, another beach bleached blonde he confessed to have spotted on the occasion of that romantic lunch with the future mother of his child. I'm sure he couldn't recall one word of what Fiona talked about that day. The elected waitress possessed large silicone breasts no man could, or would, ignore. Her mini skirt ended half an inch from her G-stringed ass, releasing two legs long enough to hang yourself with. By the time we ordered coffee, Jude had coaxed her into joining him after her shift. He didn't have to work hard. He asked her in which car she'd liked to be picked up, a Mercedes or a Jaguar? She mentioned a preference for the Mercedes and told Jude she'd be ready at five. It was that simple. One, two, three, and hop you go. Jude got the Mercedes back and rented the Jaguar, a move that cost him a small fortune.

"Well, a man's got to do what he's got to do," he told an envious Hugo.

I remember being dead sure that the only roadblock between a California girl and a one-night stand was a fancy foreign car. Hugo couldn't afford it yet, but he made Frankie promise they would come back one day with enough money to rent the right vehicle. Not only were these girls beautiful, sculpted by the best plastic surgeons in the world, but to make things even better, when the sun rose, all they asked for was to go back to their workplace or home, never asking when or whether you intended to ever see them again. Krystal, Justine, or Sunshine waved and said "see ya" the way people do when they don't mean it. A man's heaven. The California girls I was introduced to apparently knew better than to fall off balance for a French accent and a sports car. They understood what most boys want from life. A harmless hit, then a fast run. A deep touch followed by an immediate departure. Costly girls, of course, but worth every penny.

Jude introduced us to no fewer than seventeen girls in a matter of three weeks, Mercedesers and Jaguarians alike. We learned to differentiate the former from the latter. Mercedesers tended to be outdoor girls, playing beach volleyball and wearing little makeup, but the Jaguarians loved to sip fancy drinks by the pool, taking extraordinary precautions not to mess up their hair. Otherwise they both displayed the same features, the same tanned silicone breasts, the same ski-slope noses, and a particular affection for the expressions "oh, gross" and "gag me with a spoon." Fiona would have destroyed each and every one of them in a minute.

She called from India on two occasions. The first time she sounded ecstatic. She said she was happy to be "back home" with her master, a conversation that left Jude reassured. After all, as long as Fiona was happy, he didn't see why he shouldn't enjoy himself too.

But the second time, Fiona didn't have much to say, and Jude sensed she was in a foul mood. The line was bad. Noises, echoes. Jude hung up feeling uneasy and nervous. What if Fiona, his witch of a girlfriend, had detected the distant perfumes of blondes bouncing up and down on their California bed?

On countless occasions, Jude had witnessed for himself how easily Fiona picked up on these things. She was also prone to experiencing prophetic dreams. There had to be a reason for her to be angry. She was always so happy when she was around Holiji. Doubts besieged Jude's mind. What if she knew he was being unfaithful? What if Holiji knew too? Couldn't he see everything his children were doing? Jude's heart was in his throat. Paranoia emerged (largely because of his cocaine use and abuse since Fiona's departure).

He immediately got rid of the girl from the night before. She didn't seem to mind, but she couldn't find her bra. Alex found it behind the grand piano, and Hugo took her home in a hurry. She never questioned why she was hustled off so quickly. Jude flung his bedroom window wide open to get rid of her smell as well as the perfume of the others who had shared his bed since Fiona had last occupied it. He shoved the sheets in the washer, scrubbed the bathroom tiles, and vacuumed around the bed. He felt reasonably confident of having successfully erased every blond hair from the room. He checked around again—one could never be too careful. Fiona would certainly detect the faintest signs of foul play in their bedroom.

That done, Jude now kept mostly to himself. He got rid of the Jaguar despite Hugo's heart-rending pleas, and from then on he spent his days practicing yoga and meditating in an isolated cove by the beach.

Her Singapore Airlines flight landed in LA ten days later. By then Fiona's mood had weathered down from ire to profound sadness. She didn't want to talk about it.

From the moment Jude picked her up at the airport, she showed nothing but contempt toward him. However, she didn't seem eager to quarrel. Back in his holy persona, Jude didn't ask her a single question and simply did everything he could to avoid her. He could easily read the lines on the wall. When Linda asked Fiona about our beloved master, she snapped at her. "You know where he is. You go and check him out for yourself."

"Well, that says it all," we said to one another with relief. Holiji was obviously against the baby project. I blessed his most excellent judgement.

Fiona and Jude didn't fight again that summer. Fiona ignored us as if we were part of the furniture. She cried in their room for hours at a time. One morning, I found the heart to knock on her door. I have to admit that I was more than a little curious. I asked if she'd care for some fresh-squeezed orange juice. She answered with a small no, but she didn't tell me to fuck off so I stepped in. She was lying on her unmade bed, her clothes from the previous evening wrinkled all over for sleeping in them. She said she'd had enough, she was tired and didn't know what her priorities were anymore.

"I feel like something's dying in me."

"Something bad happened in India?"

Her face closed up immediately. "Nothing. Nothing ever happens in India. Reality is what happens to us every time we set foot in India. We let emotions take over, and we forget how small and fragile we are. Nothing ever happens in India, Geneviève, India happens to you ..." And blah, blah blah. The same shit she always said.

Then she started crying again. There is a form of misery in others that really gets to me, and Fiona's was no exception. I felt a lump in my throat as she crashed into my arms, sobbing. My God, what was happening to her? How could she be so miserable for not having a child with this lousy dick of a boyfriend of hers?

"You'll have a baby in time, I'm sure, Fiona," I whispered, caressing her hair.

She pushed me away. "I don't want a baby. Not in these conditions. Not with Jude anyway. Not if I have a choice. Maybe I don't want a baby after all. I just want to serve my master and nothing more. I want to live at *his* feet for the rest of my life. Maybe that's *all* I really want."

Maybe you don't know what you're talking about, girl. Maybe you just can't face the fact that Jude and you couldn't possibly be decent parents. A child's worst nightmare, more likely.

But, of course, I didn't speak my mind. What I said was, "Maybe not."

"Well, we'll see."

She went to the bathroom to blow her nose. Then she made her bed thoroughly, as if the steady movements of flattening the sheets could also straighten up everything that was wrong in her life. She opened the curtains and marvelled aloud at the calmness of the ocean. We could see the others playing ball on the beach. Jude looked up and waved.

"I love that man, but he's no good for me."

I knew better than to agree with her. With no warning, she pulled the curtains closed and threw herself on the made-up bed. She didn't ask for me to stay so I turned and left, shutting the door quietly behind me.

Chapter 58

*Listening to the Beatles singing about a couple going
nowhere special and spending someone else's money
on the way*

As summer wore on, Fiona's mood did not improve, not by an iota. She still dragged herself around, miserable, her hair undone and her nails dirty. Jude continued to act as if there was nothing unusual going on with her.

Everything—good and bad—comes to an end, and before we knew it we had to head back home. Grace, Claude, Camille, and Frankie had left at the end of July. Less than a month later, the holiday was officially over for the rest of us.

One day near the end of August, Fiona suddenly told Jude she wished to get home as quickly as possible. She was adamant about wanting to fly back to Montreal—there was no way in hell she'd go back by car. Jude asked Hugo, Alex, Linda, and me if we would mind driving the Mercedes back to Canada. Hugo jumped at the opportunity. He didn't care if he lost his job—he figured he too could find another one in no time. Alex, Linda, and I were more than happy to oblige.

Before leaving for the airport, Fiona called Leon and pestered him with questions on the renovations at Maya. She said she expected him to be there the next morning at ten. She extended my vacation for two more weeks without even an unpleasant comment. Jude gave Alex and Hugo two thick piles of cash for their expenses. Linda and I received thinner ones. The next morning, the four of us left in the Mercedes and headed for the highway.

This was when, but I only realized this much later, I should have noticed something weird going on. But my thinking was obscured by the thrill of travelling with my best pals all the way up to Montreal through the Arizona desert and the Grand Canyon. There were no conceivable reasons to worry about losing something along the way. We had plenty to smoke, money to spend, and all the time in the world.

In Nevada, Alex refused to have sex with me. In Utah, he said he wasn't in the mood. State after state he let me down. But I didn't make a case out of it. Why would I have? This kind of temporary drought happened to most couples at one time or another. And of course, Alex probably thought it would please Holiji to know we were trying harder than the others. I decided not to think about it too much.

Up in Niagara Falls, a half-day drive from Montreal, Alex dropped Hugo and Linda in front of a movie theatre, and we went out for dinner by ourselves to celebrate our fourth anniversary together. Not fourth as in four months but as in four years. A first for the both of us.

The food was overpriced and mediocre, the conversation sterile, and Alex kept glancing at the front door as if he meant to run for it. On the way back to the hotel, I was mad at him for being so distant. I told him so. He became rude. When I asked him what the hell was wrong with him, he asked me to leave him alone. When I insisted, he screamed that nothing was wrong with *him*. As he said this, he jammed on the brakes, stormed out of the car to the passenger's door, opened it, and pulled me out. Then he got back in and drove away. I stood there, dumbfounded, in the middle of nowhere. How could he leave me there all by myself? *What the fuck is wrong with him?*

I sat on the sidewalk, weeping and cursing for what seemed like hours.

The Mercedes stopped in front of me. Hugo was at the wheel, but Alex wasn't with him. I went berserk. "Where's Alex?" I screamed.

"Back at the motel." Hugo was calm. Irritatingly calm, really.

"What the fuck is the matter with him?"

I was too close to his ears to yell this way. A small vein on his temple began to pulsate nervously. He hollered, "How the fuck should I know? I don't sleep with him!"

"Well, neither do I!" I sat in the car, sobbing.

We did not exchange one word on the way to the Best Western Hotel. Hugo was humming to the radio—"For What It's Worth," Buffalo Springfield, a favourite of his.

I looked out the window and had a peek at a piece of Canada I couldn't call home. Ontario was another world for us, like the States without the thrill of being abroad. By the time we parked at the hotel, I was half pacified. Linda opened the hotel room door before I could knock. There was Alex, lying on the bed watching TV. He too appeared more relaxed. I imagined Linda had told him off for leaving me stranded out there.

"Let's go back to our room," she told Hugo.

I crawled into bed. Alex said he was sorry, really sorry. He said he didn't know what had gotten into him. He rolled a joint and offered me a hit. I took a drag, washed my face, and fell asleep while watching Johnny Carson.

We arrived in Montreal late the next evening. Alex suggested dropping me first since I was scheduled to work the next morning. That was awfully nice of him, quite a change from his jerk behaviour of the last days. I gave Linda a big hug and pecked Hugo's cheek. Alex said he'd be back within the hour.

He came much later. I woke up when he crawled into bed. He said something about an accident slowing down the traffic. Then he turned on his side, his back facing me. Within a minute he was snoring.

Later that month, Alex landed the job of his dreams, selling guitars in a music shop downtown. He was so excited. He spent most of his time "on site," as he liked to say. He almost lived at the shop. I didn't want to piss on his parade by giving him shit for ignoring me a little more every day, so I coped as best as I could, killing time with Linda.

Alex soon made friends with the members of a rock band looking for a place to rehearse. They also wanted to make a demo. Alex's boss kept a small sound studio in the basement of the store, and he told Alex he could use it under strict conditions. He expected the musicians to be very careful with the equipment and to only use the space after business hours. Alex became the band's sound engineer, and they all had high hopes of producing a big hit. Lots of work, sweat, and time was needed for Alex to become familiar with the sound board. I understood that. I kept my mouth shut. Sometimes he came home at dawn, sometimes late the next afternoon. After a long night of recording and smoking, he occasionally passed out on the couch behind the drum kit at the studio. I asked if he was snorting cocaine to stay up all night, but he swore he wasn't. I had never seen him so happy.

Chapter 59

Listening to the Who praying they won't get duped again

AROUND THAT TIME, IT must have been October by then, Odette came back from India. Odette was a dedicated devotee who had never, to my knowledge, missed a single Sunday *satsang*. Her face was heavily scarred by juvenile acne, but she was pretty enough to make you forget about it. Her eyes were slightly slanted. Her adventurous great-grandmother had abandoned her native country to pursue her true love, a Chinese tailor. According to Odette, the woman followed the Chinese man all the way to Hangzhou, where she lived as his wife. Five years later, she returned to Canada with typhoid and a baby girl, Odette's grandma. Odette was proud of the slant at the corners of her eyes, and her clothes often sported some symbol of her Chinese blood. A serious smoker, she visited the apartment regularly to stash on hash. I talked to her many times, trying to make friends, but she turned out to be a little too weird for me. She was distant with girls, and consequently they didn't like her much in return. The boys found her deliciously mysterious. There was something about Odette that made me feel as though I couldn't trust her, and she did everything she could to keep it that way. She was not the kind of person who tried to spare your feelings. She didn't care whether you liked her or not. She was blunt and never looked for sympathy. However, even at her worst, she was Holiji's child, and it was unthinkable to tell her to take a hike, even when she was rude. Especially now that she was about to bring us fresh news about the old man.

From time to time, the whole gang still met at the apartment on Jarry Street. That evening, everybody was there, including Jude, who had to talk business with Hugo. He was on his way back home from the centre, and Fiona was with him. It was an uneventful Friday, borderline boring. But Odette was about to change that.

She came in, all tanned and dressed in Indian clothes. She seemed surprised to see so many of us there. A little more stunned to see Jude and Fiona. "Hi," she said unceremoniously.

She was carrying a grocery bag. We asked her enthusiastically about Master, excited at this unexpected chance to hear about him. Odette was in no hurry. She opened the bag and took out a package of what looked like sliced ham. Big smile on her face. She took a slice of the stuff and gulped it all in one mouthful. It sure smelled good. Like ham, really. Was this a new soy product we had not heard of yet?

She took another chunk and answered, "Oh, not at all." She burped, her hand flying up to her mouth. "This is ham, all right. Lately, I've discovered I have a pronounced taste for meat."

Poor girl, she's gone insane, I thought.

Taking another slice she said, "To tell you the truth, I've been a devoted meat eater ever since Holiji grabbed my ass."

Even Hugo was shocked.

Fiona stood, strode over to Odette, and slapped her face with all her might. She was, of course, an expert at doing this. Odette staggered. Fiona ordered Hugo and Alex to throw her out, but the year was not 1750, and she wasn't the queen in command. They ignored her and stayed put. Fiona grabbed Odette by the shoulder, determined to do the job herself. Odette fought back this time. Nobody moved. Only a fool would have stood between these two cats.

Fiona got behind Odette, pulling her by the collar of her Indian cotton blouse. "You just have to take one look in her eyes to see she's lying. Holiji would never do such a thing!" Fiona was livid, almost spitting. "Take a good look at her eyes! Lying eyes! You'll meet many others like these on the road to enlightenment! Horrible liar's eyes!" Her face was boiling with rage.

Jude was as speechless as the rest of us.

Odette was choking and panting like an exhausted horse. "Crazy bitch! Your guru is a fuckin' fake!"

She took a swing at Fiona but missed. Fiona locked herself in the bathroom, and Odette walked out, slamming the door. We stood there, shell shocked. Hugo picked up the ham left on the counter and smelled it. It was ham all right.

Fiona emerged from the bathroom minutes later. She looked calmer. "I'm sorry, but I can't stand profanities. Mentally unstable souls ruining the reputation of respected gurus! Theft, rape, kidnapping, name it—they'll say anything! Accusing our father of something as vile as this! Can you believe it? It's disgusting! Insane woman! How can she lie this way? Tarnishing Holiji's name can only bring terrible karma on her. People like her drive me mad."

She turned to Jude. "And you? You just sat there, doing nothing?" This accusation was more likely aimed at every one of us. "Coward! You let people blemish his image right in front of you, and you don't say a word? Is this what you are? A traitor? A wimp?"

Jude finally opened his huge mouth. "I might be a coward, but I'm not a fuckin' lunatic. Did you see yourself? Is this what *you* are? You think Holiji would approve? You're crazy, woman!"

We were inches away from a fist fight. Hugo disappeared into his bedroom with the ham. We waited to see what would happen next, but nothing did. Jude and Fiona left—together—without saying goodbye.

I tended to agree with Fiona. The others felt the same way. We should have become involved. Odette thrived on attention, and she had always been a basket case. For instance, she had once told us how she liked to play with a Ouija board and invoke dead souls. And in the winter, she wore a woollen cape covered with peacock feathers. A nut, really. It was mean of her to do what she had just done. Mean and frighteningly disrespectful. Yeah, Fiona was right. We should have kicked her butt. My only regret was that we didn't have a chance to hear the details of her alleged accusation. It would have been interesting to see Odette's getting uneasy as she smeared her bullshit on us, her contradictions embarrassing her, her nervous hands betraying her lies. But it was too late now.

We rarely mentioned Odette's name ever again, except when we meant to insult one another. We never saw her again, not even for hash or at the satsangs. We figured she had sobered up (Hugo said she looked like she might have been drinking), understanding she had gone too far. Alex remembered she had once confided to him that her own brother had tried to rape her. We had always suspected Odette was a little sick in the head, and now we knew for sure. The guys didn't find her so mysteriously delicious anymore.

A few days later, we heard excellent news. Nothing was official yet, but there was a good chance Holiji would come back to Montreal sometime in December. He told Jude he would try to show up for a few days in the course of his second world tour. Linda was overjoyed. If he made it to Montreal, she wouldn't have to travel all the way to Asia to receive initiation.

When she heard the news, Linda cried with joy and I

hugged her. Alex did too, and I saw him whisper something in her ear. Linda blushed. When later I asked him what he had told her, he hesitated as if it weren't my business, then said, "I told her she would soon be one of us." As far as I was concerned, Linda, initiated or not, had always been one of us. I was stunned to realize Alex might have felt somehow disconnected from her just because she wasn't initiated. He'd never mentioned a word about that, and I wondered why. He certainly could have fooled me. However, I knew he cared for Linda just as much as I did. We used to call ourselves soul siblings, and we meant it. Alex was right, though—knowing the three of us shared the same guru would make our friend-ship even more special.

Chapter 60

Listening to Paul Simon singing that all dreams either
get swamped or beg to stay alive

"FIONA'S PREGNANT!" ESCAPED UNCONTROLLABLY from his fat lips as he made it through the door. Jude's face was glowing like a rooster's crest. I don't remember whether any of us congratulated him. *How could this be happening?* Hadn't Holiji been against the idea?

"Are you deaf, guys? Fiona is having my baby!"

Jude was well aware that Paul Anka had gotten shit for singing such a chauvinist statement back in '74. He sure sounded thrilled for a guy who had recently claimed he would rather get rammed in the stomach by a rhino than have a child with Fiona. Knowing Jude, he remembered his own words all too well, and that's precisely why he was reciting Paul Anka's pathetic anthem. Just another stunt to divert our attention away from his blatant contradictions and incoherence.

He didn't look upset by our lack of enthusiasm. He dished out a piece of Afghani from his pocket. A couple of joints later, speculations turned positive, and before long we were all over him, shaking hands and talking about the *good* news.

Then again, no matter how hard we tried to shoo it away, a sensation of doom lingered behind Jude's every loud laugh, like lightning in Eden.

"Holiji knows?" I think it was Grace who asked.

"Yeah, sure!"

Jude got up. "I don't think he was all for it, you know, but now that Fiona's pregnant, he's very, very happy. After all, a baby is always good news."

Silence. No one could think of anything to say.

He put on a Pat Metheny record. "To tell you the truth, at first he was a little upset."

I was stunned to hear that Holiji hadn't seen it coming. Wasn't he naturally programmed to foresee events like these? How could he be surprised? In my books, Holiji could never be surprised by anything. The idea bothered me for a split second, but I soon forgot about it. The notion was too disturbing.

Jude sat on the edge of his chair, his mouth slicing his face cheek to cheek. He had produced a miracle, a true wonder. He, a most ordinary man, had squeezed a forbidden child from heaven. I marvelled at his ability to feel completely unique in every little commonplace event happening—or not—to him. Jude rose, saying he had to return to his "wife." He stood by the door, his eyes watering. He was gaga, mushy. The idea of this child really seemed to have transformed him. Jude was right—a baby is always good news. That was an irrefutable fact. Fiona had told him so—many, many times, actually. But he'd never listened to her.

Fiona had also told Jude that according to her midwife, she was about six weeks pregnant. She promptly reserved one of the birth rooms at the Queen Victoria Hospital. This innovative revolution in obstetrics allowed for future mothers to give birth in a homey environment created for them in the maternity ward.

In the ensuing weeks, Fiona rubbed her belly as if it were

Aladdin's lamp. "This baby deserves the best and only the best. I'll see to it personally and eternally. I swear on Holiji's head!" she said to all of us.

To our amazement, the couple agreed to put their boxing gloves away—at least for the duration of the pregnancy. But Fiona still slapped Jude from time to time. Shielded by her pregnancy, she felt invincible.

Linda and I began spending a little more time with Fiona after *satsangs*. The stuffy atmosphere had loosened somewhat, and I found myself no longer dreading Sundays that in the past had found me surrounded by a bunch of uptight devotees hosted by Jude and Fiona. I could breathe and be myself a little more.

Pregnancy had a marvellous effect on Fiona. She abandoned the Shakespearian characters she usually mimicked and metamorphosed herself into a wonderfully normal human being. Even I was starting to enjoy her company. Fiona showed a side of herself we would have all bet didn't exist. After a few weeks, she stopped wearing tight dresses and high heels. The fact was that she was gaining an awful lot of weight.

"Her red-haired genes," Camille explained. "With age, red-haired women get fat. With age *and* pregnancy, they get even fatter. Do you know one middle-aged redhead who's not fat?"

I didn't know any redhead but Fiona.

Fiona lay motionless in her bed. Defying physics, she grew fatter than Milou. The midwife told her she had to stop pigging out, but Fiona said she couldn't help it.

"This baby," she said, giggling. "He'll be so strong! He wants to eat all the time. It's not me. I've never eaten this much in my whole life. It's that little person in there."

She still giggled more than I cared for, but I was learning to live with it. Flying on cloud number nine, Jude's mother visited their house every week. Fiona's own mother was on her way from the West Coast. She too couldn't wait to see her daughter's belly.

"Your father, God bless his soul, would be so proud of you!" she said when she arrived.

Strangely, Jude didn't mind her size. He loved Fiona more than ever. The baby changed everything in him. In this state, Fiona personified everything that was sacred to him. Immense power and vulnerability at the same time. He buried her with unsolicited gifts, massaged her feet to activate circulation, and rubbed her belly with almond oil to save it from stretch marks. He made sure he was home every night for dinner, and he never failed to bring Fiona a bouquet of wild flowers, her favourites. Pretty soon, Fiona didn't have to hit him anymore. We all had to admit that Jude as well was turning into a more decent and responsible human being. Fiona had been right all along. This pregnancy had indeed redeemed their relationship and turned them both into better individuals.

The centre also benefited from Fiona's pregnancy. When she wasn't nibbling in bed on cashew nuts and tahini sandwiches with alfalfa sprouts, she liked to bake shortbreads from scratch using her grandmother's recipe. The cookies still warm, she'd take a cab to Maya. Manoeuvring her immense body as lightly as she could, she hunted for customers on each floor, offering them the buttery cookies. The soundproofed boxing ring in the back room found a new vocation. Jude transformed it into a yoga room for himself and the "mother of his child." They walked out from it hand in hand, wearing smiles of loving complicity, quite a contrast from the usual shiners hidden behind dark sunglasses.

Smuggling dope was relegated to the back of their minds for a while. In fact, all illegal activities were suspended except for one deal. It was the biggest deal they had ever been involved in, a venture initiated right after or during the California trip, none of us knew for sure. On a few occasions in Laguna Beach, we dined by ourselves because Fiona and Jude had "people to see." We didn't know whether it was because of Holiji or some dope deal. We never asked questions about these things.

One thing we did know was that once this huge transaction was complete, a solid cushion of undeclared cash would allow the new parents to raise little Jade or Vincent comfortably and take care of the centre's financial ups and downs for years to come. Four other parties were involved in the deal, each of which had good reasons to want to see it come through. If the plan worked out as expected, Fiona and Jude would each pocket more than a million American dollars. Even though we knew there would be more than a million-dollar profit since other people were involved, we always referred to it as "the million-dollar deal." The couple promised to throw a big, splashy party to celebrate the successful operation.

At Maya, we were encouraged to take initiative. Leon and I explored new venues such as book distribution for a small publisher in Seattle who produced wonderful works on Tibetan Buddhism. We also added a wide variety of New Age music cassettes to the inventory. At home, Linda, Alex, and I studied the Bhagavad Gita once a week and practiced yoga every other day. Life was good again.

One morning, Jude got a call from Vermont. It was Holiji, saying he had time for a short visit in Montreal before heading back to India. This time around, Fiona was relaxed. She said she'd manage to get everything organized for his stay. She was thrilled because her mother was scheduled to be in town at the time of Holiji's visit. She too would finally get to meet him and witness for herself what her daughter's guru was all about. Though we had all assumed Holiji was against Fiona's pregnancy, he had obviously changed his mind. Perhaps our master simply wanted to see the couple happy, even if it meant bending the rules from heaven.

None of us cared one way or the other. With all the changes we had witnessed so far in Jude and Fiona, it was hard not to believe this was all for the best.

Holiji told Jude he was looking forward to initiating new devotees. Linda was beyond thrilled. He would also be there to bless Fiona's immense belly and the life cooking inside. This baby, who had single-handedly kicked out all the bad from their existences, certainly deserved it.

"By the time I give birth, Holiji will be somewhere in Australia," she calculated on her dimpled knuckles. "I'll pay a visit to the ashram as soon as I'm on my legs again."

She was no longer angry at Jude. She wasn't even angry at the girls who had stolen her bag in New York anymore. The only person she was still pissed off at was Odette, but she kept that mainly to herself.

Chapter 61

*Listening to Neil Young wishing that what he's just heard
is a tall tale*

IN EARLY DECEMBER OF 1979, my mother died. An aggressive form of cancer killed her in a matter of weeks. She promised to fight for her life, but it turned out she didn't really mean it. The idea of losing her was so unimaginable that I never thought she would fail to cure herself. She had never complained, so how could we have guessed how sick she was? At fifty-five years old, she decided she'd had enough of this life. Her children didn't need her anymore, and her husband didn't remember anything about the dreams she once had held. She had forgotten most of them herself. So she simply flew away from the pain. An overworked angel, she took off her broken wings to let them heal under a warmer sun.

I don't remember ever being so lost before or since in my life. I was aching for Holiji's soothing presence. Alex, Linda, and the rest of the gang were kind and supportive, but nothing they said could alleviate my grief. All the beautiful spiritual theories meant to make people in my position feel better seemed empty and preposterous. Only Holiji could make me feel better. I couldn't wait to see him. There were twenty-seven long days to go before his arrival. Jude promised to squeeze a moment for me in our master's busy schedule. I needed him to get rid of the emptiness and the guilt.

As if my devastation over the loss of my mother wasn't enough, an ugly snake was about to show its head in my family. My dad mourned my mom the way some middle-aged men do when they've been married for too long: a brief sadness that took place in the privacy of his own quarters. He didn't cry out loud once, at least never in front of us, and within weeks he told us he felt ready to marry again. His secretary. He said he was in love.

Drawing from the convenient inconsistencies of his vague recollections, we concluded with horror that this secretary had been his mistress for months—a little more than a year, actually. I was convinced my mother knew. She was too intuitive not to guess. Four months before her death, Simone had left home to attend university in Manitoba, and that was most likely when my mom's spirit began to plummet. She gave her empty life no chance. Why should she have? After all, none of her loved ones required her services anymore. Ever since she had said yes at the altar, attending to her family was all this wonderful being assumed she was meant to do in life.

Carl, Simone, and I discussed Dad's affair at length, each of us swearing to give him a piece of our mind. But faced with him and his new fiancée, we chickened out. This traitor was all that was left of our parental unit, the only one on earth with a claim on our umbilical cords. There was no room for additional sorrows, and quarrelling with Dad could only end up creating exactly that. I wore my mom's wedding ring on a chain around my neck as the only indication of my rebellion. I wept for days in the darkness of my room.

Once again, everybody showed up at the airport to greet Holiji. The singular vision of his face made me feel better. His soft voice, his immaculate hands, the mole on his chin,

and so many other things were already working their miracles on me.

Jude had arranged for Holiji to give a lecture in St. James
Church on St. Catherine Street. His house couldn't accommodate the expanding crowds lining up to hear the great
man anymore. St. James Church, conveniently located near a
metro station, was a slender nineteenth-century gothic struc-
ture guarded by an old army of gargoyles that still breathes
to this day, squished as it is between giant modern structures
closing in from all sides. The proud church stands defiantly
despite the pollution and the graffiti, a little haven of peace
in the middle of downtown Montreal.

It was winter already but I remember that day as being
unusually warm. The church was packed and overheated.
Sitting quietly in the pews, initiated and ordinary people
alike fanned themselves with the pamphlet handed to them
at the entrance. The brochure told the story of Holiji and
explained briefly the nature of his teachings. Live Love was
written in gold letters on the cover.

Holiji walked onto the podium as if floating on a cloud.
He was obviously pleased to count so many new faces in the
audience. I sat in the front row, flanked by Linda and Alex,
and we held hands. I was exhilarated because Jude had called
that same morning to let me know I could see Holiji right
after the lecture. The great man was sorry to hear about my
mom's death but had said I shouldn't be worrying because
she was fine. He told Jude he would meditate for her passage
through the wheel of life and death. Picturing Holiji praying
for my own mother sent shivers down my sweaty back.

At any other time, I would have been absorbed by his
speech, drinking in his every word, but the only thing on
my mind then was that I was about to meet him face to face.
I couldn't concentrate on what he was saying concerning
the salvation of our souls. I was uncontrollably nervous, a
stupid state of mind considering who I was about to meet.

My father from heaven. Why was I so intimidated by him? I couldn't stop shaking. I kept repeating the first words I intended to pronounce, words along the lines of "Oh, Master, thank you so much for taking this moment for me and my mother"—and then, blank. I wished I had never asked to meet him. My grief seemed insignificant compared with the world's crises. My mother had simply left this world, and I was monopolizing my master's precious time to help *me* get over it. I resolved to cancel the appointment, convinced that meditation alone would do the trick. *Holiji should devote all his prayers to peace and happiness on earth.*

Deeply absorbed in my internal dialogue, I failed to notice that the lecture was over. I lifted my head and saw Jude next to Holiji, pointing in my direction. My heart was pounding like the bells of Notre Dame. Master flashed his most beautiful smile and gestured for me to join him in the back. I wouldn't have been more nervous had I been on my way for a chat with the Beatles. My hands were wet with sweat. I hated that—it would make my touch slimy. Jude put his hands on my shoulders, flashing a big brother smile. *Never mind the world's crises, I really need this.* Jude signalled for me to walk into the antechamber normally reserved for priests.

Holiji was sitting on the wooden rocking chair Jude had bought for him on his previous trip. I wondered how he had squeezed the enormous thing inside the Mercedes. I bowed silently and sat in front of him. He closed his eyes and told me to let it all out—all the frustration, all the pain, all the sadness.

I talked about my mom, her disease, my dad, the secretary, the hospital, my guilt, and her death, and that's about all I can recall up to that point. I must have been yapping and crying for about ten minutes when Holiji invited me to come closer to him.

"Let me replace your mother for a moment. Let me rock you until your tears disappear. Like your mother would."

I thought he was speaking metaphorically, and he didn't really expect me to get up and sit on his impeccable whites. I assumed he wanted me to listen very closely to what he had to say and let his wisdom bathe me and soothe my pain. I sat back in meditation.

"Listen to me, my child. Come and sit on my knees." He tapped gently on his lap with his hands.

I approached him and sat on his lap, feeling a strong wave of gratitude gushing in my chest. Alex, Linda, and the others would be so envious! Holiji hugged me tenderly. He sang something sweet in Hindi and rocked me gently. He took my chin between his fingers. My tears streamed, and he wiped my face with his most perfect dry hand, saying that I had all the love I needed in the world right there at that precise moment. He kissed my tears. I smiled. He smiled back. Then he did something strange. He put his hands on my stomach and rubbed it as if I had complained about a tummy ache, an ailment I was positive I had not included in my list of sorrows. His eyes piercing mine, his hand massaged what I supposed was my belly chakra, but a second later it went a little higher. First I thought it had become lost in the loose fabric, but no—it seemed to know exactly where it was going. It was aiming for my tits while his lips were trying to kiss me at the same time. I was so stunned I almost choked. That was when he stuck his tongue in my mouth. I felt what seemed to be an erection beneath my thighs.

I pushed him away abruptly and jumped up, yanking my sweater down. For a second the room turned upside down. I closed my eyes forcefully. When I opened them, the same deceiving man sat there, winking gamely at me. I was disgusted and profoundly confused, but I also have to admit that in a weird and sick way, I was a little flattered.

"What's wrong, my child?"

"Nothing, Master."

"Don't you enjoy the love I'm giving you?"

"Yes, Master, but I have to go now. There's something I have to do. I'll see you around. Don't worry about me, Master. I feel a lot better now. I'll be fine. Thank y—you."

He didn't say much more. He watched me get my purse, grinning absently. "Go in peace, my child."

I walked toward the door, my mind flickering between disgust and insanity. I felt his eyes on my back. I wiped my face hastily with my hand before going out, closing the door behind me with silent precision as if I had been ordered to do so. The heat was overwhelming and I was flustered, close to fainting. I rose on the tips of my toes in a useless effort to catch a little more air. My friends were waiting for me. They probably thought I was about to levitate.

"So?"

Alex, Linda, Grace, Frankie, Tintin, Milou. Their shiny eyes betrayed a little jealousy. I was in no mood to initiate a storm. "Oh, it was great," I said, pretending to tie my shoe.

I felt miserable for myself and sorry for them because they had yet to be informed that Holiji was something horrible that I still was uncertain of. Something most definitely evil, a fraud. Maybe nothing more than just an ordinary dirty old man. My friends observed me intensely. I was part of the lucky ones who had encountered a tragedy dramatic enough to justify our master's personal intervention. Our own God in the flesh. I told them I had to use the washroom and would be back in a second. Milou said I'd find it at the end of the small corridor to the left.

I splashed my face with cold water and stared at my sad reflection, praying—to whom? I wasn't sure anymore. *You gotta think fast, girl.* What would I say to my friends exactly? That Holiji had aimed for my tits? What else? That I'd felt his tongue in my mouth? Or maybe I'd mistaken the whole ugly incident? For a second, I was tempted to rush back to his knees and apologize with profusion for my awkward behaviour, but my feet apparently decided otherwise because I turned my heels and aimed for the sink to throw up.

Odette.

I returned to my friends, saying I needed time to meditate on what I'd been told by Holiji. I said I couldn't talk about it because he'd asked me not to. That got them off my back and gave me some time to figure out what I should do next. Alex and Linda led me away as if I were an invalid.

Initiation Day was near. Linda was overjoyed. She couldn't stop smiling. Heaven was on its way.

Chapter 62

*Listening to the Rolling Stones singing a country song
about a girl with absent eyes*

IT OCCURRED TO ME that I didn't have to be the one exposing Holiji. Soon enough another girl was bound to be fondled by him, and she would let everybody know about it, just as Odette had done.

I couldn't bear the idea of being the outcast I damn well knew I would become if I ever summoned the audacity to open my mouth. Fiona alone would strangle me and cut me to pieces. It was much easier and safer to be wrong. Anyway, what had happened exactly? Maybe he hadn't been aroused at all, and that bump pulsating against my thighs was nothing more than a nerve acting up on its own. Wasn't it a possibility that it was nothing more than a distorted perception of mine? In North America, we see sex everywhere, don't we?

I reviewed the event second by second, from my first minute at his feet to the moment a hand brushed against my breast and a tongue probed my mouth. I tried to evaluate where I had slipped, but I couldn't come up with anything. All I knew was that I could not mention a word of it to most initiates. It would be like dropping a grenade on their faith.

I became harsher and harsher with myself. I tried to eradicate the plague I believed was contaminating my head and soul. I beat myself mentally until I had nearly replaced the disturbing episode in my mind with a picture of Holiji rocking all my worries away. My entire social life depended on this. If I dared to open my mouth, my friends would vanish forever. I'd be damned. And for what? However, I couldn't forget, no matter how hard I tried. I began to realize that *maybe* I could do without friends who wouldn't stand up for me. But this was still unbearable to contemplate.

I considered sharing my outrage with Hugo, but I changed my mind because I knew he would tell the others. Camille would have believed me too, but I didn't want to involve her. She would have had to take sides, and I couldn't do that to her. I whipped my brain into a frenzy for several days, and as time passed I couldn't help but see Holiji through Odette's eyes. Through her so-called lying eyes. I needed to discuss it with someone.

My first pick would have normally been Linda, but she was away visiting her adoptive mother in St. Sauveur. The woman was sick with what seemed to be bronchitis, and Linda's dad was worrying and needed his daughter by his side. Though this meant she would miss some *satsangs* hosted by Holiji, she didn't hesitate. "Family comes first," she told Alex and me.

Now that I had made a decision to tell someone, I couldn't wait any longer to get it off my chest. One morning, a couple of days before Linda was scheduled to come back, I awoke a hundred percent certain in my gut that I had actually been abused by Holiji. I swore to myself that I would spill the beans on some devotee's knees before the sun had time to set in the patch of blue sky I could see from our bed. It was Alex I chose to tell.

After breakfast, Alex and I took a walk to the corner store to buy cigarettes. That's when I decided to tell him.

His reaction was similar to the one I'd have expected had I told him I was planning to start my own satanic movement.

"You're making a big mistake," he said.

In other words, he didn't believe me.

Okay, so I shouldn't have told him. Linda wouldn't have reacted this way, though she would have probably advised me to shut up. She might even have warned me about Alex's reaction. After all, she knew him almost as well as I did. One thing I knew for sure was that she would have believed me. I pictured Linda, my best friend, fighting tears of rage at Holiji for betraying me. Never mind me, for betraying all of us. She would have said this was our little secret, like the other hundred little secrets we had accumulated throughout the years. She probably would have asked me to take some time to think things over, the way best friends do. It's hard to be as good a friend with your boyfriend as it is with your best friend. How many humans actually get the chance to spend the major part of their life with the person who sincerely and unconditionally cares for them the most?

"But I haven't done anything. I sat there and—"

"You shouldn't have sat on his lap."

"But he asked me to!"

"You should have stayed put. You should have simply listened to what he had to say and done exactly what he asked you to do."

I wasn't sure whether he realized how stupid he sounded. "But I *did* do what he asked me to. We should always do what Holiji asks us to do, right?"

"Depends on what you think he's saying, or what you think he's asking you."

"He insisted that I sit on his lap! Are you suggesting I provoked him? You think I'm making this thing up just to have an argument with you? Yeah, sure, Alex, I imagined the whole thing, and it wasn't his hand rubbing my left tit right here." I grabbed my breast to demonstrate.

Alex pulled his hand from mine. "You disgust me."

"I disgust you? *I* disgust you? What about him? Man, you're not being fair. It's not like I staged this! Whose side are you on, anyway? Put yourself in my shoes for a minute! For years, I called this man 'holy father'!"

His fucked-up iris was glaring at me. "What I'm saying is that it didn't happen the way you describe it. You misjudged his intentions—that's what I'm saying!"

I couldn't remember ever seeing him so mad at me. Not even that day in Niagara Falls.

"Maybe you crave that kind of attention from him. Maybe you just wished for Holiji to make a pass at you. You always bitch about Fiona being his favourite one. Maybe your jealousy is playing tricks on you. I'm sure you misjudged the expression of his holiest intentions. Maybe the moment was just too pure for you—"

"You're unbelievable. I misjudged his fucking holiest intentions? Are you kidding me? It's not like I was on acid when I walked in there. You saw me—don't you remember? I have never been so fuckin' aware in my whole life! I tell you, he was licking my gums with his tongue while fondling my breast. He had a huge hard-on. Why don't you believe me?"

Alex pressed his palms on his ears. He really wanted to strike me, but he didn't dare. Had I been a vampire, he would have known exactly what to do to make me and my sacrilegious words go away. Garlic, drops of holy water, a crucifix, daylight coming sooner or later. Something as simple as opening the window to see me fly away in the early sun. That same sun I had sworn to myself would not disappear before someone out there learned about Holiji's true nature. But there was no vegetable, herb, or soy product known under God's sky to cure blasphemy, nothing to protect you against disturbing stories discrediting the absolute perfection of a most irreproachable guru.

The Beatles had warned us about gurus. Didn't they write

a song about Maharishi Mahesh Yogi telling us to be careful about so-called enlightened masters?

I tried to mention this to Alex, but he didn't want to hear it. My own boyfriend didn't believe me, certainly not enough to want to investigate. He stood on the sidewalk and pontificated.

"Oh man, leave the Beatles out of this! You know what, Geneviève? Let's stop this discussion right now. We disagree, and that's not the end of the world. Let's not talk about this again, okay? Let's put it all behind us and go on as if nothing has ever happened, which I think is the case. But, and let me insist on this, I respect the way you interpret this—this—incident."

Strangely enough, I was relieved. I had not expected him to become so mad at me. Alex sighed and hugged me. He loved me.

But he didn't believe me. Though I was good at concealing it, it angered me deep down inside. If I hushed it, it was only because I was still too shaken to think clearly. Alex was my life and so were my friends, especially Linda, who was just about to receive initiation and was totally devoted to Holiji. Would I find the guts to walk away from them all? Did I really want to?

Though he was the one who said we shouldn't discuss it anymore, that evening, Alex, obviously still in shock, begged me to keep the story to myself. He said I would be lost without Holiji. He couldn't imagine his life without the guru's influence guiding his every step. He said I should try to locate what went wrong in my memory of the event. He couldn't conceive of the idea that the man we relied to guide us in everything from food choices to our future actions could have a flaw, and certainly not one of this nature. In short, I was the one on trial here.

"What about Odette?" I asked.

"What about her? She's crazy and frustrated. Ask Fiona."

"So you think I'm frustrated because—" I paused and took a long breath. "—we don't have sex anymore?"

"I didn't say that. Odette is frustrated spiritually, and she's mentally unstable. You're not frustrated because we don't have sex. We don't have sex because Holiji says we shouldn't, not unless we want a baby, and we don't. You understand that."

I wasn't sure I did. But obviously, Alex did for the both of us. "Can I tell Linda?"

Panic rose in his eyes. "Of course not!"

"But how can I keep something like this from her? She's my best friend, remember?"

"That's the whole point. If she's your best friend you shouldn't pollute her head with your perception of what happened."

Ouch. I knew he was trying to protect me. And her. But still, it hurt.

Linda was initiated that same weekend. "At last!" she said, sighing blissfully.

Alex and I helped her remember the words of the *simran*. She was radiant.

A couple of weeks later, Holiji left town to resume his tour. Despite his busy schedule while in Montreal, Fiona had managed to spend a couple of hours every day with the guru, meditating and talking about the baby. Jude told us that Holiji had told Fiona and him that their baby would be very special, that he or she had a grand destiny. I had never seen Fiona so wrapped up in Holiji's teachings. She seemed transformed by all those meditations, but she became edgy the moment she snapped out of it. She was surely exhausted by it all.

I saw Holiji many times after the incident, and he never seemed to be embarrassed by my presence. Sometimes I caught myself wondering if I had not imagined the whole thing after all. His smile was so affectionate, his hands so clean. Quite unfortunately, my mind remembered all too well how deadly ordinary his eyes had looked when he'd tried to force himself on me.

Chapter 63

*Listening to Steely Dan singing about a large black
domestic ruminant*

By February of 1980, Fiona could hardly move. Six months into her pregnancy, she looked as if she was about to explode. She spent most of her time in bed, her feet raised high on a stack of pillows. Jude said she looked happy but seemed preoccupied, almost upset, at times. Though Fiona told him there was nothing wrong, Jude noticed she didn't eat that much anymore. Nevertheless, her belly kept expanding.

Three months had passed since Fiona had last seen her reddish pubic hair below her stomach. She wore a T-shirt that said "Under Construction" with arrows pointing down to her belly button. Every evening before they went to bed, Jude massaged her swollen feet with a balm perfumed with a few drops of eucalyptus essential oil. He assumed she would give birth prematurely, but she told him that her midwife didn't agree. First-borns have a tendency to be lazy, reported Fiona. They procrastinate. *Des branleux,* as we say in Québec. Fiona said she was in no hurry. She loved being pregnant. She still spent hours meditating by herself every day. She tried hard to look serene and on top of things, but she was obviously exhausted.

"I have all the time in the world!" she said, giggling half-heartedly.

To preserve my mental sanity and to keep my relationship with Alex intact, I resolved anew to forget about the Holiji incident. I numbed my feelings for Holiji, and instead I focused on his teachings. I forced myself to appreciate him the way I would appreciate any other ordinary human being with great ideas but questionable conduct. Like John F. Kennedy, for example. Great humanitarian, naughty man.

Every Sunday after *satsang,* Linda and I helped Jude and Fiona in the kitchen. It became increasingly difficult for me not to tell Linda about Holiji, but I remained true to my word to Alex. I was sure Linda had noticed a shift in my spiritual behaviour, but she remained quiet. I guessed she was waiting for me to open up. Or, like everybody else, she thought I was still grieving for my mom.

Along with Alex, Linda meant the world to me. Lately, she hadn't been looking too healthy. Maybe it was the bad flu running around. She said she was feeling fine, and I hoped she wasn't saying that just to reassure me. Alex said I was worrying for nothing.

"Maybe she needs a change of air, that's all. Didn't she mention something lately about spending a couple of weeks with her parents in the countryside? That'll do the trick, I'm sure. Fresh air will do her good. You know Linda, she's frail physically, but she's tough mentally."

I didn't remember Linda saying anything about paying a visit to her family. My mind was going to the dogs.

The next Sunday, Linda, Alex, and I were driving home from *satsang* in the old station wagon Alex's father had offered him a few weeks after we returned from California. Alex said he'd take us girls to the apartment, and then he'd head for his grandmother's house to paint her bathroom, something he had promised to do for weeks. I asked when he'd be home.

"I'll see. Depends on what Yaya's cooking for dinner," he added, winking.

He looked a little pale too. If both of them had caught the flu, I'd be next for sure. I made a mental note to take some vitamin C before going to bed. I was halfway up to the front door when I noticed Linda wasn't behind me. She was still in the car. She stepped out carefully as if in slow motion. She appeared to be a little dizzy.

"You okay?"

"Yeah, sure. I'm just a little tired lately."

"Maybe it's the flu."

"Yeah, maybe. Nothing serious, I'm sure." She pulled back a little as I took her arm. "Don't worry, I'm fine," she said. Her eyes avoided my concerned gaze.

We headed for the kitchen. As Linda sat down at the table, I took a long look at her. She twisted a lock of hair between her fingers, examining the result with crossed eyes. I made another inquiry about her health.

"No, no. I'm feeling fine, really," she insisted.

I put the kettle on the stove to make tea and got something to smoke from the pantry's top drawer. I rolled a joint. Linda's strained face stared absently at my hands. It made me uneasy. Ever since my mother's illness, I approached people's apparent state of health with skepticism. You can't always tell when a deadly disease is spreading through the body of a loved one. It's very subtle, like water leaking under a shut door. Nobody notices until they step in it, and then it goes "squish, squish." I know this sound only too well, it's the voice of a doctor muttering words like "cancer." When you hear it, it's too late to save your ass or your carpet.

At first, my brain spun with the thought that Alex might have told her about my encounter with Holiji. That would explain why she had seemed distant from me in the past few weeks. Not obvious, but I could feel it. I could hardly believe

Alex would have had the nerve to tell her. But if he had, perhaps he'd only meant to warn her because he didn't believe I would keep my mouth shut. Still, if that were the case, wouldn't she be mad at me for not sharing my secret with her? What a mess. I felt ashamed to realize how saddened I'd feel if I were in her shoes, being told of a tragedy in my best friend's life weeks after its occurrence. After all, what are best friends for? What if she weren't sick at all, but confused and terribly angry at me? It was all Alex's fault, really. If he hadn't made me promise to keep it to myself, I would have told her. If only she had been around that day, she would have been the first one to know.

"Are you okay?"

"Things can be so complicated sometimes," is what she chose to answer.

I gave her a quizzical look, but she didn't go on. I poured the tea and spread cookies on a plate, waiting for what would come next. Nothing came. Linda was inspecting her hands and that lock of twisted hair dangling on her cheek.

"Linda, are you mad at me for something?"

She shrugged. "Of course not."

Okay, so what then? That's it. She's sick. "Are you sick? Like—really sick?"

She shivered abruptly as if I had nudged close to the tender spot. "Not exactly."

A minute passed. Linda opened her mouth, seeming ready to spill it all out. I held my breath. If my best friend was ill enough to die, I thought I'd die too. I certainly wouldn't get over this one, not after all that had happened to me that year. Anything else I could manage, anything. But not something happening to her, Alex, or Boogie. Linda was fidgeting in her seat like a cat about to cough up a hairball.

"I'm pregnant."

I felt a wave of relief. "Really? You're sure? Like you've been to the doctor, and he says you're pregnant?"

"I'm afraid so."

Yves, her ex-boyfriend, had never been a condom man, and I knew she couldn't resist having sex with him. Still, she hadn't talked about him in weeks, and I'd assumed she had gotten rid of him for good. Why hadn't she told me about what was going on? Then again, I'd never made it a secret that I didn't like Yves. Maybe she didn't feel like hearing the same nagging shit from me when all she wanted was to get a little sex here and there. For medical reasons, Linda couldn't take the pill, but despite Yves's preference, she always carried condoms in her purse. Yves probably refused to put them on. I imagined she had weighed the odds of getting pregnant fuck after fuck. There was no happiness in her face. She rose and paced around the room.

Poor thing. You're not alone, my dear friend. "No problem," I said, reaching out to take her hand. "We'll manage."

"No, we won't." The answer was firm, almost aggressive.

"You're not thinking about getting an abortion, are you?" When she didn't answer, I went on. "You can't do that, Linda, you know you can't! Holiji wouldn't agree! We're your friends, Alex and me. We won't let you down. We'll help you take care of the baby. We'll raise that baby together! He'll be our baby too. Please don't ever consider—"

"Alex is the father."

Chapter 64

Listening to Marianne Faithfull asking her boyfriend where he found the nerve to have sex with another woman in their own bed

"ALEX IS THE FATHER," she repeated, as if saying it a second time would make it sound better.

I looked at the ceiling, amused by the impossibility.

Linda raised her voice. "Alex is the father! It's the truth. And Holiji knows about it. He agreed to bless our union when he was here. We love each other more than words can say ... Oh, man, I don't know what I'm saying ..."

I laughed. "This is a joke—right?" *A real bad joke, right?*

Linda stood up and sat again. "I wish it was."

The floor moved under my feet. As I stood up, my chair hit the wall. Linda looked at me with that pitiful face of hers. There wasn't a drop of defiance in her eyes. She frowned and turned her face sideways as if she was expecting me to hit her. She deserved it. She was begging for it because it would have diminished her guilt, a pleasure I was not about to grant her. My stomach hurt. My head hurt. God, even my hair hurt.

She buttoned up her coat and ran to the front door.

I stayed in the middle of my kitchen floor, a cookie crumbling in my hand.

She yelled from the staircase, "I love you! I love him! But I couldn't have the both of you. You had each other, and I wanted you both. I had to choose. Can't you understand that at all? I've never been so much in love in my life and—"

I didn't want to hear. These were more or less the words I had once used on an ex-boyfriend of mine—Jean-Luc—and I had used them to make him go away.

I yelled back. "Shut the fuck up! *Shut up!* Get the fuck out of my house and shut the fucking door!"

And she was gone.

I was crying with rage. The first thing that came to my mind was to wait for Alex in the dark and stab him with a fork the moment he stepped in. I didn't know what to do with myself. Every thought burned like vinegar on an open wound. I called his grandmother's place, but he wasn't there. The yaya was confused. She heaved noisily.

"He told you he was on his way here? Well, I guess he changed his mind again."

She couldn't imagine how cruel her words sounded to me.

"Did he tell you he was on his way to paint my bathroom?" she went on. "That's Alex, I tell you! He says something one second, and then he does something else. Same thing last year with the tomatoes. He said he'd take me to the Jean Talon market, but he forgot all about it. I had to ask Mario, the neighbour's son! Can you imagine? I hardly know the boy! Have you ever seen him? He can't be more than sixteen, and his mother lets him drive her car! Isn't it outrageous, not to mention—"

I couldn't hear her anymore. I hung up, saying there was something burning in the oven when in fact it was my heart that was up in flames. I wasn't sure about anything anymore. Alex was gone. He was cheating on me with my best friend, and some bathroom walls in Rosemont needed a fresh coat of paint. That much, I knew.

I called the music shop, but he wasn't there either. I curled up in a ball on my bed, hugging Boogie. Alex was most certainly at Linda's place, feverishly expecting her return. Fucking coward. I dialled her number a hundred times but hung up before anybody answered.

How long had this been going on? When had they first kissed? I mean a real kiss, a tongue kiss, nothing like the one Holiji had given me—no, a first long kiss full of saliva and expectations. The kind of kiss that has the power to wound bystanders.

We love each other more than words can say. Holiji knows about it. The words resonated in my head like a gong gone mad. I cursed them both. Make that the three of them. I wished for her to abort, to fall down a staircase, to break her neck. How could they? I mean, love each other? Was this a valid excuse to ruin my life? Fuck them both and their love! How could they even consider falling in love with me there? How could they let this happen to me? How could they love each other so much anyway? I needed to know exactly when this crazy idea of falling in love had occurred, and who had initiated what and how and why. *Bitch! Bastard!*

Like a pathologist examining a dead body for clues of foul play, I reviewed the past year carefully, one event at a time. But digging out every detail only served to fulfill my irrepressible need to feel as rotten as humanly possible. That day in California, for example, when Linda said she was feeling too ill to join Jude and me on our trip to the bikini shop. Alex said he'd take care of her. I'll bet he did! And in Niagara Falls, when Hugo came to get me when Alex left me stranded on the road, who was in the room with Alex? Linda. All those nights he supposedly fell asleep at the studio. All lies. Lies, lies, lies. What an asshole! And her? She'd spend the evening with me and the night with him. What a fool I'd been. What weasels they were. *Fuck you both!*

Alex didn't come home that night. In fact, I hardly ever saw him again. I heard about him and Linda from time to time, but that was it. I stopped attending *satsangs,* and nobody asked to know why. This could only have meant that some of my friends knew about Linda and Alex. Who exactly? Which one of my so-called friends had been an accomplice? Someone must have witnessed something fishy going on at one point or another. I planned a giant clean-up of my social circle. Then I'd have to figure out how to use that large empty space out there, a vision that petrified me.

A few weeks later, while I was at work, Alex and Linda came to the apartment and took whatever Alex considered his. I came back home to find the place half empty. Alex had left a note telling me he'd live at Linda's place until I'd move out. The old lady next door told me she had seen Alex with "your friend, the pretty brunette," carrying boxes and furniture into a small truck.

I walked in the apartment and found Boogie on the bed. The moment she saw me she turned on her back for a tummy rub. I sat next to her and cried my eyes out. How could I possibly survive all the shit I'd had to deal with in the last months? The only thing that might make me feel better would be to kill Alex and Linda with my bare hands. That would be proof that I was over Holiji completely. I could have wiped my butt with his phony message of love and compassion.

Chapter 65

Listening to James Taylor singing some angry blues

I WAS IN NO RUSH to feel better, and I decided to indulge in a little depression for a time. A benign existential angst, one nobody could fuss about. This personal Armageddon of mine made me want to eat worms and pass out in a corner, abandoned by all. My spirit wandered below ocean's floor. I felt like an old sock you find behind your dresser a week after you've finally resolved yourself to throw away the other one. I had never missed Linda, Alex, and Holiji so much in my life. I missed the way I felt about them. I missed the security of once believing they cared for me.

Suicide was contemplated for a fat three minutes for the sole purpose of inflicting the unavoidable feelings of guilt on the consciences of every individual who had been mean to me since high school. What I prayed for instead was something bigger than the mere taste of revenge. I wanted to be happy. Nothing more. This goal appeared to be the best way to get even with everybody. All I needed was a little strength to let go of a few items in that sorry life of mine, notably Alex's unfaithfulness, Holiji's sexual urges, Linda's treason, and my mom's death. But reaching this goal would prove to be the hardest thing I'd attempted in my life up to that point. The last five years had been nothing but a big mistake, a fact I found hard to swallow since this amount of time represented more or less a quarter of my existence.

I soon discovered that Alex and Linda's affair had been going on for well over a year. And yeah, everybody knew about it. Jude, Hugo, Frankie, Milou, Tintin, Grace, Camille, Claude. Not that they necessarily condoned it, but they decided it was wiser to betray me by keeping me in the dark.

Everybody knew, that is, except for Fiona. Nobody wanted to take the gamble of including her in the secrecy. God knows why they assumed she would care. Jude told her a couple of weeks after Linda let the cat out of the bag in my kitchen. That same week she made a comment to me at work. Her words startled me.

"It's the beginning of the end when friends start lying to each other. On big issues such as these anyway. You and I would never do something that reprehensible to each other now, would we?"

I could hardly believe Fiona really meant what she was saying. I mean, the part about the two of us being friends.

"It's a double insult. You're losing your boyfriend *and* your best friend. Not to mention that this baby should be yours."

Thanks for reminding me, Fiona. Was that what friends were for? Tactlessly reminding you of painful truths?

I was more than ever determined to never let anyone know about Holiji's reprehensible conduct. I swore I wouldn't be remembered as another lying Odette. Also, that way, I could keep my day job.

My existence slipped out of orbit. I didn't plan the details of it. It just happened, like a sneeze attack or that stain on my best shirt. I shed nearly fifteen pounds. Weighing below one hundred to start with, I was a sorry sight.

I met my brother, Carl, for lunch. He said I should carry a sign reading Give. I reminded him of the starving Biafran children we saw every night on the evening news. He checked the circumference of my wrists, whistling his disbelief. He pressed the back of his hand on my forehead, apprehending fever, and grinned sadly at my pale complexion. The waitress came over. I ordered a glass of tomato juice with no ice. Four truckers in brown uniforms walked in, cursing.

"Tabarnac de colice de saint-ciboire!"

It was raining like hell out there. The waitress made a disapproving face at the swearing, the mud, and the water these men were dragging in their trails. She pointed out an empty table to them then turned her attention back to us, dutifully scribbling on her notepad "1 tomato juice with no ice." She was an old waitress. You'd think she'd have mastered the art of abbreviation by now.

"That'll be all for you, miss?"

"Yeah, thanks."

Carl looked at me the way Nehru looked at Gandhi on the thirtieth day of his fast.

"Give her something, anything, but give her something to eat."

I shrugged.

"And for you, sir?"

Carl scratched off a piece of dirt from his index fingernail. "Something bad will happen if you go on like this."

The waitress was getting impatient. She didn't care if I was about to die from tuberculosis right under her nose. She needed to know what Carl wanted to eat, and she needed to hear it now. There were four hungry men to be fed and mud to be mopped. Carl ordered his favourite, pasta with tomato sauce, probably hoping I'd take a bite or two if there were no meatballs in it. The waitress hurried back to the kitchen with a sigh of exasperation so deep it blew the napkins off our table.

"You have to eat something."

"I'm not hungry, and I feel fine."

"You'll die."

"Won't."

He tried to scare me with tales of horror on the effects of malnutrition, but I didn't want to know. I wasn't trying to kill myself. I wasn't being bad to myself on purpose. I just didn't feel like doing much anymore, including eating. Considering the circumstances, I didn't think it was so weird. I was too wired to feel hungry, and I couldn't make it better by addressing the issue openly because not one of the individuals who deserved my anger—the whole gang actually— was willing to confront me. I was puzzled by their behaviour. I thought they'd comfort me, telling me how sorry they were, swearing revenge on Alex and Linda. Instead, they avoided me, or more precisely, they avoided being alone with me. I shouldn't have been surprised, since most of them had been friends with Alex since their early youth. They considered me a vital part of the gang but if they had to choose, hell, what were they supposed to do?

I didn't see much of them anymore, and when I did it was never one on one and, of course, never in the presence of Alex and/or Linda. Camille was working again on Thursdays, and in my self-pitying logic I figured she too was avoiding me on purpose. My friends were protecting themselves the way wolves do. They circled around each other. They didn't want to look at their dirty selves. They anticipated the moment I would choose to shove a spotlight at their weasel faces. They had nothing against me personally, but I was expected to adapt myself to the situation. Some of them had already gone through this kind of ordeal, and they had all survived. Hugo when Marie left, Milou when he came back from Spain, Tintin when Milou was gone. Grace alone had surfed that wave a hundred times.

The basic principles of compassion dictate that you shouldn't allow yourself a day of rest until you have mastered a way to react with infinite kindness to everything coming your way, good or bad, difficult or easy. But I had long figured out that if I were to spend my life trying to tolerate everything that was wrong with this world, I would choke like a dog on a chicken bone. The hunger in Bangladesh, the drought in Africa, the South American guerrillas, communism, Kissinger, the mourning of a mother and a guru. Or the combined loss of a lover and a best friend—neither of them being actually dead; instead, rather quite healthily fucking each other's brains out. Calamities such as these would wear me out like sandpaper in my shoes.

There was no way around the situation: keeping my friends meant that 1) I'd have to be able to forget about Holiji's betrayal, and 2) I'd have to go back to being my good old self with Alex and Linda. In other words, I'd have to act as if nothing particularly bad had ever happened. Worse, I would have to admit, first to myself and then to the others, that this turn of events in my romantic life was in the best interests of everyone involved. I couldn't picture myself doing that. Even if I could succeed in raising sufficient inner control to sit in Alex and Linda's presence and restrain myself from aiming at their respective jugular veins with my nails, there was no way in hell I could watch them acting the way new couples do—holding hands, kissing, laughing, or drinking from the same beer. Then what? I would be expected to share a laugh with them? Perhaps I should cook a nice meal and invite the two of them over for dinner? Then I could cry myself to sleep, knowing that my boyfriend was making love to my best friend, my painfully accurate imagination depicting two intertwined bodies I knew so damn well? Of course, it would only be a question of time before someone made the inexcusable error of calling Linda by my name or vice versa. Alex would certainly do it. "Old habits are so hard to kill," he'd laugh, kissing Linda's hand.

One of us three—make that four if I included Holiji in this equation, not to mention the baby—had to go, and since patience came last on the list of my scarce virtues, I volunteered. I walked away. This move seemed logical, though nonetheless painful. No one interfered. My friends had every reason to be ashamed. As it often happens when something or someone makes people feel squeamish about themselves, he or she—or it—is usually pushed out of sight. Far from the eyes, far from the heart. Like an old aunt everybody likes a lot, but who's suddenly entrusted to a nursing home because she has recently developed a severe case of incontinence. Just too embarrassing to look at. So I disappeared.

No one seemed to notice I was slipping away for good. The transition was easier than what I had imagined because the one and only alternative was unconceivable. I sincerely tried to pile up enough compassion in my heart to be able to love every creature on earth, but—and I can't recall if I felt repentant or proud about this—there wasn't enough love in the whole universe for me to ever forgive these three assholes.

Not ever! I thought foolishly.

Time proved me wrong on that one. I forgave two of them. But it took a long time.

With the help of Carl and his beat-up car, I moved in a small studio, wondering when the new couple would move in the place I had once shared with Alex. I called Alex's father to thank him for the apartment. After all, we'd had the place for free for a long time. The old man was embarrassed and didn't know what to say. I didn't either, so I hung up the moment I was done.

I took the inventory of my life with no enthusiasm. My existence was like a broken possession, something I really valued but wasn't quite qualified to fix. Like a favourite book forgotten out in the pouring rain. A soaked, barely salvageable life. I didn't want to throw it away just yet, but I didn't want to hang on to it either. I stayed put, awaiting further events. Or with a little luck, a celestial sign.

Chapter 66

Listening to Dire Straits singing about a Shakespearian juvenile love

Back at Maya, Jude said Alex was "weak" and Linda "heartless." He said he sympathized with me for this "extremely frustrating embarrassment." His exact words. He didn't say "sad" or "devastating" or "overwhelming." None of that emotional stuff for Jude. For him that brand of "embarrassment" was catalogued as "extremely frustrating," like a tenacious piece of tape stuck on your fingers. I didn't say a word. There had been some distance between us lately. I was struggling just to keep afloat while Jude and Fiona were both busy with the baby's arrival and that million-American-dollar deal. They were in total control of every little detail in their existence, and I was a plastic bag flying on the highway on a windy day.

One day, Jude was watching me attentively as I sorted books in alphabetical order in a cart. We were alone on the floor except for one customer, an older woman, who stood in the aisle next to the tea room. Le Salon de Thé—Fiona's new addition to the centre at the time of the renovations—offered inventive chai teas in a velvety atmosphere ringing with smooth jazz or chamber music. A great place to sit and taste exotic hot liquids while flipping the pages of a book. Despite Jude's skepticism, the place was a hit in the neighbourhood.

Jude was standing behind me—I could feel him. He spoke suddenly, saying Alex and Linda were divine instruments that had been placed in my path to remind me—and everybody else for that matter—that we should never, ever take anything for granted in this physical world of ours. He took a book from a shelf.

"*Energy Ecstasy and Your Seven Vital Chakras.* Hmm—how promising!"

He should have known about that book already, a beautifully illustrated classic by Bernard Gunther. Jude read a passage silently. Then he gave me a lecture on chakras, and what he believed the Holy Scriptures said about them. I was listening with one ear. I knew from experience that the last thing Jude wanted in a moment like this was a two-way conversation. My mind drifted away for a minute.

He got my attention back in a snap. He was talking about Alex and Linda again. I interrupted him, whispering through my teeth, "Did you tell Alex you thought he was dumb, and did she cry when you told Linda she was a bitch for doing what she did to me?"

He didn't even blink. "Why the hell would I do something like that?" And he laughed.

A customer came up the staircase, glanced at us, then disappeared into the tea room. I heard Ingrid, the new waitress, greeting him. I returned my attention to my cart.

Jude grinned at me. He was toying with me, the scumbag. I couldn't tell him to fuck off. I needed that job, and he knew it. I don't think he was being consciously cruel. Jude was, most of the time, *carelessly* cruel. Like a cat playing with a mouse. Cats love to contemplate the plethora of unpleasant things they can subject a mouse to before killing it. Jude didn't mean to be mean. Unlike the cat, when he was done, he didn't go for the kill. He just enjoyed having a little fun at your expense, whenever he knew he couldn't fail.

I snatched the Gunther book from his hands and shoved it back on the shelf angrily. Jude kept smiling and waggled his index finger *no, no, no* in my face. As calmly as I could manage, I pushed his hand away and headed toward the back of the store, my cart still half full. He followed me and closed the door behind him. I ignored my boss and got busy unpacking books from a pile of boxes. I played a song in my head to bury his voice, but no matter how high I cranked up the volume I heard every word he said.

"Do you know that Holiji has forgiven Alex and Linda, and that he blessed their union?"

Books, books, concentrate on books. *Om mani padme hum. Om mani padme hum. Om mani padme hum. Relax. Breathe.* Not that I should have cared or been surprised, for that matter. He fucking blessed their union, knowing my mother had just died. What a vile thing to do! Had he actually given his consent before or after he'd shoved his tongue in my mouth?

Jude wasn't done yet. "It was the right and only thing for him to do because that's what love is all about! It's hard to accept, but everybody should rejoice, including you, my dear. It's your karma. The three of you are entangled in a karmic mess. Then again, aren't we all?"

Judging by his face, that was hilarious. His expression was begging for an insult. This bastard honestly believed I had to forgive. I stayed silent, biting my lips until I tasted blood.

Chapter 67

Listening to Leonard Cohen singing that light comes through broken things

I WENT CHASING FOR A new set of friends the way you go out looking for a new pusher. I didn't talk to just anybody; instead, I waited for references.

One afternoon at the centre, Fiona introduced me to a really nice girl named Chantal. Chantal was the girlfriend of Angelo, Jude's new partner from South America, who was also involved in the million-dollar deal. Angelo had travelled from Santiago to Montreal in 1973. He came with his mother, father, grandmother, two sisters, four brothers, a nephew, a parrot, two calico cats, and a few good ideas to smuggle dope in Canada. He was introduced to Chantal at a party thrown by a mutual friend. She was on her way to become a civil engineer, something quite amazing at the time for a girl, but she abandoned that path soon after meeting Angelo. He managed to convince her she was wasting her time. He had better plans. Travels and intrigues, a jet-set adventure filled with jumbo planes, chic hotels, cocaine, forged passports, and designer clothes.

Chantal was a French Canadian raised on the South Shore

by a couple of respectable university teachers who saw in their daughter the family's greatest academic hope. She had graduated from university with honours, and besides French and English, she also spoke Spanish and Portuguese fluently. She could read a book of three hundred pages or so in less than three hours. A smart cookie. You discovered her ocean-blue eyes whenever she lifted her thick eyeglasses. She winked a lot, something that made strangers automatically assume she enjoyed their company.

Every once in a while, Chantal came to Maya to go out for lunch with Fiona. One morning she came in unannounced, and Leon told her Fiona would be back in a minute. Our eight-month-pregnant boss was upstairs in the health food section, training a new employee. I would have loved to take this opportunity to chat for a moment with Chantal, but I was in the middle of a purchase order that had to be done within the hour. She walked around the bookstore, watching the stairs for a sign of Fiona. I wondered if she cared for the type of literature we sold. I watched her wandering in the Tantra section, her head tilted sideways over a book of ancient erotic paintings. She didn't look embarrassed one bit when a customer asked if she could recommend a good translation of the Kama Sutra. She answered jokingly that she hoped it was not just another pickup line. The man, realizing she was not part of the staff, turned red up to his ears. Or perhaps he turned red because she had seen through him. I liked that.

Chantal was like a nice version of Fiona. Or rather, like an all-year-round nice Fiona. She displayed the same strength as my boss and inspired the same respect. However, whereas Fiona had often proved to be unpredictable and alienating, Chantal was charming and engaging. She was more together than my redheaded boss. I soon learned she was just as rich and powerful, maybe even more so, but unlike Fiona she didn't seem obsessed with appearances.

Leon said he was going out to get something to eat. I saw

Chantal get herself a cup of tea from the tea room. She came over to me and talked about India, which she had visited twice already. I asked her if she was a disciple of Holiji.

"Me?" she said, shrugging. "Are you kidding? No, that's not my trip."

Great!

Her cup of Yogi tea steaming on the counter, she laughed at my jokes and seemed interested in what I had to say. Within thirty minutes, I felt I had enough evidence to consider adopting this girl as a potential new best friend—if she would have me. Chantal complained about being lonely. She said Angelo was out of town and wouldn't be back for another week. Before I could offer her some company, I heard Fiona coming down the stairs.

"I'd love to go out with you, darling, but I can't. I'm going to a midday concert at Place des Arts with my mother, remember? I told you last week, didn't I? I talked her into staying a little longer in town—can you believe that?" Fiona was giggling as she spoke. "Didn't I tell you about the concert, or is pregnancy making me senile?" More giggles. "I bought these tickets weeks ago! *Madama Butterfly,* my mother's favourite. Don't you remember?"

I turned to Chantal and blurted, "I can't go out now, but I'd love to go out for dinner with you tonight—if you want."

Chantal's eyes sparkled as if the world's most desirable bachelor was asking her out on a date. Sometimes you make friends as easily as you make lovers. Same ballet, different pleasure.

"Sure!" she said. "What time?"

Chantal came to meet me after work, and we took a taxi to a small vegetarian restaurant on Mackay Street called L'Oasis. Though I was still not hungry at times, I had started to eat more or less normally again. Also, this was my favourite restaurant in town. We ordered tofu burritos and sprouted sunflower seed salads. Chantal went ahead with the story of her life. She was moderately enthusiastic about her yoga classes ("Man, this teacher is an in-the-closet sadist") and completely devoted to her new puppy, a mutt named Che or Castro, I can't quite remember. She wanted to have a baby, and she and Angelo were working at it. From what she said, Angelo was a nice guy. She was proud to tell me he was taking her on romantic trips. As a matter of fact, they were about to leave for a three-week vacation in a tiny Mexican fishing village they were particularly fond of. I didn't grasp the name of the place—Zee-something. They intended to make up for lost time. Chantal said there was no doubt in her mind that Angelo would be the father of the three children she planned to bear.

"What about you?" she said. "Your turn."

I disclosed every little sordid detail of my life in a version I hoped was as intelligently condensed as the one she had just served me. I introduced the whole cast: my family, Alex, Linda, the gang, my dog, Holiji. The whole enchilada. She understood. She wasn't baffled by Holiji's behaviour. She said she heard stuff like that all the time, and she swore to never tell anyone. She confessed to not being very fond of Fiona anyway.

"I don't know—I feel like she can't be trusted at all time. A friend, yes, but not a good friend."

I could relate to Chantal even though she was by all means far brighter than I was. After dinner, we went to a café and talked until 1:00 a.m. Following that evening, we saw quite a lot of each other.

Angelo returned from his business trip and spent most of his evenings with Jude. Chantal preferred to stay home with a few close friends, me among them. Sometimes we went out for dinner, all expenses covered by a guilty Angelo. Despite how romantic Angelo reportedly was, she confessed to often feeling lonely and abandoned, one of the many things we had in common.

Fiona later told me that Chantal was the brains behind Angelo in the million-dollar deal. Angelo was a disorganized man, a flaw that made him lose vast amounts of money. His affairs were on the edge of collapsing when Chantal took over. She even coached him when it was time to negotiate. Fiona said she was a real shark.

One morning, a couple of weeks after Angelo's return, Chantal showed up at the centre. I was in the bookshop, examining a flyer offering shiatsu classes. She seemed extremely agitated.

"I couldn't sleep anymore, Geneviève. I had to see you! I drove all the way here so please don't disappoint me." Chantal was out of breath and apparently in a bad mood. She looked around at the few customers in the aisle, then whispered, her words coming out like hiccups. The trip to Mexico, the romantic interlude with Angelo, the vacation she had been talking about for weeks, the intimate getaway wrapped with a ribbon spelling the promise of conception, one of the many steps toward that normal life she was craving—well, it had been called off. From what I gathered, "the jerk"—Angelo, I had to assume—couldn't make it. Business to attend to. I knew how that felt. Chantal could hardly keep her voice down. She said she went crazy when he told her the news.

"I wanted to kill him! The rat! You know what this vacation meant to me. Shit, man!"

A little sob escaped her lips, and she sniffled. She took the flyer from my hands and pretended to read it in an unsuccessful attempt to fight her tears. She pushed her glasses up her wet nose. "But wait, there's more."

She said Angelo had been crimson with guilt. So much in fact, that he suggested for her to keep the tickets and take *me* along instead. "Now what d'you think of that? First I had no intention to let him off the hook so easily, but then I thought, 'Now, wait a minute, this could be great!' Imagine! Three weeks on the beach—you and me. A nice hotel in

Zihuatanejo. Don't tell me you can't, Geneviève. Please!" She made the sound of a whining dog.

A ball the size of a cantaloupe thudded into the pit of my stomach. Chantal was winking big time now. The cantaloupe slipped from my belly to my toes. I was just about to protest weakly when Chantal said she had to speak with Fiona for a minute. *Coitus interruptus.* My eyes followed her climbing the stairs.

Chantal returned half an hour later, pressing her left nostril and snorting swiftly. She winked at me. I winked back. She loved cocaine and always had a little on her. It didn't bother me. She was in control.

I instantly dove back in my tropical mood. She told me about Zee-whatever, the nice hotel, the beaches. I couldn't believe my luck.

"So what do you say?"

"I can't accept, really—it's too much."

"Come on, you have to come! I talked to Fiona just now, and she's fine with it. She said it would do you good 'considering your situation.'" Chantal drew quotation marks in the air with two fingers. We laughed. "And I can't ask her to join us because she can't travel now," she added. "You know she's duc in about three weeks."

Even better.

I called Grace to ask her if she would mind taking care of Boogie while I was away.

"Fuck, yes!" she said. "Of course! Boogie's like a sister to me."

A week later, Chantal and I flew to Mexico.

Chapter 68

Listening to Pink Floyd singing about how we miss the people we love when we are far away

APRIL 1980. ZIHUATANEJO—I EVENTUALLY mastered the pronunciation and spelling—was paradise on earth. The beauty of Mexico overwhelmed my senses. The hotel was small but posh. Each room was decorated with taste and displayed massive, gorgeous pieces of furniture and hand-picked Mexican antiques. Ours was spacious with a breathtaking ocean view.

There were a dozen or so vases filled with tiny white flowers all over the floor, even in the bathroom. A large bowl of exotic fruits sat on the wooden table in the entrance, their strong aromas blending shamelessly with the sweet scent of the unfamiliar flowers. I didn't recognize any of the fruits except for the miniature bananas on top. Chantal stuck her nose left and right. Did we have clean bathrobes? Was the room facing the ocean? She checked the phone for a tone.

I laughed. "Who could possibly call you now?"

She muttered, "Well, if Angelo needs to reach me—"

And the phone rang. It was Angelo. *Hallelujah.* She told him what a coincidence it was and how strongly they were connected, how she wished he could be there with her, and how the room was just perfect, something she had not seemed convinced of five seconds before. She covered her free ear with her palm as if the sound of the ocean was deafening. The still officially-named *jerk*—who, incidentally, was paying for this trip—appeared to be in an apologetic mood.

I wandered toward the balcony. The glass door slid smoothly. Table, chairs, cushions. A hammock shaded by a canopy of leaves was stretched on one side. *Wow.* Vines ran up on the railing, concealing the rust created by the salty air. In a ceramic pot by the door, I recognized birds of paradise. Four of them stood erect, their beaks wide open.

Under a spotless azure sky, the ocean's foamy waves looked like a crinoline beneath a rippling turquoise skirt. To the left, one lonely cloud abandoned by its herd was pinned on the top of a mountain, gutted by the peak, like a warning for the others to stay away. On the white sandy beach, otherwise deserted, a small group of children screamed with delight as they splashed in the water, their naked shoulders roasting under the violent sun and their small hands trying to catch handfuls of the zillion diamonds floating around them. I took a deep breath. I felt the blessing of a here-and-now moment and prayed for this sudden peace in my soul to never end.

Chantal came to join me, a cigarette in her hand. She said something about the phone connection being bad. She pointed at a couple of tiny geckoes pacing the wall, their smooth bodies scurrying on the stucco. She looked over the balcony. "Pretty," she said.

I opened my arms wide toward the beach, and in words that couldn't begin to convey what I was feeling, I told Chantal how fucking beautiful all this was to me. She took a long drag on her cigarette and put her arm around my shoulders. We remained silent for a moment. Chantal was probably pondering about the lousy phone connection while I was marvelling at the magnificent world surrounding me.

Pretty was not the word I would have chosen. With respect to my new friend, *pretty* sounded like the anorexic expression a peasant would use to describe Mozart's music. It felt much more than pretty, much bigger than pretty. Certainly deeper. More meaningful. Something in the line of hope.

Looking at the ocean from that Mexican balcony, I began to sense a new conviction growing in me—a belief that travelling the world with a caring and open mind would make me a better and happier human being. I swore to myself that whenever I might get stuck in the drama of my own existence, I would simply go away as far as I could afford. The goal being not to flee a desperate situation but to create a favourable space to regain some peace of mind, to balance my soul's pH, to be able to think clearly again. In a way, Chantal was instrumental to my obsession with travelling, which began in Zihuatanejo. To this day, going away still helps me to put things in perspective. How intense and simply fulfilling life can be on foreign soil! A new sensation was settling in my bones, my senses consumed with what I felt was my true connection to this world.

I've been afflicted with this condition ever since. *Dromomania* is what Michael Palin from Monty Python calls it. He too is sick with the travelling bug. Contrary to people suffering from other viral illnesses, people living with dromomania are quite happy with their fate.

After unpacking, we stepped out to take a walk. We ate mangoes from a tree and bought papayas for a few pesos from a toothless merchant on a little dirt road next to the hotel. Farther up, we bought plantains, believing they were bananas. The saleslady roared with laughter when she saw us struggle to peel the thick skin off and take a bite. At the end of the trail, we found a small fishing village. Children ran to us asking for pesos and *caramelos.* "*Por favor,*" they begged.

Chantal opened her bag and distributed Juicy Fruit sticks. Chewing ferociously, the kids disappeared. While my friend was busy bargaining for a *pareo,* I bought oranges with the intention of sharing them with the children. To my dismay, not one of them came running to me. How hungry could they have been if they lifted their noses on an orange? And if they weren't hungry, why were they begging? Wasn't it Monday? Shouldn't these kids be in school at this hour? A small boy with a tiny girl glued to his legs—his sister, I had to suppose—walked decisively toward me.

"*Caramelos o pesos, por favor, señorita.*"

"Sorry, I don't have—*je n'ai pas,* no—uh—"

"*Las chicas Americanas siempre tienen pesos o caramelos.*"

I understood one word: Americanas.

"I'm not American, *no soy Americana.* I'm Canadian. *Soy de Canada.*"

He didn't care. He wanted *caramelos* or pesos and nothing else. I had to show him the contents of my bag to prove I wasn't hiding any sweets. The boy screened my jeans pockets with suspicion. I offered an orange to him.

"*No, gracias.*" He left without a smile, his sister clinging to his shin. This was my first encounter with this type of poverty. Selective poor people who are not always happy with the scraps tossed their way by the well-intentioned rich of the world.

The sun was going down and Chantal suggested we go for a stroll by the ocean on our way back to the hotel. The sky was orange, the wind warm and gentle. It smelled as if something pure ruled the world. We sat on the sand, soaking in the impossible colours dripping around us. Before long, the sea swallowed the light and tiny rubbery crabs crawled out from their wet holes. Chantal said she felt ready for a drink.

"Something crazy with a double shot of tequila!" She winked and added, "You'll have one too, Geneviève. We're on vacation, aren't we? We're supposed to have fun and celebrate! Then we'll find something to smoke."

Her plan suited me just fine. We strolled back to the hotel, where we found a small bar by the pool. Chantal asked for two tequila sunrises. Three American couples were sitting behind us. We heard them complaining about the land development in the area. One fat guy who looked stoned out of his mind said this paradise was being ruined by "real estate assholes." Apparently, Club Med was about to build a huge complex called Ixtapa on a nearby beach. I didn't care. I sucked on the straw of my drink, savouring my renaissance.

"You see," I told Chantal philosophically, "life is made of big and small deaths, each of which creates a proportional rebirth."

Under the influence of her second tequila sunrise, Chantal seemed to find my statement absolutely brilliant. She scored grass from a busboy she bumped into on her way back from the washroom. The boy could also supply her with good quality cocaine for a ridiculous price. I couldn't wait to smoke a joint on our balcony. Chantal ordered two more tequila sunrises, and we took them up to our room.

The next morning, my new friend found me on the beach. She approached me lazily, an orange juice in one hand and a lit joint in the other. In those days, I spent as much time as I could in the sun because it tamed the acne still plaguing my skin at almost twenty-three. Surprisingly, Chantal had the same problem—one more reason for us to bond—and she chased rays as incessantly as I did.

We spent our days on one of the three beaches surrounding the hotel, a couple of lizards under a sun hanging in a sky of postcard blue. Before long, we were as brown as the locals. My appetite had fully returned, and we ate with gusto, never thinking twice about ordering too much food. Everything was dirt cheap, and we could indulge without feeling guilty. As far as I was concerned, we were in heaven.

In those three weeks, I grew to know Chantal a little better. If you really want to know somebody, travel with that person. I soon observed that Chantal was not altogether who

I thought she was. Easily irritated, she snapped at me more than once for no reason whatsoever. Cocaine does that to people. Money too. It makes them think they can afford to tell people off whenever they feel like it.

I remember feeling ineffably sad about this. I meant to talk to Chantal about it and let her know how her behaviour offended me. But time would not afford me the chance to discuss the matter with her because a freak show was on his way to Zihuatanejo, and both Chantal and I were about to become busy with much more urgent concerns.

Chapter 69

*Listening to Fleetwood Mac reminding us that the sky
only roars when it's pouring out there*

A FEW DAYS LATER, THE wind changed. The skies turned grey, and it rained heavily. A new revelation was on its way, and I suppose it was only fitting for nature to choose that day to go wild.

That morning, Chantal and I woke up later than usual. I volunteered to step out on the balcony, then ran back to confirm the obvious. The horizon was indeed dark, the ocean complaining strongly while the palm trees spent useless energy trying to whip the clouds away. This would be a perfect morning to stay in and read. Chantal had fallen asleep again when I came back into the room.

We ordered a late breakfast, room service. My second cup of coffee steaming, I grabbed my book and crashed on the couch. Chantal said she was in the mood for a long bath. I rose again to look at the mess outside. The village nearby would certainly be flooded. I heard Chantal turn the taps and could smell vanilla emanating from the tub. The rain played drums on the iron railing as I returned to the couch and cracked open a hard-cover edition of *How to Save Your*

Own Life by Erica Jong, a book I was looking forward to diving into. Chantal asked me to roll a joint. All was silent except for the raging weather and the occasional splash from her bath.

Of course, the phone rang. Some splashing happened from behind the bathroom door, and before I had time to react Chantal emerged, dressed in the white bathrobe supplied by the hotel. In her haste she smashed her elbow on the doorknob and reached for the phone angrily, her thick hair dripping.

"*Hola!*" she said curtly, rubbing her elbow and holding the phone between her head and shoulder. She turned in my direction.

"Angelo?" I mouthed.

She shook her head no. Covering the mouthpiece, she imitated the receptionist's nasally voice. "*Miz* Chantal, somebody is here to see your friend."

Me? "Me?"

Chantal shook her head as if there was no reason to be concerned. "It's a mistake," she said to the receptionist.

"What? Are you sure? Who? An American lady? Can I speak to her?"

Chantal covered the mouthpiece again. "What the hell. Let's go—this could be fun."

"Who the hell is she anyway? Can't she come to the phone?" I asked annoyed.

"The man says she stepped out to pay for her taxi."

Before I could decide whether I was up for it or not, Chantal said to the receptionist, "Okay. Tell her she'll come down in a minute."

She hung up and turned to me. "You have American friends?" She whistled as if she had just learned I was related to the Hearst family. I was as surprised as she was, and I told her so. I didn't know any American person, man or woman, who would have known where I was at that time or cared enough to follow me all the way to Mexico.

But Chantal was clearly dying to see who the mysterious intruder was. I wasn't. Not at all. I pouted. I wanted this woman, whoever she was, to go away and leave me alone with Erica Jong and the vanilla scent of someone else's bath. It could only have been a stupid misunderstanding, nobody I actually knew. Just a terrible waste of my precious vacation time. But I got dressed and joined her at the door. We went down to the lobby.

The man at the desk pointed at the bench in the entrance hall.

No, please. Not her. Not here.

CHANTAL SAID IT FIRST. "Fiona?"

So there was my "American friend." The notion that Jude's girlfriend was a witch who had the power to ruin everything I treasured was once again confirmed in front of my very eyes. The idea that she had come all the way to Mexico to join us increased my horror. But not for long.

Fiona's shaky hands betrayed her wide smile. She mouthed a silent hello. This was not a good sign. She was not about to refer to her presence as a happy surprise, a girls' reunion, or anything of the like. It would be much worse than that. She stood there, a little thing covered in leopard fabrics, lost on the marble floor of my little paradise.

She certainly wasn't pregnant anymore. Her belly looked as flat as a Saskatchewan plain, but maybe it was because of the baggy pants she was wearing. I could tell she was still a little overweight—her shirt was tighter than it should be—but the transformation was phenomenal. Chantal didn't seem to notice so I took a good look a second time. Fiona stared at us as we stared back at her. Her high heels said it all. She wasn't in Mexico for a well-deserved vacation after nine months of impersonating a sumo wrestler version of herself. Had it been the case, she would have been wearing a Gap outfit with brand-new tennis shoes and a bottle of Veuve Clicquot in her hand. "Surprise!" she would have screamed, giggling her ass off, her arms opened wide.

I couldn't see any luggage. A good omen. Whatever the reason for her presence that day, it had to be bad enough for her to be silent. She wore large dark shades, the Jackie-O style, the type that cover your face and make you look like someone who wants anything but anonymity. Her delicate sandals were torn at the heels. She probably hadn't noticed yet.

Chantal stepped forward. "But you're not pregnant anymore!"

Okay, so she was slow on this one. I still couldn't utter a single word. But I listened carefully, making sure I could see Fiona's lips. My curiosity would not be deprived of the tiniest detail of her reply. Chantal and I walked around Fiona from a distance. We must have looked like two dogs eager to sniff her behind. Chantal kissed her, and I did too, reluctantly. A couple came in with their luggage. Fiona looked at them uneasily. The sky was clearing up, and Chantal suggested we go out in the garden. God bless Chantal—it didn't cross her mind to invite Fiona up to our room. Our sacred, un-fucked-up sanctum.

Chapter 70

*Listening to Bob Dylan singing about a conversation
between a wise guy and a larcenist on a barbican*

WE WALKED AWAY FROM everyone, including the gardeners. Puddles of rain spotted our path. We carefully made our way around them. As we sat under a parasol in the garden of our hotel, Chantal tried to fill up the awkward silence. She was nervous, I could tell. Not for herself, but for me. If Fiona had covered all that distance to have a word with me, it could only be because of terribly bad news. I honestly couldn't imagine what more could have possibly gone wrong in this sorry life of mine.

"So Fiona, what brings you here? And where's your baby? When did you—"

"Look at us!" Fiona giggled, interrupting her. "Now, take a look at us!" she repeated. "We look like Charlie's Angels on a mission."

Fiona laughed and Chantal joined in, but I didn't. That reference to a trio of bimbos with guns and preposterous adversaries irritated me. I imagined that in Fiona's fantasy, she was Farrah Fawcett—of course—Chantal was Jaclyn Smith—pretty and also brainy—which would make me Kate

Jackson, the one angel people loved like a sister. The one who wasn't as hot as the other two, but was probably just as smart—nobody knew for sure.

Fiona turned to Chantal. "I'm here to give you bad news, honey."

"To me?" Chantal asked, surprised.

"I'm afraid so, dear."

Chantal turned pale. "Angelo?"

For a second, I was selfishly relieved. Fiona had not travelled all that way to ruin *my* day.

Fiona went right to the point. "He was arrested by the RCMP on his way out of—"

Chantal screamed. *"Noooo!"*

"But," Fiona said, raising her voice. "But, *but*—" She was waiting for Chantal to calm down. "He's in Montreal, out on bail, and he'll meet you in Guatemala in a week or two. In the meantime, you have to stay put."

Quite strangely, considering what Fiona had just thrown at Chantal, the first question on my mind was why Fiona had specifically asked for me at the hotel reception desk when it was Chantal she actually meant to see. I felt extremely sorry for Chantal, but I didn't see what I could be expected to do besides cheer her up while we were still in Mexico. I had no problem dealing with that, especially if Fiona swore on Holiji's head to jump on the first plane heading north. On the other hand, if her idea was to send me to Guatemala with Chantal until Angelo's arrival, she had another thing coming. That would be like her to ask me something like this in front of my friend—making it too awkward for me to decline. I had seen her do it a thousand times. I was convinced this was the reason she had asked for me. She wanted to be sure I'd be there, right in front of a very upset Chantal. *Fuck.* I didn't want to get trapped in another of Fiona's schemes.

Chantal was crying in little sobs, her nose dripping in narrow streams. She was far too much in love with Angelo to abandon him, especially now, when he needed her support. She knew too much about the million-dollar deal to walk away from this bust unscathed. The RCMP had surely followed Angelo for weeks before arresting him, which meant they knew about her. To add to her despair, she couldn't fly from Mexico to Guatemala and allow her family to assume something terrible had happened to her. How could she just disappear? She had to talk to her mother to let her know why she wouldn't return home the following week as expected.

Fiona didn't sympathize. She put her arm around Chantal. "You can't do that, dear. Not if you want to protect yourself and Angelo. We'll notify your family. But you will not call home. You can't, and you won't. For your own safety and his, you must fly from Mexico to meet Angelo in Guatemala."

"He's going to jump bail?" Chantal sounded as if she was hyperventilating. I don't think she had exhaled a single time since Fiona had dropped the bomb on her. She was drowning in open air. There was not enough oxygen in the ocean breeze to save her. Each spasmodic inhalation pushed the pain a little deeper, like a hot knife in butter.

"He has no choice, honey. Either he flees Canada, or he stays in jail for no less than ten years." Fiona's voice softened. "Don't worry. I personally took care of everything. He'll fly from Toronto with a new passport."

"Fiona! How will I explain this to my family? I mean Angelo? The dope deals? Me?"

Poor girl. Her dad and mom were about to be informed that their little genius was on the run with a drug dealer, a man they believed had recently been named salesperson of the year in some imaginary pharmaceutical company.

"The best thing to do is to let them know through one of us that you're fine. There'll be plenty of time to explain later, and we—"

"Who could possibly tell them? They'll freak out!"

"I'll see to it myself if that's what you want. Or, I could ask

Jude to call them."

"No! *No!* Not Jude! Anyone, just *not Jude!*"

Fiona nodded. "Then I'll do it. You understand that I'll have to ask them to keep their mouths shut if they want to protect you."

Chantal was not listening. "How long will we have to hide? And where? Guatemala can't be safe forever."

Fiona didn't even try to sound reassuring. "A couple of years. Maybe more. Until the RCMP have forgotten all about you. Then again, they could be on your trail forever—you never know with them. You may not be able to return to Montreal ever again."

These last words made Chantal pant like a dog. Her face turned the same colour as the roses on her *pareo.* That did it for me too, and I started crying. Chantal turned to me, and we took refuge in each other's arms. I guessed Fiona was pleased. She would have to take charge of everything, since she was the only one thinking straight here. Her expertise would be needed. She looked ready for action, and in that plan of hers there was limited room for sentimentalism.

"Now, now, everything will be just fine. You'll love Guatemala."

Chantal was frantic now, hugging her sides and rocking herself rhythmically to the sound of a long scream coming from somewhere inside her.

Okay now, go away, Fiona, I thought. *I'll take care of Chantal.*

Chantal jumped up. "This is crazy, Fiona—it's not possible," she cried. "We've been so careful. Surely this is just a bad dream? She looked at both of us helplessly. "Actually, I'm quite sure this is a bad dream. Yeah, that's it—it's nothing but a dream. In real life, you're pregnant and too fat."

Chantal was losing her mind. In that dream of hers, she felt she could insult Fiona. What are dreams for anyway but to do things you wished you could do in real life? But she wasn't dreaming. Or we were sharing the same nightmare.

I was certain Fiona wouldn't allow Angelo's girlfriend to be insolent to her. Fiona showed no signs of anger, but her forehead was crumpled in a frown behind her sunglasses. The baroness skilfully adjusted the poison dosage of her response and served Chantal her personal version of a reality check. This royal derrière had not covered all that mileage just to be told she was a bad dream.

"You're so deep in real shit, darling, you'd need chains to pull you out. Your family will learn about Angelo at one point or another. It's too late. Get a grip on yourself, for Holiji's sake! It was a stupid idea to move the dope from one warehouse to the other. I told Angelo, but it wasn't my call. Anyway, it's no use blaming Angelo, Jude, or me, for that matter. What's done is done." She looked at Chantal with no compassion. "It's time for you to save your butt and take care of Angelo. He needs you now more than ever."

Oh yeah, Fiona, sure. Miss Stand by Your Man and Hit Him if You Can.

She took Chantal's hand. I thought she'd say something cheesy like "don't you worry" or "hang in there," but she guided Chantal's hand gently to her belly and handed it back to her as if she was offering a gift.

"Regarding my baby, I gave birth a few days after you girls left. The same day Angelo got arrested, actually. Vincent," she said, smiling pensively for a second or two. "That's my little boy's name. Vincent. Pretty name, isn't it?"

I could swear I saw a glimpse of genuine fragility in her at that moment.

"My little angel, Vincent. I miss him terribly. I flew to Vancouver right after giving birth. He's with my mom now. I sensed that something bad was coming our way. I could feel it. Female intuition, I suppose." She rubbed her hands. She seemed so proud of herself. "Angelo's bust has a terrible impact on our business. Our million-dollar deal is kaput.

The RCMP came to Maya—they'd been following Angelo for some time. Luckily, Jude was in New York at the time and I—protected by Holiji, God bless his soul —was in the hospital giving birth prematurely and completely unexpectedly. Jude will stay put in the States. We have friends over there. I'm going back to Vancouver, but my little boy and I will join Daddy when things calm down a little. I can only stay here for a very short time. I'm breastfeeding, you see."

Nobody was in the mood for a description of her motherhood experience. But Fiona went on, describing how giving birth was "uneventful," something you couldn't possibly do wrong.

"Even if you have no idea of what's happening to you, your body does. Giving birth is ingrained in your female code. You just have to give in to the knowledge within. That's what I did, and I didn't feel a thing."

As if Chantal could possibly care. Of course, even in delivering babies Fiona was special, the best, the Guinness World Record holder. *Vincent, you have such a weird mother.*

Then Fiona threw a quick look at me. "Now," she said with a dramatic air, "there's another matter that needs to be addressed with the most extreme urgency. That's why I also had to see Geneviève immediately."

Okay, so this is it. Spit it out, Fiona.

But she wouldn't look at me anymore. She stared at the ocean as she spoke. "In fact, this is the real reason I'm here. We couldn't have this conversation on the phone." She hesitated. "It's too—too complicated—and too sudden." She added that she could have simply called Chantal from a phone booth to tell her about Angelo's arrest.

"But before we go any further, girls, would you mind if we went to the bar? If I don't drink something, I'll faint!" Fiona whined.

We took a table at the hotel's coffee shop, and before we had a chance to glance at the menu, Fiona ordered iced tea with lemon for the three of us. She didn't seem at ease anymore. The tea was promptly served, and Fiona tasted it. She seemed annoyed to find lime in it.

Chantal was finally getting a grip on herself. "We'll make it through this, I know it," is what I remember her saying.

Fiona dimmed the light at the end of that tunnel of hope by stressing that this bust was the worst they had suffered so far, and that she was seriously concerned about the aftermath.

"We lost everything, Chantal. Everything. The other partners are furious, and I wouldn't be surprised if they were plotting revenge at this very moment. It's better for every one of us to vanish into thin air for a while."

I asked whether I should be concerned. I was getting impatient. When was she planning to tell me what she had taken such pains to come all this way to impart?

"Of course not. The police can't possibly be interested in you"—she pouted with a mix of disdain and envy—"not for anything serious, anyway. In fact, *we* need you." She almost spat those last three words.

Chapter 71

*Listening to David Bowie singing that if you can't afford
the fare for the ride, don't expect him to pay it for you*

"The centre has to be sold," she announced. "We need
you to take it over with Leon. We have to sell it now,
and I mean right now."

I immediately remembered how Jude had flatly refused
two hundred and fifty thousand dollars for Maya the year
before. Was Fiona stupid or what? I didn't have that kind of
money, and she knew it damned well. And what about my
job? If she had chosen this moment to take my hand, I would
have bitten her.

She finished her glass of iced tea. "These are the facts,
darling," she said. "Maya is in great peril, and it's up for sale.
Its survival depends on you."

Really. "Really?"

"Absolutely," she confirmed. "Jude, Vincent, and I will be
out of the country for a year at the very least, maybe more.
Maybe forever." Her hands opened, palms up, signifying the
situation was in God's hands. Or rather, in Hulijl's. "Darling,
I don't know how to put it. We won't be able to take care of
Maya anymore, but we need to know it will go on. Don't you

want it too? For Holiji, you know …"

Of course, this argument had little weight with me. I looked at her with no emotion whatsoever. I could tell she was taken aback by my lack of enthusiasm. Nevertheless, she kept her poise. This was not the time to talk about my apparent indifference to Holiji.

"And not only for Holiji. Also for, you know, all the others—Gurdjieff, Inayat Khan, Rajneesh, Jung, Chinmoy, the health food shop, Le Salon de Thé, the yoga classes—"

I was still cold as a stone.

"Krishnamurti, Mahesh Yogi, Blavatsky, Bailey, Meher Baba, Aurobindo—"

She was trying to find a guru's name that would make my eyes light up. She was incapable of imagining me—or anyone else for that matter—leading a happy life deprived of the assistance of a guru, a teacher, someone telling you when to stop and when to go. For Fiona, life with no spiritual guidance was a pitiful waste.

I said nothing. She ordered more tea. Chantal was scribbling something on her napkin, probably a list of the countless things she had to address and figure out. Things like forged passports, lies, and hearts beating so fast you think you're going to pass out.

"For how long do you expect us to take the centre over?" I asked at last.

"For good. It's over for us, dear. Now, you of all people know as well as I do that not only is Maya a good business, it's also the only New Age meeting point in Montreal. You have a good opportunity here. Don't be a fool—take it."

"Fiona, you know damn well that I don't have enough money to buy myself a new coat, let alone a business. What do you think? That my mother left money to us? Jewels? Gold? She was no baroness, you know."

She looked offended by the sarcasm, but not enough to make me feel good.

Chantal folded her napkin neatly. She asked how safe Guatemala was.

"Safe enough," Fiona replied sternly. "But it's Central America, you know, so you have to be careful. For one thing, El Salvador is close by. Don't worry, you'll be fine. Angelo is a smart man. And you both speak Spanish." She smiled at Chantal with no tenderness, like a bored nurse. Her eyes shifted back in my direction. "How much money do you have to your name?"

I counted mentally. "Six hundred dollars, give or take—Canadian dollars." The amount was so laughable that it was my turn to giggle stupidly.

"Okay. We'll take it."

Say that again? "What? Are you nuts?"

Even Chantal lifted her nose, leaving Guatemala and the guerrillas aside for a minute.

Fiona chased a fly away. "We'll take it. Leon has a little more cash than you, but we'll do it this way. Six hundred each, that's twelve hundred. Don't get me wrong here. It's not that we need the money, it's only to make the sale look legitimate." She made a face as if greed was so far beneath her it could only make her giggle again. "We'll take the money, and upon your return we'll transfer everything to you two. Our lawyers will take care of everything. You sign on the dotted line, Geneviève, dear, and Maya is all yours. Yours and Leon's, of course."

My brain was whirling. "I don't know, Fiona …"

Fiona and Jude had given Leon and me ample opportunities to measure our abilities at managing the place. We weren't doing badly so far. But to own it? I wasn't at all sure.

Chantal looked sideway, indicating she had no idea what to say.

Fiona went on. "I'm sure you'd like to know that Alex and Linda have mentioned they'd be willing to take over the centre if there were no other takers."

I didn't need more to picture myself as a New Age centre owner. After all I had been through, this sounded like a positive turn in my life. The again, the offer was too good to be true. Fiona could not give something without either a high price tag on it or arsenic in it. She expected something in return. Or there was some other catch.

"How much in debt is the centre?" I ventured.

"Around twenty-five thousand dollars."

Wow. That's a lot of dough. "How much money is left in the bank?"

"Zilch. Jude and I took everything from the accounts, Canadian and American."

Ha ha. Of course you did. "Hmm—" Admittedly, it was difficult to be picky when I was offered a new life for six hundred bucks. "Leon is okay with all this?"

"Yes. In fact, he's very pleased. I think he'll make a good—um—business partner."

Fiona had confided in me more than once how she considered her ex-husband to be a terminally dumb subject, a loser, a sculptor with no talent, a man with no skill for business. But Leon was no threat to me. We had a good relationship, and despite his bad breath, we had learned to waltz smoothly on the centre's floor and not step on each other's feet, literally and figuratively. Of course, running a New Age centre in Montreal would not be the remedy to all my sorrows, but maybe Leon and I could make a good living out of it. Sure, the RCMP would pay us a visit or two, but they wouldn't find anything illegal going on, and they'd be on their way.

My mind ran in ten directions. So many possibilities. Owning a business. I liked the sound of that. *Why not? What do I have to lose?* I made a mental inventory of my belongings. Cheap furniture, no car, no house, a middle-aged dog, some clothes, a broken heart, and a disillusioned mind. In other words, nothing worth confiscating if business went bad. I was still on the prowl to find my mission in life, and managing a

New Age centre sounded like a good enough call to answer.

Fiona looked at her watch, waiting for my reply.

"Well, I'm not sure what to say, Fiona. I'd like to have more time to think about it." I paused for a long minute. "But since that's not possible—I accept."

Fiona sighed with obvious relief. "So it's settled, then."

She said she had to leave for Vancouver at once. She was flying early the next morning, and she thought it would be better to take a hotel near the airport. I was relieved, and so was Chantal, I could tell. Fiona paid the bill and the three of us made our way back to the lobby. She asked the reception clerk to call a taxi. Pecks on the cheek, and out she went.

We went back to our room, too freaked out to exchange another word. Chantal didn't check the phone for a dial tone this time. Angelo wouldn't call. We lay on our beds, staring at the ceiling until it was dusk. It didn't rain again that day.

The rest of our Mexican vacation was bearable, considering the circumstances. When Chantal wasn't crying, she spent her time trying to find something good in that messy situation of hers. Lying on my bed or basking in the sun, the only thought on my mind was Maya. I couldn't help it. It was unreal, in a way, to picture Leon and me as entrepreneurs. I forced myself to show more concern for Chantal, and she tried to forget about her predicament temporarily by discussing my plans for Maya, but we never really succeeded in helping each other get a clearer view of what lay ahead.

Chantal left for Guatemala the same day I flew back home. At the airport, we promised to keep in touch, but for obvious reasons, we couldn't. I was losing another friend for good.

A YEAR LATER, CHANTAL was dead. Her little penchant for cocaine, a vice she had always seemed to master with ease, got out of hand. Apparently, she quit the middle-of-the-road route soon after Angelo joined her in Guatemala, and she suffocated as a result of an overdose.

Angelo had the grace to fly back to Montreal with Chantal's body so her parents could bury their daughter in the family plot. Of course, the RCMP caught up with him. The cops put handcuffs on him the minute the funeral service was over.

Chapter 72

*Listening to Bob Dylan singing about losing precious time
with an unworthy lover*

UPON HER RETURN FROM Mexico, Fiona broke up with
Jude, though Jude was the last one to be informed. Too
much money, not enough love—these things apparently
prompted her to let him go. Jude was far from imagining
that he would never in his life set eyes on his own child.

The fact that Vincent had come into this world two weeks
ahead of time, something Jude couldn't have foreseen, especially since the midwife herself had rejected the possibility,
altered his original plans of being next to his sweaty and
swollen girlfriend at the time of the blessed event.

After speaking with Fiona—who was still at the hospital at the time—Jude didn't see the point of flying home
immediately to be with her and the baby. The show was
over. He had missed the birth of his first child. He wasn't
needed to cut the umbilical cord anymore. There would be
no picture of him holding a little bundle of bloody flesh. He
was surprised to realize how much it bothered him to have
missed the whole thing.

Unaware of Fiona's decision to leave him, he was angry at

her nonetheless. Why hadn't she waited for him? How could she have given birth without him around? How could she not have seen it coming? Why hadn't she called the moment she felt the first contraction?

When he spoke to her on the phone, he didn't ask any of these questions. He knew it would only aggravate Fiona, and God knows how she'd make him pay for it. Hate and spite came back as fast as they had vanished months before.

"Why does she always have to spoil things for me?" he fumed. He swore on his son's head that he would be in the delivery room for their next child. "Only one child in a family is unhealthy," he had often told Fiona during her pregnancy. "We'll have two." She had seemed ecstatic at the prospect.

Next time, he vowed he would stick around from the seventh month of her pregnancy. With this thought denting an almost invisible veneer of guilt, Jude went back to his drink and watched the glitter go by at Studio 54.

The next day, he went out for lunch at the Russian Tea Room. He liked to do so whenever his need for more money or fun pushed him aboard the short flight from Montreal to New York. He would have been in Montreal for the big day if Fiona hadn't strongly suggested he see personally to some business details he would have normally dealt with over the phone. He raised a glass of indecently expensive champagne to himself. He was a daddy now, something well worth celebrating. He gulped a mouthful of bubbles and swirled the amber liquid slowly into every corner of his big mouth.

The authentic Swedish twins he had been lucky enough to bump into the night before were true to their word. Jude had promised the sisters a couple of grams of good cocaine if they agreed to join him at the famous restaurant the next day. After the meal, he planned to ask them to follow him to his hotel suite for an afternoon of illicit fun. If he spent enough money on them, the girls would agree. With the hundred-dollar bills he was flashing around and the good dope he always had in his pockets, Jude could be very persuasive with flat-broke pinup-wannabe twins starving in the Big Apple.

He ordered three Brazilian coffees from the envious waiter who couldn't help but wink at him once or twice during the meal, something that pleased Jude immensely. He would leave the man a good tip. The envy could be read in every male's eyes throughout the room. This communal virile moan was the reason Jude would have sex with these twins that same afternoon. Nothing excited this boy more than the knowing that people envied him. He was always more concerned about the celebrities who could see *him* at the Russian Tea Room than the other way around.

He held in his mind the beatific picture of Fiona dressed in white, their naked son clutched to her alabaster breast. Then he thought about Fiona's second call earlier that morning telling him about Angelo's arrest. She said she had heard the news the day before, just before she left for the hospital, but had somehow forgotten all about it by the time she got to speak to him. This puzzled Jude greatly. This new father agreed that giving birth was a major event, but he felt that Angelo's bust was just as crucial. Fiona had to be in another world to have forgotten it. But he forgave her that part. After all, she had just given him a son. Jude emptied his glass in one gulp. In reality, he wasn't overly concerned, though the notion that it would take another opportunity of a similar kind to get rich enough to stop dealing irritated him. The other partners would go ape shit. For some of them, this was their very first deal. Others had invested up to their last cent in it. They wouldn't believe that shit actually happens in that business.

Jude convinced himself that he had been suspicious about the million-dollar deal since day one. Too many people were involved, and most had little or no experience whatsoever. Angelo was fucked. Some of the partners were probably fucked too. But Jude, Fiona, and the baby would be fine.

Holiji was behind this karmic tragedy, and once again the guru expected his two favourite children to draw an essential lesson from it. They both still had to figure out what it was exactly, though. This deal would have put an end to the couple's illegal business, something that should have pleased Holiji. God did work in mysterious ways.

The twins were taking forever in the restroom, likely rearranging their every aspect of seduction. They were either brushing their teeth, jacking up their tits in their pushup bras, or glossing their lips to "pay" for their meal and dope. Jude was waiting, chewing on his meaty lips. What were they doing, for God's sake?

"Damn chicks," he muttered. "All the same."

Chapter 73

*Listening to Don McLean singing about the story of
rock and roll*

THE NEXT MORNING, JUDE's mind sneaked back to Fiona. His mother was almost certainly with her, but he had forgotten to ask Fiona and he couldn't call Mrs. P in case her phone was tapped. Anyway, he'd be back home in no time. He couldn't stay away forever. Things would get better soon, and with a new passport he'd find a way to return to Montreal unnoticed and sort this whole thing out with his partners. Fiona was right—Angelo shouldn't have moved the shipment more than once. The Chilean had taken too many risks.

For the first time in his life, and though he felt protected by Holiji, an infinitesimal part of Jude's brain—the reptilian part, one can only suppose, since that's where the survival instinct kicks in—feared that the narcs might catch up with him. The notion terrified him. He was still pretty confident he could trust Angelo, that the Chilean wouldn't squeal on him and Fiona, but one could never be sure in this type of predicament.

He had been out of town at the time of Angelo's bust, and that was certainly proof that Holiji meant to protect him from the police, wasn't it? It was no coincidence. Holiji—and consequently God—had decided it still wasn't his fate to end up in prison. If he was safe and sound in New York, he only had his good karma to thank. And Fiona, somehow. The real culprit could only be Angelo's bad karma. God and Holiji would supply Jude with many other opportunities to make up for the lost million-dollar deal. A bigger deal. With better partners.

Fiona didn't seem to miss him that much. In fact, she didn't seem to miss him at all. The next time she called, it was to tell him she was about to leave for Vancouver with the baby and stay with her mother for some time. She called from the airport. She said she hadn't returned to their place for fear of being arrested. She begged him to stay in New York and wait for her instructions. Fiona's tone was formal. If he wanted to be safe, he had to stay away. A forged passport wouldn't do the trick this time because customs agents would most certainly be looking for him. They might even have pictures of him and Fiona. Jude felt he had no choice. He was snorting cocaine again, and it made him paranoid just listening to her. Fiona told him he should relax and take it easy.

"We'll miss you, the baby and me. But we all have to be patient. In the meantime, go see a Broadway show. Enjoy yourself a little. For once, let me take care of things here."

"I don't care for Broadway shows, Fiona. I want to see my child—and you," he added in haste.

"It won't take long, you'll see. We'll be together in no time."

He asked Fiona to fly to New York with the baby, but she refused. "Too risky for us and our son."

Jude liked to hear these words from her mouth. *Our son.* "My boy," he said, smiling.

He heard a baby cry behind Fiona's voice. "I have to breastfeed Vincent, honey. Talk to you soon. I'll call you from another phone booth tomorrow. Promise."

And she hung up before he could say goodbye. Vincent. How he loved that name! He had chosen it, and strangely Fiona had agreed. A delightful surprise since she rarely agreed with anything he said. He could only trust her. After all, she was the one who told him that it had been foolish for Angelo to move the dope, and he could only admire her for that. She was certainly a pain in the neck most of the time, but he was pretty sure he still loved her. Somehow.

"Might as well have some fun in the meantime," he told himself.

Jude cabled money to Fiona here and there and initiated other deals to finance a good lawyer for Angelo. Though she had promised to get back to him the next day, it was a week before he heard from her again. By then, he was frantic and imagining the worst.

She called from Vancouver. She was fine, but from what she said, their "situation" had changed from bad to worse. Jude was distraught. Apparently, the RCMP was getting closer to them. Leon had seen a suspicious van parked close to the centre and asked a friend in Vancouver to find Fiona and let her know about it. Fiona told the father of her child that she saw no other alternative but to sell Maya and stay out of Québec for a year at the very least. After a round of arguments on the subject, Jude gave his consent with no en-thusiasm. Selling the centre was not part of his plans. Come to think of it, none of this "situation" was part of his plans. But there was no point in arguing. Everything seemed to be beyond his control, with the possible exception of the Swedish twins. Fiona said she'd fly their lawyer to New York and Jude could quickly sign the papers that would transfer Maya's ownership to Leon and me.

"You think they'll manage?" Jude said.

"I don't care, Jude, but I hope so for the sake of Holiji and the city's spiritual seekers. At this point, I just want to make sure we erase all traces leading to us."

"Won't you miss it?"

"What?"

"Well, Maya, of course!"

"No, I don't think I'll miss a single thing from Montreal."

Something in her voice was odd, Jude was positive. But what?

Jude couldn't possibly have guessed that when her water broke, Fiona hadn't called anybody to take her to the hospital, not even her mother-in-law, though they had expressly agreed this would be the first thing she would do if he happened to be out of town. With no news from her daughter-in-law in days, Jude's mother became a little concerned. She knew her son was in New York, but she didn't have a number to reach him, and there was no answer at the couple's place. She called at Maya, but Leon had no idea where Fiona was. When she asked to talk to me, Leon told her I was in Mexico with a friend. Mrs. P was more than a little upset.

That day, the same day Angelo was busted, Fiona drove herself to the Royal Victoria Hospital early in the morning, holding the Mercedes' steering wheel with one hand and her belly with the other. When the nurse at the desk asked who she wished to contact, Fiona answered firmly that there was no need to alert anyone.

Weeks later, an intern who'd been working in the emergency room at the time reported to Mrs. P that the redheaded woman didn't sound like she was kidding when she said she'd make a scene if anyone attempted to reach her mother-in-law, though she had herself supplied her phone number months before. She hadn't even wanted them to contact her midwife.

"Women have given birth since the beginning of time," Fiona had said. "I'm sure I can manage by myself."

When she was wheeled in the birth room, she'd said she felt privileged to be surrounded by a team of specialists and not all by herself squatting over a muddy hole in a rice field somewhere in Asia. The hospital staff on the obstetrics floor gossiped. It was strange for a classy lady like Fiona to give birth all by herself with no family around to comfort her.

Fiona went through the painful motions of delivery with panache—"like a cat, really, no stitches," the doctor told Mrs. P later—and the next day she left the hospital with her newborn son and went straight to the airport, where she boarded the next plane to Vancouver. A few days later, she was sitting in the lobby of the Catalina Hotel in Zihuatanejo. How did she manage to do it all so fast? Simple. She was a witch. Or that's what I would have told you at the time.

From the telephone booth near her mother's place in Vancouver, Fiona explained to Jude why she hadn't called her mother-in-law at the first contraction. "We can't be too discreet with everything that's happening."

"What about the midwife? You didn't call her either?"

"No, I didn't. Oddly enough, I had a premonition at the same time I felt the first contraction. A minute later, Sammy called with the news. I'm so sure this is all Holiji's work, darling. I went to the hospital like a robot, my feet guiding me. I wasn't aware of what I was doing. I'm telling you, baby, Holiji worked for us with all his might and I believe he—"

"Who did you say called you?"

"Angelo's friend, Sammy, remember him? He saw Angelo being arrested outside the warehouse."

Jude was positive Fiona was lying, but he didn't know about what. Maybe he hadn't listened closely enough. Something Fiona would gladly remind him of, since she always complained he never paid much attention to what she said. He would ask her to explain it to him again. Once they were face to face.

"Sammy didn't get arrested too?"

"I don't know. I don't think so."

She went on. "Anyway, after he called to let us know, I realized how lucky we were. Nobody knew I would give birth that day, and you, my dear, were already in New York.

I mean, isn't that marvellous? Wasn't it wise to avoid your mother and the midwife, considering the circumstances? Aren't you amazed at Holiji's intervention?"

Jude was torn between gratitude and suspicion.

"Well, if you're not, you should be!" Fiona was obviously annoyed. "Get in lotus position and praise Holiji! He saved the three of us!"

Later that day, Jude's paranoia played tricks on him. He suddenly had the feeling that his girlfriend had never planned for him to be in Montreal for Vincent's birth. It was always a bad idea to underestimate Fiona. Could she be running away from him? With his own baby?

Very unlikely, he told himself. No, of course not! He was stark raving mad. She would never do something like that. The damn cocaine made him irrational. Hadn't he bought her flowers every day lately? He couldn't recall ever being that nice to a woman, and that included his own mother. *And* Holiji wouldn't approve. Having reassured himself, Jude slipped under the covers of his king-sized hotel bed and fell asleep the moment his head hit the pillow.

He was awakened in the middle of the night by the sound of a fire engine on the deserted street below. He walked to the window and watched the red flashing lights die away along with the siren's screech. He went back to bed but couldn't find sleep again. Fiona had never seemed so out of reach. She came up with a good excuse every time he asked her to fly to the States with the baby. Now that Jude had stored enough hours of fun to last him for a few years of boring family life, he felt ready to take the plunge. He knew he'd be great at it: an excellent father, a devoted husband, and a dedicated Holiji disciple. The less Fiona manifested herself, the more Jude grew obsessed with the picture of his future happy domestic life. She couldn't take that away from him. Holiji wouldn't allow it.

Months dragged by. Then a year. When the summer of 1981 came, Jude was still in New York by himself. Fiona always seemed to be extremely busy keeping her and their son's lives under cover, or so she said. Fiona also told him she felt her mother's house in Vancouver might be under surveillance. Jude got to speak to Fiona no more than twice a month. His son was a year old, and his dad had yet to meet him. Jude still didn't dare to make the trip back to Canada. If he ended up in prison because he couldn't hold still, he wouldn't get to see Vincent for years to come, possibly decades. He knew he had to remain cool and wait until the coast was clear. Unfortunately at this point in time, isolated from his former partners with no way of contacting them, only Fiona could let him know when the opportunity to go back to Canada would come.

After many unsuccessful attempts, he finally succeeded in persuading Fiona to meet him somewhere, make that any-where, anytime she wanted. Jude was no fool, and he knew this begging of his made Fiona feel powerful and in charge as well as a little contemptuous, but he couldn't be patient anymore. He had to see his son. This situation was about to drive him insane. He went through a lot of trouble to organize a trip for the three of them "as far away from the mainland" as Fiona had insisted on.

"Far, but not too far," she had ordered.

Jude cringed.

The first time it was in Barbados. The second time in Guadeloupe. On both occasions, Fiona showed up with too much luggage and no kid. Twice she came up with a reason-able excuse for leaving their son behind under the excellent care of her mother. In Barbados, it was an ear infection.

"Everybody knows that planes are the worst when it comes to ear infections."

She said she was delighted by this unexpected opportunity to spend time alone with him. But that was another tall tale because three days passed before she was willing to have sex. But she talked, that she did. In fact, she had never been so voluble. She told Jude she needed more money to carry on. Fiona babbled constantly, concentrating her conversation on topics that made Jude feel anxious. She wanted to know what his plans were for the future, and where and how he meant to live. Jude asked to see a picture of the baby. Fiona was sorry to tell him she had none.

"Not yet. The flash, you know. Bad for the eyes."

Weeks later, she arrived two days late in Guadeloupe. Jude had waited for her at Pointe-à-Pitre Airport for three hours. He returned two days later for the next flight from Vancouver, via Miami. Once again, Vincent was not resting in his mother's arms. Fiona was radiant, saying how happy she was to see him. When Jude requested with all the pleasantness he could muster an explanation for her lateness and Vincent's absence, Fiona turned around to inspect the suitcases at her feet as if she expected to be missing a piece. She told Jude that the baby had become sick in the car on the way to the airport.

"He had a fit at the airline counter!"

She said she had judged it much wiser to get a room in a nearby hotel and take the next flight instead. She had no idea where Jude was staying on the island so she couldn't call to let him know. Vincent's fever apparently became worse, and Fiona had to send for a doctor who confirmed the poor baby was suffering from yet another bad case of ear infection.

"So the last thing to do—" she began.

"—was to take him on a plane." Jude finished her sentence.

"Exactly, darling. So my mom came to pick him up. Next time it will work out fine, don't worry. He's your son, after all, isn't he?"

Giggle-o-rama. She said she was glad to have another opportunity to be alone with him and finally get to talk. Jude wished he knew what the fuck she wanted to talk about this time. All she seemed to want to talk about was the money she needed to keep her and Vincent safe.

"By the way," she added. "I have pictures of Vincent."

She was all smiles when she handed him the thin envelope. Jude examined each snapshot closely. The three pictures were a little out of focus, and to make matters worse, the child stood with a blinding sun setting behind him. Jude couldn't make out the contour of the boy's face. "I can't see his face. He's so far away."

"Let me see—" She leaned over the photo. "Of course you can see him. It's that stupid flash, you know. It goes on by itself. I should get a new camera, really. But you can see him, surely. You just have to open your eyes, for Holiji's sake!"

"Why didn't you take them in the house? I wouldn't recognize my own kid if I saw him on the street!" It was hard for him to stay calm.

Fiona looked annoyed. "I don't know, Jude. I took the pictures when I took the pictures. What is it? You want to fight about this?"

Exasperated, he didn't know what else to say. Every time he pressed her about the kid, Fiona became defensive.

"I took the pictures in October," she went on. "It's rare to see so much snow that early in the winter, even in the Rockies." She pointed to the blurry face on the glossy paper. "You see, he still has a little suntan left from the summer."

What was she talking about? October was too early for that much snow and too late for a fading suntan. But Jude didn't want to fight. Arguing with Fiona would only serve to isolate him further from what he considered his God-given family. Jude wondered if Vincent's dark brown hair, the same as Jude's own father's from what he could make out on the pictures, would turn red later on. Jude hoped not—in fact, he decided he would hate it if it were to happen.

WHEN MUCH LATER I asked Jude why he hadn't hired a lawyer or a detective to locate Vincent, he said the thought had never crossed his mind. "I was way too scared to go back to Canada at the time. Lawyers, detectives, I could afford them all, but then I was living under a false name, false passport, false driver's licence, you name it. I was too paranoid. I was snorting cocaine again. Also, Holiji himself asked me to leave her alone for a while. I wanted my son, yes, but I couldn't take care of him at that time. He needed his mother more than he needed me. And apparently," he said, sighing, "his mother didn't want me in her life anymore than she wanted me in my boy's life."

"Couldn't you have asked a friend to try to put some sense in Fiona's head?"

"Friends? I hardly had any friends then. Even Hugo didn't like it when I called at his place. It was such a crazy time, man. And anyway," he added, laughing half-heartedly, "I bet my friends and partners feared Fiona much more than they feared me."

Chapter 74

*Listening to Paul Simon singing he's always willing
to admit that whatever goes wrong in his love life
is his own fault*

WHEN HE GOT BACK to New York, Jude stuck his son's pictures side by side on the full-length mirror in the apartment he had finally resigned himself to rent in Manhattan. Though he loved the place and the balcony with a side view on Central Park, he felt alone like a dog at the pound. The sole reminders of his fatherhood stared at his face every morning, imploring or cursing him, he couldn't tell. Jude felt completely alienated. Fiona was a little more evasive every time they spoke on the phone, and he had no way to locate her. His mind tormented him. Was she leaving him progressively, in stages? What if she had no intention whatsoever to share her life with Vincent's father? Perhaps all she had ever wanted from this relationship was to get pregnant, only to dump him once the child was born, like a puppy in a cardboard box dropped on the side of the road. Was this all part of an exit plan?

Jude got a few deals going while Fiona vanished for weeks

at a time. Money flowed in again. Whenever she called, she hung up the moment Jude started to get angry at her for keeping Vincent away from him. She said it wasn't her fault if the RCMP was on their case.

"You want your son's mother in jail, is that it?"

Jude could have strangled her.

LATE THE FOLLOWING WINTER, via a postcard from Lake Louise near Banff, Fiona was pleased to let Jude know that his son could repeat some words of the *simran* with little effort. Vincent was a little shy of two years old by then.

What if the boy had never been told about his father? Jude wondered. The idea made his heart sink. He kept sending money to Vancouver, hoping it would soften Fiona's heart.

Soon after the postcard, he bumped into Jane, the wife of a dealer friend, in a restaurant. Jude was no longer dealing with her husband, though they were still friends, and it was by sheer coincidence that he met her that day. She explained she was in New York to visit her sister. As they were about to part, she told Jude she had seen Fiona a few months before while vacationing on Phuket Island in Thailand. Fiona was alone but told Jane that Vincent was travelling with her. The dealer's wife didn't get to see the little boy for herself. Jude was crushed but he didn't talk to Fiona about it. He knew that if confronted, she would make him pay by disappearing for God knows how much longer.

Fiona hid the kid as if she feared someone might kidnap him. Why? And she actually travelled with him. The boy was tanned in the pictures on Jude's mirror precisely because she took him places. On a plane, of course. To Asia, which topped off Jude's chagrin. The ear infection excuse was a lie, a dirty lie. She had never intended to take the boy to his father. Fucking hell, he thought. Why?

He reflected on his situation day and night. It killed him to know that should father and child ever meet, they would have to be formally introduced. Vincent would be shy and cling to his mother. After all, so far, Fleeting-Queen-Mother-Once-So-Fabulous Fiona had been the boy's sole anchor in this world. What if the little boy had heard nothing or worse, only bad things about his dad? Would Vincent become hysterical if Jude reached out to pick him up? Would he look at his father as if he was a potentially dangerous man? Would he ever call him Daddy?

Jude tortured himself, wondering what the hell he could have possibly done to deserve such a heartless punishment. Plenty, you'll say. *Hey Jude, maybe this is a little manifestation of your own bad karma?* But he wouldn't have grasped your point. This Jude didn't know how to take an unhappy song and make it better.

He eventually formulated three scenarios offering a sound explanation for Fiona's behaviour. In one, her only ambition had been for him to supply her with his sperm (because of his most excellent genes, he suspected). In that scenario, he felt dirty and abused. In the second scenario, there was another man in Fiona's life, and this asshole was raising Vincent as his own child. If this were the case, Jude would kill her. The image of Fiona's red hair bouncing up and down with two hairy hands on her magnificent breasts made his fists clench. He couldn't recall the third scenario—the first two made him too furious to think straight.

Jude was no angel. He was unfaithful himself, a fact he openly admitted to everyone but Fiona. Nevertheless, his commitment to her and their child went far beyond casual sex. It had nothing to do with him reaching orgasm in various ways with the Swedish twins after making sure they were both on the pill. For the first time in his life, Jude felt ready to be a father and a husband. That alone, he concluded, should have made Fiona content. But remaining faithful? Hell no. "Life's too short," he thought, shrugging.

Once Jude had convinced himself that Fiona was cheating on him, he could not contain his wrath anymore. Two years! He had been waiting patiently for two long years. Disregarding his safety, he placed a frenetic phone call from his New York apartment to Fiona's mother in Vancouver. He told his mother-in-law that he demanded to speak with "the woman who had my baby."

There was no response from the other end of the phone line. Fiona's mother was speechless.

"Enough of that shit, woman! I want to see my son. Do you get that?" For the first time, he added a threatening tone to his voice. "I have connections, you know."

Fiona's mother, who had seen enough evil in Europe during the Second World War, did what people do when individuals with no real authority become verbally abusive on the phone: she hung up on him. Jude threw the phone across the room, swearing he'd kill them both, mother *and* daughter. Then he could have Vincent all to himself. But of course, Holiji wouldn't agree with that, and there was enough to deal with as it was.

Chapter 75

Listening to Steely Dan going mad under a cold rain

FIONA DISAPPEARED FOR ANOTHER full year before Jude heard from her again. She finally agreed to speak with him in exchange for a large sum of money but, according to the telegram, "for no more than five minutes." Jude paid and waited for her call impatiently.

At this point, fighting the feeling that it was all over had exhausted him. For four years, their destinies had been inextricably intertwined. Then for three years, irreversibly disconnected. He had lost hope of ever living a normal life with Fiona and Vincent. However, his mind still tortured him every time he thought about why she had vanished with no explanation and then only acted like a bitch since. But it would take still more time for him to understand that he would never get to hear a sound explanation.

She phoned at the promised hour. She said she was living near Whistler, the ski mountain two hours north of Vancouver, but she refused to say more. Just like the old days, the rest of the conversation was spent swearing and cursing each other's destinies and mothers. Fiona hung up abruptly after five minutes—exactly five minutes, in fact—without the least chance to talk about Vincent.

Jude called Fiona's mother once more. She of all people surely knew her daughter's address and phone number. This time, Fiona's mother didn't immediately hang up. When Jude forced himself to shut up, not because he was out of words but because he was out of breath, the old lady calmly swore on her "dead husband's nuts" that she had no idea where her daughter was.

"She's always on the go. Just like her grandmother. Couldn't sit still for five minutes, that woman. Running all over the globe like she had worms in her underwear." Then she hung up. Jude tried to call again, but there was no answer. He wanted nothing more than to hold and hug his son. How could Fiona deprive him of this sacred contact?

Months passed, and only because Jude was once again willing to pay another large amount of money, Fiona agreed to let him talk to Vincent over the phone. Despite the fact that he'd become profoundly cynical and suspicious of Fiona, Jude felt he was getting somewhere. Unfortunately, in what seemed a calculated move on Fiona's part, Vincent was old enough to tell the stranger on the phone that he didn't want to see him, that he didn't know him, and that he was scared of him. Jude's worst nightmare was real. Vincent had never been told about his dad.

Whenever Jude complained about Fiona to Holiji during the many long-distance calls he placed to the ashram, the guru brought some fresh news about mother and child. He always tried to cheer up his favourite disciple.

"They're both fine, my son. Fiona needs this time by herself. You'll see your son in time. You made Fiona suffer very much, you know. Let her be for a while. Carry on, get a new life. Find peace with a new soul mate."

"But didn't you order us to stick together? I thought you said Fiona and I were a karmic item."

"How could I order you to stay together if you're both miserable?"

"But you did. You said we were bound together forever. Won't we have to reincarnate again just to settle this relationship?"

"Well, you probably should, but I'll make sure you won't have to."

Amen. There seemed nothing he could do but acquiesce to Fiona's whims.

WITH DOPE DEALS ONCE again occupying most of his neurons, Jude carried on. Gradually, it seemed easier to give up on Fiona and Vincent rather than undertake the apparently impossible task of reviving a family life from the chaos "that cunt of a bitch" had created for the three of them.

By the third summer of Vincent's existence, I'd long grown apart from the group. Leon and I were thriving, despite the odds, in the business bequeathed to us by Fiona. Through the grapevine, I heard that Jude moved from New York to Boston. When he finally acknowledged that Fiona would never come back to him, he pledged he would have other children of his own. To initiate a new life, he married a Latino beauty discreet enough to never inquire about his "job" or the vast amount of cash he always had available.

He'd met Daniela in Rio. He had simply bumped into her in a bar, and she mumbled some apology in Portuguese for stepping on his foot. Jude had never heard such a sexy voice in his life. She happened to be slim and tall, assets that added to his conviction that they were made for each other. They were married a couple of months later.

Daniela was marvellously patient with him. So quiet, so accepting of the fact that he was always so busy. Every now and then, Jude took her out for a movie followed by sushi and disco to reward her docile behaviour. Daniela never failed to be thrilled. She loved to digest her raw fish on a dance floor, her champagne burps mixing with the fading taste of wasabi in the back of her throat. When Jude told Holiji about Daniela, his guru was glad to hear his son had found love again.

Unfortunately for Jude, it turned out that the sweet Brazilian angel, the one who never asked questions, the same girl who coincidentally never had to answer any, that lovely twenty-five-year-old Jude had wed in a Catholic church to please her parents (who had flown to Boston from Rio for the event, at Jude's expense, of course), that beautiful angel who had given birth to his daughter Bianca (he made sure he was in the delivery room this time), that sweet, sweet *carioca,* was in fact an ex-semi-prostitute fancying heroin, a couple of facts she worked hard at denying the afternoon she returned from the hairdresser to find Jude in possession of her little golden purse, the one her good friend Marlena had bought for her in Hong Kong years before. The silk pouch that was just the right size to stash her shooting gear.

Daniela pleaded with Jude. She swore she had not used the stuff in years. There had to be some truth to her claim because Jude had never noticed a puncture mark on her celestial body. But then again, he was absent for weeks at a time, and shooting was not the only way to use heroin. His anger dictated a harsh verdict: she was lying. Confronted with the purse, she cried too much, screamed too much, pulled her hair too much. Completely out of control. He had witnessed Fiona in this state on many occasions, and she too was a liar.

Sadly, Jude's discovery occurred on a day that should have been a happy one for the couple. Following a longer than anticipated trip to India, Jude told Daniela he would take her out for an evening of fun. For the occasion, she went to the beauty salon for a new hairdo and a manicure while he stayed home to set up his new Harman Kardon amplifier.

He was pulling out a large tin box full of cables and wires from the top shelf of the living room closet when the little gold silk purse with a purple dragon stitched on both sides fell on his face. His hand fondled the bag. He felt the hard contour of the syringe through the soft fabric. He didn't want to open it, and he didn't have to—he knew damn well what was in there. His thumb found the shape of a small silver spoon. He stood there, livid.

He looked at his watch and picked up the phone. This time around, he would act swiftly to make sure the child stayed with him. He called his mother, begging her to take care of Bianca for a few days. Bianca was only a toddler at the time. From her Outremont dining room, Mrs. P accepted without hesitation. She would pick Bianca up at the airport the next day. Even though years had passed since Angelo's bust, Jude was still paranoid about his safety, and his mother was aware that people from the police might be listening.

"Our conversations must remain brief," Jude had told her on numerous occasions.

Mrs. P made no attempt to discover what was going on, figuring she'd find out sooner or later. She prayed that her new daughter-in-law wasn't ill or anything of the kind. Bianca was too young to be away from her mother for long.

According to Jude's version of events, the confrontation that took place between him and his wife that afternoon was brief but very effective. Bianca and two suitcases of her clothes and toys were hastily delivered to a friend's house nearby. This deed accomplished, Jude sat in the living room and waited for his wife. He heard Daniela's key in the front door. She was in a good spirits and ready for what she hoped would be a well-deserved evening of fun. Jude remained seated. Without saying a word, he threw the silk pouch at Daniela's feet. It landed right between the high-heeled blue suede shoes she had just bought on Newbury Street.

The shoes were meant to complement that tight indigo dress of hers, the one she was planning to wear that night.

Daniela admitted to having used the stuff in her youth, but she couldn't explain why. Her life had always been so easy. All she'd wanted was a little spice, a little adventure. Believing that honesty might pull her out of this one and fearing Jude would also find out one way or another, she confessed to having prostituted herself a few times to pay for her doses, whenever her parents had refused to give her more cash. But, she swore, it was all over. She begged him to put it all behind them.

But Jude was in no mood for compassion. "Why did you keep your shooting gear, then?"

"I don't know. It was stupid of me."

"You bet it was."

Jude couldn't control his anger. Daniela would pay for her own lies *and* Fiona's lies. He grabbed her by the hair, messing up the styling he had paid for, and dragged her out of the apartment into the hallway. Before slamming the door on her, he pulled a few hundred dollars from his pocket and threw the bills in her face. He had seen similar scenes in movies. The gesture reflected perfectly the level of his contempt. Then he told her she would never see her daughter again. That was the kind of promise Jude could make to a woman and be true to it for a lifetime.

Jude told me the story himself some years later. I asked whether Daniela had made any attempt to get custody of the child.

"I left with Bianca, not leaving a trace," he said. "She flew to Montreal to be with my mom and I stayed with a friend until I figured out my next move. I doubt Daniela would have gone to the police. When she called back the next day, as if there was any chance I'd forgive her, I told I'd kill her if she tried anything. She believed me. She was really clueless, you know. I asked my friends in Boston to check her whereabouts, and they told me she'd gone back to Rio. She's probably whoring in Copacabana to pay her monkey. Now she has a good excuse to get wasted."

I said something about the ironic parallel between Vincent and Bianca, both children being separated from one parent. He said he had never thought about it that way.

"My wife knows why she'll never see her child again. Fiona never had the balls to tell me."

"For one thing, you weren't faithful."

"I was in my heart. And I was always really careful."

"Would you have minded if Fiona had slept around but stayed true to you in her heart?"

"Of course! That would have made her a slut. There's no such word for men."

That big laugh of his.

I got to see Jude again on one of his rare visits to Montreal. Despite Leon's claim to have once spotted a suspicious van close to the centre, neither he nor I had ever seen an RCMP officer inquiring about the former owners. Maybe they watched us from afar for a time or tapped the lines. Then again, Fiona and Jude had never attempted to reach us at Maya or at home.

Then one July day Jude phoned the centre. Leon was out for lunch, and I was alone on the first floor. Had Jude known that? The city was making major repairs on the street, and every store owner complained about the noise. On the phone, Jude didn't introduce himself. He only asked if I recognized who he was, something I had guessed the moment he said hi even though the jackhammer right outside the door made his voice almost inaudible. Of course, I didn't utter his name. Good old paranoia. Jude said I shouldn't tell anyone about his call, not even Leon. He asked if I was free to meet him at a café on Prince Arthur Street. Curiosity overtook my many apprehensions, and I agreed. When Leon came back from lunch, I told him I had to step out for an hour or two to run errands.

Jude looked fine and as relaxed as a dope dealer on the run for years could be. He seemed genuinely delighted to see me. He was pleased to hear that Maya was doing well. He touched my arm affectionately in a buddy-buddy way, saying he couldn't really trust anybody anymore except for his old friends and family. He said he knew he could count on me because even though I had abandoned Holiji for motives still obscure to him, I had proven that I was able to lead a spiritual and satisfying life without—or rather, *despite,* I thought— that precious master of his. I suspected Jude and Fiona had concluded that the decline of my devotion had a lot to do with Holiji's blessing of Alex and Linda's union. I could have told him the truth that day, but I didn't feel like it.

Jude took a bite of his sandwich. A drop of mayonnaise ran down his chin. He talked, his mouth full, chewing noisily. "The cops never caught up with me, and that alone is a miracle, a clear manifestation of Holiji's unique connection with God. Every single dealer I know was caught at one time or another."

I had heard this shit so many times before. After telling me about Daniela, he added, "Another thing—I truly believe that if it wasn't for Holiji's divine work, one of these crazy cokehead dealers would have killed me already. The way I look at it, I'll always be saved because every single day of my life I pay for my bad karma through the mothers of my children."

He asked if I had heard from Fiona. I said I had heard about her but not from her.

"Anything interesting?"

"No, not really."

"You know the only thing I find difficult to forget and forgive is that my son and I are on the same planet, and that we may never meet."

I was blunt because I was long past being intimidated by this man and didn't owe him any kindness.

"Maybe it's your karma and nothing more, Jude. You lost your son in this incarnation, but you met Holiji. Fiona will make sure Vincent receives initiation and avoids reincarnation, you know she will. It's probably already done. Vincent will never come back to earth and neither will you, so you'll be together in the nowhere at one point or another."

Jude nodded. He didn't seem offended. He talked for an hour and a half, filling me in on what had happened to him since we had last seen each other. I asked if he had gone back to India since leaving Montreal.

"Many times. In the hope of seeing Fiona to be honest. But I never did. Maybe Holiji made sure we wouldn't meet."

He said it must have been in the stars for him to talk to me that day because I had made him look at his frustration from a different angle. I doubt he really meant it. Before we parted, he told me he was in Montreal only for a day or two. I didn't ask where he was heading afterward.

Chapter 76

Listening to the Who tuning to a girl's mind

I DIDN'T CONSCIOUSLY TRY TO keep track of Fiona—at first, anyway—but, as I had admitted to Jude, I heard about her many times again. There was always somebody around with some news or sizzling gossip about my ex-boss. It was like following a trail of shiny pebbles in a thick forest.

I may be wrong in my interpretations of the events reported to me throughout the years. By the time I had figured it all out (or believed that I had), nobody I knew gave a damn about Fabulous Fiona anymore. My life had changed so dramatically since 1973, it was a wonder that I still cared to find out what had become of her. Let's say that subconsciously, I was trying to find some closure with her.

Fiona had made friends throughout Montreal, and not only dealers or striptease aficionados. Her name was mentioned sporadically at a party here, at a dinner there, places where people tend to gossip about everyone and everything. Some, like me, were intrigued by her disappearance, and everybody seemed to know someone who had seen her or talked to her. I began recording every story, mentally discarding whatever seemed improbable, and added each rumour to my collection of "facts." I then sorted out the results chronologically and filled in the blanks according to my understanding of the animal (Fiona) and her typical reaction to different environments (North America, Europe, Asia). Of course, sometimes I had to indulge in pure fantasy, whenever I had no clue. I imagine that this semi-obsession of mine bloomed because of an old fear I entertained for years of finding Fiona giggling her ass off on my doorstep.

Jude's suspicions turned out to be valid. Fiona had indeed planned the whole thing out—what was to be her final exit and every single detail about it.

To start with, it was she who had demanded Jude make that trip to New York the week she gave birth, insisting he should settle some trivial business he would have ordinarily managed by phone. Fiona wanted Jude out of the way to put her plan into practice. Her initial intention was to give birth with no one around and then vanish with the baby while Jude was still in New York and the million-dollar deal almost done with. She planned to hide for some time and blackmail Jude with the kid until she got her part of the deal. Then, she meant to disappear for good with Vincent. However, with Angelo's bust and the money gone, she had to change her strategy on the spot. One thing is certain: deal or no deal, she had no intention whatsoever of seeing Jude again. I believe she had good reasons for this, other than the fact that he was a scumbag. But we'll get to that later.

I believe that Fiona did whatever she had to do to induce labour while Jude was away. Much later I read in a magazine there are ways to do this with some powerful herbs or tinctures, but it can take days before it becomes effective. Fiona might very well have begun the treatment the moment Jude left for New York. Or even some time before. Or perhaps it was only a coincidence that her water broke the same day the bust took place. One thing is certain, she meant to leave for good with the baby that week, while Jude was out of the way.

Why go through so much trouble to ditch Jude and keep the baby? She could have done this easily simply by walking out on him, especially after the deal tying them together had fallen apart. Something was missing, but I didn't know what. I'm still not dead sure to this day.

In British Columbia, she kept out of Jude's reach and tormented him with the kid to extort large amounts of money from him. The total represented a fraction of the anticipated share from the million-dollar deal, but enough to manage while she was hiding from him and the police. She let a few months pass and, typical of Fiona, one morning she got a sign. She probably tested the omen by zigzagging in and out of the country with her many passports, sometimes accompanied by her son, sometimes by herself, perhaps dying her hair and dodging each potential pitfall by rehearsing her every move three times. That part must have been easy, almost fun, after being on the run for months. Somehow she knew when she no longer had to hide.

What follows is what happened when Fiona disappeared for a year while Jude was still in New York. I pieced together these events from the rumour grapevine and someone who met her at the time.

After her forced seclusion, Fiona most certainly emerged from the British Columbia woods with a smirk of victory on her face. Months before, she had spotted a quiet community in the far end of the Western Canadian Nowhere, not too far from Whistler. She decided to settle down there with Vincent for a while. The close-knit group of hippies was smitten by her grace and her coolness. She rented a pleasant cottage fit for two not too far from a well. From the backyard, she could hear the vigorous sounds of a stream she was told was boiling with salmon and grizzly bears.

She didn't make it a secret that she wished for no one from the outside to know where she was. The village elders gathered to make a decision. She looked frail, innocent, and vulnerable, and they voted to protect her. Fiona and her son were camouflaged in the wild as efficiently as if their two bodies and few belongings had been tucked under thick bushes of moss and broken tree branches. Fiona, who could invent a past, a present, and a future in a minute, led her new friends to believe she was emerging from a difficult time with a most despotic man. They had no idea where she had come from, but the isolated community felt sorry for her.

At first, Fiona led a happy and simple existence. She benefited from the total devotion of some lost souls in the village, notably many of the middle-aged women, who were irresistibly attracted by the contents of her suitcases. Especially the largest one, the one bursting with leopard-skin fabrics, blood-red shoes, and lizard-skin boots. However, and almost before she could see it coming, Fiona's initial enthusiasm faded. She grew bored with baking bread, gardening, and showing girls how to remove unwanted fuzzy pubic hair with hot wax and strips of thin cotton. To alleviate her restlessness, she asked the elders for permission to open a dance school in the village. Classes would be free, of course. She was applauded, and the villagers let her use an abandoned barn next to the communal bungalow reserved for spiritual gatherings.

The school was a huge hit. Every single villager attended except for babies, the elderly, and the handicapped. Fiona taught modern dance classes for an hour every day, and for a time her heart was again content. However, this new venture didn't manage to capture her attention for long either.

Months passed, and she found herself eager to move on. As mentioned earlier, with Fiona there always had to be some sign from heaven that persuaded her to take a risk. A crow in the sky, a prophetic dream, or a spider on her ceiling told her that it was all over, that she had won against all odds. Once set on leaving, she asked Jodie and June, her two best friends from this peaceful episode of her life, to take care of the dance school. Fiona said she expected them to keep it open.

"This is a place of joy where the rhythm of life beats from the forest floor to our stubborn feet. Another fabulous gift from Master Holiji!"

Of course, Fiona had told them all about Holiji. They meditated in his name under the trees or in the communal space whenever the cold was too unbearable to consider sitting outside.

Vincent grew into a healthy boy. In no time he could count up to twenty, a great achievement for a child of his age. The outdoors and the fresh mountain air strengthened him. He didn't cry anymore when he fell down or hurt himself. He was his mama's pride and joy, and the villagers adored him.

Jodie, June, and the other women begged Fiona to stay, but she said she had to follow her karma wherever it led her. It was time for her and Vincent to follow their destiny. She supplied some irrefutable astrological arguments. Everybody nodded. But they tried again. "Nobody will find you here. You and Vincent will always be protected from whatever or whoever you are afraid of."

Fiona replied that if she stuck anywhere for long, she'd be found sooner or later. Jodie and June asked how much she wanted for the school—the material, the mirrors, the chairs, the mats Fiona had ordered from Vancouver when she started class. That stuff hadn't cost her much, but Fiona was not the kind of person to give if she got nothing out of the deal.

Fiona turned to them. "How much do you have to your name?"

Jodie's daughter, Amy Stone, was visiting her mother that summer, and she remembered Fiona clearly. She had taken dance classes to pass time and they'd grown quite close—these two city girls had natural affinities. The baroness told her that in another life she had run a New Age centre in Montreal. The next summer, Amy happened to be in Montreal and paid a visit to Maya, the only New Age centre there at the time, and I got the chance to talk to her. Leon couldn't have cared less about Fiona's fate. I still couldn't explain why I did.

According to Amy, the day Fiona left the hippie community, she cleaned her cottage thoroughly and donated her Holiji books to her friends, not keeping a single one for herself. She didn't need them anymore. She knew them by heart, and they were less weight to carry around and worry about. And off she went, Vincent holding her hand.

Later, an ex-runner of hers, a Québécois I had met on numerous occasions, told me Fiona had married a musician, Stanley, and the couple lived in LA. According to the runner, Stanley had no official gig, but he was the kind of guy who whispered to people who didn't care to know that he had had sex twice with Janis (Joplin, of course). He gave Fiona a bracelet and a silver ring he swore had belonged to the singer. Apparently, Fiona wore the trinkets everywhere she went until she divorced him a year or so later. I'll bet she sold the two items at a high price.

The last time I saw Fiona was around 1990. I bumped into her one afternoon in downtown Montreal. She was about forty at the time. She was still striking, and still pretending not to notice the men breaking their necks to get a closer look at her. I remember thinking how insignificant she seemed to me that day. *Has she always been this way?* Perhaps I was seeing through her for the first time.

She was alone, and I asked about Vincent.

"He just turned ten," she sighed with a big smile as if it was a miracle the boy was still alive. She said he lived in Vancouver, close to her mother's place. "I spend time with Vincent as much as I can. But I have so much to do"—I didn't care to find out what—"and, of course, he has to go to school. We go to India at least twice a year. Vincent is crazy about Holiji. He loves it at the ashram!"

(Oh yes, that giggle).

She didn't inquire about Maya. I assumed she had been told

that Leon and I had sold it the year before to a Vietnamese businessman who turned it into a health spa. If she was tempted to ask for my phone number or whether I was free to have coffee with her, she refrained from it. I should have taken that opportunity to pry, but I didn't. Mind you, had I asked, she would have certainly lied.

I could tell she didn't recognize the woman in front of her, and I'm quite sure she didn't appreciate the metamorphosis. My hair, my attitude, my clothes—everything was different to her, out of place, definitely more sophisticated. I could tell she was puzzled. She didn't agree with what she was seeing and wouldn't have known where to start if she had to explain. How could she trap me in one of her ongoing schemes if she didn't know who I was anymore?

"You changed your hair, Geneviève?" she asked, as if I had done it just to spite her.

I nodded, lost for words.

"That's so Moon in Leo of you," she said, touching my bangs.

I was stunned. How had she remembered that detail of my astrological chart? Her enthusiasm instantly vanished, and she became bored like a leopard pacing in a cage. She interrupted me in mid-sentence—I can't remember what I was saying—and glanced at her watch feverishly as if she were about to miss an audience with the prime minister. She kissed the air around my face, promising (or threatening) we would meet again, and she went on her way, wiggling her ass among the other mortals on the busy St. Catherine Street intersection. I watched her from afar.

Behind her, four Japanese girls in school uniforms walked hastily, holding turquoise umbrellas. I hadn't noticed the rain. Fiona pulled the pointed black hood of her raincoat over her head and drifted away in the crowd. The high school girls' umbrellas caught up with her. Fiona's dark hood surfed their turquoise umbrellas like a fin for a moment.

Years passed. I went back to school, completed a degree in business administration, and began working abroad occasionally. My free time was devoted to travelling, and I tried to leave for a couple of months every year. I had almost forgotten about Fiona—I say *almost* because she was not the kind of person you could ever forget about completely. My busy life had led me far away from my past. Then one day, an amazing coincidence knocked me off my feet.

Chapter 77

Listening to Frank Zappa telling a holy man to fuck off

IN FEBRUARY 2001, I travelled to India to be at the Kumbh Mela, India's largest spiritual festival. This was not my first time in India, and I was looking forward to the event, having heard so much about it. It took place in Allahabad, a town in the state of Uttar Pradesh where the Hindu god Brahma, creator of the world, is said to have offered his first sacrifice. This celebration, the grandest spiritual gathering on earth, is held every twelve years and attracts tens of millions souls. It's an awesome circus. A feast for the eyes.

Allahabad by itself is not worth the detour. However, this sacred city is home to three of the holiest rivers in Hindu mythology: Ganga, Yamuna, and the mythical Saraswati. The spot where they converge is called the Sangam, and the millions of pilgrims who make the trip to the Kumbh can't wait to take a dip in this most auspicious location. According to the Hindu faith, miracles can happen after a bath in the Ganges. You could become rich after a life of poverty, get pregnant after years of trying with no success, even erase a fatal illness. You could also die from one of the many diseases these filthy rivers carry in their waters, though the occurrence is rather exceptional.

The Kumbh does not take place within the city walls of Allahabad, but in the area surrounding it. One can stay in town and sleep comfortably in a hotel at night, but this means walking at least three hours every day just to get to the most interesting events of the celebration. The majority of pilgrims elect to spend their stay on site in a tent. That's exactly what I did.

Unfortunately, I found myself stranded on a compound operated by a disgustingly hairy and equally dishonest Westerner man who named himself Gaga Shanti. I got into Allahabad too late to get a better spot, and Gaga's campsite was my only option. Staying in a hotel far from the site was out of the question. This hirsute asshole took people's money and left them to fend for themselves without supplying the services advertised to bait them. It was a trying experience to be ordered around by this furry Nazi in the middle of a sacred celebration, and I keep an indelible bad memory of this shithead. Gaga Shit Camp—that's what I called it.

On my first day at the Kumbh, I made friends with a Dutch couple camping on the ground of the Hare Krishnas. The Krishnas' food was delightful compared with the cold rice and slimy pinkish dhal served at Gaga's campsite. So I ended up visiting the Krishnas' camp twice a day for lunch and dinner. That's how I met Lydia and Anton and learned their story.

This Dutch couple had moved from Den Haag to India in the early 1980s, leaving behind comfortable jobs and a luxurious apartment overlooking a calm canal. They were irresistibly attracted to India, a place where they expected to be taught how to live and die. This was the very base of their relationship. They rented a tiny but cozy and inexpensive "almost cockroach-free" apartment in Bombay. Lydia gave English lessons to middle-class kids while Anton learned to play the sitar with a distinguished master from Kerala.

But they quickly grew tired of Bombay's madness. After reading *Lonely Planet* from cover to cover, they decided to move to Orchha.

Orchha is a lovely village nestled in the heart of an ancient fortress a few miles south from Varanasi (also called Benares). In Orchha, Anton and Lydia cultivated pesticide-free vegetables and waited for a good idea to come their way. It came with waves of Dutch tourists overwhelmed by the size of the archaeological site. They were all looking for someone who spoke enough Dutch, German, or English to guide them through the crippled buildings. In no time, Anton and Lydia made a business of it. They later left Orchha for Radjasthan, a region renowned for its breathtaking sites and colourful folklore. With the invaluable help of wealthy Indian friends, they opened their own tour agency in Jaipur. Soon afterward, they signed a deal with a Dutch tour company operating a dozen agencies in Netherlands and in England.

Business blossomed. Lydia and Anton moved again, this time to a quaint residential area in Delhi. Their office was located a little more than a block away from the InterContinental Hotel. The hotel guests who hadn't come to the country on an all-inclusive tour, the ones who wanted to see the "real thing," didn't have to go far to book a tour that would show them the authentic India. With twelve drivers on the payroll and a fleet of twenty vehicles of all sizes, from Ambassador cars to air-conditioned buses, Anton and Lydia were doing better than they had ever hoped. Later on, in 2004, the marketing campaign titled "Incredible India" put together by the Ogilvy & Mather advertising agency was so successful that the couple opened two new branches, one in Bombay and another in Madras.

I instantly liked them. They were soft spoken and very funny. I enjoyed their conversation, their chai, their generous hospitality, and their unconditional love for India despite its many mind-boggling contradictions. I found myself accepting their every invitation for food, tea, and chillum. In fact, I ended up sharing most of my time with them.

There was a day at the Kumbh that I remember particularly well. Anton, Lydia, and I had spent the better part of the morning following the heavy crowds of pilgrims making their way toward the Sangam. The scene was from another time (make that another solar system). Elephants, fakirs, camels, swamis, babas, and endless processions from all over India approaching the water according to a meticulously preset hierarchical order. The smell of it all, I'll never forget. On the way, we saw a swami sitting on a metal swing over a large fire. He seemed to enjoy it. He didn't even sweat. I called him Shish KeBaba—we had a good laugh over that.

Suddenly, signs of an incoming dust storm swirled around us. Anton said we should get back to the campground immediately and take shelter. Lydia and I didn't argue. We were eating more dust than we could swallow. My eyes felt like two sunny-side-up eggs frying in an iron pan.

When we reached the camp, two old babas stood in front of the couple's tent. They were apparently waiting for the man of the house—or rather, the man of the tent. Anton correctly guessed they were a little curious and nothing else, so he invited them both in for a cup of chai and a chillum, miming the offer since the two men didn't seem to understand a single word of English. The orange-dressed holy men hesitated. They exchanged a few words between themselves, most probably weighing the potential danger of sitting together with Anton, his white skin, and his two white "girlfriends." But they also felt the sting of the sandy wind biting their skinny legs and, with Shiva protecting them, they stepped in. The two men sat in the smoky darkness and accepted a cup of tea from Lydia's hands, bowing their heads in wordless thanks. They drank slowly and passed the chillum around, trying hard not to stare, especially at Lydia and me. After what they considered to be a polite stay—a little more than fifteen minutes—they stood up and left, bidding us a formal *namaste*. A strong odour of sandalwood lingered in the dry air after they were gone.

The three of us sat and smoked a little more. Lydia asked me about Marie-Andrée Leclerc, a girl from Levis, a small town near Québec City, who had been crazy, stupid, or sadistic enough to assist notorious serial killer Charles Sobhraj in his murderous spree throughout Asia in the 1970s. Lydia wondered if Leclerc was still alive, information I couldn't confirm or deny. One thing I did remember was that Leclerc had spent a long time in Delhi's Tihar Jail before being released when she became sick with cancer. Lydia knew about that. She said it was not surprising Leclerc became ill considering the sordid treatment reserved for foreign female prisoners in the infamous Indian detention centre.

"Tihar is a typical third-world prison. It's crowded, filthy, and they don't feed you properly. Guards steal from you, and nobody gives a damn. They say the inmates aren't too fond of Westerners."

Anton said there was an interesting story concerning Tihar.

"Oh yeah, a great story!" Lydia said enthusiastically.

Too bad, because I was just about to roll over for a nap, but I didn't want to be rude. Lydia retrieved more chai from a big thermos in a wooden box behind her. Anton said something about a strange Austrian woman rotting in a Tihar cell. The dust storm was still raging outside.

He went on. "The story goes like this: she was arrested at the airport in Delhi two years ago and—"

Lydia disagreed energetically, stating that at least three years had passed since the incident. One more chillum passed my way. I didn't care to know about the Austrian woman. For a moment, time floated at the gentle pace of the swirling incense smoke blending with the Dutch soundtrack of their benign argument. Apparently, it was Lydia who knew the story best because she took over.

"It happened three or four years ago."

Anton didn't flinch. Lydia gave him a mocking smile and continued. "We heard the whole thing from a clerk at the Dutch embassy," she said. "Many embassies were said to be involved in the case. Anyway, this guy told us that an Austrian lady has been detained in Tihar for an undisclosed period of time. There's no solid court case against her. The woman simply vegetates in a cell. The interesting edge is that she wasn't caught on her way *out* of the country with dope or anything illegal in her luggage. No, she was arrested on her way *in* because they found a ridiculously large amount of American dollars in her luggage. How they found it, the exact amount, and why she was searched in the first place, the clerk didn't know."

"Another dumb-ass loony, if you ask me," I said, swallowing a yawn.

"Wait," Lydia said. "It gets better."

I turned toward her, feigning interest, trying not to spill the contents of my cup.

Lydia fixed one more chillum. "Anyway, it was enough money to annoy the customs officers. For some reason, they believed she was a drug dealer. The woman didn't deny it, but she didn't confirm it either. The event was reported in the newspaper, but it went unnoticed. You know, just another crazy Westerner busted at the airport, as you say. The police declared she would be detained as long as she refused to reveal what she was planning to do with all that cash. Apparently, the woman showed no resistance. She didn't argue or fight for her rights. She's been in Tihar ever since. Can you imagine?"

I opened my eyes wide to add to her pleasure. After inhaling deeply from the chillum, she handed it to me. She let out the smoke and set herself comfortably on a big cushion embroidered with a dancing Hanuman. "The clerk saw her passport picture on the office computer as well as her mug shot. He said she looked middle-aged. Pretty. One interesting feature, her hair. He said it was 'raving red.' Only a gay guy would say something like this, no? Anton says the clerk is straight, but my poor husband is blind."

Red hair? Stoned out of my brain, I sat a little straighter.

Anton finally spoke up. "It's not because he said she has red hair that he's gay!" he protested.

"*Raving* red, my dear. Of course it means he's gay! Didn't you notice how he melts in front of you?"

Anton rolled his eyes.

Lydia turned to me. "Where was I? Oh yeah, her hair."

Suddenly I had a coughing attack. I coughed. And coughed. I couldn't hear Lydia anymore, and she couldn't hear herself either. She poured more tea. I regained my breath. My face was tingling.

After a minute, Lydia assumed it was safe to go on. "As I said, nobody at the embassy knows for sure the amount of money she was carrying. When she was asked about it, she said that God had given it to her. Weird woman. But they say she's definitely not crazy."

She got up, still taking. She walked to the tent flap and tucked it in tighter.

"Many details remained obscure. For one thing, who tipped off the Indian customs? Someone definitely snitched on her, that's for sure. There's no other plausible reason customs agents would check her out. Why would they care about money? And if she had nothing to hide, why didn't she raise hell to get out? Some things just don't add up in that story. For instance, she held a passport from Austria, but she didn't speak German and didn't seem to understand one word of it when people from the embassy paid a visit to her."

"I say she's nuts," Anton said.

Lydia shook her head. "I don't know. Sometimes I wonder. What if this woman is a harmless loony who wanted to spread her fortune to wretched souls? Wouldn't you say her imprisonment was an awful injustice?"

Anton rose to check the weather. "Don't start again, Lydia, please!"

"I know, I know. But why does she let herself rot in an Indian jail? The whole thing is really odd. I wish I could remember her last name. Shit. Anton, what was it again? Quite a common name in Austria …"

Anton said he couldn't remember.

Lydia rubbed her earlobe. "Isn't it Klauser? That's it—Klauser. Mrs. Klauser!"

According to Lydia, when Mrs. Klauser was presented with the opportunity to fight for her innocence in front of an Indian judge, a man who incidentally had seen his fair share of Westerners on the stand, the red-haired lady kept her cool. She spoke English very well. There wasn't a trace of despair in her plea. She mumbled stuff about her incommensurable devotion to her guru and humankind. She sounded crazy, but one look at her apparently convinced everybody in the courtroom that Mrs. Klauser was far from being a lunatic. She was too cool. And very much in control—almost arrogant.

"Very strange," insisted Lydia. "It would have been so easy for her to come up with a good story about Mother Teresa's orphanage or some other charity. But no, she didn't even take a lawyer, and she refused to meet the one provided by the court. When the judge asked where the money had come from, the Austrian said it came to her in many illegal ways. Can you believe that? The judge didn't like Mrs. Klauser's attitude one bit, no more than he liked her passport stamped with a dozen Indian visas. He summoned the prosecutor assigned to the case to gather more information on Mrs. Klauser's activities in the country. The judge was openly irritated by the complete lack of interest from the accused."

I could only imagine that the Indian magistrate had expected a colourful display of relatives, friends, and family, dressed in their Sunday best, wiping a tear or two, begging the court to let the temporarily insane woman go. He sat on his bench that day certainly looking forward to an honest performance of repentance, including flashbacks to a time when the assumed culprit was a hero crowned with the trust of an entire community in one of the rich countries the judge might care to visit, if only he could afford it. But he got none of this. Lydia said that this lack of display of emotions in the first case of the day apparently frustrated the hell out of the judge.

Mrs. Klauser was given a few more weeks to get herself a lawyer and get on with her case. Five months later, she had her day in court again, but this time she fell asleep before the judge had time to make his entrance in the courtroom. Another six months later, she slightly improved her condition by remaining awake until halfway through the procedure. Nevertheless, they still couldn't squeeze any sense out of her. Mrs. Klauser sat in lotus position, her eyes closed, apparently meditating. The Austrian embassy declared her passport forged, another accusation Mrs. Klauser didn't even try to deny. When asked where she'd obtained it and where she was from, she said she had bought it on the black market but refused to disclose her official nationality as well as where she had obtained the falsified document.

I glanced at Anton. He had obviously heard more than enough about Mrs. Klauser. "With no clues about her past," he argued, "and nobody there to plead for her, why should the Indian legal system go out of their way to help her?"

I asked the couple if they knew the name of Mrs. Klauser's guru.

Lydia thought about it for a moment. "I don't remember."

She turned to Anton, but he had no idea. I held my breath. Lydia's eyes scrutinized the air in search of the guru's name printed somewhere in her memory, but they came back from the expedition with no results. She looked at me and shrugged. "Does it matter?"

I wasn't ready to open this jar of insanity from my past. "No, not really. Just curious."

Chapter 78

Listening to Jimi Hendrix singing about a traffic jam

Later that year, Lydia sent me a lengthy letter with more details about the mysterious Mrs. Klauser. She confessed almost apologetically that she'd had to harass one of her drivers whose sister had a friend who happened to be the cousin of the best friend of one of the prison guards working the section where the Austrian woman was incarcerated. There was also the talkative—gay or not—clerk from the Dutch embassy who never missed an opportunity to chat with Lydia and who gave her a call every time he heard something new concerning the evolution of Mrs. Klauser's case. Anton didn't want to hear about it anymore, and Lydia was happy to be able to gossip with me.

What Lydia wrote was intriguing to say the least. Let's say it caused me to open the Fiona file buried somewhere in my head. My curiosity got the better of me, and I unearthed the corpse.

Lydia explained that the Indian legal system had become fed up with Mrs. Klauser. They pleaded repeatedly with her to put an end to this nonsense. They begged her to get someone, anyone willing to help her. A lawyer, a family member, an ex-husband—in other words, anyone likely to pull her out of there. Her situation bothered them much more than it bothered her. It seemed that all she wanted was to be left alone.

She settled into her prison cell among ill prostitutes, addicts, rude guards, rabid rats, and mammoth cockroaches. According to the guard related to Lydia's driver, Mrs. Klauser was perfectly organized and strongly territorial. She gradually took control over her little mad world. The enigmatic woman who rarely uttered a word to anybody under the sun was said to be friendly and generous with the creatures sharing the sombre dampness of her quarters, except, of course, for the meanest guards, the rats, and the cockroaches. However, she still hadn't supplied a single sliver of light about herself. Inmates and guards alike soon found out she could talk a little Hindi. Sitting on my bed, I read the rest of the letter, incredulous.

> She demanded the right to live in a salubrious environment, and she cajoled the guards into providing her with everything she needed to clean up her cell. They say she has a way of making people do what she wants them to do. She even persuaded some of the inmates to help her scrub the floors, wash the walls, and get rid of the bugs and rats in the cells sharing walls with hers! The guard says her bright red hair scares these uneducated girls and they bow whenever she passes by. She hung pretty fabrics on the walls of her cell and placed a bamboo mat in a corner for her daily meditation. She's been officially declared healthy and "psychologically stable." She never gets sick and rarely complains (can you imagine, in such a dump!?) She also refuses to mingle with the

other Western women populating the prison. She pays *bakshish* to the guards to get fresh food from the market, and she cooks her own meals on a small burner. The guard says she shares her food with the Indian inmates and guards alike. In fact, she is so appreciated that there were rumours the prison administration was doing everything they could to keep her happy because they didn't want her to leave! Apparently, since her arrival life has significantly improved for everyone in that section of Tihar. The guard says she eats well, exercises, meditates, and practises yoga daily. Oh, and she sings all the time. She looks genuinely happy living the simple routine of a prisoner. She displays all the symptoms we attribute to happiness and a well-balanced existence.

I can't tell you how her resigned attitude bothers me! Maybe I'm envious. How can a human being remain cool for so long? Nobody can be happy in a prison, much less in that terrible place! Somehow our Mrs. Klauser is much more "enlightened" than I could ever aspire to be. She has no plans to go anywhere. She truly lives in the here and now of her horrific life with a big smile on her face. She told a guard, one who was nasty with her at the beginning but who has since been completely "reformed," that her soul and happiness belong to her master, her "one and only love." She said she is ready to spend the rest of her days in India begging him to dispose of her body and soul any way he wishes.

I remember you asking about her guru's name. I asked my friend at the embassy, and he didn't have a clue. In fact, he said she's never mentioned his name in court. He remembers it well because the judge was obviously annoyed when Mrs. Klauser refused to reveal it. I asked my driver to find out from the guard. He came back to me, saying that though Mrs. Klauser seemed glad to let her inmates know about her guru's teachings, she's never referred to him by name. When she's asked, she just smiles blissfully and walks away. That's one of the reasons I suppose the prison authorities believed she was a little insane.

I put the letter down. *It could very well be her.* Then again, so many people go completely berserk over their guru, giving away all their money, all their time and possessions, sometimes even their virgin daughters. Unfortunately for my investigation, Fiona was far from being the only obsessive devotee on earth.

Chapter 79

Listening to Bob Dylan singing that everybody should get high

A FEW MONTHS LATER, I paid a visit to Anton and Lydia in Amsterdam. They had just bought a spacious studio, their new *pied-à-terre* in the Netherlands that served as their refuge during the Indian monsoon season. This break allowed them to see their families and bathe in the luxuries they had once been accustomed to year round. I was still living in Montreal at the time, and it made it that much easier for us to see one another.

They seemed in good spirits despite the grey Dutch weather. I was pleased to see them again and to hear their travel agencies were doing so well. We sat around drinking Yogi Tea and sharing a joint. I thanked Lydia for the long letters about Mrs. Klauser. The saga had expanded a little more since her last missive. "The brew thickened again," she said, laughing.

Apparently, the driver with the Tihar connection was always trying to please his "lady boss," and he knew that gossip concerning Mrs. Klauser was one of the candies she enjoyed the most. It made me smile when she told me this.

I could easily picture Lydia gathering clues, squeezing her driver for a little more, being as intrigued by Mrs. Klauser as I had once been with Fiona.

"Recently, to the general astonishment of everyone, the lady has had a visitor! No need to say, the news travelled quickly within the walls of the prison ward."

Anton was in a good mood, and he played along. He pretended to be talking in an imaginary microphone. "Who's this visitor special enough to make the queen of the hive fly away from her frugal quarters?"

Lydia threw a cushion at him. "The Tihar guard who keeps us up to date on Mrs. Klauser got to see the visitor from up close because she was the one who took the individual to the parlour. A man." Lydia rubbed her hands, waiting eagerly for my reaction.

"And?" I asked, sitting on the edge of seat. Curiosity was killing me, but I wanted to remain calm.

Lydia took a long sip from her tea. "The guard described him as a young man in his early twenties who looked 'sort of Indian.' He was handsome and very polite. His fingernails were meticulously clean. He wore clothes from the West, cologne from the West, and boots from the West. His name was Vidur something. An Indian surname. He's been coming back every week ever since. He brings Mrs. Klauser gifts and other goodies, everything she asks for, actually—cosmetics, food, saris, you name it. The authorities asked the young man to volunteer some information about the woman, but he said he didn't know much about her. He claimed to be the son of a deceased friend of Mrs. Klauser. He said he was paying his respects to the lady who had 'showered an ocean of goodness' on him. His explanation must have been consistent enough because he wasn't bothered again. They must not have wanted to annoy Mrs. Klauser by harassing her unique visitor. The boy spoke Hindi and English. He told the prison authorities he had studied in the best European and

American schools, thanks to Mrs. Klauser's financial support. He calls her *Mamaji,* you know, 'Holy Mother.' The guard says the boy kisses her forehead and hugs her every time they part, sometimes he even sheds tears."

The phone rang. Lydia answered and hung up almost immediately. "Wrong number. Where was I again? Oh yeah, *Mamaji.* Here comes the surreal part. One day, Mrs. Klauser told an inmate who repeated it to one of the guards that the visitor boy was the son of a very important man. When the Indian woman pressed her to reveal the father's name, the Austrian replied in one breath—"

"God!" Anton yelled.

He fell back on the couch, laughing. Lydia was annoyed. Her husband had stolen her punch line.

Anton lit a fat joint of White Widow. He coughed and cursed as the thick blue smoke escaped from his mouth. It looked as if he were chewing on dry ice. Anton was desperate to switch the conversation back to the trip they were planning to Ladakh, but Lydia wasn't finished yet.

"Soon after, someone heard Mrs. Klauser confide to the eldest woman in her ward, a quiet lady she's apparently fond of, that the young man is her child, and that she had conceived him in a dream with her guru. That's why she's convinced he's the Son of God. She said the father himself told her so! Can you imagine? She calls the visitor her 'golden boy'! She swears he's the next avatar, the saviour of the world, the soul who will shower lasting peace and eternal love on this sorry planet of ours. Her only wish is to remain in India, anywhere in India. Close to her guru and their son, breathing the same air, drinking the same filthy water."

"And that," Anton said, "is where I draw the line between the facts and the Bollywood legend my wife is making out of that dear Mrs. Klauser."

Lydia was becoming irked. "Anton, would you please stop interrupting me?" She turned back to me. "Where was I?

Oh yes. Mrs. Klauser also told the old woman that if God meant for her to go out in the world again, he would arrange for her to escape. She said she begs God to let her resume her life serving his two chosen sons for eternity. Lyrical, no? My friend at the embassy is not so sure she isn't crazy anymore."

"Why doesn't she fight to be released if all she wants is to be reunited with the both of them?" I asked.

"Oh, I forgot to tell you that crucial part!" Lydia threw an angry eye at Anton. "We also got more details about the day of her arrest. Apparently, the customs people at the airport had been tipped off by a man important enough to be taken seriously. He told them Mrs. Klauser was a drug dealer, and he could prove it. He was Indian, according to my friend at the embassy. At the time of her trial, another informer told the police that Mrs. Klauser had been exporting hash from India to the West since the 1970s. Why did these men denounce her? I don't know. Why did the police believe them? I don't know either. Confronted with these accusations, Mrs. Klauser refused to answer. It's so weird! I can't help but think someone means to keep her in Tihar, and that individual scares her so much that she'd rather stay in jail."

Anton rolled his eyes. I felt profoundly uneasy. My problem was that I couldn't accept the possibility that there might be another woman on this earth as prodigiously stubborn and intriguing as my ex-boss. Unless, of course, this Mrs. Klauser had come from the same gene pool. Then again, I figured they'd thrown out the mould after Fiona's birth.

I wasn't ready to let my Dutch friends know yet (or ever, I wasn't sure) that I might be the one who held the key to Mrs. Klauser's true motives and nature. Somehow I didn't feel like spending hours exposing the story of my youth. I could only assume Lydia wouldn't let me off the hook until I had spat out every single detail about Fiona. Everything would be scrutinized under a microscope and labelled accordingly, an exercise I wasn't ready to go through yet. I felt uneasy just thinking about it. Jude, Fiona, smuggling money for them, the drug-dealing scene I had once been involved in, and so many other details I'd rather keep to myself. Who knows what Lydia would do with my confessions once back in India? I was sure she wouldn't be able to keep them to herself. She'd be eager to share the information with her friend at the Dutch embassy, for one thing. God knows what would come of that. Funny how I always feel my life is something I have to censor, to sift carefully, throwing away every chunk of questionable choices, actions and individuals. Lydia and Anton were devoted smokers, but they were "straight" nonetheless. Drug dealers were not necessarily their favourite breed. Since smoking pot was—and still is—legal in the Netherlands, they never really had to mix with shady characters just to get some weed. Most people using dope feel this way. Hate the fuckin' dealer, love the dope. Finding something to smoke in India is also very easy. Nothing weird about it. Not once had I talked about that part of my life with my Dutch friends. I was not about to start then.

Lydia said it was time to eat. While I set the table, my thoughts went back to Mrs. Klauser. I had seen my ex-boss about twelve years before and she hadn't seemed any different to me—definitely not delusional. She hadn't mentioned much about India besides the part about her and Vincent going to the ashram twice a year.

To hell with it, I thought, *just for fun, let's pretend for a second that Mrs. Klauser is Fiona.* If she were, that meant that more or less eight years after I'd encountered her for the last time, Fiona would have travelled to India without Vincent, since Mrs. Klauser was alone when she'd been arrested. Up to that point, things made sense. Vincent could have stayed behind at his grandmother's place, or he might have already been at the ashram at the time.

Lydia interrupted my thoughts by asking if I wanted red or white wine with my meal. I answered absently.

I sat on the couch and rolled a couple of joints while my hosts were busy with the last touches to their Indian meal. My mind raced back to Mrs. Klauser—or Fiona. Who would have tipped off the Indian customs and the police during her trial, and why? Fiona had never encountered any problems in India, entering or leaving. Someone must have wanted her to stay there, out of reach, in a place where she couldn't cause trouble. And she must have been well aware of it since she didn't fight for her release. Knowing Fiona, she would have done everything in her power to stay out of jail—that is, unless her life, Holiji's, or Vincent's, was at stake. What about that boy visiting her, the friend's son? The part about being the Son of God was so ridiculous that I didn't want to add it to the equation just yet.

The strong smell of *saag paneer* and *naan* bread made my mouth water. Anton brought some *raita* to the table. A minute later, Lydia emerged from the kitchen with smoking plates. There would be plenty of time to mull over Mrs. Klauser. For now, Anton was delighted to let me know the details of their trip to Ladakh.

After dinner, a little tipsy and her cheeks red from wine, Lydia got back to the Austrian prisoner. Anton stretched his mouth in an exaggerated yawn.

"Then again, what if this young man truly is the Son of God? Can you imagine? We could be sitting here gossiping like fools while some Jesus walks on this planet at this very moment, mortified by grief at the sight of his dear mother in prison. What if we could help him but never did? How will we be judged? I don't want to sound stupid, but weird things have happened in this world, especially in India."

Anton sighed. "Yeah," he chuckled. "We'll all burn in a piping hot Christian hell. My dear love, if ever by chance a true saviour appears somewhere on earth, people will recognize him this time around. He will not be tortured, ignored, or crucified. I have no doubts about it. History won't repeat itself. Look at the Dalai Lama—besides the Chinese, most everyone acknowledges he's a god in flesh. Forget about that crazy woman."

Lydia shook her head. "How can you be so sure? Meher Baba was an avatar, wasn't he? Did we run to him? No. Did we pay much attention? No. We read the book, meditated on his words and spent a few days in total silence. Then what? We came back to our little routine and forgot about the whole thing. Did we truly believe he was an avatar? Did we recognize this divine element in him? Probably not. Otherwise, we would still be wrapped in his teachings. What would make you, or anybody else for that matter, recognize the next avatar?"

"A healthy dose of skepticism." Anton said. "And by the way, Meher Baba was a self-proclaimed avatar."

"Aren't all avatars self-proclaimed?" I said.

"Would you need to witness a few miracles before you'd be convinced?" Lydia addressed Anton, though I sensed her question was also directed at me. "Short of a miracle, how would you know for sure? What would make you fall on your knees and beg for mercy? A word, a *darshan*? If you need the parting of the Red Sea to become a believer, you're on the wrong path, my dear. Doubting is the trap, defeating it is everything. I think you overestimate your instinct. I believe that the vast majority of humans are much too self-absorbed to have the capacity to recognize a god in flesh. The Dalai Lama got famous because he was the head of a nation. If not, I doubt we would have heard much about him. Same thing goes for Gandhi."

She looked at me. "Let's ask someone who seems impartial here. Tell me, my friend, do you actually believe you would recognize the next avatar? No matter how he looked, or what he did for a living? Or do you believe you might not be enlightened enough to identify him?"

I hated to piss on her parade, though I didn't exactly agree with Anton either. In the past years, I had developed a deep condescension toward religions and so-called avatars. This Son of God Lydia was talking about, some religion would claim him as its own. And there we'd go again. Another round of wars.

"I'm not sure I'd care, to be perfectly honest. I don't believe that such a man or woman has ever or will ever live among us. The way I see it, there is no such thing as a god in flesh. By definition, God is not flesh. Whoever has to eat, take a crap, burp, and piss can't be a god. Not in the sense of someone more advanced or perfect than the rest of us, anyway. That is, unless we're all gods, but unaware of it. No human being made of flesh and bones is in any way superior to another one. Could be morally or spiritually enlightened but not superior. I truly believe that all humans are created equal. Most of us fuck it up down here, and we call gods the one who don't. Fucking up is just as important as leading an exemplary life. Both are part of the spectrum of learning, aren't they?"

Anton and Lydia became lost in their thoughts for a minute.

As far as I am concerned, problems arise when some people start believing they understand this world better than others. Religious beliefs are like underwear—you shouldn't show them to just anybody. Brandishing your underwear— or your religious beliefs—attracts unwanted attention and criticism. It might even send you to the loony bin. It is a sure way to get stigmatized. Keep your underwear and religious beliefs to yourself, and this world will be a much better place. Or better, get rid of both. Walk in life with no underwear and no religious beliefs. Then you might be able to do some good, all the while feeling free and rebellious. All religious beliefs are stupid. Period. Religious leaders are fakes, nothing more than politicians, except, of course, for the Dalai Lama and Gandhi and a very few others who are in a class of their own. Those who have never claimed to be avatars. The rest care for something else other than peace and love on earth.

The way I look at it, faith is self-induced. Faith is the product of collective hysteria. Faith is an RTD, a Religiously Transmitted Disease plaguing people and creating intolerance, hatred, fear, bigotry, and worst of all, the feeling of having made a better choice than thy neighbour. Religion is pure evil. A drop of its poison on a planet as splendid as the one we share and *wham!* Look at what we end up with. I don't care for the second coming of Christ or any other avatar for that matter. He or she would only add to the immense confusion. There is only one rule in my heart: don't do to others what you would not have them do to you. This one alone can keep you busy for a lifetime.

But that is not what I said. I told them, "I honestly believe that the physical body is here to prove that we're all the same. People who have disciples are fakes, frauds. If you need to convince and convert others in order to live your religion and your beliefs, then you're a politician, not a holy individual. Every bowel movement should remind such person how deadly ordinary he or she is. That's why I like Tibetans and many babas in India. They don't try to convert the world, they just want to be left alone in peace. I don't believe in the second coming of anybody, except maybe the Perpetual Coming of Assholes."

Anton and Lydia laughed. Lydia stuck her tongue at me. "Okay, okay. Forget it. Oh, and one last thing about Mrs. Klauser."

She threw an apologetic glance at Anton. "Last one, promise. Our guest is just as interested as I am. It's only a detail, really, but one amusing enough. The guard says Mrs. Klauser gives modern dance lessons every afternoon at four. Everyone, including a couple of guards, attends her classes. They say she's an absolutely amazing teacher."

I took a deep breath, staring at my food. I felt a knot in my stomach. I couldn't eat anymore, though just minutes before, I was considering going for a second serving. *Could Mother Mary Klauser really be Fiona?* A redhead hopelessly devoted to her guru. A woman loaded with inner demons she never let anyone peek at. The overall weirdness of the circumstances surrounding Mrs. Klauser reflected Fiona's personality to a tee. A still lake inhabited by eerie creatures.

That night in bed, I spent most of my time tossing and turning. I recapitulated what I knew for sure. A little more than eight months into her pregnancy, Fiona had persuaded Jude he should go to New York because she meant to leave him for good and take the baby with her. She managed to go into labour while he was away. She drove herself to the hospital, gave birth, and flew the next day to Vancouver. Then, she began to extort a lot of money from Jude. These were all facts.

According to my own collection of "facts" based on the rumours I had heard over the years, I was pretty sure that by giving her all that money, Jude had financed Fiona's escape plan and made it easier for her to get away from him. I was also convinced that Fiona hadn't taken all that money from Jude out of revenge. Had the million-dollar deal gone through, I'm sure she would have demanded to get her share, and not a penny more. She hid as far as she could into the wild because at the time she probably feared someone might be looking for her (the police), or for Vincent (Jude). Once she felt it was safe, she came out of the woods. *Then what?* Perhaps she'd kept a low profile for a while, but staying in Canada, getting a "normal" job, and raising her son by herself wouldn't have been Fiona-like behaviour, and she'd certainly thought of Holiji's ashram as a refuge until she sorted things out. The police wouldn't look for her that far and if Jude ever showed up at the ashram's gate, he wouldn't dare to confront her in front of Holiji. It wasn't too far-fetched to imagine Fiona deciding to live at her master's feet as she'd always felt she should. Vincent would grow up next to Holiji, learning about the divine instead of geography and mathematics. Fiona would have loved that. All this made sense.

My mind wandered for a moment and Odette suddenly popped into my mind. I remembered Fiona's unleashed anger at her. Odette and her "lying eyes." I examined a notion that had evaded me for decades. If Holiji tried to have his way with Odette and me, why the hell had I never asked myself why he'd never made a pass at Fiona? *Surely he must have given it a shot, at least once. When she was at the ashram by herself. Like when she visited him without Jude that summer in California.* The monsoon was raging at the time Fiona left for India, giving them lots of time for intimacy inside his cottage. She returned in a foul mood and never offered an explanation, not even to Jude. I remembered how upset and confused she was. What if Fiona was already Holiji's lover by the time Odette returned from India? She would have certainly gone for the ride. This was a man who was completely worthy of her. And Odette had dared to tell her otherwise. But she forgot all about her when she learned she was pregnant a couple of months later …

Another bolt of lightning struck me between my ears. *Could Vincent be Fiona and Holiji's child? Could Vidur, the so-called son of God, be Vincent?* Lydia said the boy was in his early twenties, more or less Vincent's age at that time. She said he spoke English and had been educated in Europe and America. The notion was so enthralling that I indulged for a minute. This would explain why Fiona had done everything in her power to make sure no one from her past ever laid eyes on her son, not even in the delivery room. She might have harboured doubts about the baby's paternity until the very last minute, not sure whether it was Jude's or Holiji's.

That meant Jude wouldn't have recognized his son even if the boy was standing right in front of him. He wouldn't look anything like him!

My eyes wide open and my mind not about to allow me a minute of sleep, I took a step further in my train of thought. The Austrian woman had said her child was conceived with her guru in a dream. Smart as she was, that was exactly the kind of shit Fiona would fall for. Throw a few astrological arguments into the deal and you've got her. To be told she was the mother of God would have certainly made sense to Fiona. This charade would have immensely appealed to her vanity. It would also explain why she had been so docile at the time of her arrest. Fiona would have believed this was all part of the divine plan.

I got up and went to pee. I stared at the dark blue wall facing me. *If Vincent was indeed Holiji's child, wouldn't the guru do everything in his power to keep child and mother at bay to preserve his reputation?* What if Fiona resisted? The snitch who tipped the customs agents at the New Delhi airport and the other who contacted the police during the trial could very well be Holiji's disciples. Every Indian guru had the support of some influential individuals populating his flock, influential enough to be taken seriously by customs and police officers, and devoted enough not to question their guru's order. Holiji couldn't afford to have any of his disciples find out about Vincent's real father. Especially Jude, who represented the ashram's main source of income at the time. Not to mention that a vengeful Jude would certainly spread the news to every devotee on earth. Holiji would have a lot at stake with Fiona around. Wouldn't this whole situation have driven Fiona a little insane as time went on? Especially while confined in a Tihar cell? *Could she have been willing to suffer for the rest of her life to preserve the love of the only man she considered perfect enough for her?*

I took a peek out the window. The pieces somehow fit, but it was hard to believe all the same. Experience had shown me many times how ludicrous it was to try to understand Fiona's behaviour. Mrs. Klauser could very well have been Fiona.

And I wanted her to be. The reason for this was simple.
It fitted Fiona. It fitted *la grandeur du personnage.*
   Am I losing my mind over this shit?

Epilogue

*Listening to Neil Young singing about old friends he never
meant to keep out of sight*

I FOUND MYSELF IN DELHI again a couple of years later, and I was slightly tempted to pay a visit to Mrs. Klauser. Just to check her out. Nonetheless, I left India without fulfilling this mission. I chickened out. I was afraid my imagination had taken me too far. Or maybe I feared what Fiona would ask of me if she found me on her trail. Mrs. Klauser could very well have been no more than a demented Austrian woman who pretended to ignore her mother tongue simply because she wanted to be left alone in her prison cell. It was also possible that at that moment, somewhere in a Vancouver suburb, a middle-aged Fiona, dressed in a leopard-print outfit, was cooking a strictly vegetarian dinner with her doctor husband while Vincent, Jude's biological son, was on his way home for Thanksgiving.

Soon after that trip, Lydia lost track of Mrs. Klauser. Her contact at the embassy was transferred to another country, and the driver who was related to the Tihar guard left his job after being diagnosed with dengue fever. Lydia too thought about paying the woman a visit but she also changed her mind. There would be no more gossip about Mrs. Klauser.

Years after our breakup, I heard that Jean-Luc, my first serious boyfriend, the one I left for Jude, had remained single for a long time after our sad last date together. He eventually married, and a year later his wife gave birth to twins. People said he never touched a drop of alcohol again.

A few years ago around Christmas, I bumped into him in a shopping centre. He was divorced, and so was I. It could have been a great opportunity to date again. You'd think that events gone wrong on account of youth mixed with cheap wine would be remembered with humour. But the memory of this unpleasant evening came rushing back like the train that had almost crushed Jean-Luc to death. The uneasiness we both felt was as silently loud as the Christmas lights surrounding us. Though neither of us mentioned a word about it, it was right there creeping behind every sentence. We exchanged business cards but never attempted to contact each other.

Linda turned out to be my most precious guardian angel. Thirty-odd years later, I am still awed by the positive impact of her betrayal. Karmically speaking—if you'll excuse the expression—she is surely the best friend I've ever had. I owe my great life all to her, really, and I say this without the faintest trace of sarcasm or irony. If Linda hadn't "stolen" Alex from me, I might still be pacing a kitchen floor somewhere in Montreal, never taking the risk of wandering out on my own, away from a safe circle of friends. If she hadn't been a traitor, I don't believe I would have pushed my limits as far as I did. I like to think that subconsciously, Linda was meant to be on my path, that she came into my life to save me from a dead end. I certainly wouldn't have travelled that much. Hell, I probably would never have learned how to drive. I can only be eternally grateful for her lack of integrity. The past *is* worth revisiting sometimes. Linda and Alex still live together to this day, and it's only fair to say that they were indeed made for each other. Who knows? Maybe Holiji's blessing did them some good after all.

I heard that Frankie married a nurse, the daughter of his father's oldest friend. He went back to school to become a dental assistant but failed to graduate. He tried accounting, swapping teeth and gums for columns and numbers, but that didn't work for him either. He flunked the last exam and was seriously considering selling dope to make ends meet when Julie, his beloved wife, became ill. She died a few years later of cancer. Frankie was inconsolable, and he fell into a deep depression. Fortunately, his old friends Hugo, Alex, and Milou pulled him out. He returned to school again, learning how to drive an eighteen-wheeler this time, and he's been driving trucks ever since. I met him by accident in a Montreal restaurant a couple of years ago. A sad man in his early fifties, his skin had the firmness of youth but the brownish colours of maturation, like a prematurely aged fruit. He said he was doing fine.

Camille and Claude had a baby daughter in the late '80s. Their relationship took a turn for the worse after the birth, and Camille left Claude after she caught him in a motel room with his secretary. My dear friend had been suspecting something for a few months. Claude began coming home from work much later than usual. He also dressed differently, then he bought a new cologne—clear signs. So one day Camille rented a car and followed her husband after work. He seemed to be doing nothing more than going to a downtown bar with his colleagues. Many colleagues, his secretary among them. Camille followed her husband's car as Claude took the girl to a motel a little out of town. The couple had yet to lock the door behind them when Camille burst in, fuming. When she saw them holding each other, she went ballistic. Enraged, she beat the two of them up with a Gideon Bible. "The only blunt object available in the room," she explained.

After the divorce, she studied Tuscan cuisine and got herself a job as a chef in a family restaurant in Montreal's Little Italy. Claude's relationship with the secretary didn't work out. He told Camille he wished to get back with her.

"Fat chance!" she laughed, swearing she would never give him the time of day. The dark-eyed stallion from Naples who owned the pizzeria next door to the restaurant where she worked, the one who sent her flowers every week, surely had something to do with it. Camille has aged gracefully, and her laugh is just as contagious as it used to be. We are still friends to this day, and I'm crazy about her daughter. She is a carbon copy of Camille at the same age.

Grace chose France. In the early '80s, she joined an organized two-week trip through French vineyards and quaint stone villages. On the tour bus, she was so good at "translating" from Québécois to French—and vice versa—that the company hired her. Eventually she married a Frenchman from Lyon who thought she was adorable when she swore in her mother tongue. She subsequently dumped him for an American painter in search of inspiration in Paris.

For a time, my work sent me to France every once in a while to meet clients. On one of those occasions, I phoned Grace (Camille was still in touch with her and had given me her number), and we went out for lunch. Not a bone in her had changed. Same smile, same Du Maurier cigarettes that her mother shipped to her from Canada. We sat on a terrace in le Quartier Latin and laughed ourselves silly, drunk on white wine and memories. We planned to do it again and did a few times. I don't get to work in Paris anymore, and I've since lost track of her. Camille said Grace eventually found Jesus and raised her three children—from three different fathers—as good Christians somewhere around Paris. She still lives there.

For years now, Milou has been working as a grip on movie sets. He met a makeup girl much younger than him who remains his faithful companion to this day. His girlfriend couldn't bear children, and they didn't care to adopt. Instead they became foster parents for three white-headed baby capuchin monkeys from a destitute zoo. That's Milou, all right. I was told recently that he's in the process of writing his gogo boy memoirs. If this rumour proves to be true, I'll get a copy of that book the moment it hits the stands. It promises to be a page-turner. Milou never managed to lose the weight he had gained in Spain but he was a happy man again. There are no rumours whatsoever on Tintin's whereabouts.

Hugo remained in contact with me through all those years, if only sporadically. After months of silence, he called me when he heard that Leon and I had sold Maya. Time had passed, and I didn't hold a grudge anymore. It was nice to be in contact again. To this day, we can always rely on each other, though we rarely get to meet face to face. For some reason, our friendship kept afloat, firmly rooted in soil that has not been fertilized for years. I know I can always count on him no matter where I am, or what time it is. He still spends most of his life chasing skirts, but at a slower pace.

Leon opened his own pagan convent in the Haight-Ashbury district in San Francisco, an old hippie dream of his. I hear he still makes sculptures nobody buys. It's been years since I heard from him.

Angelo served seven years in prison. Jude picked him up on the day of his release. Two weeks later, he left Montreal and returned to Santiago along with his mother, father, grandmother, two sisters, four brothers, nephew, and parrot, but without the two calico cats who had died of old age by then. I imagine he is still there, running dope deals in his hometown.

Holiji died of heart failure in 2005, but he named a successor while he was still alive. God knows how this one is doing. By the time he passed away, Holiji was a fairly rich man with plenty of followers. It is said he had initiated no fewer than two million souls during his passage on earth. He still has devoted followers to this day. How many more girls did he try to seduce? I don't like to think about the number.

Sadhu Das, the guru who believed he was the real successor of Sant Baba Ram Singh, abandoned his small herd of followers and vanished into the mountains, never to be seen again. To this day, his followers believe he was the true successor of the great master.

Boogie, my dear dog, died in 1989, after sixteen years of a happy dog life. Losing her was a shock, though I knew she couldn't live forever. She was my buddy and an irreproachable hound. They say your domestic animals are the first ones greeting you when you migrate to the other world. I can't wait to feel her fur again.

I haven't heard anything about Fiona or Jude in ages.

As for me, I was lucky, after all. Life had a lot more surprises in store for me, most of them amazing. In 1997, I quit Montreal and began working abroad, changing occupations along the way, depending on what was offered to me at the time. I still smoke dope every day. Or at least every day I can find it, because at my age that's becoming more and more of a challenge. Whenever I visit Lydia and Anton in Amsterdam, I splurge silly.

I fell in and out of love for a long time, and it was only much later that I met the Right One.

But that's another story.

Acknowledgements

I STARTED WRITING THIS book in the late '90s. My husband and I were living in Texas at the time. One night, we went to see *Almost Famous*, Cameron Crowe's movie about groupies in the '70s. That same evening I wrote the first lines of this story. On many occasions I had to put the manuscript on the back burner for long periods of time due to work, travels, or simply because I didn't see the point anymore. However, some people believed in my writing and encouraged me to go on. Others made me want to persevere because they were willing to work with me for free. Am I lucky or what?

Here are some of those fabulous people:

Arlene Prunkl, my editor, worked her magic on my writing and made me a better writer in the process. Arlene, thanks for your constant encouragement, endless advice, and your patience. You've always been there for me. You're the best.

Emma Smart, my drum-player Kiwi angel, who amazed me with her many skills: editing, proofreading, typesetting, cover and text design. Emma, I'm eternally grateful for your remarkable talents and your prodigious generosity.

Lydia Hoekstra, my friend and partner in crime, for her fabulous collages. Lydia, you rock. A big thanks for being there when I needed it.

My husband, Martin, for allowing me to ruin most of his weekends because there was work to be done on the manuscript. Thanks for your support, your unwavering faith in my writing and for being my home, wherever we are.

I also want to thank Cameron Crowe for planting this idea in my head many, many years ago.

About the author

A MONTREALER AT HEART, Sylvie Chartrand is a self-proclaimed "old hippy" who loves to travel the world. She currently lives with her husband in Switzerland where she teaches English and pets every dog that crosses her way. *Forbidden Child: A Tale of the '70s* is her first book.